THE WOLF

J. KENNER

OLIVERHEBERBOOKS

Cover art by Dar Albert at Wicked Smart Designs

Published by Oliver-Heber Books

0 9 8 7 6 5 4 3 2 1

CONTENT WARNING

This dark romance contains elements that may disturb some readers, including:

- Possessive, morally gray hero
- Captivity themes and unequal power dynamics
- Explicit sexual content, including bondage and dominance
- Dubious consent (past and present)
- Non-consensual drugging and stalking
- Sexual coercion and manipulation
- Threats of violence and psychological intimidation
- Past trauma and emotional abuse
- Revenge themes and morally ambiguous choices

For readers who crave an intense, emotional journey with a dangerous hero who walks the line between protection and possession, this second-chance romance delivers a raw, unfiltered experience. The darkness is real—but so is the redemption.

"She had met the wolf, and he had said "good morning" to her,
but with such a wicked look in his eyes that if they had not been
on the public road, she was certain he would have eaten her up."

—The Brothers Grimm

ONE
INTO THE WOODS

The kitchen smells like heaven—brown butter and cinnamon from Granny's apple strudel mingling with coffee brewing in the ancient percolator she refuses to replace.

Copper pots hang from wrought iron hooks, and morning sunlight streams through curtains that Granny embroidered decades ago, casting everything in a warm, golden glow.

I'm curled in the window seat with my third cup of coffee, watching steam rise from the surface while Sasha demolishes her second slice of strudel, as if she's making up for the years she'd been forced to work as a model.

It's warm and wonderful, and I sigh as I take another sip. This cozy kitchen—this entire Connecticut cottage—is mine now, ever since I signed the deed just over a year ago.

But it's not just my home. It's become a sanctuary, so different from the sterile perfection of Reed Tower, where Granny and I lived for most of my life.

Here, scarred wooden counters tell centuries-old stories, and the mismatched chairs around the farmhouse table are like monuments to all the new memories I'm making here.

When Sasha suggested that Granny and I move to the Connecticut countryside to be closer to her and Liam, I thought

Granny would balk at leaving the only home she'd known for decades. In fact, she'd packed her bags only minutes after I told her I'd made an offer. Not only because we'd both fallen in love with the country charm, but because she was just as eager to escape Reed Tower as I'd been.

"You're going to make yourself sick," I tell Sasha, as she reaches for another slice. But I'm only teasing. It's good to see her eat without counting calories or worrying about what her now-dead asshole of a father would say.

She grins, licking cinnamon sugar off her fingers with zero shame, then tucking a shoulder-length lock of blonde hair behind her ear. "If I do, it'll be worth it."

"You eat up," Granny says from the stove, where she's starting lunch prep despite it being barely past nine. My grandmother never sits still—her hands are always busy, folding dough, stirring soup, making all sorts of delicious things. "A woman needs curves," she adds with a wink toward Sasha. "Liam will appreciate my strudel."

Sasha laughs. "In that case, I'll take two more slices."

"You, too, Liebling?" Granny asks, her German accent still thick even after more than four decades in New York.

I glance down at my jeans, which I've had to belt lately to keep from sliding down my hips. "Why not? I've been so busy at work that I keep forgetting to eat. Busy in a good way," I add, then turn to Granny. "Don't want to offend the boss," I say in a fake whisper.

Sasha's expression shifts to concern. "You do realize that work isn't supposed to be your entire life? Even when you're working for your genuinely amazing and extremely awesome best friend."

"Really?" I pretend to be shocked. "I never got that memo."

She rolls her eyes. "When's the last time you did something just for you? Something that had nothing to do with Lydia Cosmetics?"

"I do things for me."

"Reading industry reports doesn't count." She leans forward, that knowing look in her eyes—the one that says she sees through my bullshit and always has. "Come on, Ruby. You need to start dating."

Heat creeps up my neck. "I date."

"A long line of first dates over the course of years doesn't count." She settles back in her chair with the satisfied air of someone who's about to dissect my love life. "When's the last time you made it to a second date? Or better yet, when's the last time you wanted to?"

I force myself to meet her too-knowing eyes. "I have a third date tonight," I say smugly. "I'm going to his place and making him dinner."

She and Granny both stare at me like I've announced I'm joining the circus.

"Marcus?" Sasha asks, referring to the owner of a posh men's store whom I met through a client. "I had no idea you'd even had date number two," she says off my nod. "I'm feeling seriously gossip-deprived."

I fidget with my now-empty coffee mug, a solid anchor in a conversation I don't want to have. "My boss has been keeping me too busy to gossip," I tease, flashing a smirk her way. "But I like him. He's nice. Reliable and sweet."

It's not a lie. Marcus is kind and funny and polite. Everything all those magazines say a woman should want. And everything my first—and only—serious boyfriend wasn't.

"Nice," Sasha repeats, her voice as flat as week-old champagne. "Nice is what you say about oatmeal."

"There's nothing wrong with oatmeal."

"Hello? You hate oatmeal."

Damn. She's right. "Oatmeal isn't the point," I say as Granny wipes flour-dusted hands on her apron, then slides into the chair across from my window seat. Her eyes are bright with curiosity— the same shade of blue as mine, though hers hold decades more wisdom and mischief.

"Tell us about this Marcus," she says. "What does he do?"

I give her the run-down of the store, then add, "He's very successful, and Janae speaks highly of him." I say the last to Sasha. Janae is one of our distribution partners who also does business with his stores. Which makes her a perfect character witness for Marcus.

Sasha just meets my gaze mildly.

I clear my throat. "He's dedicated to his work. Ambitious. And we talk all the time," I add, though that one's not entirely accurate. The truth is, he texts me all the time, and I invariably get drawn into a conversation that happens in a half-focused state, with me clearing out old emails while I wait for him to finish typing out a message.

None of which Granny and Sasha need to know.

"He's stable," I blurt, knowing I sound more defensive than engaged. Which isn't what I want to convey at all, because Marcus is a genuinely nice guy who's fun to go out with and who doesn't hide the fact that he likes me. Isn't that what every woman wants?

But I don't say any of that. Instead, I blurt, "He's very together. Responsible. He even has a five-year plan for moving forward in his business and his life. And he's nice," I add. "Believe me—nice is good."

"Oh, honey." Sasha puts down another forkful of strudel, actual pity in her voice. The kind you'd use for someone who's trying to convince themselves that sawdust tastes like chocolate.

"What's wrong with being nice and responsible?" I almost point out the crazy courtship she'd had with Liam—the opposite of nice and responsible. Try wild and controlling and dangerous.

But since they're wildly, madly, deeply in love, that really wouldn't help my argument.

Instead, I cross my arms and sit back against the glass. "What's wrong with having his shit together?" I demand. "The man's focused. He knows what he wants. He plans for it. He goes after it. That's a good thing."

"Of course it is," Sasha says, the words like a placating pat on my head. "Planning is important."

I grimace. The truth is, she's not bullshitting. I know her well enough to know that she means it. But I also know her well enough to see the humor dancing in her eyes.

I cross my arms. "Well?"

"Well, what?" she asks, her tone as innocent as an infant.

I try to stare her down but fail. I sigh, giving in. "Just say it."

"No, it's nothing. Really. Planning is good."

I see the tug of laughter at the corner of her mouth and consider trading her in for a new bestie.

I narrow my eyes. "But?"

"But what's his plan for getting you naked?" she blurts, the hint of a laugh blooming into a wide, teasing grin as Granny guffaws.

Heat floods my face, and I shoot a glance at Granny, feeling all of fourteen instead of twenty-eight. "Really?" I snap, my attention back to Sasha. "Really?"

Granny laughs, the sound rich and delighted. "Please, Liebling, I wasn't born yesterday. The girl has a point—if a man doesn't make you think about sex, you should scurry away fast."

I want to crawl under the table and die. "Can we please change the subject?"

"Fine." Sasha pulls out her phone, scrolling through what's probably the endless stream of emails that never stops flowing through Lydia Cosmetics. "Speaking of naked—metaphorically—I need to find someone to handle the Maison Rouge meeting this evening. Sucks that it's a Saturday, but the buyer's only in town tonight and wants to discuss the spring campaign over drinks. Liam and I have plans we can't break."

"I'll do it," I say, grateful for the chance to talk about something other than my sex life. Or non-sex life, as the case may be. "Marcus will understand. I mean, meetings like this are literally my job."

"Nope." Sasha doesn't even look up from her phone, dismissing me with the casual authority of someone who's not only found her power, but learned how to wield it. "As your boss,

I'm officially ordering you to prioritize your sex life over spreadsheets."

My face is on fire. "Really, Sasha? Really?"

"I'm serious. When's the last time you got properly laid? I know you and Marcus haven't yet."

"Oh my God." I cover my face with my hands while Granny laughs so hard the sound echoes off the copper pots hanging over the stove. "How could you possibly know that?"

"Duh. I'm your best friend. You would've told me."

She's got me there.

"So? How long has it been? A year? Five years? Seven years?" she adds with deliberate emphasis.

My stomach twists, but I tilt my head and stare her down. "Do I need to call Darla in HR? This is like total harassment."

She just rolls her eyes and continues scrolling.

"The girl speaks truth," Granny says to me, her tone as serious as when she lectured me for sneaking a cigarette when I was twelve. "You need passion. Fire. A man who makes your blood sing."

I bang my head on the window, but not in exasperation—though I'm totally exasperated by both of them. No. I need a moment to get past the memory that has hit me like a punch to the chest. A memory of laughing green eyes that saw everything, hands that knew how to make me beg, and a voice that could make me wet just by saying my name.

Leo Grimm had been fire and darkness and everything I thought I wanted.

Until he showed me what I meant to him.

Nothing.

That's when those eyes stopped laughing for me. That's when they became a snake about to strike.

The fact that he's now my best friend's brother-in-law should make things awkward, but I've gotten good at strategic avoidance. Still, I dread the day when I can't dodge him anymore.

I shake off the thoughts, forcing a bright smile that feels like it might crack my face. "Marcus is very…attentive."

"Attentive like a golden retriever," Sasha mutters into her mug.

"There's nothing wrong with golden retrievers."

"No. But you don't want to fuck one."

"Sasha!" I'm pretty sure my face is glowing now, radiating heat like a space heater. Considering she grew up as the most sheltered person on the planet, my bestie has a wild side. Then again, she'd spent much of her youth escaping her palatial prison by hiding in a virtual world she'd built—and it wasn't filled with unicorns and puppies. More like sexy princes.

"Look," she says. "I'm sorry. Really. I know everything you went through back then, and you know I understand. But that was one man. One fucked-up guy who we all agree needs to stay away from you. I mean, Liam and I manage pretty well not having you two cross paths, so you know I get it. But just because Leo Grimm was a bomb who exploded all over you doesn't mean that you don't deserve a nice, stable guy—"

"Marcus is stable."

"—with more passion than a slug," she finishes with a glare that could freeze Hawaii.

"Marcus has passion," I mumble. He must. Everyone has some passion. And his kisses really are sweet, even if they don't make my toes curl. Besides, it's not like there's anything wrong with a slow build. After all, instant, explosive, fiery passion didn't win me any prizes back in college.

I think Sasha's about to call me out on the Marcus/passion thing, but all she does is glance at her phone again, then nod. "I'll have Melissa handle the meeting tonight. You're spending the evening with Mr. Five-To-Ten-Year-Plan and seeing where it goes. End of discussion."

I slump, defeated. The truth is, I should be excited about tonight. Marcus is everything I should want—stable and kind and smart.

Maybe he doesn't make my pulse race, but I know how life with a man like that can turn out, and I do not want to go there. Not ever again. A relationship on an even keel would be like a dream.

And even though I've never really thought of Marcus as the man of my dreams, he fits all my criteria. He's gentle and sweet and stable and dotes on me.

So what if he never looks like he wants to devour me whole, to consume me from the inside out until there's nothing left but need and surrender?

That's a good thing.

Just like it's good that he doesn't send that thrill of excitement coursing through me.

All that means is that Marcus is safe.

So, no, he's not like Liam, Sasha's husband, who's danger personified, just like all the Grimm brothers. Leo, whom I know better than to get close to again. Elliott. Alexander. And definitely Gabriel. Because surely it was that innate darkness that got the eldest brother killed.

I draw a breath. I love Sasha, and she's part of that family now, and that's fine for her. Liam's only half-a-Grimm, after all.

But me?

I'm staying far, far away.

Safe isn't settling. It's survival.

I know that better than anyone.

Movement outside the window catches my eye, and I glance up to see a figure in the tree line. Dark hair on a body that's tall and lean and—*Oh, shit.*

I look away, my pulse pounding in my throat. It takes me only a moment to draw in a breath and force myself to look again. But when I do, he's gone. I frown, peering out the window, my heart still pounding as my eyes search the area.

No one.

Just shadows and morning light that must have been playing tricks on my eyes, filtering through leaves that are starting to turn gold and magenta with the promise of autumn.

It wasn't him. It couldn't be him. Leo Grimm has better things to do than lurk in the woods outside my house.

"Ruby?" Sasha's voice pulls me back from the window, back from the sudden chill that has nothing to do with the change of seasons. "Something wrong?"

"Nothing. Just a deer." I drain my coffee cup and stand, needing movement, needing something to do with my hands. "I should head to the market. I want to get a few things for tonight."

"What are you making him?" Granny asks, undoubtedly considering which of her pots and pans I'll need to borrow.

"I haven't decided. Maybe that chicken dish you taught me." I glance at Sasha, who shrugs. Apparently, she's through trying to convince me that Marcus isn't the man of my dreams. For now, anyway.

I grab my jacket and canvas bag, then bid them both goodbye, adding a kiss for Granny. I head out through the kitchen's back door, then onto the brick path that cuts across my property. At the edge of my acreage, it connects to a county-maintained trail that weaves through the countryside, marking the route to the town square and the weekly farmers market.

The trail is popular with bikers, runners, and walkers, but this morning it's quiet and empty, and I'm grateful for the solitude as I put in my earbuds and listen to my favorite musical, *Into the Woods*, because what better soundtrack could I have for this walk? Then I let my mind drift as the familiar score fills my ears.

This trail is my favorite thing about my new home. Sure, I'd fallen in love with the cottage the moment I'd walked through the door, but it had been the discovery of the trail that had sealed the deal.

Now, this familiar route is where I come when I need to think, to breathe, to simply be.

The branches of ancient oaks and maples twine above, making the sunlight that filters through dance upon the ground. It's both beautiful and slightly eerie, like an enchanted forest that belongs in a fairy tale.

The path winds deeper into the woods, and I pause my music so that I can enjoy the way the creek babbles over the smooth stones worn down by decades of flowing water. Songbirds talk among themselves, and somewhere overhead, a hawk cries, the sound echoing off the trees before fading into a silence that's broken by the harsh buzz of my phone.

I sigh, then pause beside an oak tree as I pull my phone from my back pocket. I expect a text from Sasha with a last-minute work crisis or from Granny with some staple she needs from the market. Instead, it's Marcus.

Hey beautiful. Rain check on tonight? Stomach bug. Next week?

I stare at the message, waiting for disappointment to hit. Waiting for the frustration of wasted time walking to get supplies at the market and the sting of a ruined evening.

It doesn't come.

What hits instead is…indifference.

What the hell?

I like Marcus. I do. And I had fun on both our dates, and our phone calls always leave me laughing. But right here and right now, I don't care that he's canceling.

And the reason why? Because Leo fucking Grimm has gotten into my head. And it's a gift—a stupid, annoying, screwed up gift—that Marcus is canceling. Because Leo Grimm is like poison, and now I don't want to be around any guy. Even one as sweet as Marcus.

Right as that thought hits me, Little Red Riding Hood starts to sing through my earpods, her voice clear and crisp as she sings about how the wolf made her feel. Excited. Scared.

Yeah. I know the feeling.

That's how I felt about Leo once. I'd craved that intensity, that fire that nearly consumed me before it burned me to ash.

I'd wanted it. Needed it.

And like Little Red Riding Hood, the wolf I'd craved had swallowed me whole.

I draw a deep breath and try to get control of my thoughts as the forest seems to press closer, shadows deepening as clouds pass over the sun. A breeze stirs the leaves overhead, creating patterns of light and dark that shift and dance like living things. Somewhere in the distance, a branch snaps—probably just a squirrel, but the sound makes me jumpy in a way that has nothing to do with wildlife.

I'm typing back a response to Marcus when a shadow falls across the path. Not the dappled shadow of leaves, but something solid. Human. A runner, probably, and I look up, grateful for the distraction from my roiling thoughts.

A man steps out of the trees directly in front of me, materializing from the gloom like he's part of the forest itself.

Leo Grimm.

Tall and lean, with that deceptively lazy grace that always made me think of a cowboy who'd traded his horse for a motorcycle. Dark jeans and a button-down shirt that's rolled up at the sleeves, as if he's been working with his hands instead of lurking in boardrooms or at a computer keyboard.

His hair is dark and tousled, just long enough to show the natural curl he's always fought, as if he's run his fingers through it while waiting for me to appear.

But it's his eyes that stop my breath—green as bottle-glass, bright with that perpetual amusement that used to make my heart race and my good sense evaporate. Eyes that have haunted my dreams for years.

He's standing just three feet away, hands shoved in his pockets like he's been waiting. Like he's been hunting.

My phone slips from my hand, hitting the ground with a crack that echoes off the trees.

"Hey, Ruby," Leo says, as if there's nothing dark between us. As if he hadn't destroyed me. "We need to talk."

TWO
EXCITED & SCARED

The world tilts sideways. Like totally sideways. As if someone has reached into my chest and squeezed until there's nothing left but silence and terror.

Leo Grimm.

Here. In my woods. In my sanctuary. After so many years of careful distance. Of fleeting glimpses at charity galas. Of tense moments at events, where he'd orbit me like a wary planet. Of harsh smackdowns from my circle of friends when he got too close or tried to talk to me.

Year after year of determinedly keeping my distance. Trying to forget him.

Reminding myself how much I hate him.

And now here he is, appearing out of nowhere like he just stepped out of one of his ancestors' fairy tales.

God help me, he's still the most beautiful man I've ever seen.

I haven't allowed myself to look too closely at him over the last few years, but now—with my tongue tied and my mind muddled—I take a moment.

The years have been kind to him. More than kind. The sharp angles of his face have mellowed slightly, making him look less like a fallen angel and more like a fallen god.

His hair is still raven black, the dappled light revealing just a few hidden strands of red, as if stating that in all ways, he's the family rebel.

His clothes are casual, but from the way he carries his body, he might as well be in a tailored suit. He looks like a man who's in control of himself and his environment.

And who wants to be in control of me.

I lift my chin in defense against the thought and see the flicker of humor in his eyes. Those wildly familiar eyes. Emerald green and intense and the same as they were when he used to look down at me—sprawled naked in his bed—on so many glorious nights.

But that had all shattered on the worst day of my life—a day when I'd needed him desperately. And instead of being there to hold and help me, he'd broken up with me through a fucking note, as if all of our sweet talks and all of our wicked nights had meant nothing to him at all.

"Ruby?" His voice is low. That same rough velvet that had once made me wet simply from the way he said my name.

The spell breaks, and I draw in a breath, as if I'm sucking in courage. I'm eerily calm, standing tall and straight as I face him dead on. "Get the hell away from me."

His mouth curves in what might have been a smile had it reached his eyes. "You look good. Stronger. You're kicking ass as an exec these days."

"Yours is the only ass I want to kick," I snap. "And don't stand there and act like you have the right to comment on anything about me. You lost that right when you ripped my heart out. And now?" I look him up and down, hoping my expression shows nothing but contempt. "Now you don't know me at all."

"Don't I?" He takes a step closer, then reaches for a strand of my shoulder-length red hair. I lurch back, breaking the contact, but as I do, I catch his scent—something woodsy and male that makes my body respond despite every rational thought in my head.

"Dammit, Leo. I told you to get away from me."

He steps even closer. "I can't do that."

I lurch back, only to find myself pressed against a massive tree trunk. "You can," I say, forcing the words out, my nerves jangling as I realize I'm trapped on a secluded forest trail with this man who once destroyed me. Who could so easily destroy me again.

"You can," I repeat, rolling my shoulders the way I do to settle my nerves before I have to speak to investors or potential clients of Lydia Cosmetics. "It's easy. Just go. We both know you've done it before."

His face turns to stone, as if he wants to counter my verbal lashes but is forcing himself to hold back.

"Now," I snap. "You know damn well I have zero interest in seeing you, talking to you, or even acknowledging that you exist on this planet."

"I know," he says. "You want me gone. You want me to leave you the fuck alone."

"Smart boy."

"Not happening. Not this time."

He takes a step closer, so close we're breathing the same air, and my pulse kicks up. From fear. Only from fear.

"Just go." I want the words to hit him like a gut punch. Instead, they sound soft. Broken. Just like he'd once broken me. "Please. Just leave me alone."

He doesn't. He inches even closer—so close we're almost defying physics and occupying the same space.

Frustration curls through me. I need him gone. This is the man who destroyed me. Who had me sobbing for weeks, then on and off for the next year whenever something reminded me of him.

This is the man who'd used me. Who'd thrown me away like garbage.

The man I'd once loved but quickly learned to hate.

The man whose proximity has launched a slide show of every naughty, wicked, wonderful thing we'd ever done together.

Things I'd thought meant love and a future. But I'd been so damn wrong.

One tear snakes down my cheek, and he wipes it away. "Don't," I snarl. "Don't you dare touch me."

His brow rises as he comes closer. My heart pounds, but the rest of me...

Oh, dear god, the rest of me is all too aware of him. And in that moment, I think I hate myself as much as I hate him. "Dammit, Leo. Get away from me."

"I can't," he says.

"The hell you can't." I snap the words out, but all he does is lean in more, until no air exists between us that hasn't touched him first.

"You're in danger, Rue. Real danger."

A laugh escapes me. "That's rich coming from you. My parents died and you—"

"Would you shut up and listen? It's a legitimate threat."

I shake my head, his words landing on me like Latin, entirely incomprehensible. "What does that even mean?"

"It means that this isn't some scam I've put together to piss you off or torment you or whatever you're thinking right now. I came here to warn you and protect you."

I let his words wash over me, even as I slowly shake my head. "You don't have any conscience at all, do you? A threat? Because women who work in the cosmetics industry are so prone to danger? You honestly think I don't see through your bullshit? That I don't know that you're the only threat in my life right now, just like you've always been."

"Dammit, Ruby, you have to trust me."

"I really don't. You burned that bridge a long, long time ago."

Something flickers in his eyes—hurt, maybe, or regret. But it's gone so fast I might have imagined it.

He leans in.

"Don't." I hold up a hand, surprised by how steady it is when everything inside me is shaking.

He's lying, of course. There's no real threat against me. Even if I thought he cared enough about me to try and protect me—and I know better—he wouldn't come himself. He'd tell Sasha. Or Liam. He knows I don't trust him. And I know that this is some sort of sick, fucked-up trap.

Still, I'll ask Liam to double-check. I'm certain Leo's a shit who doesn't give a damn about me, but that doesn't necessarily mean he's lying about a threat. I can't imagine who would have it in for me, but better safe than sorry.

I lift my chin, confident in my plan and my decision. "Get the hell away from me." My voice is colder than I can ever remember.

He goes still in that way snakes do before they strike. It should terrify me. In a way, it does. But at the same time, it sends a dark thrill through my body.

I draw in a breath. *Game on, you bastard.*

"Dammit, Ruby. Would you just fucking listen to me?" His voice is level but hard. "Someone wants to hurt you."

"So you said." I bend down to retrieve my phone, grateful that the screen didn't completely shatter despite the fall. Anything to avoid looking at him, to keep from drowning in those green eyes that once saw every part of me. "Let me guess—only you can protect me. Only you can keep me safe. How convenient."

"This isn't a game."

"Bullshit." I lift my chin, then press my palm to his chest and shove him back a step. "This is your kind of game. Come at me when I'm at my happiest, then cut me down."

His hands clench at his sides. Hands I remember only too well. What they could do. How they felt on my skin. On my lips.

Inside me.

Once upon a time, I'd wanted him. Hell, I'd belonged to him.

But he won't ever own me again.

"For fuck's sake, Ruby."

"What's the threat, Leo?" I cross my arms and force myself to meet those eyes I used to drown in. "Who's after me? What do they want? Give me specifics. Prove to me this isn't just one more of your sick games. Like the ones we used to play. The innocent girl tied up by the evil prince who forced her to give in to every one of his decadent whims."

Heat tightens at my core as I remember our scenes. The way my skin felt like lightning was sizzling over it. My breasts so sensitive that a mere brush of a nipple brought me to orgasm. My core so wet and—

Stop it.

"Tell me the damn threat, Leo," I say, both to break the silence and to quiet my thoughts. "Because as far as I'm concerned, you're the only dangerous thing in my life. And you're smarter than to think I'd trust you after everything you put me through. If there was a threat, you would have told Liam or Sasha, and they would have told me. I see through you now, Leo. I see you for the user you are. Cruel and—"

"Dammit, Ruby." He snaps the words out so hard I jump.

"You want to keep me safe? Stay the fuck away or tell me what the threat is."

He doesn't answer, and the quiet lingers until I start to think he never will. When he finally does, his voice is careful, controlled. "I can't tell you everything. Not yet."

Of course, he can't. Because there is no threat. There's just Leo Grimm trying to manipulate me back into his orbit.

I take another step toward him. "This is just more of your bull-shit," I say, the word tasting like freedom on my tongue. "You're the one who destroyed my life, remember? You used me, then discarded me like trash, and made it clear that I'd never meant anything to you. And for the last seven years, you've watched me like some perv from a distance, knowing that you were making me uncomfortable every time our paths crossed at some stupid party or benefit."

I can see him searching for words, but I don't give him time to find them. "You liked it, didn't you? Liked making me squirm? You're a sick fuck, Leopold Grimm. And I know that better than anyone."

His face goes still, like a mask sliding into place. "Just let me —" he begins, but I'm already pushing past him, already running down the trail. Not the graceful, controlled exit I'd prefer, but the desperate flight of prey that's spotted a predator closing in.

He calls my name once more, but I don't look back. I can't. Because if I look back—if I see whatever expression is on his face right now—I might stop running.

I bolt through the dappled forest, my feet pounding against the path that had once been a sanctuary.

He's tainted even this. Branches catch at my jacket, and my breath comes in sharp gasps that have nothing to do with exertion and everything to do with the panic clawing at my throat.

Seven years. Seven years of working hard to trust my judgment again. To build a life that doesn't revolve around a man who saw me as nothing more than a convenient body to use when he was bored.

And he thinks he can just step out of the trees and back into my life like nothing happened?

Like he didn't break me so completely it took years to find all the pieces?

By the time I reach the edge of the farmers market, my lungs are burning and my hands are shaking. I pause at the tree line, looking over my shoulder at the path that disappears into shadows.

He's not following me.

I exhale slowly, tension leaving my chest in waves.

But I honestly can't tell if what I'm experiencing is relief or disappointment.

THREE
SIMMERING

I try to lose myself in the familiar sights and sounds of the market—vendors calling out their specials, the sweet scent of fresh-baked bread, the laughter of children on the nearby playscape as their parents browse fresh produce. But it all feels surreal after my run-in with Leo.

I pause at the apple stand, staring at the neat rows of red and green without really seeing them. My mind keeps replaying his voice. The way his emerald eyes had looked at me, like he could see straight through to my soul. A look that had once melted me. Now, it scares me.

Now, *he* scares me.

Someone wants to hurt you.

I shiver at the memory of those words. Ironic, coming from him. After all, I doubt there's anyone on this planet who could cut me more deeply than he once did.

Except that's not true.

Leo hurt me, yes.

But he also opened my eyes. Hell, maybe he even did me a favor, because now I know how cruel people can be. How hard they can twist the knife.

I still have the scars from Leo, after all. And god knows, I saw a new level of brutality in the way Victor Reed tortured Sasha.

Someone wants to hurt you.

The words are still bouncing around my head like a horrible echo, and I wrap my arms around myself despite the warm afternoon sun. I know I should dismiss it as another one of Leo's manipulations, but I can't seem to do that. There'd been something in his voice. An urgency that felt real.

So maybe Leo—

"Ruby!"

I jump, my heart pounding, then immediately relax as I recognize the voice. I turn to see Sasha hurrying over from the herb vendor's table, a small paper bag in her hand and concern etched across features made famous from years of being the face of the now-defunct Reed Cosmetics.

She's traded her battered sweatpants for designer jeans, a silk top, and a pale blue cashmere sweater. She could just as easily be shopping on Fifth Avenue as at this market.

I meet her halfway, some of the tension draining out of me at the sight of my bestie showing up like a port in a storm. "What on earth are you doing here?"

"Basil," she says, holding up the bag with a slightly sheepish expression. "I was answering emails, and then I was thinking about spaghetti sauce. You know—that recipe I found in my mom's things last year?"

"That sauce is amazing."

"Right? But it has to simmer for at least five hours, so I blew off a meeting and hurried here."

My brows rise. "Who are you and what have you done with my best friend?"

She rolls her eyes. "What can I say? I'm the boss." A smile tugs at her mouth. "Honestly, once the idea got in my head, it was all I could think of. I rescheduled the meeting. So not flaking off at all." She tilts her head. "Well, maybe a little. But the prize is a spaghetti dinner with Mom's sauce."

"At least you crave stuff that's healthy. The ones that stick in my head are usually of the candy variety. Like Tootsie Rolls." I sigh, then shoot her a look. "Great. Now I've got a craving, too."

"It's a good thing foods aren't sentient," Sasha said. "They would totally be our evil overlords."

"True that."

"Speaking of food, why aren't you holding any? Did you get lost on the way?"

I glance down at the packed dirt that defines the market's space. "No, just…" I trail off with a shrug and force myself to fight a shiver.

She leans in, her eye narrowing. "What the hell, Rue? You look like you've seen a ghost."

"It's nothing," I say, but I'm sure even the apple vendor can hear the lie.

"Have you met me?" she asks, leading me away from the table so we can talk without being overheard. "Best friend. Knows you better than anyone. Have confided all my crazy secrets to you since forever. And knows you too damn well to believe your bull-shit. So tell me what's wrong."

I want to stay silent. Hell, I want to run from the truth. But I don't. This is Sasha, after all. "I saw Leo."

I'd barely managed to whisper the words, but from the way Sasha goes completely still, it's obvious she heard me. "What? Here? At the market? Maybe he was headed to my place and stopped to buy some wine or cheese or something."

There's a hint of hope in her voice. Leo is the only brother of the four—well, three surviving— brothers with whom Liam is close. Which means Sasha is very invested in Leo not once again becoming a major ass vis-à-vis me.

"Not here," I say. "On the trail. Just a few minutes ago." I gesture vaguely in that direction. "He just stepped out of the trees like he'd been waiting for me."

"Oh, Ruby. Dammit. I wish I'd thought to walk here with you."

I shrug. "I can't call you for Leo-duty every time I go outside. Besides, the last time I saw him was over four months ago when I showed up at your house without calling first. He's not on my radar anymore."

Except he is.

Because even though I may not see him every day—and even though I hate the man with every tiny cell in my body—my sick, pathetic truth is that not a day has gone by in seven years when I haven't thought of him.

"So what happened?" Sasha spins her hand, urging me to get on with the story. "What did he want? You're sure he was waiting for you? He wasn't walking to our house?"

"He came for me," I say flatly. Then I tell her everything—Leo's appearance, his warning about danger, the way he'd admitted to watching me.

She listens without interruption, her expression growing more troubled with each detail.

"He said someone wants to hurt me," I finish. "But when I asked for specifics, he said he couldn't tell me everything. Not yet. Honestly, I call bullshit. He's the only one who's ever wanted to hurt me. And for some reason, I'm back on his radar."

"Shit." The word is almost a whisper, but still as hard as a rock. "That's so fucked up."

"Well, yeah. I noticed."

"No, I mean…" She trails off, biting her lower lip, then draws in a breath. "Look, I know how deeply Leo hurt you. What he put you through. But I've gotten to know him pretty well, and he wouldn't lie about something like that."

"Color me unconvinced."

"But why would he? Where's the profit in scaring you?"

I study her face, seeing something that looks like genuine fear in her eyes. "You really think he's telling the truth? But that's crazy. I mean, why would someone want to hurt me? Maybe a year ago, I could see your dad hurting me to hurt you. But that's all over. We're safe."

"On my side, maybe," she says. "And, yes, you're my sister in everything but blood, so that applies to you, too."

"That's what I'm saying. It's just Leo wanting to get a rise out of me."

"But what if it's not my side that's coming after you?"

I frown. "What are you talking about?"

"The Grimm family has enemies. Real ones. People who would hurt you to get to Leo, or Liam, or me. And they'd do it just because they can." She runs a hand through her hair. "You know I'm right."

A chill runs down my spine at the conviction in her voice. "Not Leo. He couldn't give a fuck about anyone hurting me. Himself included." I shrug, as if I don't care at all anymore. Which I don't. Not even a little bit.

"But I guess you have a point about you and Liam," I add before she can try and convince me that Leo gives the smallest of fucks about me. "Except why? Is there something going on with the family? Did Alexander screw a competitor over?"

The eldest living brother, Alexander Grimm, has taken charge of the family's massive, octopus-like business ever since his father fell ill and ended up in a coma. And from what I've heard, Alex has done a spectacular job emulating his father's brutal and frequently dishonest method of keeping the Grimm family businesses chugging along.

Sasha shrugs. "Knowing Alex, he probably did screw a competitor. But tying that back to a threat to you…"

I sigh. "Bottom line—neither one of us has an inkling of a clue why anyone would be after me."

"Not even an inkling of an inkling," she agrees, then cocks her head and gives me *that* look. "But it sounds like Leo might."

I want to tell her she's wrong, but I know she might be right. So I pull up my big girl panties, draw a breath, and say, "Will you ask Liam to find out what's up? The threat, I mean. If Leo won't give me details, maybe Liam can find out."

"Hell yeah, I will. He called before I left to say he was stepping into a meeting, but I'll catch him as soon as he's free."

"He probably doesn't know anything."

"Probably not, or he would have told you. But he has resources, connections. If there's a legitimate threat, he'll find out."

"And if there isn't?" I ask. "If this is just Leo playing some twisted game?"

"Then we'll know that too." She reaches out to squeeze my arm. "Ruby, I get why you don't trust him. After what he did to you… But I also know that Liam trusts Leo completely. And Liam doesn't trust easily."

I nod, understanding the weight of that statement. Liam Grimm is not a man who gives his trust lightly, especially after what his father put him through. If he trusts Leo, there has to be a reason. But Liam trusting his mercurial little brother is a lot different than me trusting the man who destroyed me.

I meet Sasha's eyes. "I don't want to be one of those too-stupid-to-live girls like in a horror movie," I say. "So I'll pay attention to whatever Liam learns. But no way will I let Leo Grimm close to me again."

"Believe me," she says, "I get it. So, we get more information. Then we decide what to do next." Sasha's voice carries the authority of someone who's learned to separate emotion from survival. And because she did survive, I know she understands. And because she's been my bestie since forever, I believe her.

"Right. Okay." I nod. "We have a plan. Sort of."

We share an ironic grin.

"Can I drive you home? I don't like the idea of you walking that trail alone if there really is a threat."

I should jump all over that offer. I don't. Because it's sparked something rebellious in my chest. "I want to walk."

"Ruby…"

I lift my chin and square my shoulders. "I need to prove to

myself that I'm not going to let Leo Grimm scare me into changing my life. I've walked that trail a hundred times, and I'm not going to stop because my ex-boyfriend thinks there might be a boogeyman in the woods."

"Except there really might be a boogeyman in the woods."

"Maybe," I admit. "But do you really believe Leo walked away when I told him to get lost?"

She meets my eyes. She and I both know that if there truly is a threat out there—and if Leo did come to warn me of it—then just because I sent him away doesn't mean that he's gone. And it sure as hell doesn't mean that I'll see him on the way home.

All it means is that I'll get home safely.

I may not trust Leo with my heart anymore. But I know that much.

After a moment, her shoulders relax, and she nods. "Okay. But call me when you get home?"

"I will."

We shop a bit longer, then part ways, Sasha heading to her car while I turn back toward the wooded trail. The sun has disappeared behind several large clouds that threaten rain, making the path seem dark and gloomy, and every creak of a branch or rustle of an animal seems to ring out and startle me.

Even so, I force myself to walk at a normal pace.

I'm not afraid of Leo Grimm. I'm not afraid of whatever threat he thinks is out there.

But as I listen to the sound of the forest, I can't deny that some tiny part of me hopes I'll see him again. That he'll step out of the shadows and demand to walk me home.

The thought stops me cold.

No.

We're over. We've been over for ages.

And that's how we're going to stay.

Some cuts are just too deep to heal. Some betrayals too fundamental to forgive. Leo Grimm showed me exactly what I meant to him all those years ago, and I'd be an idiot to forget that lesson now.

I know that. I believe it. Hell, I cling like grim death to the truth of it. But even so, my traitorous heart speeds up every time a branch rustles, every time a shadow moves in my peripheral vision. So that by the time I reach home, I'm wound tight with a tension that has nothing to do with fear and everything to do with disappointed anticipation.

He's not coming back.

And that, I tell myself firmly, is a very good thing.

The house is quiet when I let myself in through the kitchen door. I drop my one bag on the counter—I'd barely bought anything at the market, my conversation with Sasha having distracted me from my original mission. Not that I need anything now. I won't be cooking for Marcus tonight.

"Granny," I call softly, but there's no answer.

When I see that her bedroom door is closed, I assume she's napping, and I leave her to rest and head upstairs to my room.

I need a shower. I need to wash the scent of him off my skin, the memory of his touch out of my head.

In my bedroom, I strip off my clothes and catch a glimpse of myself in the full-length mirror. The woman looking back at me is different from the girl Leo knew seven years ago—stronger, more confident, with the kind of poise that comes from rebuilding yourself from the ground up.

But my body remembers him anyway. The way my pulse quickened when he stepped close. The way my skin heated when he held me tight. When he bound me. When he touched me in ways that should make me ashamed, but the memory only makes me wet.

Pathetic. I tell myself, turning away from the mirror and hurrying toward the bathroom and the promise of that cleansing spray I so desperately need.

I turn the water as hot as I can stand and step under the spray. The heat feels good against my tense muscles, washing away the stress of the day. I close my eyes and let myself relax for the first time since Leo appeared on that trail.

But relaxing is a mistake because that's when the memories creep in.

Memories of Leo's hands sliding soap down my back, his body pressed against mine under the spray of his magnificent shower. The way he whispered my name against my ear, his voice rough with want. How he'd made me come apart with just his fingers while the water cascaded over us both.

"That's it, Red," he'd murmured, his mouth hot against my throat. "Let go for me."

And I had. God help me, I'd let go completely, surrendering to him in ways I'd never imagined possible. Trusting him with my body, my heart, my everything.

The memory hits me so hard I have to brace myself against the shower wall. Even after all these years, I can still feel the phantom touch of his hands on my skin, still hear the way he'd said my name like it was a prayer.

I grab the soap with shaking hands, trying not to think about the way Leo used to soap me up. How he'd take his time, mapping every inch of my body like he was memorizing it. The reverent way he'd touch me, like I was something precious instead of just another conquest.

Stop it. I stiffen in defense against the flood of memories. Of want. Of need.

Most of all, of fury and hate and heartbreak.

None of the moments I'd cherished had been real. He'd only been playing a game. And I was the naive little girl, too enchanted by the handsome prince to see it.

He'd hurt me, and I don't want him in my head now. I don't want to think about his touch. About how he felt inside me.

And yet that's all I can think about. All I can feel. My body doesn't care about logic. My body doesn't shy from betrayal. My body simply wants to feel like that again. My nipples tight. That glorious ache between my thighs. A desperate need sizzling over me like electricity.

And his hands moving over all my secret places, hard and soft and demanding all at once.

Dammit, stop!

This time, the plea reaches the functioning part of my brain. I finish washing, angrily scrubbing away any trace of the encounter in the woods. When I step out of the shower, my skin is pink from the heat and the loofah.

I wrap myself in a towel and move back into my bedroom, feeling more clearheaded. The shower helped, even if it brought up memories I'd rather leave buried. I'm stronger now than I was at twenty-one. I won't let Leo Grimm get under my skin again.

But when I enter my bedroom, the clearheaded feeling evaporates instantly, replaced by confusion.

My laptop is open on my bed, but I'm sure I left it on my desk. And I always keep it shut and the screen locked.

Right now, something is playing on the screen. I can't see it from this angle, but I can see the light it's emitting dancing in the dim room.

What the fuck?

I clutch the towel at my chest, my heart hammering as I approach it slowly, like someone nearing an injured animal. I round the edge of the bed, and as I do, I can see what's playing. And my blood turns to ice.

A video.

Of me.

Seven years younger, naked, my hands bound above my head with silk scarves. My face is turned toward the camera, eyes closed in pleasure as Leo's hands move over my body. I recognize the moment—one of our long nights of sensual play in his suite at Grimm Tower, back when I'd trusted him completely. Body and soul.

He never told me he was recording us.

My stomach roils, and my knees go weak. I bend over, my

hand on the mattress as I slide to the floor, as lost and weak as if I'd been drugged.

But somehow, I can't look away. It's vile. It's unforgivable. And yet, a shameful thrill settles low in my belly as I watch him take me like I was his to keep.

Then reality slaps me hard in the face, and I recoil, bile rising in my throat.

Someone was in my house. Someone not only logged into my laptop, but they also loaded this horror and left it for me to find.

Leo? Or someone else?

Even as the question taunts me, text begins to scroll across the bottom of the video— *You're beautiful when you surrender. Soon, you'll be on your knees, my cock in your mouth. Exactly where you belong, doing exactly what you're good for…*

I stare at the screen in horror as the video continues to play a loop of my younger self lost in pleasure and trust, unaware that the man I loved was documenting my vulnerability for future use.

This is why he came to me today.

Not because someone else wants to hurt me, but because he wants to remind me what he's capable of. That he can destroy me anytime he wants. That he has all the power.

And he does, too. He has this tape. A tape that would have only tweaked my life when I was younger, but now that I'm a VP at the fastest-growing woman-owned cosmetics company in history—now that I strategize about how to grow our market, regularly go on news programs, and give talks all over the country about women's empowerment and how Lydia Cosmetics fits in—that tape could not only hurt me, it could completely eviscerate both me and the career I love.

And the most devastating, horrific part? Despite the violation, despite the fury and humiliation burning in my chest, watching that video brings back every erotic sensation from that day and so many others. The way he'd made me feel. The ecstasy of his body filling mine. Of his lips teasing me, his teeth biting me. His palm spanking my ass as he led me down a path to heights of pleasure

I'd never experienced before. And have only ever experienced with him.

"Bastard." I slam the laptop shut, my hands shaking with rage and something else I don't want to name.

Leo Grimm just reminded me exactly why I ran seven years ago.

And exactly why I need to run now.

FOUR
UNRAVELING

*G*ranny!

The thought hits me like a physical blow—*whoever did this was in the house with Granny.*

Cold terror courses through me, and I tighten my robe as I race downstairs, my bare feet slipping on the hardwood.

"Granny!" My voice cracks with panic. "Granny, where are you?"

Silence.

I pound on her bedroom door. "Gran? Gran!" I twist the knob, then slam the door open. "Are you in here? Are you okay?"

No one.

Just an empty room, the bed neatly made, the pillows placed exactly like she does every morning.

I clutch the doorjamb. Forcing myself to think despite the rising tide of fear. There's no sign of a struggle...but there's no Gran, either.

Please no, please no...

My eyes sweep over her room, as if I'll find her in a corner. As if the panic clawing at my throat means nothing.

Except it means everything. Because I know what happened, and as much as I want to run and hide under my bed—as much as

I want Gran to hold me and pat my back and tell me things will be just fine—I know better.

Someone took her.

Someone broke into my house, left that horrible video, and took my grandmother.

And each and every one of those things was done to hurt me. To scare me.

Leo?

But no. He's an ass—no question there. But I can't believe he'd do that.

But if not him, then who?

The question haunts me as I pat the back pocket of my jeans, only to realize I don't have my phone. I whirl around, then race out of Granny's room and back to the stairs, taking them two at a time. I'm winded when I grab my phone off my nightstand, then fumble before finally managing to hit the speed dial for Sasha.

I pace the room, holding the phone in front of me like it's some magical talisman as it rings and rings and—

"Rue?" Her voice over the speaker is sharp. "Tell me he wasn't waiting on the path—"

"Someone broke into the house." The words tumble over each other as I blurt them out. "There was a video, and now Gran—"

"Wait, what?" Her voice is sharp with alarm.

"They left a—a video playing on my laptop. And Granny's gone and I can't find her anywhere and someone was in my house and—"

"Ruby, stop. It's okay. Stop and breathe." Sasha's voice is calm, controlled.

"It's not okay. It's very much not—"

"Birgit's here." Her voice is soft. Calming. But the words make no sense.

"What are you talking about?"

"Birgit's here with me and Liam. She's fine. She walked over about twenty minutes ago. She's completely safe."

I shake my head, not understanding. "But how? Why?"

"She said I texted, asking her to come over."

"You did?" I can barely focus on her words, too relieved that Gran is safe. "What for?"

"No, that's what I'm telling you. I didn't, but you know how twisted up she gets with texting, so I just figured you sent a text asking her to come by."

"Oh. *Oh!*" Relief crashes over me with such force that my knees buckle. I sink onto the edge of my bed, pressing my free hand to my chest. "She's really okay?"

"She's fine. She's downstairs with Liam right now. But what the hell happened?" Her voice has a dark edge now. "What was on your laptop? A video of what?"

The relief that had cloaked me vanishes, twisting into a sick mixture of rage and humiliation. "Me—" I have to swallow. "Me and Leo. From—from before. When we were together."

Silence stretches across the line, long enough that I wonder if the call dropped.

Her voice is low and hard when she finally speaks. "Are you telling me someone left a sex vid on your laptop?"

"Not someone," I say, my voice hard. "I know damn well who did it. He had to hack my computer password to upload the thing." I wipe away the runaway tears that stream down my cheeks. "Leo Grimm could hack a computer before he could walk."

"That sick son of a bitch." I can hear her moving. "I can't believe he'd do that."

"I can."

She sighs. "Yeah. I guess I can, too. Rue, I'm so sorry."

"I just—I just want to curl into a ball and die."

"He's the asshole, Rue. You didn't do anything wrong."

"Except trust him."

"Yeah, well, he's the prick, and you're coming here and staying the night with me. Pack a bag. I'm going to send Liam to come get you."

"Sasha—"

"No arguments. Even if it's not Leo—and it might not be," she says, her words hard and measured and allowing for no interruption—"someone is fucking with you, and you're not staying there a minute longer than you have to."

I want to argue about Leo, because I know what I know. But I also know I'm not staying in this house alone tonight. "Where should I wait for him?"

"Where are you now?"

"My bedroom."

"Alone? You're sure?"

I glance around. The house is old enough that there's no closet. Instead, my clothes are tucked into a dresser or hanging in the wardrobe. I can't imagine a person could hide in there with all my clothes jammed in, but I check just in case. Then I take a peek under the bed, before a final glance around the bathroom. "Alone," I say. "I'm sure."

"Lock the bedroom door and don't go down until Liam gets there."

After we hang up, I grab an overnight bag and start to fill it with leggings, jeans, underwear, and a few T-shirts. I pack my laptop, too, vile though it may now be.

All in all, my luggage isn't much different than what I take on weekend vacations. Except I've never been terrified before setting off on a long weekend.

I try to shake off some of the fear as I wait, but every creak of settling wood makes me jump, and I hate Leo even more for turning my safe and cozy home into a place that feels vile and full of danger.

I'm off the bed and pacing two minutes later when my phone rings and Marcus's name flashes on the screen.

For a moment, I consider letting it go to voicemail. But at the same time, I want the distraction.

"Hi, Marcus. How are you feeling?"

"Better, actually." His voice is warm, confident. "I went to a clinic, and it turns out it's just allergies. So I thought I'd try to salvage the weekend. Maybe order in a pizza and watch a movie if you're still available tonight? Or have you tossed me aside for a hot date?"

I know he's teasing, but I cringe a little. And—damn me—my mind conjures Leo.

"That sounds great," I say. It's not a lie. Right now, pizza and wine and a movie with a nice, normal guy who isn't stalking me sounds like heaven. "But I can't," I add, hoping I don't sound like a woman about to jump out of her skin. "A work thing came up, and Sasha and I are in for an all-nighter."

"I get it," he says. "I'll just take a rain check."

"You're a really great guy," I say, meaning it. And wishing that this really great guy pushed my buttons harder.

"Want me to swing by with take-out? You don't even have to invite me in. I just want to make sure you don't forget to eat."

"You're sweet. But Sasha already ordered food." It's a horrible lie, but it pairs well with my horrible guilt. This wonderful man is offering to feed me so I can survive a work marathon. And I'm all but running away.

God. I'm so fucked up.

"Too bad," he says, and there's real heat in his voice when he adds, "I've been looking forward to seeing you again. Even if just for a minute."

Something twists in my chest—not attraction, not longing, but something uncomfortably close to guilt. Or shame. Because even as he offers to take care of me, my mind keeps returning to the images on my laptop...and the memory of how I'd felt seven years ago, tied spread-eagled to a bed frame, more than happy to let Leo Grimm do any wild and perverse thing he wanted to, so long as in the end, he made me come.

He never once failed.

"—you could come."

I stiffen. "Sorry. What?"

"I said I'm going into Manhattan tomorrow. If things aren't too crazy, you could come with me."

"Oh. I—I have back-to-back meetings tomorrow."

"Pity," Marcus says. "Well, I'll let you get back to it. If you need anything—food, an emergency massage—just give me a call."

"I will," I promise, even though I know I won't call him. Not later tonight. Not tomorrow. And when I finally do, it will be to walk away.

He's a sweet guy, but he's not for me.

Leo Grimm is not a sweet guy, and I don't want him to be for me, either. Except some seriously fucked-up part of me does. The part that's still a naive little college girl who thought she'd found the man of her dreams, only to learn that the dream was a nightmare.

That girl still lives inside me, and she still craves the man who destroyed her. And I need to figure out how to shut her up or change her mind. Because there is no way I'm getting into bed with Leo Grimm again. Not actually. Not metaphorically. Not any way.

He's dead to me. And the fact that he now seems intent on tormenting me…

Well, maybe that damn video scared me at first. But now I'm just pissed off.

And that's a good thing. Pissed off, I can handle. Pissed off kicks me into business mode, and I'm damn good at that. At pulling back. At compartmentalizing. At dealing only with the facts, the projections, the potential outcomes. Not emotions.

Because it's those ooey-gooey emotions that make everything a mess. Leo taught me that lesson back before I knew how to shut it all down.

Now? Well, now I don't have any goo left for Leo. I haven't for a long time. There's just contempt bordering on hatred. And that hate will make me strong.

The sound of tires on gravel pushes me to my feet, and I peer out my window to see Liam emerging from a sleek, black Jaguar. He turns slowly, scanning the area with the practiced eye of someone who's spent years looking for threats. Then he approaches the house slowly, hands visible, and I realize he's being careful not to spook me.

Smart man, though a bit of overkill. After all, he's Sasha's husband. My days of thinking he's an ass are over. Except for the fact that he genuinely loves—and likes—Leo. That, I just don't get.

I'm hurrying down the stairs as he knocks, but I wait until he calls out, "It's Liam," before I open the door, keeping the chain on until I can double-check that no one's crept up behind him. As if someone could sneak up on Liam. So not happening.

Then I open the door and step back to let him in.

He fills the doorway—tall, broad-shouldered, with copper hair and pale blue eyes that miss nothing. He's wearing dark jeans and a black sweater, looking more like a sexy action hero than the billionaire CEO he actually is.

"You okay?" he asks, his voice gentle despite his intimidating appearance.

That simple question breaks something loose in my chest. "No. I'm really fucking not okay."

He steps inside, closing and locking the door behind him. "Tell me what happened. Step by step."

So I do. I tell him everything, my face burning as I tell him about the video. About the violation of seeing myself so young and trusting.

"That's what your brother is capable of," I finish, surprised by how steady my voice sounds. "That's what he did to me seven years ago, and that's what he's doing now. He never once told me he was taping us. He's a monster, Liam."

Liam's jaw tightens, but he doesn't immediately defend Leo the way I expected. Instead, he runs a hand through his hair and sighs.

"There's not a hero in my whole damn family," he says quietly. "But I don't believe Leo would do this. The taping, maybe. But harassing you? That's not his style."

"You're too damn trusting of the people you love." The words come out sharper than I intended. "That's how he destroyed me before. He drew me in, and I trusted him completely. I won't make that mistake again."

"What if it wasn't him?"

"Then who?" I grab my bag and head for the door. "Who else would have access to that video? I mean, I didn't even know it existed, so who other than Leo would know about it? And besides, who else would know exactly how to hurt me?"

Liam follows me outside, waiting while I lock the door with shaking hands. "I don't know," he says, "but we'll figure it out."

"Even if you prove that someone else broke in and set the video up on my bed, I'll still believe that Leo was behind it. And," I add, looking him straight in the eye, "I think you believe that, too."

He opens the passenger door for me but doesn't meet my eyes. "We'll figure it out," he repeats firmly. "And it won't be Leo who left that vid."

I believe the first part. Liam Grimm has resources that most people can't even imagine. If there's a trail to follow, he'll find it.

But I don't believe the second part. Deep in my bones, I know Leo Grimm is behind this. And nothing Liam discovers will convince me otherwise.

FIVE
SAFE HARBOR

The security at Liam and Sasha's house is impressive even by billionaire standards, a little tidbit I picked up by not only being Sasha's bestie for basically our entire lives, but by being right by her and Liam's side when all the shit went down with them and her father. That's when Liam increased the security tenfold to be absolutely certain the security around Sasha was impenetrable.

Now, they have gates that require both a code and a biometric scan, cameras tracking our approach, and discrete but obvious armed guards at key points around the massive property. But while getting onto the property may be a challenge of *Mission Impossible* proportions, the house itself has no visible security. Nothing at all to hide its magnificence, which is all the more impressive since Liam built it himself, though I have no idea how he managed. Then again, all of the Grimm brothers are over-the-top talented and smart. Too bad only Liam is nice. Not to mention sane.

I glance over as Liam drives slowly, careful of the wildlife that darts across the long drive. The house is built into the hillside with modern lines of wood and stone highlighted by enormous windows. It's nothing short of a fortress, but it's not off-putting at all. On the contrary, it's warm and welcoming.

He parks in the circular drive, and Sasha pulls me into a fierce hug the moment I'm through the door. "I'm so sorry this is happening."

"Where's Granny?"

"Kitchen. She's baking." We share a grin. Granny bakes when she's stressed. Well, she bakes all the time, but when she's stressed, she goes all-in. I have a feeling that by bedtime, there will be enough cakes and muffins and cookies for Sasha to set up her own stall at the farmers market.

I know my way around, so I hurry to the kitchen to find Granny standing at the counter with a mixing bowl held tight with one arm while she folds chips into the cookie dough with the other. She looks up, sees me, and her face crumples with relief.

"Ruby!" She practically throws the bowl onto the counter, then wraps me in her arms. "I've been so worried."

I hold her tight, breathing in her familiar scent of lavender and vanilla. For the first time since I found that laptop, I feel like I can breathe.

"I'm sorry Leo pulled you into this. The prick," I add, despite Granny's disdain of what she calls "salty language."

"Now, Liebling, we don't know it was Leo." She pulls back to look at me with those sharp eyes. "I remember that boy from when you were dating. He was wild, yes, and perhaps his charm hid a good bit of mischief. But I never saw an ounce of cruelty." She shakes her head. "No, Liebling, I can't believe he would do such a thing."

The casual dismissal of my certainty makes something break inside me. "Dammit, Granny. He did. He's horrible."

"Ruby—"

"No." I snap out the word. "You don't know him like I do. And you definitely don't know what he's capable of. What he did to me," I add, my voice tight.

"Liebling, please. You must—"

"He left a sex tape." I shudder, hating that those, raw and ugly words have contaminated the warmth of this kitchen. "A video of me naked and tied up, from when we were in college. A video I didn't even know he was making."

The silence that follows is deafening. Granny's face goes pale, her hand flying to her mouth. Sasha looks as stricken as she'd sounded on the phone, and Liam's already hard expression darkens to something thunderous.

As for me, I just stand there under a mountain of mortification, barely able to believe what I just confessed to my grandmother.

"Oh, hell," I whisper, my chest tight. "I'm sorry. I shouldn't have told you—"

"Hush, child," she says, her voice as soft and warm as a blanket. And then she's holding me again, and I'm crying—ugly, broken sobs that I've been holding back since I saw that video, all the humiliation and rage spewing out of me.

"There's no shame in loving someone," Granny whispers as she strokes my hair. "No shame in trusting. If he did this terrible thing, then he is a chameleon, because that is not the boy I met."

"You're a good judge of character," I say when I can speak again. "I am, too. Usually. But we were both wrong about Leo Grimm. So very, very wrong."

She cups my face in her weathered hands, forcing me to meet her eyes. "And if you were wrong then, could you be wrong now?"

The question hangs in the air like a challenge. I want to say no. Want to cling to my certainty that Leo is behind this. Because if he's not, then someone else has that video. And god only knows what they intend to do with it.

I shudder, then turn to Liam. "I don't want to see him."

"Ruby—"

"But I have to," I add. The admission tastes like defeat. "I have to know what he wants from me."

"Birgit is right. It might not have been Leo." Liam's voice is low and firm.

"Of course it was."

Liam's eyes cut to Sasha, as if there's something he needs to tell me, and he's dreading it.

"Just say it." I clutch my twisting stomach. "Might as well pile it all on."

"I had three other brothers back when you and Leo were dating."

I shake my head, not understanding.

He rubs his temples, then sighs. "I wouldn't put it past any one of them to rig a camera in Leo's room. Make a tape to tease him with later. Or to keep as leverage."

I shake my head. "No way. Leo was too smart, even back then. Too careful." I cross my arms. "Could Alexander have rigged your room without you knowing it?"

The tiniest hint of pride shines in his eyes. "No."

"Same goes for Leo. So stop trying to let him off the hook."

Liam looks like he wants to argue, but he says nothing. Granny looks between us, then cups my cheek. "You three should talk. I'll be watching my shows. You come when you need me."

I nod and give her a hug before she heads to the living area.

"He wants to protect you," Liam says a few moments later, his soft voice breaking the lingering silence. "You know that."

I shrug. What Leo Grimm says and what he means don't necessarily match up. With a sigh, I tilt my head and meet Liam's eyes. "All right," I say. "You trust him, I get that. But then you tell me—what exactly is this threat that he's supposedly determined to protect me from?"

"I don't know." The admission clearly costs him. "I called, but he won't give me details either. But I don't believe that he's the one who left the video. Like I said, for all we know, he's as surprised as you that the video even exists."

I tilt my head and stare him down. To his credit, he shrugs. "Fair enough," he says. "He probably did tape the two of you. I wouldn't put that past him. But leaving it like a bomb on your bed—torturing you with something I know meant the world to him…" He trails off with a shake of his head. "I don't believe it."

"A sex tape meant the world to him?" My voice is like a sneer. "Yeah, that sounds like Leo."

"Ruby…" Sasha's voice is soft.

"Not the video," Liam says firmly. "You. Or, more exactly, the two of you. Your relationship." He pauses, his expression as serious as I've ever seen it. "He loved you, Ruby. I think he still does."

"He never really loved me." I stare at the floor, not wanting him to see the tears that now sting my eyes. Tears for what I've lost. For what I'd never really had.

And now here's Leo all over again, twisting that goddamn knife.

Love? Leo Grimm wouldn't know love if it kicked him in the teeth. And damned if I don't wish that I'd done just that. Today. Back then. Whenever I'd had the chance.

I look up to see Liam watching me. I turn away.

"I'll be the first to call Leo out if he deserves it," he says softly, like he's talking to a skittish puppy. "But I don't think he does. Not about this, anyway."

I shrug, suddenly exhausted by all of it. "Fine. Whatever. Let's give him the benefit of the doubt and say he's not behind the break-in. Let's say my creepy stalker is someone else who wants to scare me or hurt me." I look between Liam and Sasha. "Let's say Liam's right and Leo just wants to protect me." I shake my head. "No way will I ever accept protection from that fucker."

I see the pain in Sasha's eyes when she says, "Ruby…"

"No. Just no." I hold up a hand and draw in a breath. "Come on, Sasha. You know what happened. Leo Grimm dumped me on the worst day of my life. No warning. No kindness. Just *blam*. It was like he couldn't get away from me fast enough. I learned a lot about people that day. About how cruel they can be. And how fake."

I shift to look at Liam. "Sasha knows how much it destroyed

me. Trust Leo Grimm?" I look between the two of them. "Never again."

Sasha nods. I know she remembers that night as well as I do. Hell, I practically drowned us both in my tears.

I turn my attention to Liam. "How much do you know about all that?"

"The details?" He shakes his head. "I don't. I was dealing with my own shit in Chicago back then. So when he told me he cut you loose, it surprised the shit out of me."

I cross my arms. "Yeah? Why?"

"Because whenever he talked to me about you, it sounded like he'd fallen hard. The big L. I still think so," he adds, his voice going softer.

I start to protest, but he cuts me off.

"Until you, Leo was the guy who had a new fling every other sunrise. But you? He was sticking. Or so I thought. When he said you'd broken up, I figured I'd misread the signs." He looks me straight in the eye. "Now, I don't think I did."

"Why?"

"Things he's said over the years. The way he's always showing up at events you're attending." He smiles a little. "I've steered him away because you asked me to, not because I thought he needed steering."

I nod. I can't argue that Liam's been on my side. Or, he has ever since he landed at Sasha's.

"Okay, fine," I say. "Let's pretend you're right and he loved me. Then why did he dump me?"

"I don't know," he says, his voice soft and soothing. "But I know Leo almost as well as I know myself. He wouldn't go out of his way to hurt you like that. He just wouldn't."

"Oh, he would," I say.

Liam nods. "Fair enough. But whether what's going on now is him, another one of my brothers, some other stalker, or little green elves from space, the bottom line is that you're vulnerable."

I swallow, then nod.

"Best case, someone's just messing with your mind. Worst case, they want you dead. I can't imagine why, but we have to move forward as if you're in the crosshairs of an assassin's gun."

He's right. I wish he weren't, but I know he is.

"So you'll stay here while we figure it out," he continues. "I'll even double security if it will make you feel better."

"You double security, and this house will have more protection than most small countries."

"And that's a problem?"

I laugh, which feels pretty good. But the truth is, he may be right. After all, I can't go home. Not now. Maybe never. My lovely little cottage may never feel safe again.

But at the same time, I know I can't stay here. Leo will figure it out the moment he comes to visit, and Liam brushes him off.

Leo Grimm is not a fool.

I need something better. Something bolder, and I mentally flip through every possibility I can think of. Finally, I lift my head and smile. "Why don't I just disappear? Go off-grid? Then let him try and track me down."

Liam lifts a brow. "Have you met my little brother? The man's a fixer. A security expert. Implementing it and breaking it. Trust me when I say that he'll find you."

"Okay, maybe. But you can help me with a new identity, right?" I consider it. Liam may be right—Leo is damn good at what he does—and I'm pretty sure that Leo's job in security straddles the line between legal and not-so-legal.

But it's not as if I'm going to go off the grid forever. I just need to buy some time. Surely I can disappear for a few weeks, then have Liam bring me back when I've figured out what to do next.

"But where will you go?" Sasha asks, after I explain all that. "If you only need a few weeks, why not stay here?"

"Leo would expect it," Liam says before I can reply. "And you can bet he'll be showing up here later today. He probably already knows she's here. At the very least, he suspects it."

"Fine," Sasha says, though she doesn't seem happy. "And still I ask—where?"

"Still thinking." I look at Liam. "And you really won't tell him?"

"I swear. But for the record, I still think you're wrong about him."

"You have to think that. He's your brother."

Liam snorts. "If it were Elliott or Alexander, I'd be the first to accuse them. And god knows if Gabriel were still alive, it would take very little to convince me that he'd harass an old girlfriend. Leo may be the only one of my brothers I give a shit about, but if I thought he'd done this, I'd call him out." Those pale blue eyes focus on me. "And whether you want to admit it or not, you know that."

He's right. I know perfectly well that Leo is the only one of his half-brothers Liam respects. Or likes, for that matter. "I know," I say. "But you're wrong."

"And if I turn out to be right?"

"Then I guess the drinks are on me." I share a smile with him, then turn to Sasha, who looks caught between laughing and crying. "I'll be fine," I tell her.

"You better be. Because if anything happens to you, I'm going to kick your ass."

"Where will you go?" The question comes from Granny, and the three of us turn to see her standing in the doorway. From her expression, it's clear she's been there for a while. And the fact that she hasn't interrupted or insisted that I stay close gives me a new burst of confidence.

This is the right decision. I'm sure of it.

I let my gaze rake over the three of them, smiling for the first time since this nightmare began. "I know just the place."

SIX

UNDONE

The Celestial rises into the Manhattan sky like a crystal spear, all glass and steel and old money elegance. I've been here before for various conferences and events, but never as a guest. Never with a driver's license bearing the name Rebecca Stone and a fuck-you attitude toward whoever's trying to mess with my life.

I hold my breath as I check in, but everything goes smoothly. I pay cash for my room but give them Rebecca's black Amex card for incidentals. Then I take my room key from the desk clerk with a smile, tuck it into my purse, and hurry toward the elevator, hoping that the sound of my pounding heart isn't echoing throughout the elegant lobby.

"How long did it take you to put this together?" I'd asked Liam just two hours ago, as I'd fingered the proof of my new, secret life.

"An hour," he'd said with a slight smile. "The benefits of having friends in very low places."

The ease with which he'd erased Ruby Ryder and created Rebecca Stone should have been reassuring. Instead, it left me slightly unsettled. If Liam could make me disappear this easily, who knows what Leo could do? At the very least, he could seriously fuck my life. As in, even more than he already has.

Since I've decided to hide out by burying myself in luxury, I take the private elevator to the very top floor, then draw in a breath when it opens onto the Presidential Suite. The room is even more posh than I'd imagined. And much better in real life than in the photos on the hotel's website. I step out of the elevator and walk reverently to the wall of floor-to-ceiling windows. I press my palm to the glass, then draw a deep breath, feeling strangely safe at this height. As if I'm not just looking out at Central Park, but at a new life.

I don't intend to be Rebecca forever, but at the moment, it feels right and real.

Or is that just a justification for running away?

I dismiss the annoying voice in my head. I'm not running, I'm regrouping. And I'm moving myself away from the danger zone to do that. It's the smart move. The right move.

The safe move.

With that thought running through my head like a refrain, I explore the rest of my seriously awesome suite that includes a huge, ornate bedroom that boasts a bed that could comfortably sleep six people. Or one person who needs to spread out all her emotional baggage.

There's even a full kitchen with its own entrance, presumably so that the staff can come and go to prepare food without having to interrupt a guest by crossing through the dining area. I check that lock, too—just to be sure—then head back into the bedroom, satisfied that this penthouse suite is locked up tight.

Self-tour over, I sit on the bed, then bounce a little as I order a fruit and cheese plate for dinner, along with an exceptional vintage pinot noir, just because spoiling myself seems like a really good idea.

Room service arrives so quickly that I begin to think that Rebecca's Black Card has magical powers. And less than ten minutes later, I'm settled on the suite's ridiculously comfy velvet armchair, watching bad reality TV while I sip my wine and enjoy the most impressive fruit and cheese plate I've ever seen.

Then I pick up Rebecca's phone and call Sasha.

"You're safe?"

"All good," I assure her. "Or, well, you know."

"As good as you can be."

"Exactly."

There's a pause, and I know Sasha well enough to know that means she wants to tell me something that she doesn't think I want to hear. "I can still do remote work for Lydia Cos," I say. "Don't take that away from me. I'll just spend every waking hour obsessing if you do."

"No, it's Leo."

My back goes rigid. "What about him?"

"I don't think he's the one who set the laptop up in your room."

"Oh." That was the last thing I expected to hear. "Why?"

"Because we all know—and Leo, too—that Birgit goes into your room to clean, put away your clothes, and sometimes use your jacuzzi tub. Leo can be an ass—no argument from me—but he always liked Birgit. He wouldn't risk her finding that video."

I draw a breath. She's right.

"Then who?"

"I don't know. But Liam agrees."

I stay silent, not sure if I'm relieved it wasn't Leo—because now I'm certain that it wasn't—or even more scared, since that means there's someone else skulking around and fucking with my life. And how the hell am I supposed to find them?

"You okay?"

"Fine," I assure her. "Liam's on it, right?"

"All over it. I wish I could come stay with you."

"Me, too. But I'm fine." I grimace. I'm not remotely fine. In fact, now I'm more stressed than ever. But no way am I telling Sasha that.

We chat a bit more, and then I end the call, saying that the stress has tired me out, and I'm crashing early.

Instead, as two reality stars scream at each other on the giant

TV screen about nothing in particular, I pick up the nearby house phone and call down to schedule a massage. I won't indulge like this every night, but I think going overboard right now is reasonable. After all, it's been one hell of a day.

"In-room, please," I say in response to the attendant's question. "And tonight, if possible."

"Of course, Ms. Stone. Let me check the schedule."

Ms. Stone. Every time I hear the fake name, I feel a little bit safer. After all, Rebecca Stone has no history with Leo Grimm. No weird stalker leaving sex tapes. No baggage, no broken heart, no reason to be afraid. All she wants is her wine, her fruit, her cheese, and her massage.

"We have slots available tonight at eight and nine-thirty. The next availability is tomorrow at eleven. Are any of those convenient?"

I glance at my watch. "Eight tonight would be great." That's only forty-five minutes from now, and the idea of complete relaxation on the heels of the day I've had feels like a gift from the gods.

"Swedish, deep tissue, or hot stone?"

"Whatever will make me forget the worst day of my life." I wince, realizing I'd said that aloud.

"That's our specialty." I can almost hear the smile in her voice.

As soon as I hang up the phone, I take a long sip of wine, letting even more of the day's tension dissolve.

Outside, the sun has dropped low in the sky, bathing the city in a golden hue. It's beautiful and weirdly calming, and from forty floors above the city, the chaos of my life seems far away. As if all this scary bullshit is nothing more than a bad dream.

By seven-thirty, I've had a luxurious bath in the suite's humongous tub, finished off most of the wine, and changed into the hotel's plush terry cloth robe. When the door chimes at eight PM sharp, I'm feeling pleasantly buzzed and more relaxed than I have all day.

I open the door to find a man in his thirties with kind eyes and a professional demeanor. He's carrying a massage table and shoulder bag with the hotel spa's logo, and his polite smile erases the tiny, niggling doubts about inviting a stranger into my suite. He's not a stranger. He's a vetted hotel employee.

As if to prove my point, he extends a hand. "Ms. Stone? I'm David from the spa. Where would you like me to set up?"

I shake my head, clueless. "Wherever works best."

He gestures toward the windows. "If you open your eyes, you'll have a lovely view."

I nod in agreement, then watch as he sets everything up with practiced efficiency. Then he steps back. "I'll wait in the kitchen while you get settled. Just strip down to your comfort level, then get on the table face down under the sheet. I'll tap on the door before I come back in."

I nod, then wait for him to disappear into the kitchen before slipping off my robe and tossing it onto a nearby chair. I'm naked now, and even though I know David won't walk in, I hurry onto the table and position myself like he'd said. I close my eyes, draw in a deep breath, then let it out slowly. The suite is quiet, and for the first time since I found that video on my laptop, I feel something approaching peace.

A soft tap interrupts my thoughts.

"Come on in."

The carpeting is too dense to hear footsteps, but soon enough the scent of massage oil—something warm and woodsy—fills the air.

"Just relax." He's speaking in a low whisper that seems almost as intimate as a touch, and I let my eyes drift closed.

I hear him rubbing his hands together. Then warm, oiled hands settle on my shoulders, and I sigh with relief. After the stress of the last few days, this is definitely what I need.

His hands are skilled, working the knots out of my shoulders with just the right pressure. Not too gentle, not too rough. Exactly as I like it, and I'm grateful for this perfect end to a truly horrific day.

I let myself drift on the sensation of finally feeling safe and free and taken care of. I exhale, letting my mind go pleasantly fuzzy. The wine has left me feeling loose and relaxed, and combined with the expert touch, I feel like I'm floating.

"How's the pressure?" His voice is so soft I can barely hear him.

"Perfect," I murmur into the face cradle.

His hands move along my spine, and I can't help the soft sound of pleasure that escapes me. It's been so long since anyone's touched me like this. I've had kisses with Marcus, but he's playing the gentleman, and that's as far as it's gone.

Now, this gentle contact is like balm on a wound I didn't know was still festering.

"You carry a lot of tension," he murmurs.

I make a soft sound of agreement, too relaxed to form actual words. His hands continue their work, moving lower along my back, and I swear I'm standing at the gates of heaven.

When his hands reach the sheet covering my rear, I let out a long sigh, my mind drifting with pleasure. And, yes, with an inappropriate fantasy, too. Not a scene with Marcus, who should be in my thoughts, but with an anonymous man, strong and dark. A man who doesn't exist, but all too often stars in my fantasies. Because lately, fantasies are all I have in that department.

"Any requests?" The whispered voice seems like a caress in and of itself.

"Just this. It's perfect." And it is. His hands are magic, finding every knot, every source of tension. I'm not sure if it's the wine or if David is just exceptionally skilled, but I've never had a massage this good except from Leo, and I give in to the warm, glowy feeling and simply let myself melt under his expert touch as he continues working his way down my back in a way that makes me feel both floaty and hyper-aware.

When his fingers skim the edge of the sheet, I make another soft sound of pleasure—then suck in a little gasp when he pulls the sheet slowly up from the bottom, exposing one leg. He works on my calf first, then moves his hands higher until he's working my thigh in long, sensual strokes, sliding higher and higher until I start to fear that he's going to slide his hands all the way up to my core.

Then I start to fear that he won't, especially when the way he's touching me triggers so many memories. Leo's hands, both rough and soft against my skin. The slow, strong strokes with which he used to massage me. The way he'd draw it out, letting the pleasure of his touch grow and grow.

Leo.

I tell myself to stop—to let go of that fantasy. But at the same time, what's wrong with a little make-believe, especially when these long, sensuous strokes are already making me wet?

I know I should ask him to focus on my back. My shoulders. My neck. Instead, I spread my legs just a bit, hardly able to believe that I'm doing this, letting myself fall into the fantasy of Leo. Of what we used to have. Of how he made me feel. Because, damn me all to hell, I want this. I want the touch. I want the sensations, I want the memories of the touch of that man I loved. The man I now loathe.

I want to be here, locked in my fortress of a suite, and let this man touch me the way Marcus never had the balls to.

The way Leo always did.

It's been far too long since I've had this kind of attention from a man. Leo. Only Leo. And though I hate that I'm thinking of him, that's how I'm longing to be satisfied.

I'm going to hell. I'm one hundred percent going to hell.

Except I'm not. I'm an adult. And, dammit, even if it's just for the next few minutes, I want to lose myself in sensuality and this stranger's touch.

He's not a stranger. You know he's not a stranger.

I ignore the voice in my head. The little fantasy that's spinning out in my mind. Instead, I give myself over as he slowly parts my thighs, his hand sliding up my sensitive skin, leaving plenty of time for me to protest. I don't. I only sigh when he finds my core, his finger teasing my clit as I suck in air, relishing the sweet sensations that ripple through me—then I whimper as he slides one finger inside me, then teases my clit with his other hand as his finger strokes my G-spot.

Yes. Oh, god, yes.

My cheeks are burning, but I don't want him to stop. I'm probably going to hell, but I don't care. I want this. Hell, I'm relishing it. Most of all, I'm lost in the memory of a deep intimacy that I've missed…and have been craving for too damn long.

"Let yourself go," he whispers as he teases my clit and my ass. "Just shed all of that tension."

I let myself relax even more. *Feel* even more. The way my body tingles and tightens. So close. So goddamn close.

"That's it," he says. "I want to see you. You're like a goddess when you come."

Those words!

I try to roll over, but he moves one hand to my back and holds me down, the other now focused entirely on my clit.

"Stop," I beg. "Dammit, Leo, stop."

But he doesn't. With one hand, he keeps me down, and with the other, he makes me come with the expertise of a man who knows my body all too well.

A long, drawn-out, tingly, hot, vibrant, hateful orgasm rolls through me, making my body arch and quake, my nipples tighten, and my core get exponentially wetter.

"That's my girl," he says, then backs away as the last shock of the wildest orgasm of my life rips through me. I gasp, my heart pounding as I scramble into a sitting position, the sheet held against me like a shield.

"You son-of-a-bitch." I throw the words at him like knives, all the harder because I've realized that—not only has he been the man starring in my fantasies for years, but that somehow—someway—I knew it was him from that very first touch.

Not that I will ever, *ever* admit that to him.

"Good to see you, too," he says lightly. "I never realized you were so into happy endings."

My face goes hot. "How the hell did you find me?"

He laughs. "Come on, Red. If you thought you could hide behind a fake name and a posh address, then you never really knew me at all."

"That was rape."

"Bullshit. You could have said stop at any time. For that matter, you could have kept your thighs closed. Looked like a beautiful invite to me."

"I thought it was David."

"The hell you did. You knew it was me." He steps closer, and I freeze as he puts his hands on my knees, then pushes them apart, easily foiling my attempt to keep my legs locked together as my feet dangle off the table. "You wanted it to be me." He stands between my thighs, my still-wet core barely hidden beneath the sheet, and his body far too close.

"And you didn't want me to stop because you were enjoying it too much."

He's not wrong. Except for being so very *wrong*. My cheeks burn with mortification, but I stare him down anyway, hoping my eyes look hard and unforgiving.

His, of course, are dancing with amusement.

"I wouldn't have enjoyed it at all if I'd known it was you."

He tilts his head, a mannerism that always makes his smile look that much more cocky. "Sorry, Red. I don't believe you."

"Don't call me that," I snap, remembering all too well how that nickname sounded as he whispered sweet words to me in bed. "You lost the right long ago."

I flinch as he reaches for me, then runs a strand of my red hair through his fingers. "Ah, but we're not finished."

"The hell we aren't." But even as I say it, I feel my body responding to his touch. The wine, the relaxation, the loneliness—they've all combined to strip away my defenses.

"Your body doesn't seem to agree." His hand moves lower, his fingertip dancing over my collarbone. "You were practically purring under my hands."

"I thought you were David!"

"And now you know better." His voice is dark with satisfaction. "But you're not fighting very hard, are you?"

He's right, and I hate him for it. I should be screaming, clawing, doing everything I can to get away. Instead, I'm letting him touch me.

"I've had too much wine," I whisper.

"Have you?" His fingers dance along my neck in a way that makes me shiver. "Or have you been lying awake at night thinking about this? Thinking about me?"

"Hardly," I lie. Because the horrible truth is that there've been far too many nights when I've gotten off with a toy and the memory of how it felt to be touched by him. How it felt to be wanted so completely.

"Nothing between us is real," I murmur, more to myself than to him. "It never was."

"Bullshit." He snaps the word out, the force of the denial startling me. Then he flashes that grin again as he slides his hand lower, taking the sheet with him and exposing my breasts.

I stay perfectly still, not willing to give him the satisfaction of fighting, ignoring the way my nipples have peaked, now painfully hard.

He tugs the sheet lower, finally pulling it firmly from my grasp and leaving me seated naked on the massage table and fully exposed since he's already pushed my thighs apart.

His fingertips are dancing up my thighs, the touch teasing, and my arousal now impossible to hide.

"Stop," I whisper. "Please, Leo. Stop."

But he just slides two fingertips deep into my core.

"Tell me you don't want this," he says quietly. "Tell me your body isn't aching for my touch. Tell me," he repeats, "and I'll stop."

I open my mouth to say exactly that, but the words won't

come. Because despite everything—despite my anger, despite my fear, despite knowing this is exactly what he wants—my body is betraying me.

"I hate you," I whisper instead.

"I know." He slides his fingers in and out, each motion teasing my clit. "But you want me anyway."

His touch is sure, confident, and he explores my core with the skill of a master. He's always known how to make me fall apart, and god help me, I do, my hands clutching the edge of the table as he teases my clit, as he thrusts inside me, as he bends to run his teeth over my nipple. As he whispers how hot I make him, how much he likes seeing me wet.

How desperately he wants to fuck me.

And—damn me—even though this is the worst kind of violation—even though I hate him with a desperate, deep loathing—right here and right now, I don't care. All I want is for him to make me come again. And I'm close. So wildly, desperately, horribly close.

He backs away, breaking contact.

I draw in a ragged breath, frustration crawling over me like ants. "Leo?"

He lifts a brow. "Wouldn't want me to cross a line, would you?"

"You already did. Have you forgotten?"

Humor lights those damnable green eyes. "And that seemed to upset you."

"You prick," I snap. "You goddamn, miserable prick."

"You hate me," he says, handing me the fallen sheet. "You'll feel better tomorrow knowing I didn't fuck you."

He steps closer, then puts his hands on my knees as he leans in to whisper. "But don't worry, Red. I will have you. Fully. Completely. But not now. That's not why I'm here."

"Get out," I snap, completely mortified. "Get out of my room."

"No," he says.

"Fuck you," I snap.

"As I said, I will. But not quite yet." His grin is smug as he moves to the bar and pours himself a drink. "You can get dressed now."

I don't move. Can't move. I'm too mortified, too angry, too confused by my response to him. By my fury that he left me hanging. And for the still-lingering desire to feel him inside me.

What the hell is wrong with me?

"Ruby." His voice is sharp as he turns to face me, now holding a whiskey. "Get dressed."

"Why?" I clutch the sheet tighter around me. "So you can gloat? So you can remind me that you still own me?"

"So we can talk about the people who want to hurt you. About why you need my protection, whether you want it or not."

"I don't need anything from you."

"Bullshit." He steps closer, and I can see the satisfaction in his green eyes. "You were made for my touch."

"No. I—"

"You're still mine, Ruby. You'll always be mine. And if you think I'm a danger to you, imagine what someone who actually wants to hurt you could do. Because they will."

My lips part, but I can't find any words.

"Get dressed now," he orders, "or I'll dress you myself. And punish you for disobeying me when all I'm trying to do is keep you safe."

I glare, but I go. Not because he's told me to, but because I want more than a sheet between us.

That's what I tell myself, but my body is still humming from his touch, and as I cross to the bedroom, I know that he's just proven something I'd desperately hoped wasn't true—Leo Grimm still owns me. And this time, he's not letting me go.

SEVEN
TRAPPED

I close the bedroom door behind me and lean against it, my legs finally giving out. I slide down until I'm sitting on the floor and hugging my knees to my chest as the full weight of what just happened crashes over me.

He made me come.

Hell, he almost made me come twice.

Leo Grimm put his hands on my body and made me fall apart under his touch, and I let him. Worse than that—I wanted it.

All of it.

Shame burns through me like acid, but underneath it is something worse. The lingering heat of arousal that refuses to fade. The way my body still hums with the memory of his fingers on my skin. Of the total naughtiness of what I just let happen.

And of the thrill that his touch—and the circumstances—gave me.

Oh, god.

What is wrong with me?

How could I have responded to him like that? How could I have so desperately craved his touch when I know what the fucker is capable of...and yet even once I realized it was him touching me on that table, I still wanted it. I still wanted him.

61

The wine.

Alcohol reduces inhibitions, right? And I was tipsy—maybe even drunk. Not to mention stressed and scared.

That's all it was. Nothing to do with Leo himself. Nothing to do with craving his touch in those secret, lonely moments that I hate admitting even to myself.

But I have to admit it now. I have to face the truth. Because some sick, horny, spineless, hidden part of me has been craving his touch for seven years. Not the man—no, not Leo Grimm. No way. Not now. Not again.

Not ever.

But his touch…

Oh, yes.

The way he makes my body respond. The way he makes me feel, like the world is on fire and me along with it. Like my body is the center of a universe made of nothing but pleasure.

Like I'm finally, truly alive.

And I hate myself for that.

A sound from the living area reminds me that he's waiting for me. And since I can't hide in this room forever, it's time to get dressed like a good girl so we can have a civilized conversation about why he's here and why the hell he thinks that I'd ever in a million years let him protect me when he's the one person in all the world who's ever truly hurt me.

I force myself to stand on unsteady legs and move to my still-unpacked suitcase. I dig around, then find a tee and my favorite comfy sweats.

As I pull the shirt down over my head, I can't help but catch a glimpse of the full-length mirror that occupies one corner of the room.

"You're a fool," I say to the girl in the mirror. "He's playing games with you. Don't let him win."

But even as I tell her that—the poor, little twit—I know it's too late. Leo Grimm's already won this round. And this game doesn't have do-overs.

Come on, Rue. Get it the fuck together.

Right. I can do this. I handled Leo for years during college—all the way up until he handled me. But I know the man. I can play this game. I just need to be strong. Need to prove to him that I didn't surrender on that damn massage table. On the contrary. I took what I wanted from him, thank you very much. And the fact that he didn't take me all the way a second time? Well, so what? I'm more than capable of taking care of that myself.

So fuck him.

Except not literally. That would be a mistake.

I take a deep breath, then open the bedroom door to find Leo sitting in one of the living room's armchairs, looking perfectly composed. He's changed into dark jeans and a white button-down, and there's no sign of the massage table or any evidence of what passed between us. If not for the satisfied gleam in his green eyes, I might believe I'd imagined the whole thing.

"So, David?"

His brows rise.

"Let me guess. You killed him."

He chuckles. "Close. I manufactured a family emergency. Told him the spa sent me up to take over so he could hurry home."

"Please tell me it was only a scam and you didn't kill his puppy."

He meets my gaze somberly. "I'd never hurt a puppy."

I fight a smile. "It makes me feel better knowing you're only 99.9 percent an asshole."

He spreads his hands and grins. "I aim to please."

This, I realize, is the trap. The memory of how well we'd meshed. Our long talks. Our silly banter. Finishing each other's sentences and knowing each other's needs with nothing more than a glance.

I'd thought it was all real. That he was my soulmate.

I was so damn wrong.

I lift my chin and cross my arms. "You're a prick."

"True," he says with a shrug. "But for a while, I was your prick."

"We all make mistakes." I draw a shaky breath. "You almost broke me, you know. The way you left. It was fucking cruel. But I didn't break, and I'm stronger now. You don't scare me, and you don't control me. And if you ever touch me without my consent again, I promise you'll regret it."

"Noted," he says, but the corner of his mouth twitches, as if he's holding back a smug little smile. As if he's telling me that my silence was consent enough.

As if he somehow knows that he's still my weakness.

Silence hangs thick between us for a moment, then he just shrugs and gestures to the sofa. "Have a seat."

"I'm fine," I say, leaning against the television cabinet.

"Are you?"

I meet his eyes. "Yes," I say firmly. "You lost the power to break me long ago." It's a lie, of course, but I lift my shoulder in a casual shrug. "Maybe you did get me riled up. But so can a large variety of adult toys." I flash a sickly-sweet grin. "Trust me when I say you're replaceable."

"Good to know," he says. "But I'm curious about one thing…"

"What?"

"That outfit," he says. "What the hell were you thinking?"

I cross my arms. "That being clothed around you would be a good idea."

He doesn't respond, only stands. He moves to the bar, tops off his drink, then turns to me. "You're trying to hide from me. From what just happened between us."

"Nothing happened between us."

"Oh, something did." His voice is conversational, but there's heat underneath it. "And now you don't trust yourself around me," he adds, taking two steps in my direction. "Especially not after the way you responded to my touch."

Heat floods my cheeks. "So I got off. Big deal. Like I said, I have some very nice toys that can get me there faster than you. What just happened doesn't mean a thing."

"Don't be so demure, Red. We both know you've missed me." He takes a step closer, so close I can feel his heat. "And don't try the toy bullshit on me. All that says is that you're trying too hard to convince yourself you didn't feel anything."

"Oh, I felt something. Assault."

His eyes are steady on mine, unrepentant. "If I wanted to assault you, I promise you'd know the difference. But maybe now you have an idea of how easily someone can get to you."

I swallow, hating the reminder of that vile video. But at the same time, he's right. If he didn't leave it, then there's someone else out there watching me. Playing me. Maybe even trying to hurt me.

"Who?"

"I don't know," he says. "But I intend to find out. And Ruby," he adds, taking a step closer so that I'm trapped between him and the TV cabinet, "I will keep you safe, whether you want me to or not."

"I don't want you to."

He shrugs. "Like I said, your tough luck. Because you have me." He reaches up and runs a strand of my hair through his fingers, the way he used to. "And I have you."

I blink rapidly, trying to stave off tears, wishing I could melt into the damn furniture. Wishing I could turn back time. But I can't do either. All I can do is whisper, "Please. Just—just give me some space. Please."

Something hard and determined crosses over his face, and for a moment, I fear that he's going to ignore my plea, yank me toward him, and destroy me with a kiss.

He doesn't. He steps back with an almost gentlemanly nod of consent. I exhale, relieved that I'm able to breathe again.

Even so, I can't deny the tiny, buried part of me that had hoped he'd take my arm, tug me toward him, devour me with kisses, then say some magic words that would make the past disappear. That would recall the knife he'd shoved into my soul.

That would erase the fact that he'd once destroyed me completely.

I look down at the carpet, not wanting him to see any hint of that lingering fantasy on my face.

"You're beautiful," he says softly. "Even more than you were in college."

"Stop." I shout the word in my head. In the room, it comes out as a whisper.

"Why? It's true."

"Don't try to pretend like any part of the Leo I once loved still exists. I know he was an illusion. A mirage. Entirely fake and completely untouchable."

"If he were fake, you wouldn't still want him so much."

"I don't."

"You do," he says, then grins. "Trust me. I know things. And I'm hardly ever wrong."

Despite myself, I almost laugh.

"And for the record," he says softly, "I wasn't trying to break you on that massage table."

"No? What were you trying to do?"

"Position myself so that I can control you."

"Oh." That may be the first honest thing he's said all night. "Why?"

His expression is hard when he says, "I told you—someone wants to hurt you. I don't intend to let that happen. And I want to make sure you don't turn out to be your own worst enemy."

"I can handle myself."

"You can't. If you could, you wouldn't be dressed like that in baggy sweatpants and a T-shirt that hides your exceptional curves."

I shake my head, totally confused. "What are you talking about?"

"You don't trust yourself around me." He flashes a very smug grin. "Especially not now. Not after the way you responded to me. Came for me. Not after the way you showed how much you want me."

"No. No way. I was vulnerable and you crossed a very thick red line, and—"

"I did," he says simply. "And you liked what was waiting on the other side of that line. But you hate that you liked it. Thus, the afternoon-home-watching-reality-TV outfit. But you can't hide from me any more than you can hide from yourself. And I'm not going anywhere."

I say nothing. Of course, the bastard's right.

"You forgot one thing, though."

I should stay quiet, but I can't help myself. "What?"

"You'd be the most desirable woman in this hotel even if you were wearing a garbage bag."

His voice has gone soft, and my eyes sting with the tears I'm fighting to hold back. "Don't," I say.

"Don't what?"

"Don't say things like that. Don't try to be charming."

"You're still mine, Red. And you always will be."

"You're wrong."

"Strangely, I'm hardly ever wrong." He lets out a put-upon sigh. "It's a curse, but I've learned to bear it."

"We're not playing this game," I say, crossing my arms and forcing myself to meet his eyes. "You say you're here because I'm in danger. Okay, what danger? Tell me what you mean, or get out now."

His eyes narrow, but all he does is pull out his phone and move to the sofa. I stay where I am.

"Well?" he says, nodding to the spot beside him as he holds up his phone. "Do you want to see what I've got here or not?"

I go reluctantly, then frown when I see the first image. A photo of me walking out of Lydia Cosmetics, my head down, completely unaware I'm being watched. The timestamp shows it was taken five days ago.

"You took that?"

"I didn't. I'm not the threat."

"How do I know that?" I blurt out the question, but my voice lacks conviction, and he ignores me as he swipes through more images.

"Someone's been documenting your every move for weeks." He stops at a photo of Sasha and me at the farmers market, both of us laughing. We look so normal, so unsuspecting.

The thought that someone was watching us—planning something—makes me sick.

"How did you get those?"

"Someone left a USB drive for me at the front desk of Grimm Tower."

"Who?" I know how tight security is at the tower. They'd have the person on video.

"A sixteen-year-old kid. He was approached as he was walking home from high school. Someone paid him a hundred dollars to deliver it." He sighs. "I interviewed the kid, pulled every video feed around the school I could find. Whoever chose him knew the area and knew how to stay out of sight."

"That's—" I cut myself off with a shake of my head. I want to say that's crazy, but it's no crazier than everything else.

"There are more," he says, handing me the phone. I scroll through image after image of me going about my daily life, completely oblivious to my stalker.

With a shudder, I toss the phone aside, then pull my knees up and hug myself, feeling more exposed than I'd felt when I found the sex tape.

"Who?" I whisper. "Why?"

"I don't know yet. Not for certain." His voice is hard now, all business. "But whoever it is, they're professional. They know how to avoid detection. And they're patient."

"What do they want?"

"Me," he says. "Or something from me."

I shake my head. "That doesn't make sense."

"You're a pawn, Ruby. Or bait. Take your pick. Either way, if your stalker doesn't get what he wants from me, you're the one he'll punish."

I swallow. "Why?"

"Because hurting you would hurt me."

I manage a dark laugh. "I guess this stalker hasn't brushed up on Ruby and Leo history."

"It's real," he says, his voice thick with regret. "And I'm so goddamn sorry. But I will keep you safe."

I grab his phone again, then scroll back and forth through the photos, unable to process the magnitude of what I'm seeing. All these mundane moments of my life captured by a stranger's camera. Smiles. Laughs. Dozens of unguarded moments turned into intelligence for someone who's stalking me. And all because of Leo Grimm.

And isn't that just fucking perfect?

He stands and moves to the window, looking out at the city lights below. "We don't know how long they've been watching you. Which means we have to assume they know every detail of your life. We have to assume they know your weaknesses as well as I do. And that means that whenever they think it's time to drop the hammer on me, they'll have a plan for getting to you."

The casual way he says it has my temper flaring, which, frankly, is a welcome relief from the fear. "You don't know one thing about my weaknesses."

"Don't I?" There's something almost predatory in his smile. "Just minutes ago, you were naked under my hands, coming apart like you were starving for my touch. If that's not a weakness, what is?"

The reminder makes heat coil low in my belly again, and I hate myself for the reaction. "That was—"

"Honest," he interrupts. "Maybe the first honest thing that's passed between us in seven years."

"I thought you were David."

"No," he says. "You didn't."

I swallow, then close my eyes. "It was a mistake. A huge mistake."

"It was inevitable."

I open my eyes to see him standing right in front of me, his cock a hard, huge bulge in his jeans at right about eye level.

My mouth goes dry.

He takes a step closer, and I resist the urge to shrink back into the cushion. "And it's going to happen again."

"No, it's not."

"Yes, it is." His voice drops to that commanding tone that always made me want to obey him. To submit and lose myself to his will, his commands, his pleasure.

"I will have you again, Red," he says, his voice low and even. "Because I want you. I want my cock inside you. I want to hear you beg me to fuck you harder. Deeper. Faster. Because despite everything you think you know about me, despite all the reasons you have to hate me, your body knows the truth, and I want to see that truth on your face when I make you explode."

"What truth?" My words come out in a whisper.

"That you're mine." The words are soft, implacable. "That you've always been mine. That seven years of trying to forget me hasn't changed that fundamental fact."

"I'm not yours," I say, but it's only form. Right now, I have no idea if I'm lying or telling the god's honest truth.

"Your body says you are."

"My body was responding to physical stimulation," I say, then I roll my shoulders and lift my chin, determined not to lose this round. "It doesn't mean anything."

"It means everything." His eyes are intense, focused entirely on me. "It means you still want me, even though you hate me. It means you still belong to me, even though you've spent seven years trying to convince yourself otherwise."

"It means you'll stay, because deep down, you know you're safer with me than anywhere else. You'll stay because some part of you wants to be kept."

The words hit too close to the truth, and I feel something crack inside my chest. "You're insane, Leo Grimm. And you're a goddamn fucking prick, too."

"Maybe. But I'm your insane fucking prick. And right now, I'm the only thing standing between you and whoever knows that threatening you is a path to manipulating me."

"I'll stay with Sasha. They can't get to me there."

He looks me up and down. "That's what you want?"

I consider it. Sure, I could call Liam—tell him what's going on and ask him to step in. And once Sasha learns about this, she'd make him promise to stay on me twenty-four/seven.

Which is exactly why I can't call them. Because he would. He'd do it because I'm important to the person he loves most in the world.

But no way will I come between them like that. Not after all that they've already survived.

Which means that, like it or not, Leo Grimm is my fairy tale hero. The man who'll protect me from the misguided wolf who's out to hurt me just to hurt him.

Ironic since, as far as I'm concerned, Leo's the biggest baddest wolf there is. And if I get too close, he really will eat me alive.

"Well?" he says, finally breaking the silence. "Have you sorted through every possible way you can stay safe without me, only to realize there aren't any? You need me, Ruby, and I'm truly am sorry that some enemy of mine is the reason you got dragged into this.

"But don't worry," he adds, leaning forward, so close I can feel his breath on my lips. "The price for my protection may be steep, but I promise you'll enjoy it. Day and night," he says, his finger tracing my jawline and making me shiver. "In my bed and out of it."

"Price? Hello? You're the reason I'm in this mess."

He spreads his hands. "And I'll be sure to thank whoever's harassing us for that. Right before I kill him."

"Oh, come on, Leo. You can't be serious."

But he just grins, then bends closer to whisper in my ear, and I suck in a breath, craving what he's demanding despite myself.

"I'm going to stay right by your side," he says. "I'm going to have you any time I want. I'm going to fuck you mercilessly. And I'm going to make you come so hard, you'll swear you got a peek into heaven."

I swallow, hating my body for reacting so viscerally to his words. Wishing I could race out of this goddamn room and hide from him and everyone else.

But I can't. He may be the cause, but I truly need the protection.

So, yes. I'm willing to pay any price he asks. And I despise myself for knowing that I'll enjoy it.

I meet his eyes, keeping mine cold and flat. "Agreed."

That smug, possessive look fades, his brow furrows, and in that moment, I remember just how damn smart Leo Grimm is. It only takes him a second, then he says, his voice low and urgent, "What else is going on?"

I swallow, then look away.

"Rue?"

"Your goddamn sex tape," I blurt. "You fucking taped us." I watch his face as my words pummel him, hard and fast. "The damn thing landed in my house today. Somebody left it on my bed, playing like a damn porno when I got home from the market."

He's gone perfectly still, and what I see in his eyes is fury—not aimed at me, but at our unknown tormentor.

I've seen that look before. That protective fire in him that would ignite whenever anyone got in his way. Or, god forbid, got in mine.

"That son-of-a-bitch," he says, his voice harder than I've ever heard it.

A moment passes, then he says, "Whoever the hell is trying to get to me..." I watch as he shakes his head. Moving. Pacing. Then he stops, his gaze like a laser on me. "On your bed? He left a sex tape playing on your bed? A VHS? A disc? Tell me you didn't load it into your laptop."

"It was playing on my laptop," I say. "It's got a ton of security, so I don't know how—"

"Is it here?" He glances around the room, as if my computer is going to leap out and attack. That's when I realize that, of course, my prick tormenter must have added some sort of tracking or monitoring software.

"Liam has it now," I say. "He's trying to find whatever he can find."

Leo pulls out his phone and taps out a text, then paces as he waits for an answer. A few seconds later, his phone vibrates, and I watch as he scrolls down the screen, reading the text.

"Liam neutralized the tracking," Leo says. "And he found a message."

"A message?" Ice runs through my veins. "What message?"

Leo starts to speak, then closes his mouth.

"Are you kidding me? It's my computer. My life. You just told me I'm the bait, so tell me what the damn message says. Hell, Liam should have already called and told me."

"We've barely begun." He draws in a long breath. "It says, we've barely begun."

"Begun what?"

He doesn't answer. Just runs his fingers through his hair as he paces the room, making the dark strands stand up, giving him a sexy, heavy metal kind of vibe. "This changes things."

"You're the one who made that horrible tape."

His eyes flash to mine. "The tape isn't the problem."

"The hell it's not. You made a sex tape and didn't even tell—"

"Dammit, Ruby, you can be pissed off at me later. Right now, we're focusing on the asshole who's got the skills to have stolen that recording from my very secure server. The same guy who broke into your house and left it there. Who's taken hundreds of pictures of you in order to taunt me. So forgive me if I'm not in the mood to talk about a goddamn tape we made in college."

"*You* made," I say, then fall silent when he shoots me the sharpest look I've ever seen from him. "Fine," I say, holding up my hands in surrender. I can ream him out for taping us later. Right now, I'll let him do whatever he needs to do to keep my mysterious stalker off my back.

He paces another lap, then another. And another after that. Just as I'm beginning to feel like I'm watching a very slow tennis game, he stops in front of me. "You're not staying here," he says. "I got in too easily. Someone else could, too."

"A dump of a motel?" I suggest. "Cash only? Maybe in Canada?"

"Smart," he says, his voice laced with something that sounds like pride. "But no. I have just the place."

"Where?" I ask, realizing that I never doubted that Leo would have a plan. He's a prick, but he's also a clever one.

"You're staying with me."

"The hell I am."

"You are." There's steel in his voice now. He moves to the bar and pours two whiskeys, then hands one to me.

I take it eagerly, then snuggle into the corner of the couch and take a long, long swallow.

"Be reasonable. Someone is stalking you to get to me. Someone who knows our history. Someone who has the skill to hack highly secure off-site digital storage."

"You really don't know who?" I take another sip, reveling in the whiskey's bite, waiting for it to smooth out all these rough edges. Then I toss back the rest of the whiskey. Because, dammit, it's one of those days.

"I don't. But I intend to find out. And until I do, I'm sticking to you like glue."

I shake my head. "No. Not you."

"Me," he says. "There's nobody I trust more to keep you safe. I'm sticking, Red, whether you want me to or not."

"Screw that," I say. "Liam will find someone else to watch me." I try to concentrate despite the way the alcohol is hitting my system. "He'll insist, too, because I'll tell Sasha what you did tonight. You crossed a helluva line," I add, my head lolling as I wish I'd eaten more, because the whiskey is already making me loopy. "You destroyed me," I tell him. "You ripped my heart out and stomped on it."

"I know," he says. "But that was before. Now, I'm keeping you safe."

"No, you..." But I trail off, unable to keep track of the words floating in my head. Just floating there like a feather on the wind or maybe a sailboat or...I lose the thread of the thought and look up at the two Leos looking down at me. "Bastard," I say—or maybe I just think it. But it's clear now. So pretty and clear and wrong. "You drugged me."

"You'll thank me tomorrow."

I start to shake my head, but it's too heavy. And the last thing I see before the darkness takes me is Leo's face, close to mine, his green eyes filled with something that looks almost like love.

Almost.

EIGHT
SPINNING

My head throbs like someone's using my skull as a drum, my mouth tastes like I've been sucking on gravel, and every muscle in my body aches like I've been hit by a freight train. Twice.

What the hell is wrong with me?

With a groan, I force my eyes to open, certain I'm going to see fire and brimstone, because I must surely be in hell.

I'm not. I'm on a bed, a soft blanket spread over me.

I frown, fighting through fuzzy wisps of memory, then sit up like a shot when it all rushes back to me. The tape. The Celestial. The massage. The drink.

Leo.

The prick spiked my drink.

A dark fury curls through me as I remember the way his green eyes had watched me as the hotel's suite began to spin. My own horrifying realization of what he'd done. And then the bolt of terror as I lost the fight to stay awake and was pulled into unconsciousness, slipping far, far away while Leopold Xavier Grimm stood over me like some beautiful, deadly predator.

"You sick bastard," I whisper to the empty room, my voice cracked and raw like I've been screaming. Maybe I have.

I look around, moving slowly to protect my head, my eyes squinting against the room's dim light. This isn't my bedroom at home. And it's not my pristine suite at the Celestial, either. Not by a long shot.

I sit up carefully, then pad to the wall of floor-to-ceiling windows, moving slowly lest my head explode. I press a hand against the glass and look down. The city looks small from here, like an architect's model. And as I look around at the building I'm in, I see familiar green spires gleaming in the sun, along with grinning gargoyles clinging to the stonework.

Grimm Tower.

And then it all clicks…

I'm in Leo's suite. The very suite we'd come to years ago. Where he'd sneak me up through his private elevator so none of his family would know about the nobody college girl he was screwing on the side.

And I'm not just in his suite. This is the guest bedroom. The room that we'd christened as ours. Where we'd cuddle and talk and eat Italian takeout and fool around.

This is the place where he filmed me without my consent. Where he captured my most vulnerable moments and stored them away like trophies.

I'm back in the place where everything went wrong. Where he destroyed me.

And now he's going to kick me to hell all over again.

I close my eyes and clench my fists, determined not to think of that. Instead, I take stock of the room, the memory of it flooding back as I look around. The furniture is Mid-Century Modern—striking with the clean lines and bold accents, a bit like Leo himself. The art fits the period, and I recognize a Rothko and a Mondrian. Both originals. And each one is probably worth a hell of a lot more than my charming little Connecticut cottage.

And, of course, I can't ignore the king-size bed where he used to tie me up and—

Stop it.

With a start, I realize that although I'm still in the sweats that I'd changed into at the hotel, my shirt is a souvenir Broadway tee from *Into the Woods*. The very shirt he'd bought me to sleep in at his place, and which I'd left behind the night I'd bolted, my face wet with tears and my heart torn into tatters.

I grimace, remembering the song I'd been listening to when I bumped into him on the trail. That moment feels like a lifetime ago. In reality, it was barely a breath in time.

I'd compared him to a wolf then—and all things considered, I think that was a damn fine assessment.

I hug myself to ward off a shudder, but it doesn't come, and I'm forced to face what's been nudging me ever since Leo Grimm slid back into my life—that even after everything he's done, some traitorous part of me still craves his touch. Some stupid, broken part of me that never learned its lesson these past seven years.

Am I really that pathetic?

The man assaulted me in the hotel, after all. And, yes, I'd leaned into the touch. But that's when I thought it was impersonal. A stranger. An erotic encounter that would be over when the hour was up.

Not Leo. Not the man who'd hurt me so deeply the scars still feel fresh.

Except that's a lie. I knew it was him. I knew I needed to fight. But I'd let it happen. Some part of me even wanted it to happen.

And my punishment for those moments of weakness? He'd drugged me and brought me here against my will. Then topped all of that off by changing my shirt to one that used to mean something wonderful, but now just holds pain and loss.

Once upon a time, I would have told anyone who'd listen that Leo Grimm might be arrogant and controlling, but he'd never physically hurt me. Not even during the games we'd played in bed. And he would certainly never force me into anything past my comfort zone.

Now?

Now I'm not so sure.

This Leo is different. Darker. More dangerous than the man I thought I knew. The massage, the drugging, bringing me here—it's like he's shed whatever restraint he used to have.

Or maybe he never had any. Maybe I was just too naive to see the darkness that cloaked him.

I need to get the hell out of here.

Determined, I hurry out of the room to the entrance hall and tug on the door. But it's as solid as a fortress. Locked, of course.

"Shit." I lean forward, my forehead and palms pressed against the cool wood, trying to think. Maybe I could pick the lock. There's probably something in a drawer or the guestroom or the bathroom that—

The bathroom.

Not the one in Leo's master bedroom that doubles as his in-suite office or in our guest bedroom. Neither of those bathrooms has windows. But this suite's original bathroom survived the Tower's remodel. Now—or, rather, seven years ago—that original bathroom had opened off the living area. And unless there's been another remodel, that bathroom still retains the four-foot-tall, hinged window that opens onto an ancient fire escape.

Leo used to joke about it, saying it was dangerous and unmaintained, but that every time his father dropped by, he'd have to talk himself out of tempting fate by escaping that way. Because possible death was preferable to an unplanned conversation with Elias Grimm.

I hurry across the living area, my bare feet silent on the thick carpeting. The bathroom is just as I remember—gleaming marble and golden fixtures, with a huge claw-foot bathtub.

And there—in the dressing area—is that wonderful, beautiful window that's going to usher me the hell out of here.

I move closer and peek through the glass, then frown. Definitely rickety.

I swallow. Forty-three stories is one hell of a long fall.

And staying here as Leo's prisoner is its own kind of hell.

I draw a breath. *I can do this.*

I strain my arms as I try to open the latch, stiff from disuse. At first, I think it will never budge, but it finally gives way with a small click that sounds as loud as a gunshot in the silence.

I push the window open, then stick my head out to examine my escape route, which—as advertised— looks rusty and rickety as it hangs over more than forty floors of empty air. A wave of foreboding crashes over me, but that's just nerves. It may look like a death trap, but surely it was well-built. Fire code, right? And it's not as if I weigh that much.

And there's also the fact that I have no other option.

Right. Going for it.

Determined, I hook one leg over the open window frame. No way am I going back into that bedroom now that freedom is literally within reach.

"Leaving so soon?"

I freeze, one leg still inside the bathroom, the other dangling outside. My heart hammers against my ribs as I slowly twist to look at Leo.

He's leaning against the doorframe, his expression an odd mix of irritation and humor. Possibly mixed with a hint of pride. Like I'm a well-trained puppy who did as expected.

He's still in jeans, but he's changed into a tight black T-shirt that shows off the lean muscles of his arms. And the dark stubble along his jaw gives him a dangerous, sexy edge.

But it's still his eyes that make my breath catch. Vivid green and predatory as they rake over my body, still half-outside the window.

"I was wondering how long it would take you to try that," he says, as if we're chatting over cocktails. "Less than twenty minutes after fully waking. I always knew you had spunk."

"Let me go." The words come out steadier than I feel. "I mean it, Leo. This is kidnapping. It's—"

"Protection." He pushes off from the doorframe and takes a step toward me. "Come back inside, Red."

"No." I try to pull myself the rest of the way through the

window, but he's made me twitchy, and instead of going through the window, I smash my elbow hard. "Dammit," I snap, then turn on him. "I'm leaving."

"No. You're not."

My chest tightens. Not because he's threatening me, but because he's simply stating a fact. I'm trapped, and we both know it.

"You really are insane," I whisper, coming back inside. "You can't just lock me up here."

"Of course I can." He moves closer, and I step back until I'm pressed against the marble counter. "You're not in prison. You're in protective custody."

"Bullsh—"

"Someone wants to hurt you," he snaps, interrupting me. "Hurt you to get to me. And there is no way I'm trusting anyone but me to keep you safe." He puts his fingers under my chin and raises my face until our eyes meet. "And neither should you."

I push past him, needing to get away before I do something stupid like claw his eyes out. Or kiss him. With Leo, the line between violence and passion has always been thin.

He follows me back into the main room, then silently watches as I pace to the floor-to-ceiling windows that dominate the living area. The city stretches out below us, beautiful and untouchable. It's like looking at freedom through glass. I'll never be able to reach it.

He moves to stand beside me, his arms crossed, his reflection in the window looking back at me.

"Fine," I say. "Whatever. Doesn't seem like I have a choice, does it?"

"No. You don't."

I draw a breath, forcing myself to change gears. "How did you even find me? I was careful. And it was Liam who created Rebecca Stone."

He shrugs. "Liam's good at that shit." His reflection grows

bigger, and I can feel the man behind me, close enough that his breath stirs my hair. "I'm better."

The simple arrogance of the statement sends a shiver down my spine that has nothing to do with fear and everything to do with the way his voice drops on those last two words.

I hate that I still respond to him like this. Hate that my body doesn't seem to understand that he's dangerous now. That he's not the same man I once thought I loved.

Except, he never was that man. Leo Grimm was always dangerous. I think maybe I've known that all along.

I fear that maybe I liked it.

The thought hits me like a slap, and suddenly everything becomes clear. How could I have been so stupid? How could I have let him manipulate me even for a second?

"Oh my god," I breathe, turning to face him. "I am such an idiot."

Leo's eyebrows draw together. "What are you talking about?"

"For thinking there was even a chance you weren't behind all of this. The laptop, the video, the psychological games—of course it was you."

I laugh, but there's no humor in it. "Then you topped all that off by drugging me and bringing me here. You fucking prick. You're the one who ripped me apart. You're the one who ended things. You're the one who said I was nothing to you, and—"

My words cut off on a cry as tears clog my throat.

He takes a step toward me, shaking his head.

"No." The word comes out sharp as a blade, and he stops cold, as if I've cut him. Good.

"I'm done second-guessing my instincts about what you're capable of."

For a moment, he's silent. Then he turns and walks away, leaving me with only my own reflection and the city beyond. I wait a bit, then turn to see him settling on the sofa with his back to me. When he picks up the remote and starts scrolling through channels as if he has nothing better to do, it's all I can do not to scream.

Bastard.

I want to stay put. Want to force him to give in and come back to me.

But—dammit—I follow him. Because I'm not done being pissed, and being properly pissed requires an audience.

I cross the living area, then sit on the armrest of his zillion-dollar sofa, my bare feet on the cushions. "You know what the really sick part is?" I continue. "Some tiny part of me wanted to believe that ridiculous story you spun at the hotel. There's Leo, so concerned about protecting me since he's the reason I'm in the crosshairs. And poor little me, so desperately in need of a guardian angel."

"I'm no angel."

"No shit, Sherlock."

He turns his head, meeting my eyes straight on. "But I will keep you safe."

"And I'm supposed to believe you because why? *Oh,*" I say, as if the answer has just come to me. "I should trust you because of the way you drugged me. Sorry. I didn't realize that at first. Even though it's so very, very obvious."

I draw a breath, then flip him the bird at the same time that I say, "Fuck you, Leo. You haven't changed at all. You're still the same manipulative bastard who destroyed my life."

"I didn't want to destroy your life," he says quietly.

"So you were possessed by dark forces? You just couldn't help yourself?" I'm shaking now. "Just like you couldn't help yourself with that video. Just like you can't help yourself now, playing this goddamn twisted game with my life."

"This isn't a game."

"How do I know that? You say someone is threatening me to get to you, but how do I know you're not the threat? How do I know this isn't just another big set up to stab another blade right through my heart?"

I laugh again, and this time it sounds bitter as poison. "It's all so perfectly Leo Grimm." I bend forward, wishing I could burn him with my gaze. "I'm on to you, fucker. I am so on to you."

"You're not," he says. "You're spinning out, and you're wrong. Take a deep breath and listen to me."

His voice is calmer than I've ever heard it. Like he's actually a grown-up. Which is the world's biggest joke.

I raise my middle finger, then head for the kitchen. I yank open the fridge, then slam it, uninterested in anything in there. I find a container of chocolate chip walnut cookies from Levain Bakery, and shove an entire cookie in my mouth. Then another. And one more after that.

"This isn't a game, Rue," he says, moving from the sofa to sit on one of the stools, so that he's looking at me from over the pass-through bar as I lean against the far counter and continue to rage-eat the cookies.

"Somebody wants to hurt you. And even though you're starting to piss me off, I'm not the bad guy here. And yes," he says before I can truth-blast him again, "I know what I did in the past was shitty."

"You think? You broke up with me on the day my parents died. You broke up with me in a fucking note."

His shoulders sag, and something that looks like pain crosses his face.

"I had reasons. But I shouldn't have…" He trails off, looking everywhere but at me.

And, damn me, I almost feel sorry for him. "Well?"

He draws in a breath, looking almost defeated. As if someone like him could even feel regret or loss. "I hurt you, Rue. I hurt you when you were already in pain, and I've kicked myself every day since."

He meets my eyes, his expression more broken than I've ever seen. "I'm not the one out to hurt you now, Ruby. I did that seven years ago, and it pretty much killed me. Right now, I just want to keep you safe. Hell, I want to keep you alive."

I believe him.

Maybe I'm naive, but I believe him.

I'm not, however, ready to trust him.

I finish off my last cookie, then cross my arms over my chest. "You undressed me." I pluck at the souvenir shirt.

"Hey, give me points for not taking off your bra."

I just stare him down.

"You don't remember?"

"Remember?"

He almost laughs, then he slips off the barstool and comes around into the kitchen area. He stands across from me for a moment, then hops up onto the counter before holding his hand out for a cookie. I pass him the now almost empty box, then hop up on my counter, facing him. I mean, why the hell not?

"You were loopy when we got here," he says. "I forgot what a fast metabolism you have, and you were coming off the high lightning fast."

"And you thought changing my shirt would slow down the process?"

He narrows his eyes, and I have to fight not to laugh, because that's how we used to be together. Silly arguments that were more for fun. Or for foreplay.

I wince, then look down, concentrating on the cookie in my hand and not on the direction my mind has suddenly taken.

"You spilled cocoa," he says, then shakes his head. "You really don't remember?"

"Nope," I say. "But don't you think it was kind of an asshole move to put me in this shirt? I mean, hello history, bring on the bad memories while you keep me locked in this room?"

His eyes widen, and I look down at my feet as my heels kick against his cabinetry. "Well, mostly bad," I amend.

"You asked for the shirt."

"Oh." I frown, trying to remember. "You swear? On my dad's quarter?" It was our most solemn oath. Swearing on the quarter my father had kept since the Bicentennial, when he was eleven. He'd given it to me for college, and I'd kept it safe, finally having it made into a necklace that I've worn every day since he and Mom died.

"I swear," Leo says, then holds out his hand. I start to take the necklace off, then hop off the counter instead. I cross to him, lift my chin, and pull the necklace out. He wraps his hand around it, and I feel a little shock run through my body when his knuckles brush my collarbone. "You asked for the shirt," he says firmly. "I swear it."

I blink back unwanted tears as I glance down at the now iconic *Into the Woods* image.

"You still had it," I say. "I tossed that shirt into the trash seven years ago before I bolted out of here. But this is it. This is the actual shirt." I hold up my right arm, so we can both see where I'd done a crappy job of repairing a seam under the arm.

"Packrat," he says, with a casual shrug. But that's bullshit. Leo Grimm is ruthless about getting rid of things he no longer needs. He always has been. I should know. He was at his most ruthless when he got rid of me.

Except he kept this shirt.

"Enough trotting down Memory Lane," he says. "Pass me a beer and grab whatever you want. We need to talk about the rules."

"Rules," I repeat, then grab two Coronas from the fridge. I open the drawer next to the sink, grab the bottle opener that's in the same place it's always been, then pop both tops and pass one to him.

He takes it, then cocks his head. "Over here," he says, moving back to the living area, then plonking his ass down on the sofa and putting his feet up on a table that must have cost more than most people's annual salary.

I hesitate, watching him. Reminding myself that I don't want him anymore, this man who broke me. But while my head is dead certain about that, my heart still backslides. When I see that quick, arrogant grin. When he looks at me, and I see both lust and concern in those deep green eyes.

And now, when he's seated on the sofa, his feet up and his arm outstretched, marking the space where I used to sit, my feet curled under me, my body resting against his, and his arm draped around my shoulder.

"Rue?"

"Right. Sorry. Just grabbing a few more cookies." It's a bullshit excuse, and now, of course, I'm forced to eat more cookies to cover my lie.

Pity, that.

"Sit," he says as I come to the sofa bearing cookies. He pats the spot that's been haunting my memory for the last two minutes. I ignore him, then sit at the other end of the couch, one foot tucked under me so that I'm facing him, but not close to him.

Something undefinable flickers in his eyes. Regret, maybe. But more likely irritation.

"Right," he says, then takes a long swallow from his Corona. "We need to set some rules."

"Rules," I repeat. "What is this? Kindergarten?"

"If you act like a child, I'll treat you like one." His grin is a perfect mix of heat and mischief. "Trust me when I say that I believe in corporal punishment for little girls who misbehave."

I flip him off, and he laughs. "One demerit already. Someone's gunning for a spanking."

"Just tell me your damn rules." I draw in a breath, hoping he can't tell that my cheeks are burning in the room's dim light.

"No more bullshit," he says. "No trying to get out through the fire escape. No setting a fire and hoping some sexy firefighter will come along to rescue you. He won't," Leo says. "And he wouldn't be sexier than me, anyway."

"Don't," I say, suddenly exhausted by it all. "Do not flirt with me. I'm here because I have to be. Because you won't let me walk away."

"To get maimed? Kidnapped? Possibly killed? No. I won't."

"And you really think you can keep me safe?"

He flashes that Leo-ish grin. "Of course. I can do anything. Did you forget? I'm rich and I'm smart and I'm charming."

I roll my eyes, part of me wanting to smack him for joking around. Part of me wanting to hug him for taking the edge off my fear.

And it's true. Leo has a knack for not only getting along but also for making people do what he wants. For the first time, I realize how frustrating my Ice Princess persona must have been to him. Because for seven years, I've kept that wall up. And he's a man who is definitely not used to that.

Hell, he's the only member of his family who gets along with all the others. And in his wreck of a family, that's saying a lot.

Plus, he can be just about anyone. He can play the gentleman at a charity function or the fuck-up in a dive bar. On any given week, he might donate a million to charity just hours after getting into a fist fight behind a gas station.

No one ever sees him coming, and very few people have seen the real Leo Grimm.

Once, I thought I had.

Now, I'm not so sure.

For a moment, we just stare at each other across the charged space between us. I can see something burning in his eyes—anger, maybe. Or pain. The air crackles with tension, full of seven years of unresolved hurt.

"I hate you," I whisper.

"I know." His voice is soft, almost gentle. "It's safer that way."

"Safer for who?"

"For both of us."

"You think keeping me locked up here is keeping me safe?"

"I think keeping you anywhere else will get you killed." His voice is flat, final. "And I'm not letting that happen."

"You can't keep me here forever."

"I can keep you here as long as it takes." He stands, and I can see the tension in his body as he starts to pace. He's moving as if he's holding something in. Something hard and dangerous.

His eyes skim over me, then he takes a step toward me. I stiffen, but otherwise don't move. And when he shifts toward the door, it's disappointment that washes through me. Not relief.

He pauses with his hand on the doorknob, his eyes on mine. "Don't try to leave again. The only way out of this tower is through me."

"That sounds like a threat."

"Maybe it is. I suggest you don't do anything to find out." He tugs open the door and steps over the threshold before looking back at me one more time. "I'll bring you dinner later. And there are some clothes that should fit you in the guest room closet."

"Leo." His name comes out before I can stop it.

He pauses, eyebrows raised.

"Why?" The question is barely a whisper, but I need to know.

For a moment, something vulnerable flickers across his face. Something that almost looks like the man I once thought I knew.

"Because losing you once nearly destroyed me. I won't let it happen again."

The door closes behind him with a soft click, leaving me alone with the silence and the growing realization that Leo Grimm is either my salvation or my destruction.

And I'm terrified that I won't be able to tell the difference until it's too late.

NINE
GILDED CAGE

The morning sun tickles my face, and I sit up slowly, realizing that I'd fallen asleep on the sofa. And that I've got one hell of a cramp in my leg.

I remember talking with Leo—and that we reached a weird détente—and I vaguely recall the opening credits of a classic Bond film. But that's all I remember.

I roll my neck, working out the kinks, then start to push myself up. As I do, a soft, fuzzy blanket slides to the floor.

I frown, realizing I'm wearing nothing but the *Into the Woods* tee and my underwear. *Thong* underwear.

That's when I bolt upright, gasping a bit as the cramp screams in protest of both the pain and Leo Fucking Grimm's newest violation.

The bastard stripped me down.

And, no, he didn't take off my thong or my bra, but he stripped off the sweatpants, taking it upon himself to tuck me in here rather than waking me up and sending me to the guest room.

Asshole.

Except, is he really?

Some irritatingly rational part of my mind points out that yesterday was probably the most exhausting day of my life. I don't even remember lying down. Just the opening credits with the James Bond theme, a sexy woman, and then…nothing.

Since yesterday was one hell of a day, I'm going to assume that my prick of a captor didn't drug me again. Which means I fell asleep on the couch while Sean Connery was doing his thing— and Leo tucked me in.

After stripping me down.

I want to work up a fury. Lash out that it was an invasion of my privacy. But it's not as if he hasn't already done that once in the last twenty-four hours. And god only knows how many times he put me to bed when we were together. I'm notorious for falling asleep during movies.

And, in fairness, since I hadn't made a fuss when he put me in the *Into the Woods* tee, it's probably not fair to vilify him for making me sleep-ready, even as much as I'd like to.

But at the same time, we're not a couple. And his new hobby of dressing the ex probably isn't the best idea ever.

Losing you once nearly destroyed me.

I stiffen as the memory of those words returns, seemingly out of nowhere. Sweet words on the surface, but so cruel underneath. *Losing me?*

The thought jolts me to my feet, and I wince, then start to stretch, trying to work out the damn cramp as my mind spins. The bastard didn't lose me. On the contrary, I'd been wildly, passionately, stupidly in love with him. He'd been my best friend, my lover, my everything, and I'd thought I was his.

I learned the hard way how wrong I'd been, and now the weaselly little prick is trying to rewrite history. Trying to defy basic logic to convince me that breaking my heart somehow wounded his.

I'd run those words through my head endlessly last night, curled up on this sofa while Leo flicked through the various streaming options before settling on Bond. I'd fallen asleep with the beginning of the movie as a backdrop to the way hope and regret and confusion were battling it out inside me.

Because, dammit, I want to believe him. Some foolish, traitorous part of my heart wants to believe that he suffered, too. But I've heard his sweet words before, right up until the moment he decided I wasn't worth the trouble anymore. Right up until the night when I needed him most and—

No.

Not going there. Not letting the bastard manipulate me again.

Fool me once, sure.

But he's not ever, *ever*, fooling me again.

I stand up, determined not to think about him. A determination that is immediately undermined when I head to the master bedroom. I try the door, only to find it locked. I pound on it and call for him, but there's no response.

He probably left while I was asleep. Just walked past me and out into the main hall that—

Wait.

I cock my head, remembering that the master bedrooms of all the brothers' suites have their own private elevators. If I could get in there…

I frown, knowing that's impossible. And also seeing the bigger picture. He can come and go as he pleases. And he can bring anyone into his suite straight from the parking garage, then get them out again just as easily.

I swallow, not liking the direction of my thoughts. For one, I want to know if he's in there, possibly watching me wander this space over the security cams.

And even more than that, I want to know if he's sleeping alone.

It's not jealousy. It's not.

It's annoyance. Irritation. Bad fucking manners. Because he's made sure that Grimm Tower is my prison. So it would be downright rude for him to sleep elsewhere—or bring home some little bimbo to fuck while I'm trapped out here.

"Stop it," I say aloud. Because I don't give a shit about Leo Grimm. Or what bimbo he's nailing in the back room.

He says I'm in danger and that he'll protect me. Fab. Great. I'm all about staying in one piece and nailing my sex tape stalker to the fucking wall. So long as he keeps me safe, he can tomcat around all he wants. Really. Because why would I care?

Because the time he spends fucking Bimbo Babe is time he's not working on stopping whoever is using me as a lever to move Leo Grimm.

We need to find that mysterious tormentor, because once this is over, I'm free of Leo again. And this time, I'll be free of him for good.

Losing you once nearly destroyed me.

I hug myself, wishing I could believe him. But I know only too well what a good liar Leo is.

With a sigh, I head into the guest room. The bed here is also made, because, of course, I slept on the sofa. Now, I stretch out on top of the bedspread and hug one of the soft pillows to me, trying to control my zinging and zipping thoughts. Trying to pretend like everything will be fine when I know it won't be.

Yesterday's events tainted everything, and today starts a new path in my life. A path I don't want to walk, but it's the only path there is.

Get a grip, dammit.

The order is both harsh and necessary, because this isn't what I ever expected of my life. I'm boring. A lower-class girl orphaned in college. A woman who started out working for her best friend —the Reed family heiress—while her grandmother worked as the Reed family's head housekeeper.

I'd been Sasha's assistant, then pivoted into Lydia Cosmetics when she founded it. I've always been someone's daughter, some-one's granddaughter, someone's friend.

I'm hardworking, yeah. But I'm not anything special. The closest I've come is playing superhero when I was little and I'd pretend to save the world over and over.

Nice work if you can get it, but that wasn't what the world had in store for me.

I'm just Ruby, and I'm okay with that, even if part of me dreams of something bigger.

And Just Ruby is not the kind of person you'd expect to have a target on her back.

But that, at least, makes some sense. Because there is definitely one tiny blip in my life that put me on the Bad Karma radar—Leo Fucking Grimm.

I fell for him, and now here I am, trapped in a tower and held captive by a dark prince.

Am I trapped?

It occurs to me that I haven't checked the door, so I hurry that direction, grab the knob, and turn.

Nothing.

No surprise there, but I try it again, just for good measure.

Still nothing.

Frustrated and out of ideas, I head to the kitchen, find a pot of coffee already brewed and a box of donuts. Not exactly nutritious, but I'm not going to complain about comfort food.

I put two glazed on a plate, pour a huge cup of coffee, then take my goodies to the big, comfy chair by the window. I sit there, looking out at freedom as I shove carbs into my mouth and listen to the silence that fills the apartment, broken only by the distant hum of the city below, the steady rhythm of my own heartbeat, and the soft sound of donuts vanishing into my belly.

Every few minutes, I catch my mind wandering to Leo. To his claim that I'm in danger. And I have to tell myself all over again that Leo Grimm is a master of manipulation, and I need to keep that reality firmly in mind.

But despite the warnings that slip through my head, I realize that I've been listening for his footsteps in the hallway, for the sound of his key in the lock, or his bedroom door opening. For his voice calling my name.

I draw in a slow breath, not sure if I'm hoping he'll come back or dreading his return.

Maybe both.

Finally, when my legs start to cramp from sitting in the same position, I force myself to stand. My body feels strange, disconnected, like I'm moving through water. Yesterday's drama left me wrung out, but I can't just sit here snarfing donuts like some helpless damsel waiting for rescue.

I'm going to snoop.

I start in the kitchen. Not just because I want to refill my coffee, but because you can tell a lot about a person by what they stock in their fridge and pantry. Last night, I'd only scanned the stuff in the refrigerator when I'd pulled out the Coronas. Now, I take a closer look and find it fully stocked with the basics, plus a few containers of leftovers from restaurants that used to be out of my price range, and even now—with my very nice Lydia Cosmetics salary—I'd consider a splurge. There's even a bottle of champagne chilling on a shelf. Cristal. For guests, I assume, because the Coronas are more Leo's speed.

The Leo I knew, anyway.

The pantry is similarly well-stocked. Too well-stocked, in fact. Granted, he's probably grown up a bit over the last seven years, but a man doesn't change that much. There should be more microwavable snacks and a box full of menus from every restaurant in Manhattan, whether they typically deliver or not.

Instead, this kitchen is stocked as if someone might actually prepare food rather than eat leftovers or take-out. And personal growth notwithstanding, I seriously doubt that Leo has suddenly become Chef Ramsey.

And that simple fact confirms my suspicion that I'm not the only woman who's been in this apartment.

I clench my fists. Hating that revelation even as I tell myself I'm being ridiculous. And I am. The man's seriously hot, wealthy as hell, and not exactly one to go without sex. Of course, there've been other women. Why should I care? I don't. Because the more women, the better, right? Maybe he'll forget about me.

Fuck.

A lightning bolt of fury cuts through me, and I slam the pantry door closed, telling myself that I'm annoyed because he *didn't* forget me. Instead, he set his sights on me.

My irritation has nothing to do with the women he probably fucks nightly, maybe two or three at a time. Absolutely nothing at all.

Asshole.

With a hard yank, I tug the pantry door open again, then do a quick search for a package I'd noticed earlier. *Chips Ahoy.*

I find them at eye level. Two packages, in fact. I'd finished off the Levain Bakery cookies last night, and while they were amazing, Chips Ahoy has always been my comfort food, because *yum* and, well, *budget.*

I grab one, snag a napkin, then head into the living area and plonk myself down on the couch. Not exactly an FDA-approved breakfast choice—especially following donuts—but I'm stress-eating, dammit. And if that makes me talk show fodder, then so be it.

With practiced ease, I rip open the packaging, then pull out the little tray of cookies, my deepest and most enduring comfort food.

I frown, realizing with a start that the pantry had other favorites of mine, too. And so did the fridge. He even had a basket of cloth napkins sitting on the breakfast bar instead of the roll of paper towels that I used to tease him about.

And then it hits me.

This isn't a kitchen stocked for a revolving door of women. It's a room stocked for *me.*

The realization sends a chill down my spine as doubt once again raises its ugly head. Did he really bring me here to protect me from some unknown enemy?

Or is that just a load of crap that I was stupid enough to believe?

I tremble, suddenly terrified that I gave in too easily in the hotel, and Leo has been the danger all along.

After all, he made that sex tape.

He cornered me in the woods.

He drugged me.

And now he's locked me in a tower.

Losing you once nearly destroyed me…

But he didn't lose me. He walked away from me. And now he's trying to rewrite reality.

All of which adds up to the fact that Leo Grimm is a shit, and I should know better than to trust him.

Hell, I *do* know better.

And yet, despite the little voice whispering that Leo Grimm is an egotistical, arrogant ass, I want to believe him. It makes sense, too. After all, he's a billionaire. I'm pretty much invisible.

Except I'm apparently not invisible to Leo's enemy. And if I'm being honest, I'm not invisible to Leo. Not seven years ago, anyway. And not now, either.

Maybe all of this really is only about protecting me from whoever's messing with him. But he *is* protecting me.

And as much as I hate to admit it, I wouldn't expect anything less from Leo.

I take a deep breath, then order myself to chill as I let my mind drift through memories, both good and bad. The way he used to touch me so tenderly before taking me roughly, breaking me in a way that only he could repair. A way that made me his.

I close my eyes and let all those memories hit me like floodwaters, so intense, I scrunch myself into the corner of the couch. Not because the memories are bad, but because they're good. Every day in this room—every night in his bed—each was a time that I'd cherished.

Every single time, with one horrible exception—the morning when I'd learned that my parents had died in a car wreck.

I'd put the phone down, numb, then hurried into the living area to find him. Instead, I found a note. A fucking note that twisted my grief around, like it was some horrible excuse for him to finally dump me.

I heard about your parents. Sorry. And I'm sorry, too, that you need to go. We're over.

It had taken all my strength not to trash this place. Not to destroy every inch of it with my grief and fury and hatred and confusion. But instead of whirling through the place like a tornado, I'd sat on the sofa, fuming, ready to read him the Riot Act when he came back.

But he didn't come back. Gabriel, the oldest of the brothers—the one closest to Leo and the one who scared me the most—came into the suite, then told me that if I didn't walk out, he'd carry me out.

I walked.

That's how I'd learned that I'd never meant anything to him. That I'd been nothing more than the rich boy's pretty little play-thing. That all those whispers about the places he wanted to take me and the things he wanted to show me were just pretty lies to keep me compliant while he used my body until he got bored and tossed me aside in the most horrible and hurtful of ways.

Bastard.

With a shudder, I snuggle into the corner of the sofa, my knees hugged tight against my chest as I rock back and forth, trapped in this goddamn suite. The same one where we'd once spent entire weekends tangled together, talking and laughing and exploring each other's bodies with the kind of desperate hunger that comes from knowing something is too good to last.

I was right about that, at least. Way too good to last.

I've hated Leo Grimm ever since. Not just for dumping me so cruelly, but for lying to me by putting on a false face and using me for years. He's a liar. A sociopath. A brilliant degenerate.

And I will never, ever trust him enough to let him hurt me again.

But I'll stay here now because, despite everything, I trust him to protect me.

And how fucking ironic is that?

With a vicious thrust, I launch myself off the couch. There is far, far, far too much of Leo Grimm in my head.

In order to remedy that, I turn on the TV, find *Friends*, one of the most bingeable shows ever, and I settle in to watch Ross and Rachel and the gang.

By the time I'm well-past the middle of season one, I'm feeling more chill…and more than a little hungry. I head to the kitchen, slice up an apple and some cheese, then take it to the sofa. I munch on my snack as I once try to absorb the life lessons offered by the gang.

Honestly, nothing much aligns with my current situation.

With a sigh, I click off the TV, wacky antics no longer sufficient to keep my mind off all my crap. And once again, I try to wrap my head around this whole situation.

According to Leo, I'm a target because hurting me would hurt him. But how does he know that? Maybe someone really is targeting me. Maybe they sent all those pictures to him instead of to me because they're playing some sort of long game. Maybe the real target is Sasha, who I know would pay ransom for me in a heartbeat.

Except that doesn't really make sense. I'm just making shit up because I don't want to be here. I don't want to hear Leo say that hurting me would hurt him.

I don't want to believe that, because if I believe it now, what kind of a farce does that make of the last seven years?

Fuck.

I sigh. Deep down, I know he's telling me the truth. This isn't about me at all. It's about torturing him. Or trying to. After all, I'm nobody. I'm the daughter of a grocery store manager and a second-grade teacher. Both of whom died in a horrible car accident with no assets and life insurance policies that barely paid for their funerals. I'm no heiress, and definitely not target-worthy. Which means Leo's right—it really is all about hurting me to hurt him.

Frowning, I search for my purse so I can call Sasha. I need to vent. More than that, I need a verbal hug and my best friend. But when I find it, I also find that my phone isn't in it. I try the landline, relieved that there's a dial tone, but I can't manage to make it call out. Same with the phone by the door that rings directly to Grimm Tower's front desk.

Leo did this, of course. He's trapped me here, cut off from everything, with nothing to do but wait until he deigns to come back to his suite. With a sigh, I grab the remote control and settle back on the couch.

What I want now is to just forget.

Forget that someone's been taking creepy pics of me, forget that I'm trapped in this suite, forget that Leo Grimm even exists.

Since that's not possible, I start back up with *Friends*, then revel in the escapism. Which is pathetic considering Leo seems to have every streaming service known to man, not to mention one hell of a DVD collection in the cabinet under the TV.

Still, *Friends*, it is. Easy comforting. And I snuggle into the couch for a full season, letting the entire day slip away as I lose myself in Ross and Rachel and the rest of the gang.

It's early in Season Two, and the afternoon sun is streaming through the windows when I finally turn the show off. Because that's when I realize something—it's not someone else's story I want.

It's mine.

Not only that, but I want him to come back. I'm pissed and confused and want to kick him in the balls, but I'm willing to set all of that aside for answers as to what my creepy tormentor wants from him, and when Leo's going to either have the fucker arrested or give in. Because I don't intend to stay in the Leo Grimm version of protective custody forever.

And I want to know very, very specifically how he intends to keep me safe until all that happens.

Most of all, his plan damn well better be more refined than *lock you in a tower and keep you there.*

I'm struggling to picture what an alternate plan would look like when I hear the beeps of a lock code. I twist to face the entryway, my heart racing as the door swings open to reveal Leo standing in the doorway.

His hair is tousled and damp, as if he's fresh from the shower. He's wearing gray sweatpants that cling to his thighs in a way that makes my memory tingle. His seriously ripped torso is bare except for the two ends of a white hand towel hanging around his neck.

This is a Leo I'm familiar with. The one who runs to the gym when he's working out a problem.

I fight a grin, certain that today wasn't a problem at the office.

Today, was all about me.

He takes a step closer, and my eyes dip to his chest and that sexy smattering of chest hair. Even now, I can recall the way my fingers felt when I used to draw designs on his skin, my fingertips tracing over his chest, down his belly, then even lower to ease under the band of his briefs, where my goal was a completely different kind of design.

I smile at the memory, then stiffen when I realize how closely he's watching me.

"Strolling Memory Lane?" he asks, his voice sharp enough to convey that he knows the direction of my thoughts.

"Not for the reason you think," I say. "Just trying to gather up a few memories so I can have the pleasure of shredding them one by one." I flash a simpering smile. "It'll feel so good to kick every one of my memories of you out of my head."

I say the words to hurt him, but I mean them, too. I want those memories gone. And not just the ones filled with hurt and pain, but even the good ones. *Especially* the good ones. Because now I know they were just stuff and nonsense, of no importance at all to the man I once loved.

I let my eyes rake deliberately over him, then cock my head as I meet his eyes, my gaze as hard as granite. "Glad abducting me didn't interrupt your workout schedule."

As his brows rise, I turn my back on him, pick up the remote, and turn the television back on. I click around, stopping when the second installment of *Twilight* shows up on the screen. It's one of my favorite flicks, and I used to make Leo watch the trilogy with me over and over and over.

"I can make popcorn," he says.

Even after ODing on *Friends*, the idea's just a little too appealing, so I click the remote, navigating through the channels until I find a classic movie station that's airing *Jaws*. "Sure," I say, "if you're up for this. I'm relating a lot more with those unknowing swimmers today than I am with Bella and her love triangle."

A muscle in his cheek tightens, but all he says is, "Butter?"

"Lots. And salt."

"I remember." He holds my gaze even after he speaks, and—damn me—my heart picks up tempo.

I turn away. I remember, too. The difference is that I don't want to. Why hold tight to the memory of a man who no longer exists? Who was maybe never anything more than an illusion?

I focus on the television, hugging my knees as that iconic theme plays, the music seeming to underscore the sound of Leo moving around in the kitchen, measuring kernels, stirring the on-stove popper that's probably the same one he bought in college.

After a few moments, he comes into the living area with a tray holding a carafe of wine, two glasses, a huge bowl of popcorn, and about a billion napkins.

I nod to the latter. "You remembered."

"You wiped your hands after every buttery bite, and you never reused the same napkin. You were an environmentalist's nightmare. And I assume you still are."

"Guilty," I say. "But I make up for it in annual donations. And I recycle religiously."

"Yin and Yang," he says, and I have to look away. That had been another one of our in-jokes. How the two of us had balanced each other out.

"Now it's prisoner and captor," I say sharply.

"More like mark and protector," he counters. "I'm not locking you away."

"Hello? Locked door. I checked."

"I'm keeping you safe," he says firmly. "Safe and hidden."

"That is such bullshit."

"Dammit, Rue, it's not."

I sit up straighter at the harsh edge to his voice, then frown when he sighs and drags his fingers through his still-damp hair, making it stand on end. It's a habit I recognize. It's what he does when he's worried.

I pull my knees up onto the sofa again, then hug them tight. "All right," I say slowly. "Tell me."

He doesn't want to. Leo Grimm may have the reputation of being the wildest of the Grimm brothers, but that's partly because he does what he wants—and only what he wants—moving forward toward his goals without asking for permission or help. And always, always, hitting the mark.

Uncertainty makes him crazy, as does sharing anything before he's ready. All of which is why I'm certain I'm going to have to push to get the answers I want.

"You're keeping me prisoner. At least have the common decency to tell me why."

"Don't you get it? I can't hunt this threat if I have to worry about whether or not you're safe. Grimm Tower is strategic. All the business floors have stellar security, but it's even more impenetrable up here in the residences. From the thirtieth floor all the way up to the penthouse, it's like being in a lockbox."

"So I'm just supposed to stay here like your pet rat?"

"Or you could go home and spend your time wondering when a sniper will hide in one of those gorgeous oaks that surround your cabin, then take you out in your kitchen. Or, worse, take out Granny."

I don't say anything at first because my chest is too tight. "Granny," I finally manage. "She hasn't gone back to the cabin, has she?"

"She's staying with Liam and Sasha until this is over." His voice is surprisingly gentle, and I nod.

"Okay. Good."

"Listen, Rue," he begins, his voice as matter-of-fact as if we were discussing the weather. "This asshole isn't going to give up hunting you just because you're hidden away. Eventually, this is going to come to a head, and when it does, you'll need to be ready."

"Hunting me," I repeat slowly. "Hunting me to get to you. Golly, I sure was lucky that day I met you on campus."

"No," he says, his voice soft. "But I'm too selfish to regret ever meeting you. And I will keep you safe. Or I'll die trying."

I swallow, suddenly unable to breathe as something like a fist squeezes my heart. "Leo…"

He presses a finger to my lips and shakes his head.

I sigh, then pull my feet up onto the sofa and hug my knees. "Have you learned anything new?"

"Still no demand."

"Then let me go. I can't stay here forever."

"If there's still danger? Hell yes, you can."

On the one hand, I want to smack him for suggesting he'd keep me a prisoner forever. But at the same time, I want to pull him close and lose myself in his arms, for exactly that same reason.

"Why?"

"Because I'm not taking chances with you. Keeping you here is keeping you safe."

"Are you sure?"

"That I'll protect you? Absolutely."

"No, that whoever's doing this will try to hurt me."

"I'm sure." His eyes meet mine, flat and no-nonsense. "Whoever sent those photos has been watching you for a long time. He wants something from me. He must. But I don't know what it is. It might be a thing. Something tangible. Or it might be a reaction."

I shake my head, not understanding.

"Your stalker might not want anything like money or information. This might be retribution for something I did. And they're going to punish me by hurting you."

"Why the hell would they believe you care?"

"Think what you want," he says softly. "But about how to torture me? They've got it right."

I say nothing, then go stiff when his palm rests lightly on my shoulder. "I never claimed to be a good man, Rue." His voice is soft, and I feel the whisper of his breath like a soft breeze on my hair. "I'm sorry if knowing me painted a target on your back."

His voice is low and even, almost emotionless. But I know this man well—or I thought I did. And I can hear the regret.

"And you're really sure about that?"

"You know my family's history, Rue. I know what I know." My blood runs cold, and I know he means it. The Grimm family definitely leans toward the original, darker versions of their ancestors' fairy tales. This is not a family of sweetness and light.

"Hell," he continues, "it's what got Gabriel killed," he adds, referring to the oldest Grimm brother, who was also Leo's idol.

I shudder, but shift on the couch so I'm looking straight at him. "They have us wrong," I say. "But I believe you. They'll hurt me because they think you care."

"I do care."

"Only because you don't like to lose."

"I won't lose—and neither will you, because you're going to do as I say. And that means you stop even thinking about how to try to get away from me. You can't do it, anyway, but even if you did, the moment you were out of this tower, they'd grab you. But they won't kill you," he adds, his voice low and hard. "Not right away. They want you to suffer first. They want to hurt you in ways that would make what happened to your parents look merciful."

The casual mention of my parents makes my blood run cold. The memory of how they'd burned alive, trapped in their car after a horrible accident. I hug myself, warding off the memory and my increasing fear.

"So you're keeping me here for my own good? Leo Grimm

stepping in to play the hero?" I shake my head and scoff. "I gotta say, I don't think you're right for the role."

"Sarcasm. Good. You're pissed."

I scowl. The man really does know me.

"Stay pissed. At me. At our anonymous prick. That anger's a weapon and a shield. Use it."

"Oh, you bet I will." I stand up and start pacing. "In case you hadn't noticed, I'm trapped here. Locked in. No phone. No way to reach anyone. But I'm supposed to just believe it's for my own good?"

"Christ, Rue. You're the one who sailed through college with nothing below an A. Try using that amazing brain to think. If I wanted to hurt you, I would have done it already. If I wanted you dead, you'd be dead. If I wanted to torture you, I'd have started the moment you woke up."

"Maybe you like drawing it out. Or," I add, sweeping my arm to indicate the luxurious suite, "maybe keeping me locked in a golden cage while you play mind games is your idea of the perfect revenge."

"Revenge for what?"

I falter—because he's right. For what? But I can't back off. I'm scared and I'm pissed and Leo Grimm is my personal punching bag right now.

"For—for surviving," I finally say, suddenly realizing how I must have destroyed all his plans. "For putting my life back together after you broke me, rather than spending the rest of my life curled up and whimpering."

I take a step toward him. "I survived after you dumped me, you miserable fuck. I not only survived, but I thrived. And all without you."

"I know," he says, and though I know it must be my imagination, I think I hear a hint of pride. "But this isn't about us. This is about me. This is about someone using you to get to me."

"Well, then, like I said, I guess I really am in danger, because god knows you haven't given a fuck about me since that day you jammed that knife into my heart."

I wait, watching his face, expecting him to argue. To tell me he had a good reason to destroy me and then walk away. To convince me that he's loved me all this time, and the past seven years have been a huge misunderstanding.

But a full minute passes, and he doesn't say a damn thing.

"So what's the actual plan?" I ask when I can no longer stand the silence. "Keep me locked up here forever? Wait for this mysterious enemy to get bored and move on to an easier target?"

"The plan is to keep you alive while my people hunt down whoever's been stalking you." His voice is hard, implacable. "Which means you stay here, in this suite, where I can protect you."

"Protect me or control me?"

"Both." He doesn't even try to deny it. "You're going to follow my rules, Ruby. You're going to stay where I put you, eat what I give you, and do exactly what I tell you to do. Because the alternative is watching you be tortured or killed in a way that will haunt me for the rest of my life."

The raw honesty in his voice catches me off guard, and I think I see something that might be genuine fear in his eyes.

But then I remember who I'm dealing with. Leo Grimm is a man with celebrities and politicians in his pocket. A man who can phone anyone in the government and have them return his call. A man who keeps a low profile because he doesn't need to be splashy. He's known by the people who count, and, like the Wizard, he works behind a dark curtain of secrets and lies.

Leo Grimm is a master at manipulation and covering things up. Security is his official business, but he trades in information and the currency of power.

He's not weak. He's not vulnerable. And he's not the type to scare easily.

He looks scared now.

But damned if I can tell if the fear is real…or if it's a ploy to get me to fall into line.

"What if I don't want your help? What if I'd rather take my chances than stay locked up with you?"

Leo's smile could cut steel. "Then I'll tie you to that bed and keep you there until this is over."

The casual way he delivers the threat sends chills up my spine, and I have to look away, too overcome by the flood of memories spotlighting our wildly sensual games.

"You wouldn't dare," I say, but only for form. He means it.

"Oh, I would. I'd even enjoy it." He moves to stand right in front of me, and I can practically feel his heat. He brushes his thumb along the curve of my jaw, and it takes all my willpower not to moan. "I'll do a hell of a lot more if that's what it takes to keep you alive."

I jerk away from his touch, but there's nowhere to go. I'm trapped between his body and the sofa, pinned by his proximity and the weight of his words.

"You're insane."

"Maybe." His smile is pure predator now. "But right now, think of me as your insane bodyguard. And I'm the only thing standing between you and a very ugly death."

The possessive way he says *your insane bodyguard* makes something clench low in my belly, and I hate myself for the reaction. Hate that even now, even seeing the worst of him, my body still responds.

"So here are the rules," Leo continues, moving back just enough to let me breathe. "You don't leave this suite—not that you could. You don't try to contact anyone—again, you can't, but don't bother trying. You don't do anything that might give away your location. No messages tossed from broken windows, no taking apart the TV to try to build a transmitter."

I cross my arms and lift my brows. "Seriously?"

He grins. "I did say you're clever." He hooks a finger under my chin and lifts my face to his. "You're going to obey every order

I give you without question. And, Ruby, you're going to share my bed."

The last makes me shiver, and not in a bad way.

Annoyed with myself, I roll my shoulders back and stare up at him. "And if I disobey?"

His eyes narrow, then he twines a strand of my hair around his finger. "Please do. I'd love the chance to punish you." He leans in. "I still jack off to the way you moaned when I spanked that sweet rear. Can still remember how hard you came when I twisted your nipples while fucking your ass." The finger traces over my lips. I can barely breathe.

"I'll do whatever it takes to keep you safe."

"Why?" The word is a whisper as I try to hold back tears. "You walked out on me, remember? You destroyed me, and you never even looked back once."

"You have every reason to hate me," he says.

"Hell, yeah, I do."

For a moment, I think he's just going to leave that hanging. Then he sighs and says, "I'm not a good man. I do what it takes and screw the consequences. But I also protect what's mine."

"I haven't been yours for a very long time."

"Maybe. Maybe not. But you're here now, and you're under my protection. That makes you mine."

He follows the curve of my jaw with the pad of his thumb. "But I don't do anything for free, Red, and I will take my price, whether you're willing to pay or not." He steps back, then looks me up and down. "I think you will be."

Something warm and disturbing sizzles through me, and I shake my head. "Fuck you, Leo Grimm."

He grins. "Yeah, Red. That's the idea."

His eyes rake over me one more time, then he turns and walks out of the room, leaving me standing there, breathing hard, and hating myself for wishing that he'd turn around and come back.

TEN
BREAKING POINT

I spend the bulk of the next day doing nothing. Literally nothing.

At first, I thought I might get some work done. Diving into the ever-growing pile of Lydia Cosmetics paperwork would keep me busy. But since I can't contact Sasha, I can't get the documents I need.

I could ask Leo to contact her, then task Liam with delivering the paperwork. But even if Leo surprises me and lets me have the documents, I still wouldn't be able to get any work done because almost everything I do requires access to the internet. And there's no way in hell that Leo will agree to that. After all, I might try to send a message begging Liam to help me rather than staying stupidly loyal to his idiot brother.

And, yeah, I would *so* do that. Which Leo damn well knows.

That, of course, is why the day passes with me getting no work done, responding to none of the billions of emails that are surely piling up, and sending zero SOS messages to Liam.

Damn.

I don't even get any reading done. I tried to focus on the leather-bound book of Grimm's fairy tales I'd found, but only managed to read the beginning of *Little Red Riding Hood* over and over and over, never managing to get past the first page. Instead, my mind inevitably wandered to my run-in with Leo on the trail—and the irony of how I'd pushed him away, only to find myself his captive just one short day later.

Finally, I end up flipping through magazines and wandering the suite, trying desperately to just keep busy. That's when it hits me. I can't focus on anything because I'm totally and completely preoccupied with listening for Leo's footsteps.

I am so fucked up.

That horrible realization pushes me to my feet and into action. Anything to get him out of my head. Which is how I end up in my bathroom taking what will probably turn out to be the longest shower in the history of time.

Fortunately, Grimm Tower seems to have an endless supply of hot water. Which, frankly, is the only perk of this prison that I can find.

Well, that and the cookies.

I let my mind wander as the spray pounds down on me, then use the loofa to rub body wash over every single inch of skin. Once I'm soaped up and slick, I reach up to remove the shower-head from its anchor, then aim the spray at my legs, my back, my chest, relishing the sensation of the water pounding at the tight knots that are tormenting my aching body. So much fear and tension. And—so help me—so much need.

No, no, no. Don't go there. Don't think of him.

You came in here to escape thoughts of him.

Except how can Leo not be in my head? This is the suite I remember only too well from all those years ago. This is the shower where he'd told me to press my hands against the marble wall. Where his rough, warm hands had cupped my breasts. Where he'd slid one hand down to anchor me.

I close my eyes, wishing I could push the memory away, but it's taken root and now plays like a porn video inside my head. The way he'd held me tight around the waist as his fingers plunged deep inside my slick, wet pussy. The way his cock teased the crack of my ass before he took me there, too, hard and deep. Wild at first, then finding a rhythm, his arm around me and his free hand on the wall, keeping us steady as he fucked me dirty, reducing me to nothing but glorious, overwhelming pleasure made all the more potent because it was tinged with pain.

Yes. Oh, god, yes.

I don't remember moving to sit on the shower's marble bench, but that's where I am now, my back arched, my legs spread, and my hand aiming that pulsating spray between my thighs as I let my mind go back to those months with him. Three years when he'd been mine and I'd been his. When I'd believed that Leo was the reward for something incredible I'd done in another life, because why else could I deserve a man like him? A man who loved me so wholly, so openly. So completely that I was never quite sure where he ended and I began.

Bastard.

With a sharp gasp, I slam back to the present, then toss the shower head onto the tile floor as if it's a cobra I'd accidentally picked up.

Then I stand up, my hand on the safety bar because my legs are too damn weak.

I don't want him. *I don't.*

It was just a memory. Just stress relief.

It doesn't mean anything.

It can't mean anything.

I'm still telling myself that ten minutes later, when I open the steam-fogged door, grab a towel, and dry off. Then I get out of the shower and use the moisturizer that was probably left over by some other woman Leo's fucked.

It's only after I've combed out my hair and traded the towel for the comfy robe that I realize the bathroom door's cracked. Which wouldn't be a big deal, except I know I closed it. I like steam. Lots of steam. And I've never once left a door open when I was in the shower.

Leo.

I should be furious at him for sneaking a peek. And I should definitely be mortified by the thought that he might have seen me with the shower head.

I'm not.

Quite the opposite.

And while I chastise myself for being a horny little exhibitionist slut, I also sigh from the way the robe I found behind the door slides over my body, the soft material stroking my nipples like the way he used to do with his tongue before he'd—*No.*

I put my hands on the sink and stare at my somewhat foggy reflection, silently warning myself not to become a woman with a hefty dose of Stockholm Syndrome.

He. Fucking. Drugged. Me.

Then he locked me in his palatial suite of a prison.

And except for showing me those surveillance photos so I'd break and trust him, he's staying completely silent about what he knows.

No way am I going to fall prey to his charms. Not again.

Having thoroughly schooled myself, I stand up straight, tighten the belt on the robe, then head back into the guest room. I glance at the bed, debating whether I want to simply nap my way through this ordeal.

But no. He may have locked me in, but he's not stealing my life. My time.

It may be absurd, but I'm going to act like I'm in control. Maybe if I put on a good enough show, I will be.

With a sharp nod of approval—witnessed only by my reflection in the mirror over the dresser—I head to one of the huge windows that look out over the world I'm no longer part of. Every square foot of Manhattan below me seems to pulse with life. People going to work, meeting friends for lunch, living their normal lives while I'm trapped here, a voyeur, only able to look down on life, with no way to actually live it.

Not long ago, I'd felt sorry for Sasha, trapped in Reed Tower by her controlling prick of a father. Now I'm the one who's trapped. Not by my father, dead and gone for the last seven years. But by Leo Grimm, the man who destroyed me so completely on the night my parents died.

Stop it. Just stop it.

I force myself to follow my own advice, then shove all thoughts of Leo, my parents, and the past out of my head.

Moment by moment. That's the only way I'm going to survive.

With renewed determination, I find a clean pair of sweats and a Rolling Stones T-shirt in the dresser. I pull them on, then wander back into the living area, my mind still spinning and my body restless and edgy. I can't seem to settle. Not with a book, not with the television. I can't even get excited about snooping through his drawers and cabinets.

I want him here.

The realization cuts through me, and though I hate it, I can't deny it. I want Leo here. Not for sex—though my body seems to have its own opinion about that. Not because I'm bored and lonely and need a distraction to keep my mind from drifting to the fact that somebody has it in for me. Not for answers, though god knows I need those.

Not even because I'm scared.

Or at least, not entirely.

With a frown, I realize that I'm pacing, as if my body's unable to stay still in the face of the revelation that's leaped up and is now dancing around the room, jeering at me.

I want him because he's my person.

Or, at least, he used to be.

With a small shudder, I wipe away the tears that are trickling down my face and force myself to examine that revelation more closely. Because surely not.

Except…yes.

I want him.

I want him here because he used to be the one who could make everything better. He'd tutored me when advanced calculus left me fearing I'd lose my scholarship. He'd rocked me when I fought with my roommate. He'd stroked my hair when I stressed out about having five papers due in one week, and he'd made me laugh whenever I felt low.

The only time he wasn't there for me was the time he broke me. My parents' death. That horrible note, all the more horrible because it was so brutally unexpected.

His cold, unfeeling behavior during that nightmare should have erased every kind thing he ever did. And god knows, drugging me and kidnapping me from the Celestial should earn him a few demerits, too.

And it does. All of that does. Leo Grimm is a prick. A harsh, rude, vile, controlling prick.

But some fucked-up, pathetic part of me still wants to see him as a comfort instead of a threat.

Stupid, stupid, stupid.

I shake my head, then march back into the kitchen, needing a culinary hug, pathetic as that might be. Not that I find much in the way of comfort food other than the Chips Ahoy. But I'm getting tired of those.

I start opening and closing the cabinets and am delighted to find yellow cake mix and a can of chocolate frosting shoved into the back of a high cabinet that I'd missed in my earlier foraging.

I pull them both out, then hesitate. I want the cake—right now, sugar and freedom are about all I want—I'm just not sure I want the memories.

Surely it's a coincidence. Surely his maid or someone stocked the kitchen—not Leo himself. Not with those two items.

Not unless he was trying to be subtly sentimental.

Or deliberately cruel.

With a frown, I shove the box and the can back into the cabinet, well-hidden behind a package of saltines and a stack of canned black beans.

I grab more cookies, then take them to the sofa and settle in to read. But I can't. I keep thinking about the day so many years ago when I'd knocked on the dorm room next to mine on the first day of classes, intending to ask the girl who'd lived there if she had a fresh box of cake mix, because I'd destroyed my only one, and I was trying to make a cake for the cute guy from my Intro to Psych class.

Except my neighbor hadn't returned that semester, and Leo Grimm was in that room. Then, for some inexplicable reason, when he'd asked me what I needed, I launched into a full-on explanation. "There's this guy," I'd said, "and he's coming over 'cause we're going to go see *Star Wars* at that revival theater, so I made a cake. Or a deformed wreck of a cake." I'd frowned. "So now I need to make another. My mom always says you offer guests something sweet."

"We don't have ovens," he'd said, his green eyes starting to dance. "And microwaves are pretty useless for cake mix."

"So I've discovered." I'd shrugged. "Thanks, anyway."

I'd started to turn away, but he'd caught my elbow, and the shiver from that contact had gone straight through me.

"Did it explode in the microwave? Or does it just look lumpy and weird?"

I cocked my head. "You sound like a guy who's walked this road before me."

He grinned and spread his hands, looking so adorable, I wanted to call Psych Guy—*what was his name?*—and cancel on the spot. "I've walked many roads," he'd said, then stepped into the hall and pulled the door shut behind him. "Show me."

So I had. And though he'd tried to hold back the laughter when he saw the yellow cake blob sitting by the can of chocolate icing, I could tell he was on the verge of losing it.

"Cake blocks," he said. "Tell your date it's a new thing. Very hip."

"Cake blocks?"

"Sure," he said, then used the knife to demonstrate by cutting a square, slathering icing, then putting it on the paper plate. He did two more—a rectangle and something that might have been a cylinder—before I settled in to help.

"Food art," he said.

"You are some sort of evil genius," I told him.

His grin was pure mischief—and sexy as hell. "How well you know me," he'd said, and we both laughed.

Then I'd jumped at the knock on my dorm room. "Damn!" The word slipped out, and my eyes went wide. And then my cheeks flamed when he'd looked at me, that crooked half-smile lighting his whole face.

"Stay," he'd said, rising to his feet, his wagging finger silencing my *pro forma* protest before he went to the door and cracked it open.

"Oh. Hey." The voice came from the boy on the other side of the door. My date. "I'm looking for Ruby."

"Listen, I've got to apologize for her." Leo's voice was firm, but consoling. And I scooted back to make sure Date Boy—was it Aaron?—couldn't see me. "Turns out she has a conflict. A whole evening of libertine activities that she really can't bail on."

Libertine? Wasn't that…

"Libertine?" Aaron—or maybe it was Eric?—said. "You mean, like politics and stuff?"

"Whatever you say. Raincheck, yeah?" And then he'd shut the door, leaving Eric or Aaron—and me—utterly confused.

"Libertine?" I'd said when he sat down on the floor next to me. "Do you even know what that means?"

"Yeah," he'd said, his eyes drifting over me in a way that made me very glad I didn't have a roommate. "I do. Do you?"

I didn't answer. Just bit my lower lip as he dragged his finger through the chocolate frosting. Then he leaned forward, his finger extended. "Lick it off," he'd said. And so help me, I did.

Over the course of the evening, we'd finished off that jar of chocolate frosting, licking up every bit, even though not a single ounce landed on my freakishly formed yellow cake.

Now, I shiver—both from the memory and from the touch of my fingers between my legs. Fingers I hadn't meant to put there, but must have drifted there as my mind had wandered to places it shouldn't go. Places and times when I'd loved Leo.

When I'd thought he loved me.

I draw in a sharp breath.

Fuck it.

I shove the cookies across the table, pull up my knees, and snuggle into the sofa's corner, a blanket pulled up to my neck. Then I scroll through the various channels until *Orange is the New Black* pops up.

I stick there. What the hell, right? Isn't today's theme captivity?

I'm not familiar enough with the show to know what's going on, so my mind drifts as I watch. And by the time I hear the door opening, it's past seven and I'm still in the robe.

I stand, intending to go get dressed, but that's when Leo enters, preceded by a mesmerizing aroma that must be coming from the take-out bags he's carrying.

He catches my eye but says nothing as I watch him cross to the kitchen area, moving with that predatory grace that always made my pulse skip.

"Dinner," he says, setting the bags on the kitchen counter without looking at me.

"How nice for you to be able to go out and order anything you want," I say, crossing my arms. "Maybe chat with the folks behind the take-out counter. Or just interact with other human beings. Maybe, oh, use that newfangled gizmo folks call a phone."

He studies me, his face flat and expressionless. "You know why you're here."

"Well, seeing as you *drugged* me, I missed the actual getting-here part."

"Dammit, Ru—"

"Of course, I know why I'm here. I still say it was a dick move to knock me out, but I get it. Keeping me safe. And I'm all about not dying. But dammit, Leo, you're playing your goddamn power games with me."

He just blinks at me. Like he's an innocent little puppy with no idea what I'm talking about.

"I don't have my computer," I say, my words sharp and cold. "I don't have a phone. I don't even have you—though that's probably a blessing. I'm trapped here by myself like some new breed of zoo animal you're trying to acclimate." I stalk toward him, then poke my forefinger against his button-downed chest.

"But I'm not a fucking koala bear," I continued with gusto. "I mean, what the hell? You can't even let Sasha come by? Or let me chat with her on the phone?"

"For fuck's sake, Rue. Someone got into your home. They hacked your laptop. They've been stalking you for god knows how long. And you're being pissy because you can't call your bestie?"

"Yes!" I snap the word out. "I am seriously fucking pissy. Because you're being a jerk. This isn't about protecting me. It's about *you* protecting me."

I edge closer to him. "This is about you going through the motions of stepping up. About you trying to make up for all those years ago." I have to swallow the tears that have formed a knot in my throat. "Someone's got me in their sights, and, yeah, you're stepping in to keep me safe. But not because of me. That's not what you're about."

My tears are flowing freely now, and I wipe them away with my fingers. "You destroyed me, Leo. You fucking destroyed me seven years ago. And keeping me locked up in some fucked up attempt to keep me safe isn't going to fix what you broke."

I see the tension as it moves through his posture, shifting him from the laid-back man half-slouching against the kitchen counter and into a corporate warrior—his posture ramrod straight, his eyes missing nothing, and his entire body warning the world not to fuck with him. Or with what belongs to him.

Right now, he thinks I belong to him.

But the warrior has got that wrong.

He takes a single step toward me, his eyes roaming over me

with a cool look of ownership. "You've had your say. Now I have a question for you."

I cross my arms and cock my head, waiting.

"So what?" he says.

"Excuse me?"

He moves closer, and my heartbeat picks up its tempo. "I said *so what*. I don't give a fuck what you think, Rue. You say I can't keep you safe, but you're wrong. I will keep you safe. And I will keep you alive. And I'll do whatever it takes, even if that means gagging you and strapping you to a chair for the duration. Which," he adds, raking a heated gaze over me, "might be very entertaining, but would also mean abandoning my other plans for passing the time. And that would be a shame."

I lift my chin, hoping he hasn't noticed the way the heat in both his voice and his gaze has made my nipples tighten. "Prick," I murmur.

"I've been called worse." He takes another step closer. So close that my fingers could reach the buttons of his shirt. I don't reach out, of course. But I hate myself for wanting to.

"Whoever sent you those surveillance pics is an idiot. We both know you don't give a flying fuck about me. You don't love me. You never have."

A muscle in his jaw tenses as I keep going. "I was just your plaything. Your little toy. The pretty little doll you destroyed, pulling off limb after limb, then tossing me away once you'd finished playing with me."

His sharp green eyes lock onto mine. "This isn't about love. It's not about our past. It's about keeping you safe. That's what I'm going to do, and you're going to follow my instructions and stick to my rules whether you agree with them or not. Disobey, and you will be punished."

He takes a step closer. "And just so we're clear—if I'm not doing this out of love, then it must be for my own selfish interest."

He reaches out, then runs his fingers from my neck down along the V of the robe to my cleavage. I take a step back, but he grasps the robe tie and pulls me back to him, then he undoes the bow and lets the robe fall open. He meets my eyes, as if in challenge, and though it takes every ounce of my strength, I force my hands to stay at my sides even though I want to draw the belt tight around me.

He arches one brow, the corner of his mouth rising even as his fingers stroke lightly over my breasts, then slip lower and lower until he slides his hand between my legs and fingers my shamefully wet pussy.

"I never loved you?" he asks, thrusting two fingers deep inside as I try not to moan. "I just used you? Well, buckle up, baby. Because I'm going to use you all the more."

My traitorous body is clenching around him, and my cheeks are hot when he uses his free hand to lift my chin, forcing me to look at him.

"I'll keep you safe, Ruby. That, I swear. But you're going to pay my price. And," he adds, thrusting another finger inside me and making me cry out. "I think you're going to enjoy it."

I start to protest, but he presses a finger to my lips, his expression making clear he'll brook no argument. Then he leads me to the far wall, until we're standing in front of one of the two floor-to-ceiling windows that dominate this room.

"Leo…"

"I'm going to take you here, baby. Where anyone looking can see." He nods to the other window, where he has a telescope set up. I know he's done the very thing he's talking about. I know, because I did it with him. Turning that lens toward other windows. Finding couples fucking beyond the glass. Our hands on each other as we'd mimic them, until we got so hot and wild we didn't give a fuck about what they were doing across the street, only what we were doing to each other.

But I'd loved him then. I'd been playing the game with him—foolish, maybe. But damn if it hadn't been hot.

Now…

I swallow. "Leo, no."

He doesn't answer. Just pushes the robe off my shoulders. As it slides off me to the ground, his fingers slide back inside me.

"You're so fucking wet. Tell me how much you want me."

I shake my head. "I don't."

The corner of his mouth twitches, and I gasp as he pinches my clit. Hard.

"Don't lie, baby," he says, moving his fingers in and out of my very wet pussy until I can't hold back and my body clenches, trying to hold him in. "Don't ever lie about what you want. And never to me."

I bite my lower lip as he turns me so that I'm looking out at the city, glittering under the setting sun. I'm naked, my breasts pressed against the glass, my palms flat on either side of my face, and the city spread out in front of me.

My legs are spread, and his fingers thrust inside me again. I tell myself I hate this, but my body is a damn little slut, and my core clenches tight around him.

He chuckles, then slides his fingers free, the motion wrenching a moan of protest from me.

His gaze catches mine in the faint reflection—sharp, knowing. His mouth curves in that slow, dangerous way that makes my pulse spike.

"You don't want me to stop," he murmurs.

"Yes, I do," I lie.

"No," he says, his chest pressed against my back as his fingers paint my inner thighs with my own wetness. "Your mouth says no. But your body's begging me."

A shiver runs through me, and he feels it. Of course he does.

"God, you're soaked. Tell me you've been waiting for this."

"I haven't."

"Liar."

He moves closer, his clothed body pressing against my naked flesh. His hands rest on top of mine, his cock—straining against his pants—presses against my bare ass in a way that makes me want to beg him to take me right there, right now.

But I won't beg. I won't give him the satisfaction.

His lips brush my ear as he speaks. "Look," he whispers. "One wrong move and this window gives way, and we're both falling through the Manhattan sky."

My heart lurches. "Leo—"

"Does that scare you?" he asks, almost softly.

"No," I murmur, my word barely a breath.

"Don't lie," he whispers. "Not to me. I can smell the fear on you. See it in the reflection of your face." He leans in closer, his breath teasing my ear when he whispers, his voice darker, "Fear looks so fucking good on you. And damned if it doesn't get you hot."

And then his hand is between my thighs again, plunging back into me, harder this time. I gasp, my palms splaying on the glass, cold and slick under my fingers, my nipples like pebbles against the window.

"Imagine it," he murmurs. "This window shattering. The whole city watching you come for me as we fall."

"Stop," I whisper, but the word melts into a moan when his fingertip teases my clit.

"You like it," he says, thrusting his fingers deeper, curling them just right. Making me whimper. "The danger. The thought of being caught. The thrill of knowing one slip and you're mine forever."

A helpless sound escapes me. I hate it. I hate that he's right. That he still knows me so well. That I still crave the decadent, sensual pleasures he taught me.

I don't want to want it. I want to push that all aside. I want a safe life. A safe man.

Because this man with his fingers in my cunt isn't safe at all.

But oh, god, how I crave him.

"Say you hate this," he challenges. "Say you want me to stop."

"Stop," I say, but my body makes the words a lie as I arch back against him, craving more. *Needing* more.

"That's what I thought," he growls, pumping his fingers faster, rougher. "Come for me, Red. Explode like the sexy little slut you are."

The combination of his touch and the danger and the dirty talk does me in, and the orgasm slams through me, violent, and wild and wonderful—and I cry out, my forehead pressing to the glass, trembling as he wrings every shudder from me.

My knees go weak, and I start to sag. He catches me, then spins me around, whispering, "Oh, no. I'm not done with that sweet little pussy." I'm facing him now, my bare back and my ass against the glass, my nipples still tight from both arousal and the lingering cool touch of the windowpane.

In front of me, Leo takes off his belt, then opens his fly. He's huge and harder than I've ever seen him—and I'm reminded that he's a dangerous man now, not a college boy.

He takes a step toward me, and I don't even look at his face. Just focus on his cock and swallow. Huge, yes. But I'm wet enough. And—damn me—I want this.

"Rue," he says, and in the same moment that I lift my head to look at him, he picks me up, ordering me to wrap my legs around him. I do, then gasp as he enters me, his hands on my hips slamming me down onto his cock in one hard thrust that makes me cry out in a combination of pleasure and pain.

"Fuck," he groans. "Still so fucking tight. Still mine."

Then he steps forward, and my bare back is pressed hard against the window.

I gasp, the glass vibrating slightly under the force, the city lights blurring behind me.

His pace is merciless from the start, driving me into the glass with every thrust. The faint vibration makes it worse—makes it better. I don't know. All I do know is that I haven't been this aroused since…well, since forever.

"You feel that?" His voice is low. Dangerous. "The glass isn't made for this. One hard slam and it could give."

A whimper slips from my lips.

"You're scared," he whispers, pounding harder. "Scared it'll break. Scared they'll see you. And it makes you so fucking wet for me."

"No," I choke out, but it's a lie. A horrible, beautiful lie.

"You love it," he whispers. "You love the danger. You love knowing the whole city could see you riding my cock like this."

The glass creaks faintly with the force of his thrusts, and I let out a small, startled cry.

"Oh, you like that," he groans, slamming even harder. "You like not knowing if it'll hold. You like me fucking you on the edge of it all. You like the danger. Hell, you crave it."

I whimper, then suck in a breath as his hand slides up my body, closing lightly around my throat—not choking, just holding me still as he turns my head to look at the city. "Look at all those people down there. Clueless. If only they knew everything I'm making you feel right now."

"Leo," I gasp, my nails clawing at his arms.

"Say you're mine," he growls, pounding deeper.

"I'm not—"

"Yes, you are." He thrusts harder, relentless. "Say it, or I'll fuck you against this glass until it cracks."

A helpless moan tears from my throat. My body betrays me, tightening around him, my climax building fast and sharp.

"That's it," he rasps, voice raw. "Come for me against this fucking window."

The orgasm rips through me, stealing my breath, my thoughts. I scream, trembling against the cold glass, every nerve lit up, my cunt pulsating against his cock.

"Fuck, yes," he growls, driving through it, dragging it out until I almost pass out from the intensity.

A few more punishing thrusts, and he groans low, deep, spilling inside me with one final, hard slam that makes the glass shudder again.

Then stillness.

I'm pinned, bare, my ass and back against the window, the city sprawled beneath me. My breathing is ragged, desperate.

His eyes meet mine, and I tremble under his satisfied smile. Then he bends forward, his mouth brushing my ear as he whispers, "The glass didn't break, but you did."

"I didn't," I say. "I never said it."

His eyes roam over me, and he slides his hands between my legs, then thrusts two fingers inside, making me gasp and tense, my body craving more.

"You didn't have to say it out loud, baby. That's just the way it is. You'll always break for me, Ruby. Always."

ELEVEN
AFTERSHOCK

I t's remarkable how time can seem to expand when you're being fucked by a man who knows what he's doing.

Not that I intend to share that little commentary with Leo. If the price for protection is sex, I can live with that. But I'm sure as hell not going to admit I enjoyed it. Not to him. Not ever.

"Dinner," he says, as I return to the living area, now wearing shorts and a tank top.

He has the takeout bags from earlier, and now he's pulling out a series of foil containers, each of which has a magnificent aroma.

I watch, trying to seem uninterested, as he places them on the long sideboard that takes up one wall of the living area. I breathe in the scent of tomato and garlic, and my mouth immediately waters.

"We've got a bit of everything," he says. "Come help yourself."

I shrug. "I'm not hungry," I lie, though I'm not sure why. Probably because doing the opposite of whatever Leo wants feels really, really good.

"Eat anyway. You need the energy."

"For what? My daring escape? Don't worry. I know the terms. You're protecting me, but only so long as I let you fuck me." I lift a shoulder in a way that I hope seems nonchalant. As if what we just did wasn't the best sex I've ever had. As if he hasn't gotten my emotions in a tizzy, making me mourn even more what we lost all those years ago.

"Let?" he repeats, his eyes raking over me. "Sweetheart, consent is not a factor in our arrangement."

I see heat in his eyes, but also humor. I don't know if he's teasing or threatening. I stand up straighter, then meet his eyes. "Guess that saying's wrong," I say, aiming what I hope is a sickly-sweet smile his direction.

His brow furrows. "Saying?"

"Chivalry really is dead," I explain. "At least in the Grimm family."

He flinches. Just barely, but I see it.

I wait for satisfaction to wash over me, but it doesn't. Instead, I just feel tired. "What?" I demand, when I see him looking at me.

For a moment, I think he's going to answer. Then he shakes his head before going to stand in front of the window where he'd just given me the most amazing orgasm of my life.

After a moment, he turns back, then strides across the open area to the kitchen. I settle onto the sofa, one foot tucked under me, and my back angled away from him so that I'm looking at that same window. My handprints are still visible, along with a faint print left by my breasts, the sight of which makes my nipples tighten all over again.

I cross my arms—not wanting Leo to see what would normally be hidden under a bra—then draw in a tremulous breath. Something else I don't want him to see.

On the surface, what he did was horrible. Controlling and vile. A payment he forced from me because I had no choice, and I resent the hell out of him because of it.

But in the moment…

I draw in a shuddering breath as I let the memory wash over me. Thinking back to when he was inside me…when there was nothing between us and that deadly void except a thin piece of glass, and how seriously fucking erotic that was…

I'd been more turned on than I can ever remember by the way he took control with such intensity. Such power.

But that is not something I intend to mention to this man. A dangerous man who, at worst, betrayed me. And at best is very, very, *very* bad for me.

Barely any time passes before he returns, a glass of wine in each hand. He puts one on the coffee table, then offers the other to me.

I take it. I'm not entirely sure that introducing alcohol into a situation where my emotions are already raw and confused is the greatest idea in the history of the world, but I don't care. I want the damn drink. And I want it so much that my first swallow is not a sommelier-approved sip, but a giant gulp.

He chuckles, then sits beside me. "I guess that hit the spot," he says.

I consider turning away so I can keep my back to him, but the truth is that I don't want to. The harder truth is that I don't know what I want.

I put my wine on the table and hug myself, my mind drifting to our encounter on the trail—and my lack of disappointment when Marcus had to cancel on me.

I hadn't let myself think about it then, but now—after fucking against that sky-high window—a wave of self-loathing crashes over me, dark and brutal.

Because Marcus is a good man. A kind and caring man. A man who would make a good father. A good husband.

What's wrong with me that I don't want him?

More, what's wrong with me that my body craves a man like Leo? A man with no code. A man who willingly and brutally sliced up my heart only seven years ago. A man who's now holding me prisoner, supposedly for my own good. And even if I believe him that the danger is real—and, damn me, I do—what kind of a fucked-up man demands sex in exchange for chivalry?

And what kind of woman not only gives in to his demands, but enjoys it?

"—you?" he asks, and I jump, suddenly terrified I'd been thinking aloud. Then I see him holding up the wine bottle.

"What?"

"I said, I'm having another glass. How about you?"

I realize with a start that I'd downed the entire thing while I'd been lost in my thoughts. I extend my glass, wanting the wine a hell of a lot more than I probably should. "Granny always said you could drive a woman to drink. Guess she was right."

He chuckles. "Smart woman, Birgit. I hope she's well. I have a bit of a soft spot for her."

"She's fine," I say, my voice tight because this is the trap. Small talk. Little life details. Mundane chit chat. All designed so he can worm his way back into my life. So he can get close, then destroy me all over again.

I draw a breath, then meet his eyes. "I'm here because you promised to keep me safe, and I believe you can. I know better than anyone that you're a dangerous son-of-a-bitch. But this isn't an opportunity for a walk down memory lane. You already named your price for keeping me safe. And because I need you, I agreed. But just because you're fucking me, we're not lovers. We're not a couple. We're not in a relationship. And we aren't friends."

He says nothing for so long, I begin to think he's decided to just tune me out. I'm about to rage at him for being an arrogant asshole of a prick, when he cocks his head, looks me straight in the eye, and says, "Do you think I'm a stupid man?"

The question is so unexpected that I blurt out the answer, immediate and honest. "God, no."

He grins. "Good to know," he says, as I cringe, expecting him to try and steal some advantage. But all he says is, "Only a stupid man would throw a woman like you away. Only a stupid man would say things so hurtful that they'd all but destroy you. Do things so vile they'd haunt you for years."

I shake my head, understanding the words, but not the meaning. "Leo?" My voice is soft, as if this moment demands some sort of reverence. "What are you saying?"

He shrugs. "Just that only a stupid man would hurt you the way you were hurt. A stupid man," he stresses again. "Or one with a very, very good reason."

I look down at my knees. My chest is tight, and it's suddenly hard to breathe. This is the danger, I realize. This man's charms. His cleverness. The little tricks he'll use to manipulate the situation to his favor.

And all of them swirl together to make a dangerous flavor of Kool-Aid that I desperately want to drink.

No.

With the word pounding in my head, I clench my fists so tight that my fingernails cut into the soft flesh of my palms. Thus armed with pain, I tilt my head up to look at him. But I focus on his chin. Not those green eyes that used to see me so clearly.

"Don't even try to pretend that you ever gave a flying fuck about me," I say, my voice low and flat. "You proved otherwise a long time ago."

"Oh, I don't know," he says. "That was a pretty amazing flying fuck we shared at the window."

I bark out a laugh, caught off-guard, and when I look at his face, my breath catches simply from the way he's watching me. Those green eyes raking over my body in a way that makes my skin flush with a heat I don't want to feel.

"That didn't mean anything," I say, my tone carefully neutral. "That was just seven years of unfinished business." I shrug as casually as I can manage.

His expression hardens. "*New* business," he says. "Protection services. And that barely covered the down payment."

"Fine." I fire the word at him like a weapon, then stand and go to the sideboard, where the various food containers are spread out. At first, I pay little attention as I serve myself portions of the various containers. But then it dawns on me...

Pasta al Pomodoro. Penne alla Arrabbiata, Risotto alla Milanese. Even a beautifully *displayed Caprese* salad.

All my favorites dishes from *Mangia*, the restaurant he'd taken me to on our first real date. The place that had been ours for the three years we'd been together.

I haven't been back since the day my parents died. The day he ripped my heart out and fed it to the wolves.

"Dig in," he says.

I want to protest. To tell him that he doesn't get to try and woo me with Italian food and sweet memories. Not after what he's done.

Not after what he destroyed.

But I say nothing. This day is too surreal already. And, frankly, I'm starving.

So, I pile my plate up, then bring it back to the sofa, remembering how we used to sit on the floor, our backs to the couch, our meals spread like a picnic on a blanket in front of us.

This time, though, I sit primly on the seat cushions, then take a bite, wishing I could erase that burst of memory. The way we shared french fries, or fed each other bites of pasta. The way he'd stand, a hand down to help me rise, then later that same hand helping me strip.

Most of the time, he'd lead me to his bedroom, then take me— soft and sweet or hard and wild—on his huge bed.

Sometimes, we wouldn't get that far. Our kisses would turn too intense. Our hands too eager, and he'd fuck me hard on this couch, both of us so desperate we didn't even care if we kicked over the food from our makeshift picnic.

All that had mattered was us. The joy of being together. The power of knowing we belonged to each other. That together, we were stronger.

That nothing in the world would ever come between us.

How many times had I come in his arms? How many times had he emptied himself into me, his face that glorious mixture of pain and pleasure?

How many times had we sat quietly, staring into each other's eyes, both of us amazed that in all of this huge and confusing world, we'd found each other?

So many times.

And each and every one, a lie.

As if he realizes the direction my thoughts have taken, he takes my now-empty plate away, then stands up, his hand lowered to help me to my feet.

I stay put.

"Are you ready?"

I shiver from the tone in his voice. "For what?"

He doesn't answer right away. Instead, his eyes skim slowly over me, his gaze like a physical touch, before he finally meets my eyes. "For what comes next." His voice is low. Hot.

And I honestly don't have a clue whether he's serious or joking. "Um, didn't what comes next already come first? Because I remember the coming part…"

His brows rise, and I see amusement dance in his eyes. And right then, I want to slap my own face. I just joked—*joked!*—about his fuck-for-payment-protection plan.

But he says nothing, just wiggles his fingers in a silent command.

I comply, then slip my hand into his, trying to ignore the memories that keep haunting me. They're hiding around every corner in this once-familiar place, ready to haunt me with sweet memories I wish I could forget.

As he pulls me to my feet, what I hear in my head is *good girl* in that intimate voice I can still conjure when I lie in bed, waiting for sleep to take me. A voice that hints at both praise and punishment. Kisses and spankings.

A voice that seems to curl through me, then settle between my legs in a way that I don't want.

Except maybe I do.

He doesn't release my hand once I'm standing. Instead, he

draws me closer as we walk to the bedroom—the room filled with so many memories. "Leo…"

He stops, then turns to face me straight on. "The price for today's protection." His eyes are full of heat, and his smile shows gleaming white teeth. The better to eat me with.

I swallow, the dark promise I see in his gaze making my stomach clench with need even as I want to slap his face for putting a price on protection. Even though it's a price I'm willing —even eager—to pay.

And that, of course, is the real problem. I want him. Hell, I crave him.

I'm not a stupid man.

It's true. He's not.

He's brilliant, in fact. And he's not a man who does something without a reason.

So what was the reason he broke my heart?

TWELVE
WANTING

"Do you remember?" he asks, pausing just inside the room, then turning to look at me. "All the things we used to do in here? How you'd cry out my name? How you'd beg for more?"

I cross my arms over my chest, wishing I'd changed into a long-sleeved tee rather than this stretchy tank top that emphasizes my very perky nipples.

"Oh, yeah. You remember," he says, his voice like a low, sexy purr.

I swallow, then tilt my head up to face him. "I used to remember," I say. "I could remember every tiny thing that happened between us. There was a time when every moment with you meant the world to me, and every memory meant more than gold."

I push the words out one by one, hurling them like darts. "But I worked hard—so damn hard—to try and forget you, Leo Grimm. To shove every one of our moments together into the trash, because that's where you belong."

I expect to see shock and hurt on his face. Instead, he nods, almost with sympathy.

"Part of me hoped you'd forget," he says. "Hell, part of me hoped I would. But I couldn't." He takes a single step toward me, his expression almost tender. "You'll never forget me," he says. "Sometimes, I wish you could. Mostly, I'm glad you can't. Because the truth is, Red, I can't forget you. Not a single detail. It's all burned into my mind, and it plays like a porno through my head every damn night."

A porno. "Because it was all just sex to you. Of course it was. That's why it was so easy for you to walk away."

"Dammit, Ruby," he begins, his voice sharp. "You haven't got a—"

He waves his hands, as if physically cutting off the sentence. As I watch, his expression seems to harden, and when he meets my eyes again, the softness I'd seen only moments before is completely gone.

"You know what?" he says, his voice low and edgy. "Think whatever the hell you want. It doesn't matter, does it? There's nothing but history between us now. History," he repeats as he takes my wrist and tugs me toward him. "And our arrangement."

He gives me no time to respond. Instead, he whips us around, then picks me up at the waist and tosses me on the bed. He puts his hands on my knees, and I have to hold my breath as he tugs off my shorts, then tosses them aside. I tell myself this is just a bodily function, the way my sex throbs and my thighs scream to be touched. The way my breath seems to come more rapidly as he steps into the space between my legs, then bends over me to put his hand on my shoulders.

I tremble, and for a moment, I fear I'll burn from the heat in his eyes. "I remember everything about you," he whispers. "How you like it rough, first, then soft and sweet for round two. How you cry out my name when you come."

I want to tell him to shut up, but now he's pulling my tank top off, his hands stroking my breasts as he pulls the stretchy material up and off.

I swallow, naked now as he drops my shirt to the floor.

"Beautiful," he says, his voice low and soft, almost like a prayer.

He's standing at the foot of the bed, and he grabs me above the knees and tugs me down to him, then moves his hands to my knees spreading me wide. He steps back, and I snap my legs closed.

"Oh, no, baby," he says. "Soles of your feet together. Knees wide. I want to see your cunt. I want to see how wet you are for me."

I swallow, but don't move, and he bends over me, his shirt brushing my bare breasts as he whispers, "Obey, or I'll take you like this down to the lobby. I'll send you out into the world with only the clothes on your back. Oh," he adds, with a sound of mock surprise. "You don't have any clothes on your back."

I want to retort that he wouldn't, but that's the Leo I thought I knew. This Leo—the one letting me see all his hard edges…well, this Leo probably would.

I stay silent, my eyes closed as I put my feet together as he'd ordered. I know I should fight this—should hate this—but the horrible truth is that I'm more turned on than I can ever remember being. I want to close my legs, yes. But mostly so that Leo won't see the evidence of my desire. So that I can try to staunch the growing heat between my thighs. The desperate need that courses through me.

But I can't say anything. All I can do is whimper.

All I can do is want.

And—damn me—what I want is Leo.

I fight a moan as he traces his fingertips along my inner thighs, his expression wonderous, like an explorer who's just discovered the new world. "God, I've missed this. You're so fucking beautiful," he says. "And when you're turned on, you light up like a flame. The way your back arches when you're close. The way your cunt contracts, drawing me in. God, Rue, I could paint a picture of your nipples tightening, the cords in your neck, the way your collarbone looks so fragile against the violence of what you feel when I make you come."

"Please," I whisper, though I have no idea if I'm asking him to stop, or begging him to touch me more.

His fingertip slowly teases my clit as he whispers, "Most of all, Red, I remember that you never ran out of juice. I once made you come six times in less than an hour." He bends over, his tongue teasing the edge of my ear.

"Tell me, baby. Is that just how you're wired? Or is it only me you surrender like that for? I think it's me." His voice has lost that seductive tone. Now it's hard, with a very sharp edge.

"You like the danger," he continues. "The heat. The risk. The way I'd take you under the stairs in the dorm. Against the window over the parking lot. Blindfolded and tied up."

I whimper as he runs a fingertip from my breast to my clit. "Let me up," I demand. "You've already collected your goddamn payment for the day." Except I don't mean it. I hate myself, but I want this. Want *him.*

I just don't want to want it.

"The hell I have," he whispers. He bends closer, his face just inches from mine.

"We had a deal, remember? Payment for protection. If you want to break the deal, just say so. I can have one of the guards escort you out of the building right now."

I swallow. "You know I can't."

"I do," he says. "But I know more than that, too."

I lick my lips, hating the way my pulse has kicked up just from that edgy tone in his voice. I want to pretend I don't care what he says or what he thinks. But instead of telling him to just fuck me and get it over with, I ask him what the hell he means.

"I know that you craved the danger as much as you craved me. Hell, you craved me because I was the danger."

"No," I say, twisting to one side and surprising him enough to free myself. I scoot back until my head is against the bookcase-style headboard, and I'm clutching a pillow over me for modesty.

He only chuckles. "I know what I know."

I shake my head, fury making my skin tingle. The bastard is

trying to rewrite history. Our relationship was never dangerous. Or, at least, I never believed it was. The sex was rough, sure. And we'd played bondage games and all that light BDSM stuff that I'd read in the pages of romance novels.

That's what I'd liked. The fiction. The presentation.

I'd liked the fantasy, but all the while, I knew it wasn't real.

Real would have scared me.

"Would it?" he asks when I tell him all that.

"Don't you get it? I got off knowing that you would never let anything happen to me. Never risk us getting caught, me getting embarrassed. The danger? Hell, yeah. But only if it was fake."

I draw in another breath, then try to reel my temper back. "If it had been real, I would have run far and fast."

"I wonder," he says, and I want to kick his ass. Mostly, because I wonder, too, especially after the encounter in the woods. The way I'd felt after meeting Leo on the trail juxtaposed against my indifference to Marcus canceling our date.

But I say nothing. Those are moments I'm not willing to analyze too deeply.

Leo runs his fingertip down my cheek, then lower along the curve of my neck. My breath hitches as the digit goes lower still, finally teasing my very erect, traitorous nipple.

"You liked it just now," he continues, tugging me off the bed to stand in front of him, his thumb still stroking my nipple.

"The danger," he continues, in that low voice that seems to rumble through me like an erotic storm. "Getting fucked against the window. It made you so damn wet and your skin fiery hot. I know your body, Red, and that did it for you. The world just millimeters away. The risk of being seen. The risk of falling. And me, right there, fucking you from behind."

He leans in closer. "I think the only thing that would have gotten you off faster was if I'd fucked you in the ass."

I bite my lip and force myself not to whimper. As he'd been speaking, his left hand had been snaking down my back. Now, his fingers slide further still to tease my ass in a way that makes me want to beg for more. For everything.

Instead, I lift my chin and look at him, forcing my voice to stay steady as I say, "You're a fabulous fuck, Leo. But that's about all you're good for." I shrug as if I don't have a care in the world. "As for dangerous… That little power play of yours at the window? Please. We both know the glass wasn't going to break. And I'd lay odds that no one had a camera with a telescopic lens aimed at that window."

He steps back, and I silently mourn the loss of his touch even as I give myself a mental high-five, feeling smug. Finally, I've gained the upper hand.

Then I see that familiar spark light his eyes. The heated determination when he comes back, slides an arm around my waist, then slides two fingers from his other hand deep inside me.

"Maybe there were no telescopes," he says, teasing my g-spot with a finger and my clit with the pad of his thumb. "No guy holding binoculars with one hand and jacking off with the other. No amateur photographer with a long lens."

He continues to stroke me, as I fight to stay still. To not let him know how much his touch is affecting me.

"But you imagined them there, didn't you?" His voice is low. Edgy. "Office workers at their windows, looking out at the naked woman being fucked against the glass. You imagined it, and it made you hot. It's making you hot now, just thinking about it. Don't try to deny it. I can feel the way your cunt's clenching around my fingers. Your body begging me to take you. To fuck you deep."

I whimper. He's not wrong. Right now, my entire body is so sensitized, I think he could brush my shoulder and I'd shatter completely.

He bends closer, thrusting his fingers in even deeper and making me cry out—not with surprise or pain, but with pure, raging desire.

"You liked the thrill. The possibility. Liked balancing on that knife-edge between danger and safety."

"No." I snap the word out, but it's a lie. Yes, there was a thrill. A clenching in my pussy. A wildness in my blood that kicked up once he had me pressed against that glass. Once I was naked and exposed to the world for Leo's pleasure. And for my own.

But damned if I'll admit that any more than I'll admit that he's the only man who's ever made me feel like that. The only man who's ever seemed to get me. To understand how far he could push me.

Maybe that's why he's the only one who ever truly destroyed me.

With a hard jerk, I break free and scurry away, snatching a throw to cover myself, then glare at him.

"You idiot," I say, my voice low and intentionally cruel. "You want to know what I fear? It's you. Because you're the only one who has ever—*ever*—truly hurt me."

"I know," he says, as easily as if I'd accused him of hogging the ketchup.

"Then why? Why are you demanding a price to help me? Why are you helping me at all?"

A muscle near his jaw twitches, as if he's forcing himself to think before he speaks, something that never came easy to Leo.

I'm just about to give up on him answering at all when he says, "Maybe I want to make up for walking away. Maybe I think you need someone watching your back." He shrugs, his eyes locking on mine. "Or maybe I just want the chance to fuck you again," he adds, as if the earlier words were just throwaways.

"Leo…"

"Does it really matter?" The question is hard. Terse. "I'll take my price, and I will keep you safe. I'll find whoever is playing this goddamn game with us, and I will make it my mission to destroy them. Do you believe me?"

"Yes," I whisper. Because despite everything that has passed between us, I do.

"Once it's over, I'll walk away. Until then, I'll take what I want, and you can either give it to me willingly or not. But if you can't deal with that, I'll give you one chance to walk away. Just say the word right now," he orders. "Because once I count to ten, this deal is locked in, and you're all mine, Red."

I want to. I want to throw it all in his face. To tell him I'm not currency to cover a debt any more than I'm his damn sex toy.

But I don't say that.

But whether it's because I want to pay the price or because he's the only one I truly trust to keep me safe from whoever is taunting him…well, that I really don't know.

And he doesn't give me the chance to find out. Because now he's right in front of me, his fingertip tracing my collarbone he counts down to ten. When he hits zero without me having said a word, he smiles. Not like a man who's just made a business deal, but like a pauper who's won the lottery.

I lift my chin, trying not to think about this choice I've made.

"Ruby," he says, standing so close I can feel his breath on my skin. "Get on the bed. Eyes closed. Legs spread."

THIRTEEN
PAYMENT

I did as he asked, because that was the deal I'd made.

I'd expected him to be impatient. To pin me down and take me hard, making it all about him, and me just the toy he used to get off.

Expected it, yes. Maybe I'd even wanted it, the thrill of being completely and thoroughly used without any thought of what I wanted. Just the eroticism of being there only for his pleasure.

But that wasn't what happened. Instead, he'd cupped my head, then kissed me. A long, slow kiss—a gentle kiss—that had opened me up, making me crave and want and wish.

I hadn't felt like something he'd bought, but like something he cherished. His gentle touch. His tender caress. His mouth. Soft and swee.

At least until it isn't.

And god, when it isn't soft anymore, when Leo's control finally snaps and he claims me with the kind of desperate hunger I remember from our best nights together, it's like coming home to a part of myself I'd forgotten existed.

He starts so gently, his hands mapping my body like he's relearning every curve, every sensitive spot that makes me gasp and arch beneath him. His mouth follows the path of his fingers, pressing reverent kisses to my throat, my collarbone, the sensitive spot where my neck meets my shoulder—a place that always makes me shiver.

"I remember this," he murmurs against my skin, his voice rough with want. "The way you taste here. The sound you make when I do this."

And then he proves he remembers exactly what *this* is, his teeth grazing that spot with just enough pressure to make me cry out, my body arching off the bed as sensation shoots straight through me.

That's when the gentleness shifts into something more primal, more claiming. Leo's hands become more demanding, his mouth more possessive, like he can't get enough of the taste of my skin, the feel of me responding to his touch.

"Christ, Red," he breathes as he works his way down my body, his voice filled with something that sounds like wonder. "Do you have any idea how much I've missed this? Missed you?"

I'm too lost in sensation to answer, especially when his mouth finds my breast, his tongue circling my nipple until I'm writhing beneath him, my hands fisted in his dark hair, holding him against me.

He takes his time there, worshipping first one breast then the other, using his teeth and tongue in ways that have me making sounds I'd forgotten I was capable of. The combination of gentle reverence and raw hunger is intoxicating, making me feel both precious and desperately wanted.

"Please," I whisper when I can't take the teasing anymore, when every nerve ending in my body is singing with need.

"Please what?" Leo asks, lifting his head to look at me with eyes that burn like green fire.

"Please touch me. Please don't stop. Please make me remember what it feels like to be yours."

The last words slip out without permission, but instead of making Leo pull back, they make him growl low in his throat, a sound that's pure possession and satisfaction.

"You are mine," he says, his hand sliding down between my thighs to find me already wet and ready for him. "You've always been mine, Ruby. Even when you hated me, even when you were trying to forget me—you were still mine."

His fingers find my center then, stroking and teasing until I'm gasping his name, my hips bucking against his hand as he builds me toward a climax that feels like it might shatter me completely.

"That's it, baby." His voice is dark with satisfaction as he watches me fall apart beneath his touch. "Let go for me. Show me how good I make you feel."

The first orgasm tears through me like lightning, every muscle in my body clenching as waves of pleasure crash over me. But Leo doesn't stop there. He works me through it, then keeps going, using his fingers and mouth to build me toward another peak before I've even recovered from the first.

By the time he finally moves over me, his cock rock hard, I'm desperate and shaking, so ready for him I can barely form coherent words.

"Look at me," he orders. "I want to watch you break apart, and then I'll put you back together, Red. Because you're mine. You always have been. Say it."

"Yours," I say, gasping as he starts to enter me. Slow at first in a way that has my body screaming for more. For harder. For deeper. For everything.

Then, when I think I can't stand it any longer, he thrusts inside me, filling me completely. Claiming me in a way that makes me feel whole. A way I'd forgotten was possible.

We both go still for a moment, breathing hard, lost in shared need. In wild desire. And even in the memory of a past filled with nights like this.

"Fuck," Leo breathes, his forehead pressed against mine. "You were made for me, Red."

"Yes," I whisper back, wrapping my legs around his waist to pull him deeper. "I was made for you."

When he finally starts to move again, it's with the expertise of a man who knows my body only too well, his strokes and thrusts calculated to drive me even more wild with wanting.

"This is what I dream about," he murmurs against my ear as he drives into me with increasing urgency. "Having you again. Watching you fall apart in my arms."

"Leo," I gasp, as he sets me climbing toward release again.

"Come for me," he commands, his hand sliding between us to find my clit. "Come on my cock, Ruby. Show me you're mine."

The combination of his fingers on my most sensitive spot and his cock hitting that perfect place inside me sends me flying over the edge again, this orgasm so intense I actually scream his name, my nails raking down his back as my body clenches around him.

Leo's own release follows immediately, a low groan torn from his chest as he buries himself deep and fills me completely. We cling to each other as the aftershocks roll through us, both breathing hard, lost in the remnants of pure, sensual pleasure. And despite knowing perfectly well that he'd just taken his payment for my protection, I feel warm and snuggly and very well-fucked.

"You look smug," he says minutes later, coming back from the kitchen with two glasses of wine, his naked body making my skin tingle all over again.

He grins, then lifts a brow as if he knows what I'm thinking.

The sight of him walking toward me, completely comfortable in his nudity, all lean muscle and confident grace, makes my mouth go dry. Even after what we just shared, I want him again. Want to pull him back down to this bed and lose myself in the feel of his hands on my skin.

"Insatiable," he teases, clearly reading my expression.

"And you're not?"

He chuckles, setting the wine glasses on the nightstand before sliding back into bed beside me. "Touché. But rest first. You wore me out."

"You? Damn, I must be good."

"You are," he says, the heat in his voice sliding straight between my legs. His hand finds my thigh, his thumb stroking over my skin in a way that's both soothing and arousing. "Better than I remembered. And I remembered you being pretty fucking incredible."

Deep inside my head, some voice of reason tells me to be careful. This was a payment. This isn't flirting. It isn't a relationship.

That's not a road I'll walk again.

Leo Grimm once stabbed a knife through my heart, and I need to remember that.

True words, but at the same time, something feels like it's shifted between us. Our banter feels like the old Leo and Ruby, back when he hadn't just been my lover, but my best friend. Back before he'd pulled the rug completely out from under me.

I still don't understand how he could have been so cruel, but at the same time, that was seven years ago, and we've both changed. So maybe it is time to let him back in, at least a little. A tentative detente. A trial run.

Because even though I'll never admit it to him, the truth is that I've missed him. Not the Leo on that last day, the Leo who'd destroyed me. But the man before. The one who'd loved me. Cherished me.

Protected me.

That Leo would never have hurt me. And I think—I hope— that maybe a little bit of that Leo is back.

Or, maybe I've got a massive dose of sex-induced brain mush.

"Deep thoughts?" he asks, passing me one of the two glasses. His fingers brush mine as I take the glass, and the simple contact sends warmth shooting up my arm.

"Just post-coital meanderings," I say before taking a sip.

"Oh? Should we go for another round and really get your imagination going?"

I laugh. "See? You're insatiable."

"Only with you." He shifts closer, his thigh pressing against mine, and I can feel the heat radiating from his skin. "Always only with you, Ruby."

There's not just heat in his voice, there's something softer. Something gentle. Something that feels like truth, and my heart twists a little.

For a moment, I think that he's going to kiss me again, and I feel the anticipation surge through me. His eyes are focused on my mouth, dark with want that mirrors my own. For years, I've considered him the spawn of Satan, albeit a very sexy spawn.

Now, I'm more in a The Devil You Know kind of mindset.

I sag a bit with disappointment when I realize it's not me he's reaching for but the remote. "Movie?"

We share a grin, and I know we're both remembering the way we used to wear ourselves out in bed, then stay up watching movies, snuggling and touching and teasing until we couldn't focus anymore, and the movie became background noise to another round of lovemaking.

All of which explains why I've seen the first two acts of a lot of movies...but totally missed the climax. That was okay, though. I had plenty of climaxes of my own.

"So, no movie," he says, his voice full of heat as he sets the remote aside without turning on the TV. "Interesting."

I look away, feeling weirdly shy. "Yeah, well, maybe I was thinking we could just skip to Act Three."

"Baby, you read my mind." He cups my neck and pulls me toward him, his thumb stroking over my pulse point in a way that makes me shiver. Then his lips are hard on mine, his tongue hot and demanding, his fingers twisting in my hair as he draws me closer, and I lose myself again in the heat of him. The pressure of his lips.

This is the Leo I'd fallen for. The man I could laugh with, talk with, make love with. I don't understand why it all fell apart back then, but right now, with his hands roaming my skin and his mouth teasing mine, I know that I'm right to give him another chance.

I gasp as he rolls me over, then straddles me, his rock-hard cock pressed against me. I spread my legs, anticipating his kiss, the violent thrill of him thrusting inside me, then the sense of losing myself in the blanket of pleasure I know will wrap around both of us.

Except it doesn't come. Instead, he sinks onto me, then rolls off with a frown. At first, I'm confused. Then I hear it, too. A strange chirping noise underscored by a familiar low buzz.

It takes a moment for my sex-stupid brain to get with the program, which is why I'm one step behind when Leo sits up with a silent curse, then says, "Godammit, my fucking phone is blowing up," even as another vibration sets it to shivering on the table.

Out of habit, I roll over to look for my phone, only to remember that Leo took it from me as part of our protection deal.

"If this is Alex or Elliott bugging me," he says as he snatches it up, "I swear I'm going to—Oh, fuck."

I watch his face change as he picks it up, confusion giving way to something that looks like horror.

"What?" I ask, but he doesn't answer. Just keeps staring at the screen with an expression I've never seen before.

The wine turns to acid in my stomach. "Leo, what is it?"

He still doesn't respond, too absorbed in whatever fresh hell is unfolding on that screen. "Leo!" I snap, loud enough to get his attention.

He looks up, and the devastation in his green eyes makes my breath catch. "Ruby—"

"What. Is. It?"

He opens his mouth, closes it, then seems to make some kind of decision. Without a word, he turns the phone so I can see the screen.

At first, I don't understand what I'm looking at. Social media feeds scrolling past at lightning speed. Videos playing in small windows. Hashtags trending with millions of interactions. View counts climbing so fast they're a blur of numbers.

Then my brain processes the familiar angle. The familiar bedroom. The familiar faces.

My face.

Leo's face.

And both of us lost in ecstasy, completely naked, completely vulnerable, and on every social media platform imaginable.

FOURTEEN
VIRAL

Bile rises in my throat, and I'm pretty sure I'm going to vomit as I stare at the screen, nauseous and cold and utterly destroyed.

It's the same goddamn video. The one Leo made. The one some sick bastard left playing on my bed.

And now it's trending on every social media platform known to man. And—considering who Leo is and who I work for—I'm pretty sure that if we're not already on the mainstream news, we will be pretty damn soon.

"Oh my god," I whisper, feeling sick to my stomach. But I can't look away. It's pure agony, but my eyes are locked on that damn screen.

There I am, young and completely trusting, letting Leo do things to me that I thought were private. Sacred. *Ours.*

There I am, moaning his name. Arching beneath him. Coming apart in his arms while he whispers promises he never intended to keep.

And there are the comments. Thousands of them. Scrolling past faster than I can read, but I catch enough to make my stomach churn.

damn she's hot af 🔥 🔥

is this the cosmetics chick?? RUBY RYDER OMG
bro Leo Grimm's ex is WILD 😈
Someone's getting fired from Lydia Cosmetics lmaooo
GRIMM TOWER SEX TAPE trending #1 💀
Daddy's money can't buy privacy apparently
this is literally revenge porn but go off I guess

Each comment is a knife to the chest. Each view is another violation. Each share is another stranger seeing me at my most vulnerable, most intimate moment, and I pull the sheet up, using it to cover myself, as if that's somehow a shield against all this horror.

"How many views?" I ask, even though I don't really want to know.

Leo's throat works like he's trying to swallow broken glass. "Five point two million. In the last four hours."

The number doesn't compute. Five million people. Five million strangers have watched me naked. Have seen me young and trusting and completely unaware that my most private moments were being recorded for posterity.

Five million people have watched Leo take my virginity.

The thought hits me like a physical blow, and suddenly I can't breathe. Can't think. Can't process the magnitude of what's happening.

"What the fuck did you do?" I hear myself ask the question, but my voice is coming from very far away.

"I didn't do anything." The words explode out of him, sharp and defensive. "I didn't release this. I would never—"

"But you made it." I turn to face him, my vision blurry with tears I refuse to shed. "You made it, you fucker!" I suck in air, trying to breathe despite the tears clogging my throat. "You made it," I repeat, my voice harsh with accusation, "and now it's out there."

"My server hasn't been breached," he says. "I'm certain of it." He crosses the room, then opens his laptop, navigates somewhere, then points to the screen. "No access. Not for months, and that was me. *Dammit.*" He punches the wall so hard, I'm surprised there's not a hole. Then again, considering how old the tower is, I'm surprised he didn't mangle his hand on the brick behind the plaster.

"Then how?" I demand, my body still shaking, but my voice ice cold. "How did your secret little sex tape get out if your precious security is so fucking perfect?"

He runs his hands through his hair, making the dark strands stand on end. "I don't know."

"Bullshit." I take a step toward him, fury giving me strength. "You know something. I can see it in your face. Tell me what you know."

"I don't—"

"Don't you dare lie to me!" My voice breaks on the words. "Not about this. Not when five million people have seen me naked because of something you did."

He stares at me for a long moment, his green eyes filled with something that might be pain. But then his expression shutters, going cold and distant.

"I have to go," he says, already reaching for his shirt.

"What?" The word comes out strangled. "Go where?"

"I need to make some calls. Track down how this happened. Get rid of that goddamn feed."

"Leo, no." I grab his arm, desperation making me cling to him. "You can't fix this. It's on every platform. You can't make five million people unsee it."

"I can try."

"How?" I'm screaming now, my voice raw with fury. "How exactly are you going to un-fuck my life? How are you going to make this go away?"

"I don't know, but I have to—"

"You have to stay." The words tear out of me. "I need you to stay with me. This isn't going to do a damn thing to your reputation, but it's going to destroy me. Don't you get it? I need you to be here while my world burns down around us."

Something flickers in his eyes. Something that looks almost like regret. But it's gone so fast I might have imagined it.

"Dammit, Rue, I can't sit here and do nothing while whoever did this gets away with it."

"So comforting me is nothing? Staying with me is nothing?" I'm crying now, great heaving sobs that strangle my words before I can get them out.

"Ruby, please."

"We're in this together," I manage to choke out. "We should be facing this together."

"I have to go." His voice is final, implacable. "I have to fix this."

He pulls on his pants with quick, efficient movements, and I realize he's actually leaving.

Actually going to walk out while I'm standing here wrapped in a sheet, watching my life explode across the internet.

"Don't." The word is barely a whisper. "Please, Leo. Don't leave me alone with this."

He pauses in the doorway, his hand on the knob. For a moment, I think he might turn around. Might choose me instead of running away and lying to himself that he can fix this. He can't.

And he knows that as well as I do.

"There's something else," he says without looking at me. "Something you need to be prepared for."

Ice floods my veins. "What?"

I see the way his body straightens. The way he looks at me like a man doing a duty he's required to perform. Then he draws in a breath, meets my eyes dead on, and says, "There are other videos."

The words hit me like a punch to the gut. "How many?" I can barely whisper the question.

"Six. Seven total." His voice is quiet, factual.

The room tilts sideways, and I have to grab the headboard to keep from falling. Seven videos of me naked. Of me being fucked.

Of me trusting him completely while he violated that trust in the most fundamental way possible.

"Seven videos," I say. "Gee, did you forget seven times to mention that you were filming us?"

He doesn't answer. He doesn't need to.

"And you've kept them all this time? What do you do? Pull them out and jack off to them? Invite your friends over so they can join in the fun? So you can show them the naive little girl you fucked for all that time, who never had a clue what an absolute shit you are?"

He says nothing.

"And now they're with some psychopath who can just release them whenever he feels like fucking up my life even more."

"I won't let that happen. I will find him. I will stop him. And I will fix this."

"Fuck you, Leo. You already *did* let it happen!" The words explode out of me, fueled by rage and betrayal and seven years of buried pain. "You created this situation. You made those videos. You kept them. And now you're leaving me here to deal with the aftermath alone."

"I'm going to fix it."

"What? You're going to get rid of something on the freaking internet? Are you stupid?" I shake my head and wipe away tears. "No, it's me. I'm the one who's a fucking idiot. I let myself believe you were going to help me. To be there for me through all of this stalker bullshit. But I forgot who you are, Leo Grimm. You're the guy who walks away when it gets tough. And somehow, I always seem to be the one you leave in your rearview window."

Something breaks across his face—pain, maybe, or regret. But I don't care anymore.

"As for your protection?" I straighten my shoulders and lift my chin. "Fuck that. I'll take my chances on my own."

"No." The word is sharp, final. "You won't."

"Watch me," I say, hurrying toward the living room, not even caring that all I'm wearing is a sheet.

He cuts me off before I reach the door, and for a moment, his mask slips. I see something raw and desperate in his green eyes.

Then it's gone, replaced by cold determination.

"You're not leaving this suite," he says quietly. "Not until this is over."

And then he walks out, the door clicking shut behind him with a finality that echoes through my chest like a gunshot.

I stand there for a moment, staring at the closed door, my entire body shaking with rage and humiliation and grief.

Then I grab the nearest object—a half-full crystal wine decanter that probably cost more than most people's cars—and hurl it at the wall. It explodes in a shower of glittering fragments, the sound satisfying in a way that nothing else could be.

But it's not enough. Nothing could be enough to match the destruction inside me.

I hurry back to the bedroom to get dressed, then come back and try the door. Locked, of course. Once again, I'm trapped. I pace the living room like a caged animal, my slipper-covered feet crunching on broken glass and a wine-soaked carpet.

For the first time ever, I'm glad I don't have my phone. Because I'm certain it's probably imploded by now just from the shock of zillions of horrific notifications.

When the house phone rings, I lunge for it. "Leo?"

"Ruby? It's Sasha."

I nearly collapse with relief at the sound of my best friend's voice. "Sasha. Oh god, Sasha. I was hoping Leo was calling to say he'd managed to get it taken down."

"I wish that were it. Are you okay?"

"No." The word comes out as a sob. "I'm so far from okay I can't even see it from here."

"I know. I'm so sorry."

I wipe my eyes with the back of my hand. "How are you calling me? I'm Leo's little prisoner here, in case you didn't know."

"Liam called Leo. I told him you'd need to talk."

"Understatement of the year," I say. "The prick just walked out and left me here. Like he's got some magical power that can turn back time or erase the damn internet."

"He's probably as freaked out as you are."

I make a snorting noise. "Five million people, Sasha. Five million strangers have seen me naked. Have seen me…" I can't finish the sentence. "And Leo thinks the way to help is to pretend like he can make it all go away. He can't."

"I know. But you're going to get through this."

"How? How do I come back from the entire world seeing my most private moments? And what about work? Not exactly the vibe you want for Lydia Cosmetics."

"You let me worry about that. As for you, you take it one day at a time," she says firmly. "One hour at a time if you have to. And you reach out to your best friend whenever you need to."

I sink onto the couch, pulling my knees up to my chest. "He has other videos. Seven total. What if this is just the beginning?"

"Then we'll deal with that, too."

"I can't. I can't survive this."

"Bullshit. You're the strongest person I know, Ruby. You've survived worse than this."

"Have I?" I laugh bitterly. "When?"

"When your parents died. When Leo broke your heart. When you had to rebuild your entire life from scratch." Her voice is fierce now, full of conviction. "You survived all of that. You'll survive this, too. Trust me. I know a little bit about surviving."

I have to smile. She really does.

"But I don't want to survive it. I want it to go away. I want to wake up and have this all be a nightmare."

"Wouldn't that be great? But since that's not how this works, we're going to figure out how to move forward."

"Leo thinks he can fix it," I say, my voice flat with exhaustion. "He went charging off to track down whoever did this, like he's some kind of action hero."

"Maybe he feels helpless," Sasha suggests gently. "Maybe

hunting down the bad guy is the only way he knows how to deal with something like this."

"I don't give a shit how he feels." The words come out harder than I intended. "I needed him here. Either that, or I needed to be in it with him. Helping him. Doing *something*. But all he did was metaphorically flip me off and go racing out the door to play he-man games."

"Maybe—"

"*No*." I cut her off. "I don't want to hear about how he's hurting, too. I don't want you to make excuses for him. He left me when I needed him most. Just like he did seven years ago."

Sasha is quiet for a moment. Then, "Do you want Liam to come get you? Bring you back here?"

The offer is tempting. So tempting, I almost say yes. If anyone can get me out despite Leo's edict, it would be Liam. "No. I want to be here when he comes back," I say. "I want to tell him exactly what I think of his hero complex."

"Are you sure?"

"I'm sure." And I am. Whatever happens next, I'm not letting him off until he hears exactly what I think of his manipulative, a-hole bullshit. I stayed silent seven years ago. I won't do it again.

We talk for a few more minutes, and by the time I hang up, I feel marginally more human. Still destroyed, still humiliated, but not alone.

I'm cleaning up the broken glass when I hear the beep of the key code. My head snaps up, and I'm suddenly grateful I'm holding a dustpan full of crystal shards. The urge to throw them at Leo's perfect face is almost overwhelming.

He walks in looking grim and determined, his hair disheveled like he's been running his hands through it. His eyes immediately go to the destruction in the living room, taking in the broken decanter and wine stains.

"Find your bad guy?" I ask, my voice dripping with false sweetness.

"I have a lead," he says, not quite meeting my eyes. "Someone I need to track down."

"Of course you do." I take a step closer, and he actually backs up. Good. He should be afraid of me right now. "Let me guess—you're going to charge off into the night again, leaving me here to deal with the fallout."

"Ruby, this is important—"

"More important than me?"

The question hangs between us, and I can see him weighing his answer. Calculating what will get him what he wants with the least amount of resistance.

It's exactly the kind of cold manipulation I remember from seven years ago.

"I need you to stay here," he says finally. "I need you safe while I handle this."

"No." The word comes out flat and final. "I'm done being handled. I'm done being protected. I'm done being locked away like some precious object while you make all the decisions about my life."

"You don't understand—"

"I understand perfectly." I'm advancing on him now. "I understand that you're still the same controlling bastard who thinks he knows what's best for everyone. The same man who broke my heart because he couldn't be bothered to explain himself."

"That's not—"

"Save it," I snap, cutting him off. I'm close enough now to see the gold flecks in his green eyes. Close enough to remember how those eyes used to look at me with love instead of calculation. "There was a moment last night when I thought maybe you'd changed. That maybe there could be something real between us."

Pain flashes across his face, but I push forward anyway.

"But you're still the same selfish, unfeeling prick who pushed me out of his life when I needed him most. You have no soul, Leo Grimm. And I'm glad—so fucking glad—that I was reminded of that before I made the mistake of trusting you again."

"Ruby, please."

"As for your protection?" I step back and straighten my spine. "Fuck that. I'd rather take my chances with whatever psychopath is after me than spend another minute locked in here with you."

His face goes white. "You're not leaving."

"Watch me."

I start toward the door, but he moves faster, blocking my path with his body.

"I said no."

"Get out of my way, Leo."

"Not happening."

We stare at each other for a long moment, the air between us crackling with tension and unresolved pain. Then he steps aside, and for a moment, I think he's going to let me go.

Instead, he walks to the master bedroom.

"You bastard," I breathe.

"I'll be back," he says without looking at me. "Try not to destroy anything else while I'm gone." Then steps inside, closing and locking the door behind him.

Then I hear the subtle hum of the private elevator in that room, and I know that he's gone, leaving me alone with my rage and my humiliation and the growing certainty that Leopold Grimm is exactly the monster I always knew him to be.

FIFTEEN
REVELATIONS

I'm still seething when I grab the remote and collapse onto the couch, my whole body vibrating with rage and hurt and the kind of bone-deep exhaustion that comes from having your life implode in the span of a few hours.

Not to mention having the bastard who did the imploding walk out on me again. All so he can go off and play hero while he tries to hunt down whoever's responsible for posting that damn sex tape.

Meanwhile, I'm left alone to deal with the wreckage of my life.

Fine. It's not as if I want Leo beside me, anyway. He's the man who chewed me up and spit me out, and ridiculously good sex isn't going to change that.

If Leo Fucking Grimm wants to abandon me when I need him most—again—then I'll distract myself with mindless television until my brain stops freaking out about the five million strangers who've now seen me naked.

Probably six million by now.

Or more.

Fuck.

I take out some of my fury on the poor, battered remote as I click violently through the channels, searching for something to drown out the voice in my head that keeps replaying those vile comments from strangers who have nothing better to do than reduce the most intimate moment of my life to snarky hashtags and vile comments.

I'm trying to convince myself that a rerun of *Law & Order* is both mindless and familiar enough to distract me, when a piercing alert tone cuts through my spiraling thoughts. As I wince, I look up to see that the screen is filled with the words GRIMM TOWER SECURITY ALERT against an ominous red and black background.

I immediately stiffen, then look up at the smoke detectors as my mind scrolls through possible emergencies—fire, bomb threat, lost toddler, and who knows what else?

Out of curiosity, I flip to another channel, but the same message appears, and I'm starting to get a little worried. Is there a protocol I should be following? Some sort of evacuation procedure that residents and workers at the tower already know about?

I'm about to get up and check the house phone when the tone fades, and the alert screen begins to dissolve into something else. A street scene, I think, and I wonder if the alert is supposed to notify Tower occupants of an accident near the property. I'm only half-watching, more annoyed than curious, when the video starts to come into focus. It's grainy and washed out, but it looks like traffic, and there's something familiar about the location, though I can't place it right away.

I'm curious, though, so I start to I flip through more channels, wondering if the image will be clearer. The channels all have the same image, but it's starting to sharpen at a faster rate. I lean forward, watching the pixels as they seem to shift from fuzzy to crisp, curious now as to what mysterious image is hiding in that fuzzy, old-fashioned, grainy gray image.

That's when the door explodes open and Leo bursts in, his hair disheveled and his eyes wild with something that looks like panic.

Immediately, I leap to my feet. "Oh, god. Is it a fire?"

He doesn't answer. His attention is entirely on the screen, his face as white as death. Not pale—*white*. Like someone's just drained every drop of blood from his body.

"No!" He lunges for the remote, practically ripping it from my hands with such force I'm surprised he doesn't dislocate my wrist.

The screen goes black, the TV now off.

"What the hell, Leo?" I snap, more from reflex than actual anger.

He's staring at the dark screen like it might come back to life and attack us both. His hands are shaking—actually shaking—and when he pulls out his phone to check something, his shoulders sag like he's carrying the weight of the world.

Silence stretches between us, thick with tension I don't understand. Leo looks like he's just watched someone die. Hell, he looks like he's dying himself.

"Leo?" My voice comes out smaller than I intended. "What's going on?"

"Nothing," he says. "Just nothing."

I cross my arms and lean back as I gape openly at him. "So, you always leap across a room like a Ninja on crack for nothing?"

"Fuck." He practically spits the word, dragging his fingers through his hair at the same time. "Fuck, damn, shit," he snaps, then hurls the remote across the room.

I can only stare. "Seriously, Leo. What's going on?"

As I watch, he draws a breath, then lets it out slowly. He repeats that four times before finally nodding at the sofa. I sit, a little leery, and watch as he does the same.

"I couldn't let you see that," he says, his voice barely above a whisper as he looks down at his hands.

"A security alert?" But even as I say it, something cold and nasty is unfurling in my stomach. Because Leo doesn't panic. Ever. He gets frustrated. He gets mad. And he damn sure gets headstrong. But I have never once known him to panic.

He lifts his head to face me, and I've never seen him look so broken. So utterly destroyed. It's like looking at a man who's been hollowed out from the inside.

"That video," he says slowly, as if each word is being dragged out of him with pliers, "it's your parents' murder."

I hear the words, but I can't process them. It's like he's speaking Russian at the bottom of a swimming pool.

"He taped it," Leo says. "And the fucker kept the tape."

It feels like an hour passes before I can manage a reply. "What are you talking about?" My voice sounds strange, and I realize that my hands have gone to the top of the robe, and I'm holding it tight together at my neck.

"My parents weren't murdered."

"They were," he says, in a voice so full of compassion it almost breaks me.

"No," I say, shaking my head as my eyes fill with tears. "No, no, no."

"I'm so sorry."

"*No.* A drunk driver hit them on the freeway." I have to drag the words out, as if they're hiding behind my memory of that horrible day when a dark-eyed cop came to campus to tell me the news. "They burned to death because they couldn't get out of the car. I identified their bodies. I planned their funeral. I—"

"No." The word is flat. Final. "They were murdered. And the bastard who took them out is playing games."

The room tilts sideways, and I have to grip the arm of the couch to keep from tumbling off into space. My vision is doing something weird, like I'm looking through water, and there's a ringing in my ears that makes Leo's voice sound like it's coming from very far away.

"What happened?" The words are barely a whisper. "And how —how do you know?"

Pain seems to fill his eyes as he says, "My father didn't approve of us dating." His voice is mechanical now, like he's reciting facts from a police report. Like emotion is too dangerous to let anywhere near these words.

He moves to sit on the coffee table in front of me, then leans in. But he doesn't touch me. Just meets my eyes as he continues.

"Father made a big deal about your family being working class. Your dad was a mechanic. Your mom worked the front desk at a motel. In Elias Grimm's mind, you weren't good enough for his son."

I swallow, holding my breath as he goes on.

"He told me to end it, or he'd—he'd make sure it ended permanently." Leo's green eyes are filled with a pain so raw it takes my breath away. "I thought he was bluffing, and I told him no. I told him I loved you, that I wasn't going to let you go."

I loved you.

The words I'd wanted so desperately to hear back then. The words I'd dreamed about, fantasized about, cried myself to sleep wishing for.

Now, they're destroying me.

"He had them k-killed." Leo's voice breaks on the words, and I watch a tear slide down his cheek. "I never thought he'd go that far. Ruby, please believe me, I never thought he'd do anything like that."

"No." I'm shaking my head violently, trying to dislodge his words before they can take root in my brain. "No, that's not—that can't be right."

"It's true," Leo says, his voice sounding dull and dead. "My father had your parents murdered because I wouldn't give you up."

I shake my head, as if that will make the words disappear, and the truth along with it. Because I know it's the truth. As much as I want to scream and cry and call Leo a liar, I can't. All the pieces are clicking into place. The way the police had been so quick to close the case. The supposed drunk driver who'd died in the crash, making it impossible to question him. The way the insurance company had paid out without even the hint of an investigation, as if they wanted the whole thing to disappear.

My parents were executed by Elias Grimm, one of the few men in the country—hell in the world—with the money and the pull to get away with murder.

"That image on the screen? The one I stopped you from seeing?" His voice is getting stronger now, like this confession is giving him power. "That was security footage of their deaths. My father had it recorded. Kept it as a fucking trophy."

The words hit me like blows, each one driving the air from my lungs. I can't breathe. Can't think. Can't process the magnitude of what he's telling me.

My parents died because I fell in love with the wrong man. They died because of me.

"It's my fault," Leo continues, his eyes bloodshot and his expression pained. "If I'd just walked away when he told me to, they'd still be alive. If I'd been smart enough to see what kind of monster my father really was, maybe I could have done something."

"*Stop.*" The word rips out of me like a scream. "Just stop."

But he can't stop. Now that the dam has broken, it's as if everything is pouring out in a torrent of guilt and self-recrimination and seven years of buried truth.

"The day he killed them, he threatened to kill you, too, if I told you the truth. Or if I stayed with you. He said if I wanted to keep you breathing, I had to cut you loose."

His voice is raw now. Broken. "So, I made you hate me, Rue. I ripped you apart when we broke up because I had to. I had to make sure you'd run far and fast and never look back. That you'd want nothing to do with me ever again."

The note. That horrible, cold note waiting for me in his suite when I needed him most. When I was drowning in grief and needed him to hold me while I fell apart.

I'd called him in tears after the police left, but only got his voicemail. I'd left a message, but never heard back. But I'd found that horrible note.

"I couldn't trust myself to stay away from you," he whispers. "I loved you too much. I knew if I saw you cry—if I held you while you grieved—I'd never be able to let you go. And he'd kill you, Rue. I knew he would. Hadn't he just proved it? And the only way to protect you was to make sure you never wanted to see me again."

I'm sobbing now, great heaving sobs that feel like they're tearing me apart from the inside. Tears for my parents. Tears for seven years of not knowing the truth. Of missing them so desperately, and not having a clue about why they really died.

Seven years of torture served up by Elias Grimm, and I never even had a clue.

Seven horrible years of believing that Leo didn't love me, when the truth is that he destroyed us to save my life.

"Who?" I manage to choke out between sobs. "Who did your father's dirty work?"

"I didn't know at the time. I found out years later. His name's Carson Nash. He'd been my father's fixer for years. When I was young, I thought of him as an uncle. I learned the truth much later." Leo's voice has gone hard now, dangerous in a way that makes the hair on my arms stand up.

"What?" I whisper, though I fear I already know.

Leo draws in a deep breath, then lets it out slowly. "He's the man who's been stalking you, I'm certain of it. He's the one who released the video."

Even though I'd expected it, my blood turns to ice. The faceless threat suddenly has a name. A history. And a body count that includes my parents.

"But your father's in a coma. Are you saying Alexander set him loose on me?" Alexander is the eldest living brother, and he's been running the Grimm family businesses since Elias became ill. I was never under the illusion that Alexander particularly liked or disliked me. Honestly, I'm not sure he ever even knew I existed. And I'm not at all sure why he'd think I was some kind of threat now.

"Not Alex," Leo says. "Nash wants something that he thinks I can get."

"What?"

"I don't know. Not specifically. He hasn't demanded anything yet. But I know how he thinks. More than that, I have access to Father's private vault. Nash has mad skills at hacking something digital, like information stored on a server. But Father kept actual paper records in his vault. And I think Nash wants access to material that can incriminate him."

"In my parents' death?"

"Among many, many other things. Father would have kept it. If it's something that could be used for protection or blackmail, he would have kept it in his vault."

I only nod, still shell-shocked.

He draws in a breath, then meets my eyes. "I couldn't tell you before. I couldn't risk you knowing. Now, I think I can't risk you staying in the dark."

I bite my lip, seeing so clearly now all the guilt he's been carrying. All the fear that's been driving every decision he's made for seven years.

"So he's told you he wants you to open the vault."

"Not in so many words. But he will."

"What about Alexander or Elliott?" I don't mention Liam. I know perfectly well that Elias Grimm wouldn't give his illegitimate child access to his most personal information.

"They don't have access. Alex has oversight of the business, Elliott of the family's personal finances, and I was given responsibility for being his second on the vault."

"Okay, but why now?"

"Father's health. He's in a coma, and the prognosis isn't good. Once he's dead, his attorney will have authority to open the vault."

I nod as everything falls into place. "There's something in there that Nash wants before the attorney goes through everything."

"Exactly. And," he continues with a sigh, "Nash is already pushing hard for me to open it."

"But you just said he hasn't made that demand."

He runs his fingers through my hair. "Baby, don't you see?

He's trying make his case that he can get to you. That I can't keep you safe or keep your life private. But that I can buy your safety with information." He takes my hand. "You're my pressure point, Red. And Nash damn well knows it."

My blood goes cold. A killer is trying to manipulate Leo by threatening to kill me. No, not to kill me. That would end it. He's threatening to hurt me.

The Leo I'd once loved so deeply would have done anything in his power not to let that happen. This Leo, too, I think. Because now I understand what he didn't let me see before. That he blew me off to save me.

"Ruby, I never wanted to hurt you."

My entire body has gone completely numb. "You lied to me about how my parents died."

"And I'd do it again. It was the only way to keep you safe." He steps closer, and it's only when he cups my cheek that I realize I'm crying. "Please tell me you understand that."

I nod. "I do. It hurts like hell, but. I really do." I blink back tears. I'm sorry," I whisper.

His eyes widen. "What on earth do you have to be sorry about?"

"I—all this time. I had it so horribly wrong."

"Oh, baby," he pulls me into his arms and I sag against him. "I just wish I'd come up with another way. I left you alone to grieve —and to keep you safe. And I'm so, so sorry."

My tears are flowing freely, and my nose is running, and I'm probably making a mess of his shirt. "Me too," I say, then hug him even tighter. "But you're here now."

He strokes my hair. "Yeah. I'm here now."

I step back, then wrap my arms around myself as if I can hold all the broken pieces together through sheer force of will.

"You should have told me about your father. About him not wanting us to be together."

"Maybe," he says. "I don't know. I did what I thought was best at the time."

I nod, still feeling numb. "I know. I really do. But I need time to process this. I need to figure out how to live with the fact that I'm the reason my parents are dead."

"Oh, baby. You're not the reason," he says, the words lashing out as he squeezes my hand. "My father is."

I just shake my head. "I need space."

"I can't give that to you." His voice is gentle but implacable. "I'm sorry, but I can't let you out of my sight. Not now."

"Leo, no."

"Hate me all you want," he says, stepping closer. "Scream at me, hit me, whatever you need to do. But I'm staying right by your side until Nash is dead."

I shake my head, then hug myself, not sure why I don't want Leo to be my protector.

Except I do know—for seven years, he let me believe he didn't love me. And maybe some part of me understands now why he left that horrible note. Maybe I even believe that he still really does care.

But he turned his back when I needed him the most. And maybe that's not fair, but the last seven years haven't been fair to me, either. And now that I know the truth, I'm determined to take care of myself.

"I'll hire some of Liam's people to protect me," I say.

"The hell you will," he says. "We have an arrangement, remember? You agreed to my terms."

"No. No way are you calling the shots about my life."

He stalks closer, getting right in my face. "I'm protecting you, Ruby. We've already discussed this, and we're not going to rehash it." He skims his finger down the front of my robe, tracing the edge of the V that reveals my neck and making me shiver. "You will continue to abide by the terms we agreed to," he says. "And I will keep you safe. I don't trust anyone else to keep you alive. Not even Liam."

"You don't get to make that choice for me."

"I didn't. You did when you agreed to my terms. We're not

voiding that deal now." His green eyes are fierce, blazing with determination and something that looks like desperation. "I failed to protect your parents. I failed to protect you from seven years of pain and lies and thinking you weren't good enough. But I will not—*will not*—fail to protect you now."

I stare at him for a long moment, this man who's been the source of my greatest joy and deepest pain.

"I hate you," I whisper, and mean it. Because right now, I hate him for not trusting me enough back then to hear the truth. I hate him for making me grieve alone. I hate him for letting me think I wasn't worth loving.

"I know," he says softly, and there's so much love in those two words that it breaks my heart all over again. "But you're alive. We have a deal. And as long as I'm breathing, you're going to stay that way."

SIXTEEN
BARE

He'd spent seven fucking years dreaming about this moment. Not the horror. Not the pain. But simply the moment when she was his again.

The smart part of his brain—the part that usually kept him alive—was screaming that this was wrong. That he should walk away, give her space, let her process the devastating truth he'd just laid at her feet.

But that voice was drowned out by something darker, hungrier. Something that had been starving for her since the moment he'd thrown her unceremoniously out of his life, intentionally twisting the knife so that she wouldn't come back.

So that she'd hate him.

It had worked. She hated him. She'd just told him so, and maybe she always would.

He could live with that. If hating him had kept her safe, he could live with that forever.

But right then, he couldn't live another moment without claiming what was his. Without feeling her heart beat against his. He wanted to look into her stormy gray eyes when he took her and see understanding reflected back at him. Understanding what she meant to him. Of what he'd sacrificed to keep her breathing.

He wanted to tug loose the tie that held that damned robe closed. Wanted to push it off her shoulders and see her standing naked before him, knowing the truth now. Knowing that every moment apart had been agony.

Wanted to sink his cock deep inside her and hear her cry out his name, not in ignorance this time, but in full knowledge of everything he'd endured to protect her.

He wanted it. He needed it.

And, yes, he would take what he craved.

He had to, because this was Ruby, and how could he turn away from her now, when she finally knew the truth about everything—and still needed his protection?

She was his. She'd always been his. And it was time he reminded them both of that most basic of facts.

"Come here," he demanded, even though he was only an arm's length from her.

His eyes were on her face, and he saw the exact moment she realized what was about to happen. The way her breath caught, the way her pulse fluttered at the base of her throat. Fear and want and something new—understanding—warring in those stormy eyes he'd been dreaming about.

She knew now. Knew why he'd left. Knew what it had cost him. And still she wanted him.

Good. She should want him. She should remember exactly what kind of man she'd made a deal with. What kind of man had loved her enough to destroy himself to save her.

"Time to collect," he said simply.

He moved toward her with the grace of a predator, and Christ, the way she looked at him—half terrified, half hungry, and completely aware of who he really was—made his cock so hard it hurt. Blood pounded in his ears, drowning out everything except need. Seven years of need, seven years of wanting until it was a physical ache in his chest and his cock.

"The robe," he said when he was close enough to smell the

lingering scent of his soap on her skin. Close enough to see the way her nipples were already hard beneath the terrycloth.

Close enough to see that despite everything—despite learning her parents had been murdered, despite his lies, despite her hatred—she still responded to him. "Take it off."

"Leo, no."

"I believe we have a deal. Are you telling me you're reneging?" He flashed what he knew was a wolfish grin. "Because disobedience comes with punishment, and I promise you I'll enjoy it." He let his eyes rake over her, noting how she stood straight and proud despite everything, her chin lifted even as her hands shook.

She knew what he was capable of now. Knew the lengths he'd go to. And still she stood her ground.

"You bastard," she whispered, but her hands were already moving to the belt of the robe. "You knew. You knew Nash killed them, and you never told me."

"Seven years I grieved them, thinking it was senseless."

Her hands were shaking with emotion now as she worked at the knot, and Leo had to clench his fists to keep from ripping the fabric away himself. He loved seeing her like this—angry, fierce, fighting back instead of cowering. This was the Ruby he'd fallen in love with, the one who'd challenge him even when she was afraid.

"I was protecting you," he said, his voice low and dangerous.

"You were protecting yourself." The robe fell open, revealing the body that was finally, truly his—no more lies between them, no secrets—and Leo's control became a distant memory.

"You couldn't stand the guilt, so you made sure I'd never know what you'd cost me."

"What I cost you?" The words came out sharper than he intended. "Ruby, I gave up everything to keep you alive. I destroyed *us*—the only thing that mattered to me—because my father threatened to kill you, too."

"And you never gave me the choice." She shoved the robe off

her shoulders, letting it pool at her feet, standing naked and magnificent in her fury.

"You decided for me. You chose for me. You took away my right to know why my parents died."

Perfect. She was fucking perfect. Fuller than she'd been in college, more woman than girl now. And when his gaze traveled lower, he could see the flush spreading down her neck, the way she was pressing her thighs together, shifting her weight. Already aroused for him. Already primed, despite the anger blazing in her eyes.

"Look at you," he murmured, his voice wrecked. "Furious with me and still wet. Your body knows who it belongs to, even when your mind is fighting it."

"Go to hell."

"I've been there for seven years." He stepped closer, close enough that she had to tilt her head back to meet his eyes. "And you know what's kept me sane? Knowing you were alive. Knowing you were safe. Knowing that every day you hated me was another day my father couldn't touch you."

"Don't you dare," she said, her voice shaking with emotion. "Don't you dare make this about love. You let me carry guilt that wasn't mine to carry."

"Guilt?" He had no idea what the fuck she was talking about. "Guilt about what?"

"I thought—" Her voice cracked, and he saw tears threatening at the corners of her eyes. "I thought maybe if I'd been a better daughter, if I'd visited more, if I'd called them that day instead of being with you, then maybe they'd have been at home and not driving on that road, at what I thought was the exact wrong time."

The words felt like a slap. All this time, she'd been blaming herself.

"Ruby, god no. You loved them, and they knew it. It wasn't your fault. There's no universe in which it could have been your fault."

He moved closer, wanting to pull her to him and shoulder some of her pain, but she reached out, pressing her hands against his chest.

"No," she said, but she didn't push him away. Just held them there, his heart beating beneath her palms. "You don't get to comfort me. Not when you're the reason I've been torturing myself."

"I never wanted you to blame yourself. God, how could you even think that?"

"I was broken, dammit. If you wanted me to think rationally, you should have told me the damn truth." The words came out as a sob, and something inside Leo's chest cracked open. "You should have trusted me with the truth and let me decide what to do with it."

"I couldn't risk you."

"That wasn't your choice to make." She looked up at him, tears streaming down her face now, and Leo had never seen anything more beautiful or more heartbreaking. "You talk about keeping me safe, but you were making decisions about my life without asking what I wanted."

The accusation stung because it was true. He had made choices for her. He'd decided what she could and couldn't handle.

Oh, god. Did that make him as controlling as Elias? Surely not.

Or maybe a little. *Shit.*

"I'm sorry," he said. "I'm really, truly sorry."

"Sorry doesn't give me back seven years."

"No. It doesn't."

For a moment they just stared at each other, the weight of seven years of lies and hurt and love hanging between them like a live wire.

Then Ruby's hands fisted in his shirt, and she pulled him down to her level.

"I hate you," she whispered against his lips.

"I know."

"I hate that I still want you."

"I know that, too."

"I hate that knowing the truth doesn't change anything. That I still—"

She cut herself off, but he heard what she wasn't saying.

That she still loved him.

"Show me," he said, his voice rough with need and something deeper. "Show me how much you hate me."

Her kiss was brutal, punishing, full of seven years of accumulated rage and hurt and desperate need. She bit his lip hard enough to draw blood, and when he groaned into her mouth, she took advantage, her tongue invading, claiming, conquering.

She was trying to hurt him the way he'd hurt her, and fuck if it wasn't the most erotic thing he'd ever experienced.

"You want to know what I think about at night?" she said against his mouth, her nails raking down his chest through his shirt. "I think about all the ways I want to hurt you. All the ways I want to make you pay for what you took from me."

"Tell me," he said, backing her toward the door. "Tell me how you want to hurt me."

"I want to tie you up and leave you wanting. I want to bring you right to the edge and then walk away." Her back hit the solid wood, and she was trapped between his body and the unyielding surface. "I want you to know what it feels like to lose everything that matters."

"You did that seven years ago," he said, his hands braced on either side of her head against the door. "The moment you walked out of my life, even though I'm the one who pushed you away. You completely destroyed me."

"Good." The word came out vicious, satisfied. "I hope it hurt. I hope it hurt every single day."

"It did." He pressed his forehead against hers, breathing hard. "Every fucking day. And I'd do it again if it kept you safe."

"You arrogant bastard." She reached between them and gripped him through his jeans, hard enough to make him groan.

"You think that's romantic? You think sacrificing everything makes you some kind of hero?"

"No," he said, his hips bucking involuntarily into her touch. "I think it makes me a man who loves you enough to destroy himself for you."

"Stop saying that." Her grip tightened, and stars exploded behind his eyes. "Stop saying you love me when everything you did was about control."

He caught her wrist, stilling her movements. "Ruby, look at me."

She did, and what he saw in her eyes nearly brought him to his knees. Not just anger, not just hurt, but confusion. Fear that everything she'd believed about their relationship was a lie.

"I loved you," he said quietly. "I loved you so much it scared the hell out of me. And when my father threatened you, when he showed me what he'd done to your parents, I knew I'd do anything—lie, cheat, break your heart, break my own—to keep you breathing."

"That's not love," she whispered. "That's obsession."

"The hell it is. But it doesn't matter, because that's the only kind of love I know how to give." He released her wrist and stepped back, giving her space. "And if you can't live with that, then walk away. Right now. Walk away and I'll let you go."

She stared at him for a long moment, breathing hard, and Leo held his breath waiting for her answer. Waiting to see if she'd choose to stay or choose to run.

"I can't," she said finally, and the words sounded like they were torn from her soul. "God help me, I can't walk away from you."

"Then don't." He moved back to her, pressing his body against hers, trapping her against the door. "Stay. Fight me. Hate me if you need to. But stay."

"You don't deserve it."

"No. I don't." He slid his hands into her hair, angling her head exactly where he wanted it. "But I'm asking anyway."

When he kissed her this time, it was with seven years of desperation and need and love that had never died despite everything that had happened between them. She responded immediately, her arms wrapping around his neck, pulling him closer even as she bit and scratched and tried to hurt him.

It was violent and desperate and completely without mercy. She was trying to punish him with her mouth, with her teeth, with her nails, and he let her. He welcomed it. Because her anger was better than her indifference, her violence better than her absence.

"I hate you," she gasped between kisses.

"I know."

"I hate that you made me love you."

"I know."

"I hate that I still do."

The boldness of the admission hit him like a freight train. She still loved him, and she was willing to tell him. Hell, to tell herself. Despite everything, despite the lies and the hurt and the seven years of believing he'd never cared about her, she still loved him.

"Ruby—"

"Shut up." She reached for his shirt, yanking it open so violently that buttons scattered across the floor. "Don't talk. Don't think. Just feel what you did to me."

Her hands were everywhere—scratching, claiming, demanding. She raked her nails down his chest hard enough to leave marks, and when he groaned she did it again.

"This is what you're getting," she said, her voice fierce and broken and beautiful. "Not forgiveness. Not absolution. Just this desperate fucking need that won't go away no matter how much I hate you for it."

"That's enough," he said, spinning them around so she was facing the door, her palms flat against the wood. "That's more than enough."

He kicked her legs apart, positioning her exactly where he wanted her, and when she tried to look back at him, he pressed her face against the door with one hand while the other worked at his belt.

"You want to hate me? Fine. Hate me." His jeans hit the floor, and he pressed himself against her from behind, letting her feel exactly how much he wanted her. "But you're still mine, Ruby. You're still going to take everything I give you."

"Bastard," she breathed, but when he slid his hand between her legs, she was soaking wet.

"That's right," he said, stroking her with rough fingers. "Call me whatever you want. It doesn't change the fact that your body knows who it belongs to."

He slid two fingers inside her without warning, and she cried out, pressing back against his hand despite herself.

"Fuck, you're tight," he said, working her with fingers that remembered exactly how she liked to be touched. "Seven years and you're still so tight. Have you been thinking about me, Ruby? When you're with other men, do you close your eyes and pretend it's me?"

"Go to hell."

"Answer me." He crooked his fingers against that spot that used to make her scream, and she bucked against his hand. "Do you think about me when other men touch you?"

"Yes," she gasped, and the admission seemed to surprise her as much as it did him. "Goddamn you, yes."

"Good." He added a third finger, stretching her, preparing her, and she threw her head back with a moan that nearly made him come right then. "Because I've thought about you every single day. Every single night. No other woman has ever come close to making me feel what you do."

"Liar."

"Truth." He pulled his fingers out suddenly, and she whimpered at the loss. "You're the only woman I've ever loved, Ruby. The only one I've ever wanted this much."

"Then why—" She cut herself off, but he knew what she was asking.

Why did he leave her? Why did he hurt her? Why did he choose his father's threats over fighting for their love?

"Because I was a coward," he said simply. "Because I was twenty-four years old and I'd never felt anything like what I felt for you, and it terrified me. And when my father showed me what he'd done to your parents, when he told me you'd be next if I didn't end things, I chose the sure thing over the risk."

"The sure thing?"

"Your life." He positioned himself at her entrance, his cock hard and aching and desperate for her. "I chose knowing you'd be alive and hating me over the risk that fighting back might get you killed."

She was quiet for a moment, processing his words, and Leo held himself still even though every instinct was screaming at him to push inside her, to claim her, to make her his again.

"Would you make the same choice now?" she asked finally.

"No." The answer came without hesitation. "Now I'd fight. Now I'd trust you to fight with me. Now I'd choose us over safety every single time."

"Why?"

"Because seven years without you taught me that a life without you isn't worth living." He pushed into her slowly, inch by devastating inch, and she gasped at the intrusion. "Because I'd rather have one day with you and die than spend another year without you."

She was so tight, so perfect, and when he was finally seated fully inside her he had to rest his forehead against the back of her neck and just breathe.

Home. This felt like coming home. Like forgiveness. Like redemption.

"Seven years," he said, his voice wrecked. "Seven fucking years I've wanted this. Wanted you to know the truth and still choose me."

"I'm not choosing you," she said, but her body was already

moving against him, taking him deeper. "I'm just taking payment for seven years of lies."

"Call it whatever you want." He started to move, pulling almost all the way out before sliding back in. "But you're here. You're mine. And I'm never letting you go again."

"You don't own me."

"Don't I?" He snapped his hips forward, driving into her harder, and she cried out. "Your body says otherwise."

He fucked her against that door like he was trying to prove something. Like he was trying to show her and himself that this connection between them was real, that it was worth the danger and the heartbreak and the seven years of agony.

"This is what you agreed to," he said, his hips bucking against hers. "This is your payment. My cock inside you whenever I want it. However I want it."

"Yes," she gasped, and the word hit him like lightning. "God, yes."

She was meeting him thrust for thrust now, pushing back against him with a desperation that matched his own. Her nails found his shoulders, digging in deep enough to draw blood, marking him the way he'd marked her soul seven years ago.

"Harder," she demanded, her voice fierce and broken. "If you want to claim me, then claim me properly."

The challenge in her voice drove him wild. He gripped her hips bruisingly tight and gave her what she wanted, driving into her with a force that made the heavy door shake in its frame. Each thrust sent her higher up against the wood, and she had to brace her hands flat against it to keep from losing her balance.

"Is this what you wanted?" he growled against her ear, his teeth finding the sensitive spot where her neck met her shoulder. "Is this hard enough for you?"

"More," she gasped, her body arching back against him. "I want to feel this tomorrow. I want to remember exactly what you did to me."

Christ, she was going to kill him. Her demands, her fire, the way she met his brutality with her own. And now with no lingering secrets between them. Christ, it was everything he'd dreamed of and more. The sound of their bodies coming together mixed with her moans and his harsh breathing, and Leo had never heard anything more beautiful.

"You feel that?" he said, reaching around to stroke her clit while he fucked her. "You feel how perfectly you fit around me? Like you were made for this. Made for me."

"Shut up," she said, but her voice was breathless, broken. Her inner walls were fluttering around him, and he could feel how close she was to the edge.

"Seven years of other men," he said, his fingers working her clit while his cock drove into her again and again. "And none of them could make you feel like this, could they?"

"You arrogant—" Her words cut off in a moan as he found just the right rhythm with his fingers.

"Say it," he demanded, slowing his movements until she whimpered in frustration. "Say none of them could touch you the way I do."

"Go to hell."

"Say it, or I stop." He stilled completely, and she tried to push back against him, but he held her firmly in place.

"You bastard," she panted, trembling with need.

"Say it."

"Fine!" The word exploded out of her. "None of them—none of them could make me feel like this. Happy?"

"Ecstatic." He resumed his brutal pace, and she cried out in relief and pleasure. "You can hate me all you want, but your body knows the truth. It knows who it belongs to."

She was close—he could feel it in the way she tightened around him, see it in the way her body tensed. But when she started to fall over the edge he pulled out suddenly, spinning her around to face him.

"Not yet." He lifted her without warning, her back against the door, her legs wrapping around his waist automatically. "I want to see your face when you come. Want to see that you know exactly who's making you feel this good."

The position put her cunt directly against his cock, and when he pushed back inside her, the angle was devastating. Deeper. More intense. More possessive.

"Look at me," he ordered, his voice rough with need.

She did, and what he saw there nearly brought him to his knees. Not just want, not just need, but something deeper. Something that looked like love, even wrapped in all that anger and hurt.

"I hate you," she whispered, but her hands were fisted in his hair, holding him close.

"I know."

"I hate that I still love you."

"I know that too."

"I hate that this doesn't change anything. That tomorrow I'll still be angry and you'll still be a lying bastard and I'll still want you anyway."

"Then we'll figure it out together," he said, his rhythm becoming more desperate, more claiming. "We'll fight and fuck and figure it out as we go."

"Promise me," she said suddenly, her eyes locking on his. "Promise me no more lies. Promise me no more choosing for me what I can and can't handle."

"I promise," he said, and meant it. "No more lies. No more choosing for you. We do this together or not at all."

"Swear it."

"I swear on your father's quarter," he said, remembering their old oath. "I swear on everything that matters to me. No more lies, Ruby. No more secrets between us."

Something in her face cracked open at that, and she pulled him down for a kiss that was desperate and claiming and full of seven years of love that had never died.

"Then make me come," she said against his mouth. "Make me come knowing that you love me. That you've always loved me.

That everything you did was because you couldn't bear to lose me."

That was it. The last of his control snapped like a broken wire.

He fucked her hard and fast against the door, his hands gripping her ass, holding her exactly where he wanted her. The sound of her back hitting the wood with each thrust mixed with her moans and his harsh breathing. Every movement drove him deeper into madness, deeper into need.

"This is what love looks like," he said, his voice dark with satisfaction and desperation. "This desperate fucking need. This willingness to destroy everything to keep you safe."

"Yes," she gasped, and he could hear something breaking in her voice. Not from pain—from the overwhelming intensity of finally knowing the truth, finally understanding what he'd sacrificed for her.

"Come for me," he commanded, reaching between them to stroke her clit. "Come on my cock knowing exactly who I am. Who we are. What we mean to each other."

She shattered with a scream that echoed off the walls, her whole body convulsing around him. The sensation of her coming apart in his arms—the sound of his name torn from her lips while she looked directly into his eyes—sent him over the edge with a violence that left him seeing stars.

He collapsed against her, both of them shaking, both of them breathing like they'd run a marathon as they slid down the door to the floor. He held her close, letting himself believe this was real. That she was here because she wanted to be, not just because someone was trying to kill her. That knowing the truth hadn't destroyed everything between them.

For a long moment, they just breathed together, her face buried against his neck, his arms wrapped around her like he could keep the world at bay through sheer force of will.

"I'm still angry," she said finally, her voice muffled against his skin.

"I know."

"I'm still hurt."

"I know that too."

"And I still love you, you bastard."

He pressed a kiss to the top of her head, breathing in the scent of her hair, her skin, the lingering traces of their desperate coupling.

"I love you too," he said quietly. "More than you'll ever know. More than I ever thought possible."

"Show me," she said, pulling back to look at him. "Every day for the rest of our lives, show me. No more lies. No more secrets. No more choosing for me."

"I promise," he said, and sealed it with a kiss that tasted like forgiveness and second chances and the kind of love that survives everything.

She was finally his again.

And this time, he was never letting her go.

SEVENTEEN
GAME ON

I wake up in Leo's arms for the first time in seven years, and for a moment, I let myself pretend that everything is normal. That we're just two people who found their way back to each other, not two people trapped in a nightmare of murder and threats and viral sex tapes.

I watch as the morning light dances on his jet-black hair, and I'm amazed at how quickly things seem to have turned around. How he's back—the Leo I loved. The man who sacrificed both of us to save me.

I desperately wish there'd been another way, but at least I understand why he did what he did.

Beside me, Leo shifts, his green eyes opening slowly, and when he sees me watching him, his lips curve into that devastating smile that still makes me go weak.

"And isn't this a nice way to wake up?" he says, then leans over to kiss me. It's your basic morning peck, but I close my hand over the back of his head and pull him closer, wanting to start this day off with a bang.

He resists long enough to meet my eyes, and I see both heat and mischief dancing there as he pulls me closer—only to curse when his phone chimes on the side table.

"Hold that thought," he says. "Let me silence this little bastard."

He reaches over to pick it up, but the moment he sees the screen, it's like the bottom falls out of his world. His face goes white, his jaw clenches, and every muscle in his body goes rigid.

"Leo? What the hell? Who is it?"

"No one important." His voice is carefully neutral, but I can see the lie in the way he won't meet my eyes.

"Don't," I say. 'Not after everything we just went through. You promised."

He stares at me for a long moment, and I can see the internal war playing out across his features.

I sit up with a sigh, clutching the sheet to my chest. "Really, Leo? You said we were going to face things together. Or were those just empty words to get me to shut up?"

Finally, he sighs and hands me the phone.

Enjoying the show? This is just the opening act. We need to talk, Little Buddy. - N

Oh, god. *Oh god, oh god, oh god.*

The words blur as panic tries to take hold. *Nash.* The man who killed my parents. Who's turning my life into a public spectacle.

"Ruby," he begins, but I lift my hand, cutting him off. Then I calmly hand him his phone. "All right," I say. "So we deal with this. How?"

I hold my breath, waiting for him to go all alpha male on me and say that there is no *we* in this equation. But he doesn't. Maybe it's the fury on my face or the fire in my eyes. But for a moment, he says nothing at all. Then his expression hardens with resolve.

"Get dressed," he says, already out of bed and moving toward his closet. "We need help."

Twenty minutes later, we're standing in the elevator on our way to Alexander's floor. I've only met this brother once, but I remember the same raven black hair all the Grimm men except Liam have. Not to mention those striking good looks, and that hint of danger that hums around them like some special frequency giving off alpha male vibrations.

The elevator doors open with a soft ding, and Leo leads me down a hallway that looks exactly like his—expensive, intimidating, designed to remind everyone who enters that they're in the presence of real power.

Alexander opens the door before we even knock, like he's been waiting for us. He's dressed in a perfectly tailored suit despite the early hour, and his pale green eyes—so like Leo's— assess me with the kind of sharp intelligence that makes me feel like he's reading my thoughts.

"Ruby," he says with a slight nod. "I'm sorry about what you're going through. This situation is…unfortunate."

"Thank you," I manage as he ushers us inside. To be honest, I'm a bit thrown by his politeness. Alexander Grimm is known as the hard-edged heir who's been running Grimm International with the same ruthless determination as his father had. Then again, what did I expect? That he'd tell me to quit fucking his brother and kick me back into the elevator? That he'd let Leo enter, but would slam the door in my face?

Not really likely.

The living room is as opulent as I expected—all dark wood and leather and expensive. But at the same time, there's something about the space that makes it feel lived-in and comfortable.

"Where's Elliott?" Leo asks, settling onto one of the couches and pulling me down beside him.

"Handling some business in London. He's coming back soon." Alexander moves to a bar cart and pours himself what looks like coffee from a silver service. He doesn't, however, offer any to us. "I assume this visit has to do with your overnight developments?"

Leo's phone buzzes, and he glances at it with a grimace. In addition to the morning's wake-up text from Nash, it's have been blowing up with the fall-out from the damn viral sex tape—more social media alerts, news outlets requesting a comment, everyone wanting a piece of the story.

"You might as well get a new phone and sign out of all your social media," Alexander says. "A sex tape involving one of the Grimm brothers? That's not going away any time soon."

"We're not here about the damn tape," Leo says. "Nash is back. The prick reached out."

Alexander goes very still, his coffee cup halfway to his lips. "Nash has been dead for three years."

"Then I guess hell has a good cellular plan."

"Someone spoofing him. Trying to get a rise out of you."

Leo holds out his phone. "It's him, Alex. He called me by that damn nickname."

Alexander moves from the coffee service to take the phone from Leo, and I see his expression shift as he reads the message. "Someone else could know."

Leo shakes his head. "You, me, Elliott, and Father. And I don't think Father's texting from his coma bed. And we both know it's not Elliott."

Alexander nods, his expression shifting from skepticism to something much darker.

"The psychological warfare, the timing, the way he's targeting Ruby to get to me—it's exactly his playbook." Leo's voice is getting harder, more focused.

"The fucker faked his death." Alexander's voice is a low, hard whisper. Then he squares his shoulders and nods toward Leo's phone. "He hasn't called you that since we were children."

"And when I was a kid, I wasn't nearly as strong as him. Didn't know even a tenth of what he did. That's what he's saying now. That he's got the jump on me. Me, or all of us."

"Doesn't matter," Alexander says. "You're the one he's going to pressure the hardest."

"How do you know?" I ask, then cringe back again when Alexander turns those laser-sharp eyes on me.

"Because, Ms. Ryder, at this particular moment in time, only Leo has a pressure point."

I shake my head, not understanding. Alexander just raises a brow.

"Oh," I say, feeling like an idiot as Leo squeezes my hand. "You mean me."

"Welcome to the hell we call our home, Ms. Ryder. Never a dull moment."

I almost laugh—one of those weird reactions they teach you about in psych class. But I'm distracted by another thought. *Little Buddy.* I turn the words over in my head, the realization coming at me like a punch to the gut. Nash wasn't just their father's employee—he was part of their lives. Someone Leo trusted, even loved like an uncle loved.

And I know better than most anyone how deeply that kind of betrayal can hurt.

Alexander's phone rings, interrupting my thoughts. He glances at the screen and sighs. "I need to take this," he says, aiming a sour look between me and Leo before he steps out of the room.

I scoot closer to Leo, feeling a bit steadier when his arm tightens around my shoulder. "This is the first time I've had an actual conversation with Alexander," I say. I knew Elliott somewhat, and Liam, of course, since he and Leo have always been tight. They're half-brothers, but their friendship is even stronger than the family bond. "And I never met Gabriel. He was alive when we were together, wasn't he?"

Leo nods, his expression so melancholy I wish I hadn't said a thing. "He'd been living in London, shadowing the execs over there to learn our European operations. He was back a few years before he died, though." A tremulous smile touches his lips. "I miss him."

"What happened?"

"He was betrayed," he says simply. "He loved her, and the bitch betrayed him."

My heart twists. I'm about to ask what happened to her—something must have, because the Grimm family is not one to sit back and take betrayal lightly—but Alexander's return stills my tongue.

"That tape of you two is causing quite the PR headache for the company," Alexander says, his gaze skimming over me. I tense as he turns his attention to Leo. "I hope she was worth it."

"Dammit, Alex. Really?"

"That fucking—no pun intended—video is everywhere. #RubyRyder is trending in forty-three countries. From a PR stand-point, we're looking at a complete disaster."

I slide down into my seat, wishing I could curl up and die.

"Every board member, every investor, every politician in our pocket is going to be asking questions about why intimate footage of a Grimm family member is circulating on the internet." Alexander's voice gets sharper with each word.

That's it. I sit up straighter. "Maybe if your family didn't have so many politicians in their pocket, you wouldn't have to worry about explaining your personal lives to them."

Alexander pauses, then lets out a short laugh. "Fair point." He meets Leo's eyes, and I see his brows raise just slightly. Leo squeezes my hand, and I realize that I just earned at least a tiny bit of respect from Alexander Grimm. Interesting.

"As for this new text from Nash," Alexander continues, his tone turning serious again, "none of us has any idea what his next move will be. We need to assume he's planning something bigger than just releasing another tape." He looks hard at Leo. "I assume there are other tapes?"

Leo looks miserable, but all he says is, "I never do anything by halves."

"What should we do?" I ask, not sure if I'm trying to deflect Alexander's wrath away from Leo, or just get the topic off any subject that has a naked version of me at the center.

"Stay on guard. Be ready to go on the defensive, at least until we can figure out how to turn the tables and gain the upper hand." Alexander moves back to the bar, refilling his coffee. "The question is, what does he want?"

Leo once told me that Alexander has always been good at reading people, at seeing connections others miss. It's what makes him effective as the family's de facto head of strategy. I can see that analytical mind working now, processing possibilities and probabilities.

"You must have an idea," Leo says to his brother. "You always have an idea."

Alexander chuckles. "As a matter of fact, I do. I think he wants access to our father's private vaults."

Leo looks at me, then tilts his head.

"What?" Alexander asks.

"I just told Rue the same thing."

Alexander shrugs. "Well, it makes sense. Elias kept detailed records, and Nash was doing Elias's dirty work for twenty years. There's bound to be evidence that could destroy him."

"Including proof that he arranged my parents' death," I say quietly.

Both brothers look at me, and I can see the sympathy in their eyes. But there's something else there too—recognition that I'm not going to back down from this.

"That's what I want, too," I continue, my voice getting stronger. "Proof that he killed them. I want that bastard in prison for the rest of his life."

"We'll get it," Leo says, his voice fierce with promise.

"Why not just open the vault yourselves?" I ask. "Use what's in there to turn the tables on him?"

"Too risky," Alexander says. "He'll insist on being present to ensure he has every single damning document. And that means he'll insist on looking at everything in the vault."

"And that could be some really bad stuff," I say, understanding where he's going.

He nods. "What's in that vault is undoubtedly damning. For the company. Probably for all of us. The entire Grimm conglomerate."

I start to say that the Grimm family already has a rep of being brutal, but I hold my tongue. The rep is true, but it's only whispers. No one has ever brought forth any legitimate proof.

So, yeah. No way will Alexander agree to full disclosure. For that matter, I doubt Leo would, either.

"We need to be careful," Alexander warns, thinking aloud. "Nash isn't just some hired gun. He was Carson Nash—our father's right hand for decades. He's laid low for years. The man's patient and strategic, and he knows each of us intimately."

"How so?" I ask, curious for details.

"He was like an uncle," Alexander says. "He taught Leo how to fight, how to think strategically, how to compartmentalize emotion when making difficult decisions." He pauses, his pale eyes fixed on his brother. "He always took special interest in you. Mentored you. Knew about Ruby from the very beginning."

The implications hit me like a freight train. Nash didn't just know about our relationship—he watched it develop. Maybe even encouraged it, knowing he could use it against Leo later.

"He's someone who knows your history," Alexander continues, his voice carrying a warning. "Your weaknesses. Your psychology. Someone who was around seven years ago and has been watching you from a fake grave for years."

Leo's phone buzzes again. He glances at it, and when his face goes ashen, I lean over so I can see the screen.

Time's running out, Little Buddy. Tick tock. - N

"Him," I whisper.

"If Nash is targeting Ruby to get to you," Alexander says, "then you need to be very careful about your next moves. He knows you. He knows how you think. He knows—"

"He knows that I'll do anything to protect her," Leo finishes quietly. "Including giving up anything he wants to know about the family business."

"That's exactly what I'm worried about," Alexander says sharply.

Then he looks at me, really looks at me, and I see understanding dawn in his eyes.

"She's your weakness," he says to Leo, but his gaze never leaves my face.

"Yeah," Leo says. "I know."

He'd told me that already, of course, but I hadn't understood then the depth of what he was confessing. Now I look at Leo and see the truth written in every line of his body, every shadow in his green eyes. Alexander is right. Leo would burn down everything —his family, his empire, his own life—to keep me safe.

I should be flattered. Touched. Grateful.

Instead, I'm terrified.

Because if Nash knows Leo as well as they think he does, then he already knows exactly how to win this game.

And that means Leo's been right all along—I really am the prize Nash is playing for.

EIGHTEEN
COMPLICATED

"Don't you dare tell me this is for my own good!"

I'm pacing the living room like a caged animal, my bare feet silent on the hardwood as I rage at Leo, who's standing by the windows with his arms crossed and that infuriatingly calm expression on his face.

I'm convinced he had a personality transplant overnight, because there is no way the controlling bastard standing across from me is the same man who took my arm as we left Alexander's suite and promised that we were partners. That we were in this together.

The same man who looked me in the eye as we left Alexander's suite and said we'd get through this together, as equals.

The lying hypocrite who made me believe, for one stupid moment, that he actually understood what I needed.

"Ruby, come on. This isn't about us. It's about your safety. Hell, it's about your life."

"My life? Because from where I'm standing, it looks like you're the one making the decisions."

I gesture wildly at the suite around us, at the new security measures I discovered this morning when I woke up alone. Motion sensors in every room. Cameras that weren't there yesterday. And when I tried to leave for coffee and a bagel from the shop in the lobby—something Leo said I could do, something we agreed was normal—I found two of Liam's men stationed outside the door.

Two. Like I'm some kind of high-security prisoner.

"The situation's changed," Leo says, his voice maddeningly reasonable. "Nash escalated the threat."

"So you took it on yourself to escalate my prison sentence?"

"Protection, Red. Not Prison."

I flip him the finger. "Fuck you, Leo. You did all of this without asking me or even discussing it with me. You didn't give me even the tiniest say in how my own life gets to be lived!"

"Because you would have said no."

The casual admission makes me want to throw something. "Of course, I would have said no, you idiot. Because this is insane. This is you going full-on control freak because your brother pointed out that I'm your weakness. Nice to hear, but really not nice in the way you put that little factoid into practice."

"You are my weakness," he says, his voice heavy with meaning. "Alexander was right about that."

I sag a little, then dial back my own vitriol. "I get that. I do. But that doesn't mean you can just lock me away like some precious object that might get damaged."

"My goal is to keep you alive."

"At what cost? My sanity? My autonomy? My right to make decisions about my own life?"

His brows rise in the kind of *duh* expression that I'd expect if I'd asked him if Earth orbits the sun. "If that's what it takes," he says, "then hell, yes."

The honesty of it's like a slap to my face. At least he's not pretending anymore. At least he's admitting what he really is. A controlling bastard who is about to drive me utterly and completely insane.

I draw a breath, thinking about yesterday when we'd left

Alexander's apartment. About how he'd held my hand and whispered that we were stronger together.

And I think about the way he'd touched me last night. The way he'd pulled me close and promised that things would be different between us.

Then I think about how quickly he'd abandoned every single promise the moment his fear took over, turning me into a problem to be solved rather than a person to be consulted.

And *then* I think about how quickly he'd reverted to treating me like property the moment he understood I was Nash's weapon against him.

He takes my wrist and pulls me to his side. "What's best is for you to stay alive."

"Alive is good," I agree. "But it's my life. *Mine.* And I'm entitled to have a say in how that happens."

"Not when your life is at stake."

"Excuse me? I don't get a say in my own life?"

"Not when you're going to make the wrong choice."

I gape at him. "Are you kidding me? The wrong choice according to who? You? Because, hello? My. Life. Or did that little detail escape your notice?"

"According to who?" he repeats. "According to fucking reality, you little idiot. Dammit, Red, Nash is a professional killer. And according to *that*, you have no idea what you're up against."

"But you do?"

"Hell, yes, I do." Leo moves in even closer. So close I can practically feel the frustration radiating off him, and I can see the dangerous spark that flares in his eyes.

"I know exactly what Nash is capable of," he says. "I know how he thinks, how he operates, how he destroys the people he targets. And I know that if you try to fight him on your own, you'll die."

I want to throw my hands up and scream. Instead, I force myself to speak calmly and rationally. "I don't want to fight him on my own. I want to be with you. Partners, like we said."

"Partnership is a luxury I can't afford. Not when your life is at stake."

I sag, weary with this argument. Exhausted by trying to make him understand. "Don't you get it, Leo? You've decided I'm too weak to be trusted with my own life? But that's not something you get to decide. Not on your own."

Finally, my words seem to hit their target. I can see it in the way Leo goes very still, the way his hands clench into fists at his sides.

"If that's what it takes to keep you safe," he finally says, "then yes."

I sag, furious and disappointed all at the same time, because I thought we'd finally gotten somewhere. I thought he finally—truly—understood.

But he still doesn't, and all I can do is stand there feeling numb as a tangle of fury and disappointment curl inside me. Then I move toward him, my eyes wide as I try to stave off tears. "What happened to you? What happened to the man I thought I was learning to trust again?"

His expression is hard as he says, "That man was naive. That man doesn't understand what we're up against."

"That man loved me enough to trust me."

"That man loved you enough to get your parents killed. That's not a history he'll let repeat itself."

The conversation is spiraling into territory that's too dangerous, too raw. But I can't seem to stop myself from pushing, from trying to find some crack in his armor.

"And this man?" I ask, waving my arm to indicate his body. "What does this man want?"

Leo's eyes go dark. "To keep you alive. By any means necessary."

"Even if I hate you for it."

He meets my eyes. "Any means necessary."

"How romantic," I say, my voice dripping with sarcasm. "The great Leo Grimm, willing to be hated for love."

"Mock me all you want. It doesn't change anything."

"Doesn't it?" I move closer, close enough to smell his cologne, close enough to see the exhaustion in those emerald eyes. "Because right now, standing here looking at you, I can't decide if I want to hit you or kiss you."

Leo goes very still.

"I hate everything you've done to me," I say, clinging to the only weapon I have and knowing that I have to shatter him. His stupid pride. His ridiculous control.

"I hate everything you've taken from me, and I hate that you're enough of a bastard to believe you have the right to make choices about my life."

I take a step closer, staring at his stoic face. "I hate that you're probably right about Nash. About what would happen if I tried to leave."

"Ruby…" He trails off, a warning tone in his voice.

"Mostly, I hate that I still want you despite all of that."

His eyes widen slightly.

"I want you. I do. I want to hurt you the way you've hurt me. To make you feel powerless and trapped." I reach up to trace the line of his jaw, and he doesn't pull away.

"I want to take your control," I say, cupping my hand over his rock-hard cock. "I want to take you to the edge. To make you desperate."

His breath is quick. Shallow. I see the heat in his eye and smile sweetly. "And then I want to walk away. To leave you wanting and needing and knowing that you can't have what you want because I won't give it to you. Just like you've done to me. Just like you did when you turned your back on me seven years ago and walked away."

I can see the moment when my words hit home, when Leo realizes exactly what I'm proposing. Not reconciliation. Not forgiveness. Revenge.

For a moment, he does nothing. Hell, he's barely breathing.

Then he pulls me to him, his mouth claiming mine in a violent kiss that has my entire body melting and my cunt throbbing.

When we finally break, we're both breathing hard.

"Do it," he says quietly.

"What?"

"Take your revenge. Make me desperate. Show me what it feels like to be powerless."

The unexpected capitulation throws me off balance. "Why?"

"Because you need it. Because maybe I deserve it. Because this thing between us has to go somewhere, and right now this is the only place either of us can handle."

He's right. We're both too broken, too angry, too full of hurt and betrayal to manage anything healthy. But this—this game of power and control and revenge—this we can do.

"The bedroom," I say.

He cocks his head, questioning.

"If you want to give me control, then you give me all of it. We do this my way, on my terms, or not at all."

Leo nods slowly. "Your way."

I turn and walk toward the bedroom, not looking back to see if he follows. I can hear his footsteps behind me, can feel the weight of his attention like a physical touch.

In the bedroom, I turn to face him. "Take off your clothes."

Leo doesn't hesitate. He pulls off his sweater in one smooth motion, revealing the broad expanse of his chest, the lean muscles I've mapped with my hands and mouth. His jeans follow, along with everything else, until he's standing naked before me with an expression that's part defiance, part vulnerability.

"Now what?" he asks.

I move to the dresser and pull out several silk ties—the same ones he used on me when we were in college. When he made his goddamn tapes. The irony isn't lost on either of us.

"Now you get to find out what it feels like to be completely at someone else's mercy."

I can see Leo processing the implications of what I'm proposing. See him weighing the loss of control against whatever need is driving him to agree to this.

"Do you trust me?" I ask.

"Hell, no," he says immediately. "Not when you're angry."

"Good. Because I don't trust you either. But I want this anyway."

"Why?"

I drag my fingers through my hair. "I don't know. Maybe I need to know that I can break you the way you broke me."

He shoots one heated glance at me, then moves to the bed and lies down, his arms extended toward the headboard and his cock hard and huge.

"Break me," he says.

I force myself not to react. I move businesslike to secure his wrists to the headboard, taking my time, making sure the restraints are tight enough to hold him but not tight enough to cause real damage. When I'm satisfied, I step back to look at him.

Leo Grimm, dangerous billionaire, bound, helpless, hard, and completely at my mercy. The sight sends a surge of power through me that's almost intoxicating.

"How does it feel?" I ask. He doesn't answer, but it doesn't matter. His arousal is hard to miss.

I climb onto the bed, still fully dressed, then straddle his thighs, as I begin my slow exploration of his body. I trace patterns on his chest, kiss his neck, run my hands over his skin—everywhere except where he wants it most.

"Tell me about the security measures," I demand as I continue my torture.

"Motion sensors. Cameras. Guards," he gasps out, his breathing becoming labored as I work him over with deliberate slowness, my jeans-clad rear rubbing just a bit against his cock.

I can see his control fraying, see him getting desperate beneath my touch. It's intoxicating, this power I have over him. For the first time in days, I feel like I have agency.

"My life, my choices," I whisper against his lips after kissing him hard.

"Ruby…" He lets my name hang there, the rest of his words lost in passion.

"Say it."

The war plays out behind his eyes, but finally he whispers, "Your life, your choices."

Victory courses through me. I've broken through his defenses, made him admit what I needed to hear.

But then something shifts in his expression. Something dark and calculating that should warn me, but I'm too drunk on my temporary power to notice.

"You know what?" Leo says, his voice suddenly steady despite his position. "You're right."

"What?"

"You should have choices. You should have control." His eyes lock on mine, and there's something almost predatory in his gaze now. "So here's a choice for you, Red. You can untie me right now, and we can continue this game where you pretend to have power over me."

I frown, sensing a trap, but not understanding it.

"Or," he continues, his voice dropping to that dangerous register that always makes my pulse race, "you can leave me like this and find out what happens when I decide I've had enough of playing along."

"You're tied up," I point out, though something cold is starting to settle in my stomach. "You can't—"

With a movement so fluid it seems impossible, Leo pulls his hands free of the silk ties. The knots I thought were secure fall away like nothing, and suddenly he's sitting up, his hands free, his eyes burning with an intensity that makes me realize I've made a terrible miscalculation.

"How did you—"

But I don't finish the sentence because his hands are on my wrists now, holding me still.

"You think I'd give up control when Nash is hunting you?"

Everything has flipped so fast it makes my head spin. One moment I was in charge, the next I'm the one who's trapped, straddling him while he holds my wrists in an unbreakable grip.

"I let you think you were in control because you needed it. But Ruby? There's a difference between giving you what you need and actually being powerless."

"Let me go."

"No." The word is firm, final. "We're going to finish this. But we're going to finish it my way."

Before I can protest, he flips us, and suddenly I'm the one on my back with my wrists pinned above my head. The reversal is so complete, so overwhelming, that for a moment I can only stare up at him in shock.

"This is what real control looks like," he says, securing my wrists with the same ties I thought I'd used on him. "This is what it means when I say I'll do anything to protect you. Even from yourself."

"You bastard," I breathe, but there's no real anger in it. Just awe at how completely he's outmaneuvered me. And, yes, an insane level of heat and desire.

"Oh, I'm a bastard, all right. But you knew that when you started this game."

His hands are everywhere now, touching me with the same deliberate control I'd tried to use on him, but magnified. Every caress is calculated to drive me crazy, every kiss designed to remind me who's really in charge. And like magic, he has me out of my clothes, my legs spread, and my cunt wet and throbbing and needy.

"Tell me you understand," he demands as he brings me to the edge again and again without letting me fall.

"Understand what?"

"That this—" he enters me with one devastating thrust "—is how it works between us. You can fight me, you can hate me, you can try to break me. But at the end of the day, I'm the one who decides how this goes."

"Leo—"

"Say it." His pace is relentless now, driving me toward a climax I can't control, can't stop, can't do anything but accept. "Say you understand."

"I understand," I gasp, because what choice do I have? He's proven his point completely.

"Good girl." The praise sends heat rushing through me, and I want to slap his face even as I want his mouth hard on mine. "Now come for me, baby. Show me who you belong to."

My release crashes over me with a violence that leaves me shaking, and Leo follows immediately after, his own control finally snapping as he drives deep and stays there.

We collapse together, both breathing hard, both sweat-slicked and wrung out. But when he unties my wrists and pulls me against his chest, his embrace is gentle. Protective.

"I'm not sorry," he says. "And Red? Don't ever forget that you're mine."

I should be furious. I should feel manipulated, used, betrayed. Instead, what I feel is something closer to relief. Because as much as I want control, there's something deeply satisfying about belonging to a man who's strong enough to handle me when I'm falling apart.

"I still hate you," I whisper.

"I know," he says softly. "But you're mine anyway. And, Ruby? I'm yours, too."

I snuggle closer, my frustration ebbing away. Not disappearing entirely, because I know there'll be more fights over agency, my opinions, hell, even about what TV show to watch. But that's okay. It's even right. And for the moment, it doesn't matter. We're together. A team, even. And that feels pretty damn good.

"Leo?"

"Hmm?" his voice is soft. Sleepy.

"I— Nothing. Just, good night."

His arms wrap tighter around me. "I love you, too, Red."

I blink back tears. "You always could read my mind."

He chuckles, "Yeah, well—"

The sharp ping of his phone cuts him off. "Dammit. Sorry. Hang on." He fumbles around, finds his phone, then gasps. I sit up, clutching the sheet as if that can protect me from what's to come.

"What?" I whisper, seeing the dark fury blooming on his face. He passes me the phone. It's an image of me. And underneath, the words *Tick, tock.*

NINETEEN
SAFE HARBOR

Sasha and Liam's Connecticut home has everything I could possibly need—comfortable furniture, reliable communications, a well-stocked kitchen, and a beautiful guest suite that feels more like a luxury retreat than protective custody. Not to mention my best friend right here with me.

What it doesn't have is enough space for the restless energy that's been building in my chest since Leo and I decided that this was the best place for me to stay while he and his team doubled down on finding—and stopping—Nash.

The house is surrounded by acres of carefully monitored land, with Liam's security team maintaining a discreet but professional presence. Multiple layers of gates, cameras, and motion sensors create a perimeter that should keep Nash at bay without making me feel like I'm living in a fortress.

I should be basking in relief. Instead, all I feel is a kind of suffocating restlessness that makes me want to claw at the windows.

"You're pacing again," Sasha observes from the couch, where she's pretending to read while actually watching me have what might be a breakdown.

"I'm thinking."

"You're wearing a hole in Liam's very expensive carpet."

"You're married. It's your very expensive carpet, too."

"I know." She grins. "Isn't that just the coolest thing ever?"

I have to laugh, and I stop pacing long enough to really look at my best friend. She's so calm, so centered, like being inside this ridiculously secure property while dangerous people hunt her best friend is just another Tuesday.

Still, I can see the tension in her shoulders and the way she keeps glancing at her phone.

She's scared, too. She's just better at hiding it.

"How do you do it?" I ask, dropping to sit on the ottoman in front of her.

"Do what?"

"Act normal when everything's falling apart."

Sasha sets down her book and gives me her full attention. "Okay, Rue, what's really going on? Because you were finally in a good place with Leo, and now you look like you're ready to tear your own head off."

I abandon the ottoman for the opposite end of her couch, then hug one of the soft throw pillows to my chest. "I'm just twisted up, I guess. Leo's been calling every day, updating me on their progress—or lack thereof. Nash has vanished. No trace, no leads, nothing." I drag my fingers through my hair. "And I'm stuck here, safe and useless, while Leo puts himself in danger every day trying to track down a ghost."

"It's only been five days."

"Five days of nothing. Five days of Leo out there while Nash could be anywhere, planning anything." I lean forward. "What if Nash doesn't want to be found? What if he's just...waiting?"

Before Sasha can respond, Carter Thompson, Liam's head of security, appears in the doorway, his expression serious enough to cut through our conversation like a knife.

"Ladies, I need you to move to the secure room. Now."

My blood turns to ice. "What's wrong?"

"Security breach. No immediate danger, but we're not taking chances."

Another guard joins us with Granny, and we all follow Thompson through corridors I hadn't even known existed, my mind races. Nash. It has to be Nash.

The secure room is windowless, reinforced, and boasts its own air supply and communication equipment. The clinical efficiency should be reassuring. Instead, it feels like a tomb. Even with the exceptionally comfortable furniture. Courtesy of Sasha, I'm guessing.

"What kind of breach?" Sasha asks the moment the door seals.

As Granny takes a seat in the rocking chair, Thompson moves to a bank of monitors, his face grim. "We found surveillance equipment. Professional grade, hidden in the trees about a quarter mile from the gate. Been there at least forty-eight hours."

My heart stops. "Someone's been watching us."

"Someone's been watching *you*," he corrects, pulling up photos on one of the screens.

The photos are of me. Some are straight-on, as if taken from a distance by a very long lens. Others are from above. Drones, I realize, and shiver again.

The photos are like a chronology of my time here. Arriving at the compound. Walking through the gardens with Sasha. Sitting by the window with my coffee. And in each and every one, I'm completely unaware that someone is documenting my every move.

The last photo is the one that makes my blood freeze. Sasha, laughing at something I've said, totally unguarded and happy.

"He's watching," I whisper, which is a ridiculous understatement, but the only rational thought my mind seems able to conjure. "Nash. He's stalking me. And threatening everyone I care about most."

"It would certainly appear so." Thompson's expression grows even more serious. "Understand that he wanted us to find this.

The equipment was hidden well enough to avoid casual detection, but not well enough to avoid a professional sweep."

"Why? Just to add yet another layer of horrible creepiness?"

"It's a message," Thompson says. "He wants you to know he can reach you anywhere."

The words hit me like ice water. Nash isn't just hunting me—he's playing with me. Stripping away every illusion of safety. He wants me paranoid, desperate.

And it's working.

"Why? Why watch me? Why let me know?"

"Because of Leo." Sasha's answer is soft, but firm. "The more scared you are, the more Leo's focus will split."

I swallow. She's right. "And when he does kill me," I whisper, "it will destroy Leo even more."

I meet Sasha's tear-filled eyes. She nods.

"He's never going to stop," I say quietly, pacing the room because I have to move. Have to *do*. "This could go on for months. Years. Nash watching from the shadows while everyone I care about lives in fear."

"Ruby," Granny's voice cuts through my spiral. She's been sitting quietly in the rocker this entire time, watching me process this with the patient expression of someone who's seen this kind of crisis before. "Come here, Liebling."

I move to sit near her, and she reaches for my hand, the way she used to when I was a little girl. Her thumb strokes the back of my hand, warm and steady, and my racing pulse slows slightly.

"It's not going to end," I whisper. "Nash will keep escalating until he gets what he wants. And what he wants is Leo, devastated and useless. So he'll start with everyone I love, because hurting me will hurt Leo. And when there's no one left—and I'm completely shattered—he'll destroy me, too. That's what he wants. To destroy Leo by destroying me."

"And what do *you* want, Liebling?"

Granny's soft question stops me cold, and I sit up, forcing

myself to feel strong. To know—*really know*—that I can handle this.

I draw a breath, then let it out slowly. "I want this to end. I can't live this way. Neither can Leo. Neither can you," I say, looking from Granny to Sasha. I draw a deep breath, then look my grandmother straight in the eye. "I want Nash dead or locked in a windowless box for eternity. I want my life back. I want to stop being afraid."

"Then do it," Granny says. "Stop being afraid."

I cross my arms and cock my head, trying not to feel like I'm seven all over again and being scolded. "It's not that simple."

"Isn't it?" Granny's eyes are sharp, knowing. "What would Leo do if he were the one being hunted?"

I think about that. Leo wouldn't hide in safe rooms waiting for the threat to find him. He wouldn't let Nash dictate the terms of their confrontation.

"He'd take control of the situation," I say aloud.

"Hold on," Sasha says, her voice heavy with concern. "What are you thinking?"

"I'm thinking that maybe the only way to protect everyone is to stop letting Nash hunt me."

"You want to intentionally put yourself in danger?" Her voice rises with incredulity.

"I'm already in danger," I remind her. "I want to intentionally fight back. It's time I had some agency in my own protection."

The room goes quiet. Thompson and Sasha exchange glances, but Granny is nodding slowly, like this is exactly what she's been waiting for me to figure out.

"What would that look like?" Thompson asks carefully.

"I don't know yet. But I can't keep hiding while Nash terrorizes me and everyone I care about." I stand up, energy coursing through me. "I'm tired of being Nash's victim."

"You want to be Leo's true partner in this," Granny says quietly.

I roll my eyes. "I'm not trying to be Rambo. I just want a say in what happens to me."

"That's not what I meant." Her voice is gentle but knowing. "You and Leo—before I lost my son and your mother—do you think I don't remember? You were partners in every sense of the word. You made decisions together. You faced things together. You laughed together. You trusted each other completely."

Something twists in my chest at the memory.

"That was different," I say quietly.

"Was it? Or did you just forget what it felt like to be a team?"

I stare at her, and suddenly I can see it—the way Leo and I used to move together, think together, plan together. Maybe not about life and death things, but our dates, our weekends, our everything.

But that was before everything went wrong.

"You can be again," Granny says simply.

"What are you proposing?" Thompson asks, bringing us back to the immediate problem.

It's a good question. "Exactly? I don't know." I shrug. "But waiting for Nash to make his next move doesn't do us any good. I agreed to come here so that I'd be safe, but I'm never going to be safe. But what I can be is an asset."

I meet Granny's eyes, then see her very small nod as she realizes that I've figured it out.

I look from her to Thompson. "It's time we give Nash exactly what he thinks he wants. Me."

TWENTY
PARTNERSHIP

L eo stared at his phone for a full minute after Ruby hung up, trying to process what just happened. Ruby—his Ruby, who just a few days ago had been demanding answers while tears streamed down her face—had just calmly informed him that she was done hiding and wanted to get out there and hunt Nash.

More specifically, the woman he loved had just volunteered to use herself as bait to eliminate a professional killer.

Bait.

Every protective instinct Leo possessed was screaming at him to get in his car, drive to Liam's compound, and lock Ruby away somewhere Nash could never reach her. His hands actually shook with the need to act, to override her decision and handle Nash his way—with overwhelming force and zero risk to Ruby's safety.

But he'd promised he would trust her judgment, include her in decisions, treat her as his equal instead of his beautiful prisoner.

Clearly, he was a fucking idiot.

"Yo, bossman." Rover's voice crackled through the intercom. Leo's second in command at LG Security, Rover was also one of his best friends and most trusted employees. Technically, his name was Roger Thorp, but with the big puppy dog eyes that had women melting for him in college, the nickname had stuck.

And he'd been on the com when Ruby had dropped her bomb.

"Still here," Leo said.

"You gonna tell her she's out of her fucking mind?"

He heard the tension in Rover's voice. It wasn't every day an untrained woman volunteered to be bait. Add in the fact that the untrained woman was the one he craved—no, loved—and he was having a hell of a time formulating a damn response.

"Boss?"

"Give me a goddamn minute," he snapped, then immediately regretted it. This was a mission. Emotions really didn't have a place.

Which, of course, was a solid reason to keep her out.

He clenched his hands into fists, took a deep breath, and told himself that he could do this. That he was strong enough to keep his promise. And that he was good enough at his job to train her...and to keep her alive.

At the same time, his gut told him to screw the detente that he and Ruby had reached, then toss her back into a holding cell with a TV and every streaming service on the planet until this crisis was over.

His gut also told him that she'd have his balls for breakfast if he did that.

Sometimes you find your assets in the craziest of places, baby bro. And when you do, you need to trust them.

He blinked, fighting back tears as the memory washed over him—Gabriel taking him out on a job to nail a team of professional thieves they'd learned was planning a heist on a Grimm property in Oregon.

Leo's best friend at the time had been a college gymnast who'd recently won an Olympic gold. And he had exactly the skillset that they needed. Gabriel knew it. Leo knew it. But he hadn't wanted to risk his friend.

"Would you do it for him?" Gabe had asked. "Take a risk if he needed you?"

And that had made the decision. Because of course he would.

He did.

And Eric had not only been instrumental in stopping the heist, he'd been so damn fired up that he'd stayed on at Grimm Enterprises, becoming a key part of Grimm Enterprises' London operations.

"Fine," Leo muttered, wishing more than anything that Gabriel was still alive. The eldest of the brothers, Gabriel had been more like a father to Leo, the youngest. And Leo missed him dreadfully.

He'd always taken Gabe's advice. Why change now?

Especially since Ruby would kick him in the balls the next chance she got if he tried to keep her out.

He drew in a breath, then let it out slowly. No more locking her away. No more trying to control her every move.

It was scary as shit, but he was a Grimm. He ate fear for breakfast and made a yummy snack out of danger.

He'd hate it. He'd probably fuck it up a bit. But, dammit, he'd try.

And somehow, someway, he'd make sure she made it through this hell of a mission alive.

"We're changing our approach," Leo said into the radio. "She'll push the date back a bit to buy us more time, but Ruby's going to her meeting in Los Angeles. And I'm going with her."

"Whoa there, cowboy," Rover said. "Given the escalation in Nash's surveillance—"

"I know the score," he snapped, his voice sharp with fear. Because this was a huge risk. But Ruby was right. It could also reap one hell of a reward. "We're not running from Nash. We're forcing him to come to us."

There was a pause on the other end, and Leo could practically hear Rover recalibrating. "We're using her as bait."

Leo had to clench his hands in defense against that horrible truth. Horrible, but accurate. Like his Rue had said, this was the best way to nail the bastard.

"We're giving Nash what he thinks he wants. Which gives us what we need."

For a moment, there was just static on the radio. "Taking the fight to him," Rover finally said. "Setting the location. Controlling all the variables."

"Got it in one, buddy."

"I'll get things prepped," Rover said, then signed off.

Leo ended the call and turned back to the window of his Manhattan office, looking out at the city that had been his kingdom for so long. Somewhere out there, Nash was watching, waiting, planning his next psychological assault. Probably his next physical one, too. And somewhere else, Ruby was probably pacing Liam's compound, working through strategies and contingencies with the same focused intensity Leo recognized from his own planning sessions.

She was breaking his heart and rebuilding it at the same time.

The realization hit Leo like a physical blow. It seemed like only five minutes ago, he'd locked her up to keep her safe, not seeking her opinion about that plan or even asking for it. Today, she was a woman who'd made the choice to walk straight into danger. And even though he was starting to understand why she needed to do that, it still fucking terrified him. Christ, he ached to scoop her up and hide her away, keeping her locked up and safe.

But he'd already tried locking her away. He couldn't do that. Not anymore.

Not if he wanted to keep her. Not if she was going to truly be his.

He sighed, still trying to wrap his head around all that. He got it. He understood it. He just didn't *get* it.

Maybe he never would. Not really. But he was damn sure going to try.

He let out a small chuckle, realizing that Gabriel would have totally understood where Ruby was coming from. Hell, Gabriel could probably have found the words to knock that same way of thinking into Leo's thick skull.

After all, Gabriel had been the one who taught him that sometimes the people you love surprise you with their strength. That keeping them safe might mean letting them be dangerous.

Then again, Gabriel had been betrayed. Quite possibly because he trusted too much.

His phone buzzed with a text from Elliott: *Heard about Nash surveillance and Ruby. Can come back early from UK if you need me on security. Just say the word.*

Leo's fingers tightened on his phone. His brother's first instinct was the same as his had been—surround Ruby with enough security to stop a small army, make her so safe that Nash couldn't reach her.

But Nash had already proven he could reach her anywhere. He'd gotten surveillance photos of Liam's compound, one of the most secure facilities in the state. What made them think more traditional security would be any more effective?

Maybe the answer wasn't making Ruby more secure. Maybe the answer was making her more dangerous.

He tapped out a quick response—*Under control. But thanks.*

Then he called Ruby. "I've been thinking about what you said about not hiding away," he began.

"And?"

"And I think you're right. The answer isn't hiding. It's hunting."

He heard her soft intake of breath before she said, "I'm listening."

"Nash has been watching you for months. He thinks he knows your patterns, your weaknesses, your breaking points."

"So?"

"We use that against him. That, and more."

"What do you mean?"

"We let him think he's getting the Ruby he expects. A corporate warrior for a cosmetics company. But we'll give him a different kind of warrior."

For a moment, she was silent. When she spoke again, he could hear the interest in the single word—"How?"

Leo grinned despite the circumstances. His girl definitely had some cojones. "Easy," he said. "We teach Nash the difference between hunting a victim and hunting my partner."

There was a pause on Ruby's end, and when she spoke again, her voice carried a note of anticipation that sent heat straight through Leo's body. "What did you have in mind?"

"I think it's time Nash learned that threatening you doesn't make me weak. It makes me lethal."

"Flattering to hear you go all alpha, but I thought you said this was about me?"

He chuckled. "Oh, baby, it is. We train you. And you get to prove that being my partner means being just as dangerous as I am."

"Leo, I—" She cut herself off, her voice cracking with emotion. Not fear, he thought, but anticipation.

He waited, giving her time to think.

"I want to do this," she finally said, her voice barely a whisper. "I really do. But what does it mean that I'm terrified?"

"It means you're not an idiot. And if you want to walk away, I will take the fucker out without you, I swear."

"No," she said, the word seeming to burst out across the line. "I'm in. I'm with you."

"And I'm with you, Red," he said, thinking that right then, she was the bravest person he knew.

"So, um, how do we do this?"

"We go to Los Angeles, and we make sure that it's publicly known that you'll be heading that way soon for meetings at Lydia Cosmetics. But before we set foot on a plane, we get you ready. Then we bounce to LA and you do your job. And we make sure Nash knows exactly where to find you."

"Won't that put my co-workers at risk?"

"We'll tighten security at the Lydia Cos offices. Force him to make his move at my LA house."

"Or on the street," she said, and from the quiver in her voice, he knew she was thinking of her parents.

"We'll be careful," he said, his voice soft. "Are you okay?"

"More than," she said. "Really. But your house? Won't that be obvious to him?"

"I hope so. Title's buried under quite a few corporate names. He'll have worked it out, but he'll think I believe it's a safe place to hole up. He'll think he's choosing the battleground."

"He'll be wrong," she said.

"Exactly. Nash has been dictating the terms of this confrontation since day one. Time to change that."

"And if he takes the bait?"

"Then we eliminate him. Permanently."

For weeks, he'd been reactive, defensive, trying to protect Ruby from Nash's bullshit while waiting for the bastard to switch from taunts to action. But Nash had made one crucial mistake— he'd opened Ruby's eyes. And his own.

Now he was going to show Nash exactly what happened when someone threatened his woman. A woman he'd train to fight back.

TWENTY-ONE
BAIT

"**I**f we're really doing this," Leo says, a few days after our phone call about hunting Nash, "then you need to be properly prepared."

He's standing by the windows of his office, coffee in hand, looking out at the city while I review tactical plans. The LA trip is coming up fast, and I can feel the nervous energy radiating off him despite his controlled exterior.

"I thought we covered the basics already," I say, looking up from my laptop.

"The basics, yes. But if you're going to be bait for a professional killer—and I really hate saying that out loud—you need more than the basics."

"Fair enough. And I'm only bait. Remember that. I'm not going to end up as his catch."

Our eyes lock, and we share a small smile. Then he gives a quick nod and draws a breath, and I know he's coming to terms—again—with letting me do this.

"I just want to make sure you can handle yourself if something goes wrong."

"I'm all over that," I assure him. "Proceed to educate me."

He grins, and an hour later, we're in the firing range located in the basement of LG Security's Manhattan-based headquarters. The space is state-of-the-art—multiple lanes, different target distances, even tactical obstacles for training scenarios.

"You're pulling left," Leo says, moving to stand behind me. We've done this before, and the memory from college washes over me. A night of cuddling on the couch watching some action movie, and me teasing Leo, asking him if he thought I could be as badass as the sharp-shooting, ass-kicking heroine of the film.

He'd told me I could be anything I wanted to be, and I'd laughed. My ass-kicking skills stemmed from Gymboree when I was little, and the only pistol I'd ever held was filled with water.

He'd taken me to a range the next day, and over the course of a week, he'd not only taught me to shoot, but I'd gotten reasonably good at it. As for the kicking of asses, well, that was even more fun. Granted, I didn't have the ballet-like athleticism of the film's heroine, but my legs were strong, and he taught me how to use my legs, my feet, my elbows, and even my forehead to ward off an attacker.

The lessons had been fun, but the adrenaline rush had been extraordinary, and every hot and sweaty lesson had ended up with us back in the dorm, getting an entirely different kind of workout.

But those outings had been only for the thrill—and for the reward that came after when we were both high on the pretend danger. No one had been truly out to hurt us back then. Or, more accurately, we hadn't known about the danger lurking in the wings.

Now I know, and Leo and I are trying to turn my nascent skills into serious bad-assery.

I try to ignore that visceral memory as his chest presses against my back while he adjusts my grip on the pistol. "Feel that? Your dominant hand is doing all the work. Let your support hand carry some of the weight."

I make the adjustment, and immediately the gun feels more

balanced in my hands. More like an extension of my body instead of a foreign object I'm trying to control.

"Better," Leo murmurs against my ear. "Now breathe. In, out, and squeeze on the exhale."

I follow his instructions, focusing on the target twenty-five yards downrange. This time, when I fire, the shot hits closer to the center than any of my previous attempts.

"Nice," Leo says, and I can hear the genuine approval in his voice. "You always did have a knack. Now do it again."

We keep at it for well over an hour. This isn't about Leo teaching me the basics—not this time. This is about teaching me to be more than merely competent with a weapon. To understand ballistics and stance and breathing, to get comfortable with pulling the trigger, not to mention all the other things that separate who can shoot from someone who's truly dangerous.

"I'm thinking about what you said before we started training," I say as I reload the magazine with practiced movements. Leo's been making me do this part myself, and I'm getting faster at it. "About Nash studying the old versions of us."

"What about it?"

"He's been watching me for months, right? Cataloging my routines, my reactions, my weaknesses." I slide the magazine back into the grip with a satisfying click. "But he's never seen me do this."

"No, he hasn't." Leo's smile is sharp, predatory.

"And surveillance? Do you think he knows we're down here? That he suspects what we're doing?"

He shakes his head. "The subterranean entrance is relatively new. If he's watching my office, he'll have been looking in the wrong place. And I'm confident he hasn't tracked us from the Tower to here."

"Confident? Why?"

He grins. "That's what I do. Watch. Evaluate. And take action." He nods, silently indicating for me to fire again.

I raise the pistol, settling into the modified Weaver stance Leo taught me. This time, I fire three rounds in quick succession, all hitting within the eight ring.

"Beautiful," Leo says, and I can hear the pride in his voice. "You're a natural at this, Red. You have good instincts, steady hands, and the kind of focus that can't be taught."

"Is that your professional opinion?"

He moves behind me, his body pressed to mine as he bends over to kiss my hair. "That's my completely biased opinion of the woman I'm in love with, who also happens to be naturally gifted with firearms." He bends to whisper in my ear. "And yes, it's also my professional opinion."

I can't help but grin as he steps back and I pick up the pistol again, enjoying the weight of it in my hands. When we'd started this, it made me nervous. I'd been out of practice and unsure. A bit overwhelmed at the thought of carrying something deadly.

Now it's a tool. And I intend to put it to good use if Nash even so much as breathes on me.

"Teach me something else," I say.

"Like what?"

"Something tactical. Something useful if Nash gets too close." I meet his eyes steadily. "Because let's be honest, Leo. He knows we're going to LA. The entire freaking world knows."

We'd decided to make use of that hated video, and Leo had created a fake account, reposted the damn thing, and including the tidbit that I was heading to Los Angeles soon—along with speculation that maybe I was going out there not for Lydia Cos meetings, but to shoot a porn video.

I'd hated the idea of all that going viral again…but I also knew that it would work. No way would Nash miss that post.

"He's probably there right now," I say. "Probably setting his trap. I don't intend to get caught in it. But if I do, at least now I'll feel more confident about having a way out."

Something shifts in Leo's expression, something that looks like respect mixed with desire. And the tiniest hint of worry.

"All right. Let's work on shooting from unconventional positions."

Over the next few days, Leo teaches me to shoot accurately while kneeling, while prone, while using cover. He shows me how to clear a malfunction quickly, how to reload under pressure, how to assess multiple threats and prioritize targets.

It's challenging in a way that engages every part of my mind, requiring the kind of strategic thinking I use in my work, juggling meetings, advertising, placement, employees, and crises. This is just more deadly.

The really weird thing? I genuinely enjoy it, and each improvement—each new skill mastered—gives me a sweet little thrill.

"You're a quick study," Leo says as I successfully complete a drill that involves engaging three targets in rapid succession from behind a barricade. "Most people take weeks to get this comfortable with tactical shooting."

"Most people aren't about to use themselves as bait for their parents' killer."

"True." Leo's expression grows more serious. "Ruby, I want you to know that I'm not teaching you this because I expect you to need it. I'm teaching you because you need the tools to protect yourself. But if you never have to pull your weapon, all the better."

"I know that."

"Do you?"

Something in his tone makes me set the pistol down and turn to face him fully. "What do you think this is about for me?"

"Revenge, mostly," he says with a casual shrug. "For your parents. And for now. Nash hunting you. Us."

"All true," I say. "But mostly it's about you treating me like someone who can handle the truth about your world instead of someone who needs to be protected from it. It's about you trusting me enough to teach me skills that might save my life someday, instead of just hoping I'll never need them."

Leo covers my hand with his own, leaning into my touch. "Is that what you want? To be my partner in this world?"

"I want to be your partner in every world," I admit. "I've wanted that since college. We took one hell of a detour, but, Leo, it's only ever been you."

"I know," he says.

I move closer, until there's no space left between us. "I don't want to be the woman you have to worry about. I want to be the woman who can take care of herself so you can focus on what needs to be done."

Leo's eyes darken with something that might be pride, but could also be desire. "I love you," he says, and I slide in for a long, slow kiss. Followed, of course, by another hour of working on tactical scenarios, despite the fact that his kiss had me thinking of very different kinds of tactics.

Still, I can't deny that I get off on the thrill of shooting while moving, engaging multiple targets, and learning to use cover effectively. By the end of it, I'm exhausted but exhilarated. For the first time since we started planning this insane mission, I'm confident that I can hold my own if something goes wrong.

"How do you feel?" Leo asks as we pack up the gear.

"Dangerous," I say, and mean it.

His smile is fierce. Proud. "Good."

As we head out, I catch sight of myself in the mirror that runs along one wall of the range. I look different than I did on the day we started this training. More confident, more grounded.

I look like a woman who could face down her parents' killer and walk away.

The girl in the mirror, I think, looks fierce. And she looks like me.

TWENTY-TWO
CITY OF ANGELS

The private jet's cabin feels cramped despite its luxury. I try to focus on the documents spread across my laptop and tablet and the otherwise empty seat between Leo and me. I try to enjoy the beauty of the sprawling lights of middle America below us.

I can't.

My mind keeps racing back to what we're flying toward.

A trap. One we've set ourselves, but still a trap.

Leo's been watching me for the past hour, the tension so thick I can practically taste it in the recycled air. Every time I glance up, those green eyes are studying me like he's memorizing every detail, like he's afraid this might be the last time he sees me whole and safe.

"You're staring," I say without looking up from my notes.

"I'm monitoring the situation."

"The situation being my ability to read marketing reports?"

"The situation being that we're essentially painting a target on your back." His voice is rough, strained. There's something wild in his eyes that I've never seen before—not anger, not his usual controlled intensity, but genuine fear.

"I want to turn around," he says, practically growling the

words. "I want to lock you up someplace safe. Not parade you around Los Angeles where that prick of a bastard can snatch you out of a crowd."

I draw in a breath, not much liking that scenario, either. "You can open the vault. Give him what he wants."

Thirty-six hours ago, the Grimm brothers had announced to the press that their father was not only in a coma—a fact they'd so far withheld—but also the lie that Elias Grimm had taken a turn for the worse, and that his medical team expected that he had only a week to ten days left. To most of the world, the announcement was simply news about a famous billionaire.

To Nash it would mean that details of his many, many crimes at the behest of Elias Grimm would be revealed when that vault was opened upon death by Elias's attorney. And that's when hard copies of documentation detailing every one of Nash's crimes would be revealed, including killing my parents, a death that—in the grand scheme of Nash's portfolio—pretty much ranks as crossing a street against the light.

In other words, once that vault is opened, Nash is screwed. Elias Grimm was no fool, and that vault was his protection against a dangerous man turning on him

"Nash is going to try to grab you. He's going to try to force my hand by taking you. I agree to give him the contents, and I get you back. Otherwise—"

"Otherwise, he'll torture me. I know. We've talked about this eight billion times."

"He'll torture you," Leo repeats, "and he'll make sure I know it."

"Leo…" I can see how much this is costing him. This choice not to lock me away but to let me step up. I start to speak, but he puts a finger to my lips, something flickering across his face. Heat, possession, and something darker. Something that looks like fear.

"Come here." The command in his voice sends electricity down my spine, but there's a tremor in it that tells me he's not as controlled as he wants me to believe.

I set aside my electronics, then empty the middle seat of papers so that I can comply. As I do, I can't help but notice how his hands clench and unclench on his thighs. And the moment I'm within reach, those hands frame my face, his thumbs brushing across my cheekbones with barely restrained desperation.

"I can't lose you," he murmurs, and there's something raw in his voice that makes my chest tight. "Ruby, I can't—if something happens to you because of my choices, because I dragged you into this—"

"You didn't drag me anywhere." I thread my fingers through his dark hair. "I chose this. I chose you."

His brows rise, and I see the hint of a smile, probably from the steel in my voice.

"And you won't lose me. You've trained me, remember? You trusted me enough not to toss me into a locked room to keep me safe. Instead, you taught me skills, and you did a good job. You made me strong and capable. And, yeah, I'm scared, but I'd be stupid not to be. You gave me that, too. A way to get past fear. To use it, even. To turn it all around into power."

"Ruby." My name sounds like a prayer on his lips before he kisses me, desperate and claiming. There's nothing gentle about it —just need and fear and the terrible knowledge that this LA trip might change everything.

I can taste his desperation. Can feel the way his control is fraying at the edges. When I pull back, his breathing is ragged. "Leo, I need to tell you something."

"What?"

"I'm not afraid anymore." The admission surprises even me with its truth. "Not of Nash, not of dying, not of having the people I love ripped away from me. And not of what we're walking into. Do you know what that feels like? To not be afraid?"

His hands tighten on my face, and I look deep into his eyes.

"It feels like power." I slide my hands down his chest, feeling his heart hammering beneath my palms. "You gave me that."

Leo's control cracks, just for a moment, and I see something wild and possessive flash in his eyes. "You're going to drive me insane."

"Good." I nip at his jaw, feeling him shudder. "I like you a little unhinged. A little desperate."

"Ruby." There's a warning in his voice, but also hunger. Raw, desperate hunger.

"What? Scared you can't handle me now?" I tease.

The words hit their mark, and I see the spark of amusement—and heat—flare in his eyes as his hands slide into my hair, gripping tight enough to make me gasp. "The only thing I'm scared of is losing you."

I see the truth in his eyes. The darkness. The fear. "You're trying to figure out how to lock me up somewhere safe."

His jaw clenches. "And if I am?"

"Then you're an idiot." I shift closer, pressing my body against his. "Because the woman you fell in love with in college? She would have let you. She would have hidden and let you fight her battles. But that woman is gone, Leo. I killed her."

Something shifts in his expression—surprise, heat, and something that looks like awe.

I slide my hand between us to cup his cock. "The woman sitting beside you now? The woman you're going to fuck tonight, and who's going to stand beside you tomorrow and watch Nash burn? Right now, she's going to take what she wants."

"And what does she want?" His voice is barely a whisper.

"You. All of you. Every desperate, possessive, dangerous part of you." I lean in until our lips are almost touching. "I want you to fuck me like you're afraid you'll never get the chance again. Because maybe you won't."

The words unlock something primal in both of us. Leo's control doesn't just crack—it shatters completely. He lifts me, carrying me toward the back of the plane where the bedroom waits behind a closed door, his mouth already working at my throat.

"You don't know what you're asking for," he growls against my skin.

"I'm asking for everything." I bite down on his shoulder, hard enough to leave marks.

He kicks the bedroom door shut behind us and sets me down on the bed, his hands already working at the buttons of my blouse with shaking fingers. But I catch his wrists, stilling his movements.

"Let me," I whisper, and begin unbuttoning my own shirt with deliberate slowness, watching the way his eyes darken as each inch of skin is revealed. "I want you to watch."

Leo's breathing turns ragged as I let the silk fall to the floor, as I reach behind to unclasp my bra and let it join the growing pile of fabric. When I hook my thumbs in the waistband of my skirt, his hands clench into fists.

"Ruby." My name is a broken plea.

I look up at him. "Tell me you want me."

Instead of answering, he closes the distance between us, his mouth crashing down on mine while his hands roam my body with desperate hunger. But I push him back, my palms flat against his chest.

"My turn." I begin working at his shirt buttons, my movements just as deliberate as before. "Seven years, Leo. For all of those seven empty years I thought about this. About having you at my mercy."

"You've always had me at your mercy," he whispers, but his hands are gripping my hips like he's afraid I'll disappear.

"Have I?" I push his shirt off his shoulders, my nails raking down his chest. "Then prove it. Show me how much you need me."

Something wild flashes in his eyes. Before I can react, he's pulling me up, then pressing me back against the wall beside the bed. His body cages me in, all heat and hard muscle and barely leashed power that rivals the thrum of the engine that runs through the jet.

His mouth crashes down on mine, all teeth and tongue and desperate claiming. There's nothing gentle about the way he kisses me—it's possession, pure and simple. His hands are everywhere, mapping my body like he's trying to memorize every curve, every sensitive spot that makes me gasp.

When his fingers find the edge of my panties, I catch his wrist again.

"Not yet." My voice is breathier than I'd like, but I'm not giving up control. Not when I've just claimed it. "I want to hear you say it first."

"Say what?"

"That you need me. That you're terrified of losing me. That you've been going insane thinking about what might go down in LA."

For a moment, I think he won't answer. Then his forehead drops to mine, and when he speaks, his voice is raw with honesty.

"I'm fucking terrified," he admits. "I've never been more scared of anything in my life than I am of losing you because of this op. The thought of Nash putting his hands on you, of him hurting you..." His hands shake as they frame my face. "It makes me want to burn the world down."

"And?"

"And I need you so much it's killing me. I need to be inside you, to feel you alive and whole and mine. I need to mark every inch of your skin so that even if—" His voice breaks. "So that even if something happens, you'll know you belong to me. That I love you."

The rawness in his voice, the genuine fear, breaks something open in my chest. This is what I wanted—not just his desire, but his vulnerability. His complete surrender to what's between us.

"Then take me," I whisper against his lips. "All of me. Everything."

This time, there's nothing controlled about his touch. It feels like his mouth and hands are everywhere at once, and I shimmy desperately out of my skirt. As soon as I've kicked it aside, he hooks his fingers in my panties and tears them away, and I thrill at the violence of it.

"Mine," he growls against my throat. "Every fucking inch of you is mine."

"Prove it." The challenge in my voice makes him look up, and what I see in his eyes makes my breath catch. It's not just desire—it's desperation. Love so intense it borders on obsession.

"Ruby." He says my name as a promise as his mouth begins its descent down my body, marking a path with his teeth and tongue that leaves me trembling. When he reaches the apex of my thighs, he looks up at me one more time. "You're sure about this? Because once I start, I'm not stopping. I'm going to take everything."

Instead of answering with words, I thread my fingers through his hair and guide him where I want him. The first touch of his mouth against my core makes me arch off the bed, his name a broken cry on my lips.

"That's it," he murmurs against me. "Let me hear you. Let me know how good I make you feel."

He works me with his mouth and fingers until I'm sobbing his name, until I'm so close to the edge I can barely breathe. But just when I'm about to break apart, he pulls away, moving up my body to claim my mouth again.

"Not yet," he breathes against my lips. "When you come, I want to be inside you. I want to feel you fall apart around me."

He reaches for his belt, and I watch through heavy-lidded eyes as he strips away the last barriers between us. When he settles between my thighs, the weight of him, the heat, makes me feel small and protected and claimed all at once.

"Look at me," he commands, and when I meet his eyes, there's something fierce and possessive there that makes my heart race. "I love you. Whatever happens in LA, whatever comes after—I love you."

"I love you, too." The words come out broken, desperate. "Leo, please—"

When he enters me, it's with a groan that sounds torn from his chest. For a moment we're both still, overwhelmed by the knowledge that this might be our last time.

Then he begins to move, desperate. Wild. A claiming that borders on violence. Each thrust is accompanied by broken words—promises, threats, declarations of love and possession that make my blood sing.

"Mine," he growls against my throat. "Say it. Say you're mine."

"Yours," I gasp, meeting him thrust for thrust, my nails raking down his back hard enough to leave marks. "But Leo—you're mine too. Say it."

"Yours. Completely fucking yours."

The admission breaks something loose in both of us. Leo's movements become more desperate, more claiming, and I can feel myself spiraling toward an edge.

"Ruby, I need—" His voice breaks, and something wild flashes in his eyes. His hand slides between us, finding that perfect spot that makes me cry out, while his mouth claims mine in a kiss that's more battle than caress.

"Come for me," he commands against my lips. "Let me feel you break apart."

When the orgasm hits, it's with an intensity that steals my breath, my vision, my sanity. I scream his name, my body arching as wave after wave of sensation crashes over me. He follows a heartbeat later, my name a broken prayer on his lips as he buries himself deep and holds me like I'm the only thing keeping him anchored to this world.

We lie tangled together afterward, skin cooling in the climate-controlled air, both of us trembling with the aftershocks of what just happened. Leo's fingers trace lazy patterns on my back while I listen to his heartbeat, hearing the gradual return of his control.

And that's when I feel it. That knowing, that certainty that something has shifted between us. Something fundamental and irreversible, and very important.

I snuggle close, tracing the marks my nails left on his chest, feeling a dark satisfaction at the evidence of my claim on him. "Leo, whatever happens tomorrow—"

"We're going to survive this." His voice is fierce, certain, but I can hear the edge of fear underneath. "Both of us. And then we're going to have the rest of our lives to figure out what comes next."

"And if we don't?"

"We will."

I want to believe him. I choose to believe him. But more than that, I believe in myself—in the woman I've become, in my power to shape what comes next.

When we emerge from the bedroom an hour later, hair mussed and skin still flushed, the plane is beginning its descent into Los Angeles. I can feel the shift in Leo's demeanor as he transforms back into the dangerous man who's spent years in the shadows.

But now I'm not just his mission. I'm his partner. His equal.

And we're going to end this once and for all.

TWENTY-THREE
BUSINESS AS USUAL

I wake to the sound of waves crashing against the cliffs below and Leo's arm heavy across my waist, his skin still warm from sleep. For a moment, I let myself drift in that perfect space between dreams and consciousness, where the intensity of everything that's happened feels like it's rewriting my DNA.

Then reality seeps in with the morning light, and I remember exactly why we're here.

I'm bait.

Today, I walk into the world as Ruby Ryder, corporate VP—while actually serving as a lure for the man who murdered my parents.

The thought should terrify me. Three weeks ago, it would have sent me into a panic spiral. But snuggled here beside Leo as I watch the Pacific stretch endlessly beyond the glass walls of his Malibu fortress, I realize it's not fear I feel. Not even close. Instead, it's anticipation mixed with power.

And I like the way it tastes.

"Hey, there," Leo murmurs against my shoulder, his voice rough with sleep but already edged with a now-familiar tension. I can feel it in the way his fingers flex against my ribs, the barely perceptible tightening of his muscles as consciousness brings back the reality of what we're facing.

"Morning." I shift to see him better, studying the way the light catches the sharp angles of his face. Even sliding out of sleep, he looks and feels dangerous. There's something predatory about the way he holds me—possessive, protective, ready to destroy anything that threatens what's his.

"Sleep okay?" His thumb traces my cheekbone with a gentleness that contrasts sharply with the intensity burning in his eyes.

"Better than I should have, considering." I glance toward the massive windows where the infinity pool seems to blend seamlessly with the ocean beyond. "This place is incredible."

"Secure, too. Motion sensors, thermal imaging, pressure plates on every approach." Leo's voice is matter-of-fact. He lives in a world where that stuff is normal. And now, I live in that world, too.

He strokes my arm, his touch both soothing and electrifying. "Nash might make his move today," he says, relaying what I already know.

"Or it might be tomorrow or not until next month. I know, Leo. I'm right there with you." I start toward the shower, but Leo's hand catches my wrist, pulling me back against him. "Right there with me? Then where are you going?"

I laugh, but struggle to get away. "Work. Job. Bait. Ringing any bells?"

"Lots," he says, his voice rough with something that goes beyond desire. "Come here."

"You're trying to get one more in because you think it might be our last," I tease, even as I let him pull me back into his arms, even as my body responds immediately to his touch.

His mouth crashes against mine, hard and desperate, swallowing whatever smart comment I was about to make. When he pulls back, his eyes are fierce.

"Never think like that," he says, his voice hard as steel. "*Never.*

We're going to get through this, and we're going to have thousands of mornings just like this one."

The conviction in his voice, the raw need in his kiss, strips away any pretense of casual teasing. This isn't about sex. This is about claiming, about anchoring ourselves to each other before I walk into potential danger.

With incredible speed, he moves us, so that he's over me on the bed, then inside me with that perfect stretch that makes me gasp as he fucks me with the desperation of a man who's terrified of losing what matters most. It's empowering and humbling, and when I arch beneath him—when I meet his intensity with my own —it's with the fierce joy of a woman who knows she's becoming who she was meant to be, and who's with the man who owns her Just like she owns him right back.

Afterward, as we lie tangled together, both breathing hard, Leo's phone buzzes with a text from someone named Davis: *Car ready when you are. Route cleared and secured.*

"Davis?" I ask, reading over his shoulder.

"Your driver today. And security, obviously."

"Right. Because duh." I laugh, shaking my head at my own question. Of course, Leo wouldn't send me out with just any driver.

An hour later, I'm dressed in professional armor—a sleek charcoal suit that makes me feel competent and untouchable—while Leo paces the living room like a predator stalking the perimeter of his territory. The contrast is stark—me preparing to play the role of a harmless businesswoman while he radiates barely contained violence in dark jeans and a black Henley.

"Davis and his team will monitor the exterior of the Lydia Cos building," he says, checking his phone for the third time. "I'll have eyes on the building's security feeds, as will Davis. Every camera angle, every access point."

"I know the plan, Leo."

"And you'll check in—"

"Between every meeting. And at regular intervals." I walk

over to him, smoothing my hands over his chest, feeling the tension thrumming beneath his skin like a live wire. "I'm going to be fine."

"You're walking into the lion's den."

"I'm walking into Century City to discuss quarterly projections and ad campaigns." I meet his eyes, letting him see my complete confidence. "This is what we planned. And it's a good plan."

But even as I say it, I can feel the shift in my body—the hyper-awareness that comes with knowing I'm about to step outside the protective bubble of Leo's security. I'm up for this, I tell myself. I believe myself, too.

I only hope my confidence is justified.

The drive to Century City takes forty minutes in LA traffic. The entire time, Davis stays professional and alert behind the wheel while I try to review notes in the back seat. But my mind keeps wandering, not to last night, but to the strange dissonance I'm about to experience. How do you sit in a conference room discussing marketing when every nerve in your body is primed for violence? Not to mention when half the world's seen you naked in a sex tape?

I've spent weeks learning to shoot, to fight, to think tactically. To clear my mind and focus not on my own emotions, but on danger and threats. Now I'm supposed to flip a switch and care about conversion rates and brand positioning? The thought makes me restless in a way I don't entirely understand.

My phone buzzes.

How are you feeling?

Like I want to get this over with.

Patience. Nash will make his move when he thinks he has the advantage.

And if he doesn't? What if we're wrong about all of this?

The three dots appear and disappear several times before his response comes through: *Then we adapt. But trust me, Ruby. He's coming.*

The LA offices of Lydia Cosmetics are located in the Century Blade Building, a gleaming tower of steel and glass, the kind of place where billion-dollar deals happen over artisanal coffee and mineral water. "Any trouble, you hit the panic button," Davis reminds me, referring to the little device tucked in at my waistline. "The team will be positioned so we can see all the exits, and Leo and I are tapped into the building's security cams. We'll be watching you and keeping an eye out for Nash."

I nod. I'll be keeping an eye out, too. Leo shared a photo of Nash a few days ago, and I've memorized it, along with a few computer-rendered images of him with his appearance adjusted through wigs, facial hair, and theatrical make-up.

Basically, I'm as ready as I'll ever be.

The first meeting is surreal in its normalcy. I sit in a conference room on the thirty-second floor with Lydia Cosmetics' West Coast distribution team, discussing the holiday campaign rollout while part of my brain maps escape routes and calculates how long it would take security to respond to a threat.

"Ruby, the numbers on the new foundation line are incredible," says Janet Dane, our regional manager. "We're looking at a forty percent increase in shelf space at major retailers."

I smile and nod, diving into the data with expertise that feels automatic now. But there's a strange disconnect happening—like I'm watching myself perform the role of Ruby Ryder, VP of Marketing, while the real me hovers somewhere above, alert and predatory and waiting for something to happen.

My phone buzzes. Leo: *Status?*

Discussing color matching algorithms. Riveting stuff.

Smart-ass. Any unusual activity?

Just executives excited about profit margins.

I can practically feel his tension through the phone, the way he's monitoring security feeds and fighting every protective instinct he possesses.

The meeting drags on, numbers and projections that should capture my full attention sliding off my consciousness like water. I catch myself checking the time obsessively, not because I'm bored, but because I'm waiting. Every footstep in the hallway makes my pulse spike. Every unexpected sound has me calculating distances to exits.

But it's not fear driving this hypervigilance. It's anticipation mixed with something that feels dangerously close to hunger.

And since that's something I don't want to examine too closely, I'm glad when we shift conference rooms for yet another meeting. This one about supplier negotiations that require my complete focus, but somehow feels like background noise to the constant awareness thrumming under my skin.

We're discussing packaging costs for the spring launch while I monitor every person who enters or exits the conference room, every shadow that passes by the glass walls.

"Ruby?" The voice of our packaging vendor pulls me back to the conversation. "Thoughts on the sustainable materials proposal?"

"Sorry, just making strategic notes." I focus back on the presentation, but the restlessness is growing stronger. I want Nash to make his move. It terrifies me, yes. But I want this waiting to end so I can stop pretending to care about biodegradable compacts when what I really want is to face the man who destroyed my family.

During lunch, I escape to the bathroom and call Leo, needing to hear his voice, to ground myself in the reality of what we're doing.

"How are you holding up?"

"I feel like I'm living in two different worlds at once," I admit, lowering my voice even though I'm alone. "Everyone's talking about market penetration and I'm thinking about actual penetration."

"Sex?" Amusement rolls off his voice.

I roll my eyes. "No, dummy. As in, how Nash might try to breach building security."

Leo's laugh is short and tight. "That's good. That kind of thinking's what keeps you safe."

"What if we got this wrong? What if Nash isn't even in LA? What if he's in New York orchestrating some completely different plan while I'm sitting here pretending to care about quarterly projections?"

"Then we adapt. But my sources say he's here."

"Tell me."

"No details. Just word from a few rats that he made a trip to LA yesterday evening. There's no guarantee, of course, but my gut tells me this is the right play."

"I'm tired of waiting. I want him to make his move so we can end this." The words are true, but truth is a strange thing. Bendable. Stretchable. A year ago, those words would never have left my lips. I'd have wanted to hide under the covers, wallowing in my fear. Now…

Well, now I don't want to be a victim. More than that, I want to be proactive. And it's driving me nuts that this is such a waiting game.

"I know," Leo says when I tell him that. "But patience is part of that game. He'll come when he thinks he has the advantage."

"And if that's never?"

"It won't be. Trust me."

The afternoon sessions blur together, and I feel like I'm wearing a costume that no longer fits, playing a role that belongs to someone I used to be.

I love working for Lydia Cosmetics, and before, I loved working with Sasha at the now-defunct Reed Cosmetics. The work had energized me. The problem solving and dealing with strategy.

But that's what Leo does, too. And with much higher stakes. And now, knowing that somewhere in this city a killer might be planning my capture, I can't deny that my old life feels diminished somehow. Like I've been living in black and white and only just discovered color.

The woman who used to find complete satisfaction in demographic analysis doesn't exist anymore. The woman sitting in this conference room, hyperaware of every sound and shadow, thinking tactically while discussing lipstick sales—she's someone new. Someone who belongs beside Leo, matching his intensity, becoming dangerous.

My phone buzzes with another text from Leo:

Everything okay? You're two minutes late for check-in.

All good. Just finished with the sustainability presentation.

Any problems?

Only that I keep hoping Nash will try something so we can get this over with.

Careful what you wish for.

But that's the thing—I'm not wishing carelessly. I want this confrontation because I'm finally ready for it. The old Ruby—the one Nash thinks he knows—doesn't exist anymore.

By four-thirty, I'm exhausted from maintaining dual mental tracks, but it's a good exhaustion. The kind that comes from discovering you can function in multiple realities simultaneously, even if one of those realities feels increasingly foreign.

"This has been incredibly productive," Janet says as we prepare to go into the final session. "When can we expect your full analysis of the West Coast expansion?"

"End of the week," I promise. We're walking toward the large conference room when Patricia Morrison from accounting steps directly into my path.

"Ruby." Her voice is clipped, disapproving. "I'm frankly astounded that Sasha didn't terminate you immediately."

My steps falter. "Excuse me?"

"That video." Patricia's mouth purses like she's tasted something sour. "Absolutely disgraceful. Vulgar. Everything Lydia Cosmetics stands against. We've built this brand on female empowerment, on dignity, on—"

"On a woman's right to make her own choices," I interrupt,

my voice steady despite the way my stomach has dropped to my shoes.

"And yet our company hashtag is trending alongside your… performance." She practically spits the word. "Do you have any idea what this does to our reputation? What it says about our values?"

For a moment, I feel exactly like I did seven years ago when Leo left that damn note—small, ashamed, wanting to disappear. The old Ruby would have apologized, would have slunk away to hide in her office.

But I'm not that woman anymore.

I straighten my shoulders and meet Patricia's judgmental gaze head-on. "You know what, Pat? You're right. About one thing, anyway. Lydia Cosmetics *is* built on female empowerment. On the radical idea that women get to decide what's right for their bodies, their own lives, their own relationships."

A small crowd has gathered, other employees slowing their steps to listen.

"That video was made seven years ago, in private, between two consenting adults who loved each other." I don't mention that I hadn't given consent to the video. That's *really* not the point. "We were in our own space, and I was with the man I loved, then and now, and what we chose to do there was our business. No one else's. I'm not the one who did anything wrong. That would be the asshole who stole the tape and released it. And you, too, Pat, for thinking that sex is shameful. It's not. The shame goes on the person who violated our privacy."

Patricia's face flushes. "But the company's image—"

"The company's image should be about supporting women. All women. Even women who have sex. Even women who enjoy sex. Even women who—shocking thought—might actually be proud that the man they love finds them desirable enough to want to capture those moments."

Someone in the crowd—I think it's Elizabeth from Legal—lets out a quiet, "Yes."

"I'm not ashamed of that night," I continue, my voice ringing clear down the hallway. "I'm not ashamed of loving Leo Grimm, or of him loving me. The only thing I regret is that someone violated our privacy by releasing something intimate and beautiful, and that I have to stand here defending myself to people who think sex is some terrible secret.

"It's not," I say, looking around at the faces watching me. "It's part of being human. It's part of being alive. And I refuse to be ashamed of being fully, completely alive."

The hallway erupts in applause. Janet is clapping openly, and even some of the younger guys from Digital are nodding approvingly. Patricia looks like she's swallowed a lemon, but she steps aside as I walk past her, my head held high.

"Meeting in five," I call over my shoulder, and the crowd disperses, several people giving me encouraging smiles as they pass.

Janet's grinning as we head to the final meeting—quarterly projections—which has a different vibe today, with everyone seeming more attuned to what's usually dull. I bite back a laugh, wondering if I should shout, "You're welcome," to the audience.

I don't, but I like the fantasy of it. And I'm still on a bit of a high for having said my piece. It felt really, fucking good.

My phone buzzes, and I look down to see a text from Leo. *You're incredible.*

My cheeks go pink and I realize that somebody must have taped my impromptu speech. I have a feeling it's going viral, too.

I reply with a quick heart emoji, then force myself to focus on the projections.

Half an hour later, I'm finally in the elevator, having said my goodbyes and accepted more than a few *atta-girls* from co-workers who now feel more like fans.

I can't help but smile. Then, when I see the text from Marcus, I can't help but frown. I'd basically blown the poor guy off, and now there's a sex tape out there to rub in his face.

Not a great image, but...

With a bit of trepidation, I open the message, and my heart twists as I read it.

Just saw the video of your hallway speech. Ruby, that was absolutely brilliant. I'm sorry someone violated your privacy like that, but your response? Pure class and courage. I'm glad you found him again. Really glad. Your friend always, Marcus.

I smile, then tap back a message. *Thanks. You're truly one of the good ones.*

Then I hit send, feeling, somehow like everything is as it's supposed to be.

That feeling, of course, lasts only until I reach the lobby and find Davis waiting there, a reminder that everything is *not* as it's supposed to be. And it won't be until Nash makes his move.

"How'd it go?" he asks as we walk toward the parking garage.

I shrug, biting back a smile. "Just another day at the office." I draw in a breath. "Is it horrible that I almost wish Nash had leaped out from around a corner?"

"The waiting's always the hardest part," Davis says. "But it won't last forever."

As we drive back to Malibu, I watch the Los Angeles sprawl give way to winding coastal roads and try to process the strange day I've had. The relief that nothing happened is real, but so is the frustration. I'm ready for this confrontation. I want to face Nash and prove to him—and to myself—that I'm not the same broken woman he's been studying.

My phone rings as we turn into Leo's long driveway that weaves through the hills. I answer before it can ring twice.

"I'm back safe and sound."

"So I see. How are you feeling?"

I hesitate, thinking about the tape, my speech, and Nash. "Like I have a dual personality," I say, then correct myself. "No, more like I'm finally becoming real." Davis pulls up to the front entrance, and I see Leo's silhouette in the doorway, the tension in his posture even from this distance.

"And Leo? It doesn't matter when Nash makes his move, because I know I'm truly ready for him."

TWENTY-FOUR
WAITING

The moment Ruby stepped through the front door, Leo pulled her against him with the kind of desperate relief that spoke to hours of barely controlled worry.

"God," he breathed, his mouth finding hers before she could even speak. The kiss was hungry, desperate, full of all the tension that had been building in him while he'd watched security feeds from Lydia Cos's offices and imagined every possible threat. He could taste the fear he'd been fighting all day, the barely controlled need to lock her away from danger.

This was the downside of her walking in his world—the fear. The blood red terror. The knowledge that something could happen to her. Something he couldn't stop or protect her from.

But it was too late. He couldn't push her away any more than he could ensure her safety. She was his, now fully part of his world. And if that meant that fear now lived in his veins? Well, maybe that fear would make him sharper. Maybe he could turn it into an asset.

He'd have to. Because he damn sure wasn't pushing her away. Not ever again.

"Fuck, Ruby." His voice was rough, almost broken. "Do you have any idea what it was like watching those security feeds all day? Seeing you in those meetings, looking completely normal, while I knew Nash could be planning anything?"

He let her strip the jacket away, along with the panic button and the professional facade she'd been wearing all day. Underneath, she was still her—the woman who'd discovered she liked being dangerous, who'd spent the day discussing cosmetics marketing while part of her mind stayed alert for threats.

She was incredible. And she was his.

"I liked it, you know. Living in two worlds." She rose on tiptoes and brushed a kiss over his lips. "But I like this world better. The one where I'm with you."

The confession broke something loose in him. He kissed her again, harder this time, with the kind of possessive desperation that had her sagging in his arms and sent fire racing through his veins.

This was what he'd been craving all day during those endless hours of watching and waiting—this intensity, this feeling of completely claiming the most important person in his world.

"I need you," she whispered against his mouth. "I need it hot. Hard."

"Whatever thet lady wants," he murmured, his cock so hard it was painful, and with one wild grab, he lifted her, her legs wrapping around his waist as something primal and desperate clawed at his chest. A day's worth of suppressed terror and need crashed over him like a tsunami, and he pressed her back against the front door with barely controlled violence, the windows along the front of the house open onto the stretches of Malibu hills.

She'd been in a damn cosmetics office, and he'd been about out of his mind with worry.

And how will you survive when she's in the field?

He didn't know. He just knew he had to. This was Ruby. *His* Ruby. And he was seeing her more clearly now than he'd ever seen her before. That heat that burned him. That streak of darkness that matched him.

His hands made quick work of her blouse, buttons scattering

across the hardwood floor with sharp little clicks. Then he made quick work of the rest of her professional armor, stripping away her skirt and blouse until she was standing in nothing but black lace panties and the kind of confidence that came from knowing exactly how much she was wanted.

"Look at you," Leo breathed, his voice filled with something that sounded like worship. "You have no idea what watching you today did to me. Seeing you handle yourself, seeing you become exactly who you were meant to be."

She laughed. "I was a cosmetics exec today."

"You were a fucking powerhouse." His mouth found her throat, and she arched against the door, letting him mark her skin while his hand slipped inside her panties. This was what power felt like—having Ruby choose him, choose this dangerous life, choose to become something that matched what he was.

"Tell me," she demanded, her hands fisting in his hair. "Tell me what it did to you."

"It made me realize I don't just love you," he said against her collarbone, his teeth grazing sensitive skin. "I'm proud of you. Proud to call you mine."

"Yours?" she repeated, a tease in her voice. "Better lock it in, Leo. If you want to keep me, you're going to have to show me just how deeply you own me."

He knew she was only teasing, but her words ripped something inside of him, and a wolf emerged. Dangerous and claiming. Needing. Longing.

He'd never wanted her more than he did in that moment, and in one harsh movement, he lifted her higher, positioning her exactly where he wanted her.

Anyone monitoring the property could see them, but he didn't care. Let his security team see Leo Grimm claiming his woman. Let them see what he had—what he loved—and what was worth fighting for.

Them.

His fingers slid under her lacy thong, making her gasp and

arch against the door. She was already wet, already desperate for him, and when he realized how ready she was, his control snapped completely.

"Fuck, Ruby. You're soaking for me." His voice was pure gravel, pure possession.

"God, yes," she managed. "Please," she begged, making him go even harder as his fingers worked magic against her most sensitive spots.

Then he bent forward, his mouth crashing against hers, swallowing her moans as his fingers brought her closer and closer to the edge. But just as she was about to fall over, he pulled back, working at his belt with shaking hands.

"Not yet," he growled. "When you come, I want to be inside you. I want to feel you fall apart around me. To see that you're mine. To know that you fucking match me."

"God yes," she said, even as he thrust inside her, filling her completely, stretching her in the most perfect way. The angle felt desperate, primal—her pressed against the door, him holding her up with nothing but his strength and his need.

"Christ, you feel incredible." He had to force the words out, his forehead pressed against hers as he gave her a moment to adjust. "Perfect. Like you were made for me."

"Move," she demanded, wrapping her legs tighter around his waist. "Leo, please. I need—"

"I know what you need," he growled.

When he started to move, it was with the kind of desperate rhythm that spoke to hours of pent-up tension, to a day spent watching her walk into potential danger while fighting every protective instinct he possessed. To seeing her hold her own in that wonderful speech when she'd told the world she loved him.

Each thrust pushed her harder against the door, each movement a claiming that went deeper than physical.

"This is what we're fighting for," he said against her ear, his voice rough with exertion and emotion. "This. Us. The right to choose each other every fucking day."

"Yes," she gasped. "God yes."

His pace increased, becoming more desperate, more claiming, and he could feel her starting to shatter. The combination of his words, his possession, the danger and excitement of the day, all building to this moment of perfect connection.

"Come for me, Red," he commanded, his hand sliding between them to where they were joined. "Come for me and show me exactly how alive you feel."

The moment his fingers found her clit, she broke apart. Her orgasm tore through her, her cunt clenching hard around his cock as she cried out his name, her back arching off the door, her nails raking down his shoulders as her body milked his cock.

"Fuck, yes," Leo groaned, his rhythm becoming erratic. "That's it, baby. Take what you need."

His release followed seconds later, a low growl torn from his chest as he buried himself deep and filled her completely. For a moment, they stayed joined like that, both breathing hard, clinging to each other.

"I love you," Leo finally said, pressing his face into her neck. "I love who you've become. I love who we are together."

"I love you, too," she whispered, running her fingers through his sweat-dampened hair.

He set her down gently on the sofa, both of them still breathing hard and trying to catch their breath. But before they could fully return reality, his phone buzzed in his back pocket. He met her eyes as he reached to pull it out— *Showtime.*

TWENTY-FIVE
THE TRAP

I lean over so I can see Leo's Caller ID — *Rover*

"Thought you were on downtime," Leo says.

"I fucked up, buddy," he said, his voice edgy and hard. "The asshole got one over on me."

Leo meets my eyes. "What happened? Are you hurt?"

"I was in the Rough and Ready, that bar way up PCH. Was walking to the beach, waiting for this hot waitress I know to come spend some time, you know?"

Leo and I exchange a look. From Leo's amused expression, I think he knows Rover's habits very, very well. "Anyway, she came out, but got called back in to pick up her tips." Static crackles through the line, and Rover's voice cuts in and out, like he's moving through a building with poor reception. "I was watching her walk away when the fucker tranqued me. Now he wants to make a deal."

Leo's entire body goes rigid beside me. "What kind of deal?"

"He says he'll let me go, but he has terms. Won't tell me what. Says that's for you to hear."

"And?"

Rover sighs. "He says you're to get your ass to the warehouse on Fifth Street. Red brick building with the loading dock on the east side. He wants to negotiate—says he's tired of the games and ready to end this. He said you can bring one person. Show of faith. No tricks, just talk."

Leo meets my eyes, and I shake my head, every nerve in my body screaming *danger*.

"Rover, this sounds like—"

"I know how it sounds," Rover interrupts, and there's desperation in his voice now. "But Leo, I can see his men. This isn't a bluff. He says he doesn't want the vault codes or anything else—he just wants to talk. Face to face."

Leo meets my eyes, and I can see the same terrible calculation I'm doing. This could be exactly what Rover says it is—Nash finally ready to negotiate instead of playing psychological warfare. Or it could be the trap we've been expecting.

"How do I know this is really you?" Leo asks, his voice carefully controlled.

"Fuck, man, seriously?"

"Yeah," Leo says. "Seriously."

"Aw, Christ. Okay, how about this—you keep a photo of Ruby in your wallet that you think nobody's seen. Wrong. We've all seen it. Which means we all know you're a sentimental prick. Good enough?"

"Yeah," Leo says, glancing sideways at me. "Good enough."

I bite back a self-satisfied smile, but that's more about Leo's reaction. The truth is, voice manipulation technology has gotten incredibly sophisticated. Someone could have been recording their conversations for weeks, probably even gotten a peek at Leo's wallet.

"Where am I going exactly?" Leo asks.

"Fifth Street warehouse district. Building 47, red brick with the loading dock. Nash says just you and one other—if he sees additional security, he takes me and disappears."

"Rover—"

"Dude, listen up. This needs to go down. Nash—I think he's finally ready to end this instead of dragging it out. There's a pause filled with static. But if you don't come, I think he'll kill me just to prove that he's the one in charge."

The line goes dead.

Leo immediately starts dialing, his fingers flying over his secure phone. "Davis? I need you to ping Rover's location. Now."

I watch Leo pace while he coordinates with his team, trying to trace Rover's call, checking with their surveillance assets, attempting to verify the story. But twenty minutes of frantic searching yields nothing definitive.

"His phone's dark," Leo says finally, ending his latest call. "Either it's been destroyed or it's in a location that blocks our tracking."

"What about the warehouse?"

"Davis is sending a drone, but it'll take forty minutes to get there and set up surveillance." Leo runs a hand through his hair, the gesture betraying his frustration. "We don't have enough intel to know if this is real or a trap."

"So what do we do?"

He's quiet for a moment, then he sighs. "We prepare for both possibilities," he says with a shrug. "If Rover's really being held, we'll need extraction protocols. If it's a trap…"

"If it's a trap," I say, "Nash gets exactly what he wants—both of us in a location of his choosing."

"Not both of us."

The words hit me like a slap. "What do you mean?"

"Ruby, you're not going to that warehouse."

"Like hell I'm not. If Rover's in trouble—"

"If Rover's in trouble, he needs people who can help him. You've had three weeks of training. You can shoot targets at a range and you understand basic tactical concepts, but you're not ready for a live operation."

The dismissal stings, even though I know Leo's right. "I could help. I could—"

"You could get yourself killed and distract me from saving one of my closest friends." Leo's voice is firm but not unkind.

"Rue, this isn't about you not being brave enough or strong enough. This is about training and experience. I wouldn't send any new operative into a situation like this, regardless of who they were."

I want to argue, want to insist that I should be part of whatever happens next. But Leo's right. I've learned to shoot, but I've never been in a firefight. I understand tactical concepts, but I've never executed them under pressure. I'd be a liability, not an asset.

"Fine," I say, hating how small my voice sounds. "But I want to be kept informed. I want to know the moment you have any information."

"Of course."

Leo moves with the kind of efficient precision I've come to associate with him in crisis mode. He coordinates with his team, reviews building schematics, and plans multiple extraction scenarios. Within an hour, he's ready to leave.

"Stay here," he says, checking his weapon one final time. "Keep the doors locked, the security system active. Mitchell is monitoring from the perimeter," he says, and I nod, remembering the muscular blond man Leo had introduced me to when we'd first arrived.

"How long until you know something?"

"Two hours, maybe three. If Rover's really there, we'll have him out before midnight."

When he kisses me goodbye, I can taste the tension in him, the fear that this might be exactly the trap Nash has been planning. And when he leaves, the Malibu house feels impossibly quiet, like all the life has been sucked out of it.

I try to distract myself with work, reviewing spreadsheets and client reports, but I can't concentrate. Every few minutes, I find myself pacing, then checking my phone for updates that don't come, then pacing some more. Leo and his team have gone dark, operating under radio silence to avoid detection.

By ten o'clock, I'm pacing the living room like a caged animal. Fifteen minutes later, I'm sitting at Leo's desk, staring at his computer screen without seeing the words. That's when I hear it —a sound that doesn't belong.

A footstep on the deck outside.

I freeze, every nerve in my body suddenly alert. Mitchell is supposed to be monitoring from the perimeter, but this sounds like someone moving carefully across the wooden planks that lead to the sliding glass doors.

I frown, remembering the security specs that Leo explained to me. There are pressure pads on the back porch. So why isn't the alarm beeping?

I reach for my phone to call Mitchell, but it's not where I left it. In my pacing, I must have set it down somewhere else in the house. I send a message over the computer to tell him about the footsteps and the possible breach of the system. Then, I ease open Leo's desk drawer. I'm looking for the number for property security, but my hand closes around cold metal.

A gun. The one Leo keeps in his desk for emergencies.

The footstep comes again, closer to the house now. Definitely human. Definitely trying to move quietly.

I pull the gun from the drawer, my hands shaking slightly as I eject the clip to ensure it's full, then partially pull back the slide to make sure there's one in the chamber. No surprise, there is. Leo's weapons are always ready for use.

The sliding glass door to the deck rattles softly, like someone testing to see if it's locked.

I move away from the desk, positioning myself behind the couch where I have a clear line of sight to the windows but some cover if shooting starts. My heart is hammering so hard I can hear it in my ears, but my hands are steady on the gun.

The door slides open.

A man steps into the house, moving with the kind of careful precision that screams professional. He's tall, lean, with graying hair and the kind of face that would be forgettable in a crowd. But I recognize him from the photographs Leo showed me.

Carson Nash.

"Well, well," he says, his voice carrying a slight accent I can't place. "Little Ruby Ryder, all alone in her fortress."

I keep the gun trained on him, trying to remember everything Leo taught me about sight alignment and trigger control. "You're not supposed to be here."

Nash laughs, a sound that makes my skin crawl. "I'm exactly where I'm supposed to be. Your boyfriend fell for the oldest trick in the book—create a crisis elsewhere to draw the protection away from the real target."

"Rover—"

"Is perfectly safe, having drinks in Santa Monica. Probably getting laid by now. Voice manipulation technology is quite impressive these days, don't you think?"

The confirmation that this was all a setup hits me like a slap. Leo walked into exactly the trap Nash wanted him to walk into.

"You see, Leo thought he was so clever, keeping you hidden away, surrounding you with security, making you untouchable." Nash takes a step closer, and I can see the predatory gleam in his eyes. "But everyone has cracks. Even Leo Grimm."

"Stay back," I warn, raising the gun higher.

"Ruby, sweetheart, do you even know how to use that thing?"

"You're going to find out."

The bastard laughs. "There's a difference between shooting at paper targets and shooting at someone who's shooting back."

His hand moves toward his jacket, and instinct takes over. I pull the trigger.

The shot goes wide, punching a hole in the wall behind him. Nash doesn't even flinch. Instead, he reaches for his gun as he lunges toward me. I fire again.

And his time I don't miss.

The bullet catches him in the shoulder, spinning him around and sending his gun sliding across the floor. But that doesn't stop him. He comes at me with a roar of pain and fury, and suddenly we're fighting for my gun, my heart pounding as adrenaline floods through me.

Nash is stronger than me, but he's also bleeding, and I have the advantage of desperation. I manage to twist away from his grabbing hands, putting space between us as I free the gun from his hands, then scoot back even as I scramble upright.

"You little bitch," Nash snarls, lurching toward me.

I empty the clip into him, my ears ringing, my body going hot and rigid.

Shot after shot, watching him jerk and stumble with each impact, until he finally falls and goes still.

My legs give out and I sink to the floor.

Nash is dead.

The man who killed my parents, who terrorized me for months, who was going to murder me to hurt Leo—he's dead by my hand.

And I feel…powerful.

TWENTY-SIX
AFTERMATH

I'm still holding the empty gun when Leo bursts through the front door twenty minutes later, his own weapon drawn, his face a mask of controlled panic.

"Ruby!" He stops short when he sees Nash's body, his eyes moving quickly from the corpse to me to the empty gun in my hands. "Jesus Christ. Are you hurt?"

"No." My voice sounds strange to my own ears, distant and calm. "I'm fine."

Leo holsters his weapon and crosses to me, his hands running over my arms and face, checking for injuries I don't have. "What happened? How did he get past security?"

I tell him everything—Nash's entrance, his gloating about the fake Rover call, the way he moved toward me with deadly intent. Leo listens without interruption, his face growing darker with each detail.

"He said you fell for an obvious trap," I finish. "That Rover was never in danger."

Leo's jaw tightens. "Rover's fine. But he took Mitchell out. Bullet to the back of the head."

"Oh." A chill runs through me. "I'm sorry."

"So am I. He was a good man. I'll contact his brother in the morning—he didn't have any other family." Leo runs his hands over me again, as if to prove to himself that I'm really here.

"*Fuck*." The word sounds torn out of him. "I should have left more security here. Should have anticipated that you'd be the real target."

"Leo." I reach out to touch his face, and he goes still under my fingers. "I handled it."

Something flickers in his eyes as he looks at me—really looks at me. Taking in my steady hands, my calm demeanor, the way I'm not falling apart after taking a life.

"How do you feel?" he asks carefully.

I consider the question. How do I feel? I should feel sick, traumatized, horrified by what I've done. Instead, I feel…empty. Hollow. Like I'm waiting for some reaction that hasn't come yet.

"I don't know," I say honestly. "Strange. Like it hasn't hit me yet."

"That's normal," Leo says, but I can see him processing this version of me. The woman who just killed a man and isn't falling apart. "Shock can delay the emotional response."

"Maybe." I look down at Nash's body, then back at Leo. "He was going to kill me. To hurt you through me. I stopped him."

"You did." Leo's voice is carefully neutral. "Are you scared of what that means?"

"Should I be?"

Before Leo can answer, Rover bursts through the front door, followed by Davis and two men I don't recognize.

"Christ," Rover breathes, taking in the scene. "You okay, Ruby?"

I nod, though I'm not entirely sure it's true.

The next few hours pass in a blur of controlled chaos. The cleanup crew works with professional efficiency—Nash's body will disappear into the kind of void that swallows inconvenient corpses. They'll clean the blood from the floors and fix the bullet holes in the walls. By morning, it will be like the gunfight never happened.

Except it did.

I keep waiting to break down. To feel the need to throw myself across the bed and sob. To turn ice cold as shock descends on me. But the numbness persists, broken only by occasional flashes of... something. Not satisfaction, exactly. More like relief that it's over.

"You okay?" Leo asks for the dozenth time, his watchful eyes sliding over me. His voice is carefully controlled, but I can feel the tension radiating from him.

"I think so." I take his hand and squeeze it. "I keep waiting to fall apart, but..."

"But?"

"I just feel empty. Like I'm waiting for the other shoe to drop."

He frowns but nods. "That's not uncommon. The mind processes trauma in different ways."

It takes another hour, but finally everyone is satisfied that the house is clean and secure. As soon as they clear out, Leo takes my hand and leads me to the back patio. We sit on the edge of the infinity pool and look out over the Pacific.

"I watched the security tape," he says, and when I turn to look at him, I see something burning in his green eyes that makes heat settle low in my belly.

"And?"

"Ruby, what you did back there—the way you handled your-self against a professional killer..." His voice is rough, strained. "You've got amazing instincts."

"Should that scare me?"

His answer is immediate and devastating. "It's the hottest fucking thing I've ever seen in my life."

The words hit me like lightning, sending electricity straight through my core. Suddenly the emptiness is gone, replaced by something warm and alive and thrilling. This man—this danger-ous, controlled man who's seen more violence than I can imagine —is turned on by what he saw on that tape.

"Show me how hot," I whisper.

Leo's control shatters like glass. One moment we're sitting by the pool having a careful conversation, and the next his hands are fisted in my hair and his mouth is crushing mine with desperate, claiming hunger.

This isn't gentle. This isn't soft. This is possession, dominance, the kind of raw need that comes from surviving something that should have killed you.

"Fuck, Ruby," Leo growls against my mouth. "Do you have any idea what it was like seeing you refuse to be a victim? Watching you become exactly what Nash never expected?"

"Tell me," I demand, my hands already working at his belt. I need him. Need this. Need to feel something other than the strange emptiness that's been sitting in my chest.

"Inside," he says, but his hands are already pushing up my shirt, finding the clasp of my bra. "Now. Before I fuck you right here on the pool deck."

We stumble toward the house like animals in heat, hands everywhere, mouths fused together, both of us desperate to get closer. But we don't make it to the bedroom. We barely make it through the door before Leo has me pressed against the wall, his mouth on my throat, his hands mapping every inch of exposed skin.

"I watched you kill him," Leo breathes against my collarbone as he works my bra off completely. "Watched you empty that clip into the bastard who killed your parents. And all I could think about was how fucking incredible you looked doing it."

His words send fire through my veins, filling the hollow space inside me with something that feels like power. The way he's touching me—reverent but desperate, gentle but claiming—makes me feel alive again.

"I liked it," I confess, the words surprising me even as I say them. "God help me, Leo, I think I liked killing him."

"I know you did." His hands are working at my pants now, pushing them down my hips with urgent efficiency. "I could see it in your eyes even on that recording. The determination. Fuck, Ruby, you were magnificent."

He lifts me easily, my legs wrapping around his waist as he presses me harder against the wall. The numbness is completely gone now, replaced by heat and need and the intoxicating feeling of being wanted not despite what I've done, but because of it.

"This is what you do to me," he says, grinding against me through the thin fabric of my panties. "Watching you take that prick out—Christ, I've never been harder in my life."

I reach between us and work at his jeans, needing to feel him, needing this connection that makes me feel real again. When I wrap my fingers around his length, he makes a sound that's pure animal.

"I want you inside me," I tell him, my voice coming out husky and demanding. "I want you to fuck me like I'm someone dangerous."

"You are," he says, then tears my panties away with one sharp motion, the fabric giving way like tissue paper.

He drives into me in one smooth thrust, and I cry out at the sensation of being completely filled. Ssuddenly I'm not thinking about Nash or death or what I might have become. There's only Leo and the way he's looking at me like I'm something magnificent and terrible.

"Yes," I gasp, my nails digging into his shoulders. "God, yes. Like that."

Leo sets a rhythm that's both punishing and perfect, each thrust driving me harder against the wall. There's nothing gentle about this, nothing careful. This is raw, primal, and it fills the emptiness inside me with something that feels like life.

"Look at you," Leo growls, his mouth against my ear. "Taking everything I give you. So fucking perfect. So strong."

Each word sends electricity through my system, building pressure low in my belly. This is what I needed—to feel powerful instead of hollow, claimed instead of empty.

"Harder," I demand, raking my nails down his back. "I'm not going to break."

"No, you're not." Leo's pace increases, becoming more desperate. "You're going to come for me instead."

The words send me flying over the edge. My orgasm tears through me like lightning, every muscle in my body clenching as waves of pleasure crash over me. I cry out Leo's name, feeling more alive than I have since I pulled that trigger.

Leo follows seconds later, his own release torn from his chest in a groan that sounds like something shifting between us.

For a moment we stay joined like that, both breathing hard, both trying to process the intensity of what just happened. But when Leo starts to pull away, I stop him with a hand on his chest.

"We're not done," I tell him, surprised by the hunger still coursing through me.

"No," he agrees, his hands already moving to lift me again. "We're definitely not done."

This time we make it to the bedroom. Leo sets me down and immediately drops to his knees in front of me, his hands sliding up my thighs with purposeful intent.

"I need to taste you," he says, looking up at me with eyes that burn. "Need to worship the woman who eliminated our biggest threat."

Before I can respond, his mouth is on me, his tongue finding my center with devastating precision. I cry out and thread my fingers through his dark hair, holding him against me as he devours me like a man starved.

This is different from the desperate claiming against the wall. This is reverent, worshipful. The emptiness inside me is completely gone, replaced by heat and sensation and the intoxicating knowledge that I'm wanted.

"So sweet," he murmurs against my flesh. "So perfect. My strong, deadly woman."

The combination of his words and his skillful mouth sends me spiraling toward another climax. But just as I'm about to fall over the edge, Leo pulls away.

"Not yet," he says, rising with predatory grace. "I want to feel you come around my cock again."

I start to get on the bed, but he tugs me back, then turns me around and bends me over the edge. The position is dominant, claiming, and when he slides into me from behind, it's with the kind of possession that makes me feel owned in the best possible way.

"This is how I want to take you," Leo says, his hands gripping my hips. "Hard and wild, like the dangerous woman you are. Not some fragile thing that needs protecting."

"Yes," I gasp, pushing back against him. The words feel true in a way that surprises me.

"You're perfect," Leo murmurs, one hand sliding around to find my clit. "You are so fucking perfect for me."

The dual sensation sends me flying again. This orgasm is deeper, more intense, and it wipes away the last traces of numbness, leaving me feeling raw and alive and completely claimed.

When we finally collapse onto the bed together, Leo pulls me against his side with gentle hands that contrast sharply with the intensity of what we just shared.

"How do you feel now?" he asks, his voice soft but serious.

I think about the question carefully. The emptiness is gone, replaced by something warm and satisfied. But underneath that satisfaction is a question I'm not ready to examine too closely.

"Better," I tell him honestly. "More like myself."

Leo's smile is warm and proud. "Good. Ruby, what you did tonight—"

"Was necessary," I finish. But even as I say it, a small voice in the back of my mind whispers a question: was it the killing that made me feel powerful, or was it Leo's reaction to what I'd done?

I push the voice away and focus on Leo's warmth, on the way he's looking at me like I'm something magnificent. Tomorrow I can worry about what I've become. Tonight, I just want to be the woman who survived.

TWENTY-SEVEN
SLEEPING BEAUTY

Leo watched Ruby sleep and tried to process what had happened tonight. Not just the clusterfuck with Nash. Not the mistake he'd made leaving Ruby, never thinking that Nash had set a trap.

No, what was keeping him from sleep was what he'd witnessed when he'd returned to find Nash's body sprawled across his living room floor and Ruby right there with an empty gun, as calm as someone who'd just finished brewing coffee.

She'd transformed from the Ruby who needed protecting into someone who could eliminate threats without hesitation, who could stare death in the face and emerge victorious.

It was the most beautiful and terrifying thing he'd ever seen.

For years, Leo had surrounded himself with professionals—men and women who could kill without blinking, who understood that violence was sometimes the only solution to complex problems. He'd respected their competence, relied on their skills, but he'd never felt this bone-deep satisfaction watching any of them work.

Because Ruby wasn't just competent. She was his.

Now, she shifted in her sleep, and Leo tightened his arms around her automatically. She felt different now. Not physically—she was still the same soft curves and silky skin that drove him crazy. Was still the woman whose body fit against his like they'd been designed for each other. But there was something in the way she'd carried herself earlier—and even now as she slept—that spoke to newfound confidence. *Power.* The kind of strength and bold confidence that came from discovering you could handle anything the world threw at you.

The woman who'd emptied a clip into Nash's body wasn't the same woman she'd been yesterday or last week or last year. She was someone harder, more dangerous. Someone who could stand beside him as an equal instead of hiding behind him for protection.

She'd become the woman she'd said she wanted to be. And she was the woman he'd fallen in love with years ago, transformed into someone who could survive his world.

And wasn't that the truth of it? Leo had been with other women over the years—beautiful women, intelligent women, even dangerous women. But none of them had ever made him feel like this—like he'd gotten back what he thought he'd destroyed forever. Like the love he'd sacrificed to keep her safe had somehow found its way back to him, stronger than before.

The sex they'd just had reminded him of their intensity in college, but deeper now. Not just because she was older, more experienced—though she was—but because she'd grown into someone who could match his darkness instead of being afraid of it. Someone who could be violent when necessary and feel satisfaction instead of guilt.

Someone who understood that sometimes the world required harsh solutions and didn't flinch away from implementing them.

Leo had spent his entire adult life being the one who made the hard choices, who got his hands dirty so others could sleep safely in their beds. Her freshman year, Ruby had seen bits of that in him and loved him anyway—but she'd been too innocent, too vulnerable to survive what loving him meant. He'd had to push her away to keep his father from destroying her.

But this Ruby—this Ruby had looked him in the eye after killing Nash and he'd seen it on her face. She'd been satisfied.

Not guilty, not traumatized, but satisfied that she'd eliminated a threat to the people she loved.

She understood him the way she always had. But now she was strong enough to handle that understanding.

Ruby murmured something in her sleep and pressed closer to him, and Leo felt himself getting hard again just from the contact. The woman was addictive. The combination of softness and steel, of intelligence and deadly instinct, of everything he'd been looking for without knowing he was looking for it.

He wanted her again. Wanted to wake her up and worship every inch of the body that had housed such perfectly controlled violence.

But more than that, he wanted to make sure she understood that what had happened tonight didn't change anything between them. If anything, it made him love her more. Made him want her more.

Leo's phone buzzed with a text from Rover who was overseeing the cleanup crew in the other room:

Done. No trace left. Ruby okay?

Ruby's perfect.

She damn sure handled herself.

The pride in Rover's response made Leo smile. His team understood what had happened tonight. What Ruby had proven about herself. They'd seen plenty of people freeze up in their first life-or-death situation, but Ruby had kept her head, used her training, and emerged victorious.

She was going to fit into his world better than he'd ever dared hope.

Another text came through, this one from Alexander:

Heard about Nash. Impressive work. Ruby's tougher than I gave her credit for.

Leo set the phone aside with satisfaction. If Alexander was

impressed, that meant something. His brother didn't give praise lightly, especially when it came to civilians entering their world.

Ruby stirred again, her eyes fluttering open to meet his in the darkness. Even half-asleep, she was beautiful—hair tousled, lips slightly swollen from their earlier kisses, skin glowing with the kind of satisfaction that came from being thoroughly claimed.

"Can't sleep?" she asked, her voice husky.

"Just thinking about how incredible you were tonight."

Something flickered across her face—satisfaction mixed with something that might be uncertainty. The confidence she'd shown immediately after killing Nash was giving way to something more complex, and Leo realized she was starting to process what she'd done.

"You mean that?" she asked, and he could hear the vulnerability beneath the question.

"I mean every word." Leo rolled her onto her back and settled between her thighs, feeling her body respond immediately to his proximity. Her legs parted automatically, welcoming him into the cradle of her hips. "You were magnificent, Ruby. Powerful. Exactly what Nash never expected to face."

"And that turns you on?" There was something in her voice he couldn't quite identify. Not quite insecurity, but close. Like she was testing him, seeing if he'd be honest about his reaction to her violence.

"Everything about you turns me on," he told her, leaning down to capture her mouth in a kiss that was soft and claiming at the same time. "But tonight? Watching that tape? Seeing you become exactly who you were meant to be? That was the hottest thing I've ever witnessed."

And it was true. She hadn't just survived—she'd conquered. And that was hot as fuck.

He could feel her relaxing beneath him, melting into the kiss and the praise. This was what she needed to hear—that her transformation didn't make her a monster, it made her perfect. That he didn't love her despite her capacity for violence, but because of it. Or at least that was one part of a million reasons he loved her.

"Show me again," she whispered against his mouth. "Show me how much you want this version of me."

Leo grinned. "Whatever the lady wants."

He took his time, worshipping every inch of her body with hands and mouth until she was writhing beneath him, desperate and begging. He wanted her to understand that every part of her —the soft skin, the gentle curves, the deadly hands that had killed their enemy—was exactly what he wanted.

He mapped her body with reverent touches, marking every sensitive spot, every place that made her gasp and arch beneath him. Her breasts, soft and perfect in his hands. The curve of her waist. The smooth skin of her inner thighs. He wanted to memorize all of it, to prove to her that she was precious to him not despite what she'd done tonight, but because of it.

"You saved yourself tonight," he murmured against her throat, feeling her pulse flutter beneath his lips. "You faced down a killer and won. Do you understand how incredible that is?"

"I used what you taught me," she whispered, her hands fisting in his hair.

"You used your own strength. Your own courage. I just gave you the tools—you're the one who wielded them."

When Leo finally slid inside her, it was with the kind of reverent possession that made her gasp his name like a prayer. He set a slow, thorough rhythm that built the tension between them gradually, letting the pleasure build until they were both shaking with the need for release.

This wasn't just sex—this was a claiming, a celebration, a recognition of what they'd both discovered tonight. That Ruby wasn't just strong enough to survive in his world, she was strong enough to thrive in it.

"I love you," Leo told her as he drove into her deeper, harder. "All of you. The soft parts and, the dangerous parts and every-thing in between."

"I love you, too," she gasped, her nails digging into his shoulders hard enough to leave marks. "God, Leo, I love you so much."

When they came together this time, it was with the kind of synchronized intensity that made Leo understand exactly how perfect they were for each other. Two dangerous people who had found something worth protecting in each other. Two souls who'd recognized their match and weren't letting go.

Afterward, as they lay tangled together, both breathing hard and covered in sweat, Leo couldn't resist pressing one more kiss to her temple.

"Sleep, my love," he murmured against her skin. "Tomorrow we figure out what comes next."

But Leo already knew what came next. Ruby and him as partners in everything. In business, in life, in whatever violence the world threw their way.

He'd walked away before and it had almost killed him. This time, he was never letting her go. And now, for the first time in his life, Leo Grimm wasn't facing the darkness alone.

And that changed everything.

TWENTY-EIGHT
MIRROR, MIRROR

I wake up to the sound of Leo's voice in the kitchen and squint. The morning light streaming through the windows feels too bright, too normal for the day after I killed a man.

The memory hits me like a physical blow. Nash's body jerking under the impact of each bullet. The way his eyes went empty. The blood spreading across the floor.

The satisfaction I felt watching him die.

My stomach lurches, and I have to press my hand over my mouth to keep from being sick. What kind of person feels satisfaction when they take a life? What kind of person enjoys the moment when someone stops breathing because of their actions?

"Good morning, beautiful," Leo says from the doorway, carrying a cup of coffee like this is any other morning. Like I didn't become a killer last night. "How are you feeling?"

The innocent question makes everything worse. How am I feeling? Powerful. Alive. Like I could take on the world and win.

And that terrifies me more than anything Nash ever did.

"Fine," I lie, accepting the coffee with hands that shake slightly. "Just tired."

Leo sits on the edge of the bed, his eyes scanning my face with the kind of attention that misses nothing. "Ruby, last night was intense. It's normal to have complicated feelings about what happened."

"Is it?" The words come out sharper than I intend. "Is it normal to enjoy killing someone?"

"You didn't enjoy killing," he says carefully. "You enjoyed surviving."

But that's not true, and we both know it. I didn't just survive Nash's attack—I obliterated him. I put bullet after bullet into his body even after he was dead, and every shot felt like justice. Like power.

Like coming home to myself.

"Ruby." Leo's voice is gentle, concerned. "Talk to me. What's going on in your head?"

How do I explain that I'm terrified by how natural violence felt? How do I tell the man I love that I'm questioning everything about myself, including why he was drawn to me in the first place?

"You keep telling me how incredible I was last night," I say instead.

"Because you were."

"But what does that say about me?" The question bursts out of me like a confession. "What kind of person is magnificent at killing? What kind of person has that kind of violence just waiting inside them?"

Leo goes very still. "Ruby—"

"And what does it say about you that you're attracted to that?" I continue, the words tumbling out faster now. "What does it say about us that watching the playback of me killing someone was a huge turn-on for you?"

The silence that follows is deafening. Leo sets down his coffee cup with careful precision, and I can see him choosing his words carefully.

"It says that you're stronger than you ever gave yourself credit for," he finally says. "And it says that I love every part of you, including the parts that can keep you safe when necessary."

"Safe." I laugh, but there's no humor in it. "Is that what you call what I did? Safe?"

"Nash was going to kill you. You stopped him. You saved yourself, Rue."

He's right, logically. But logic doesn't explain the dark satisfaction that filled me when Nash's body went still. Logic doesn't explain why I kept pulling the trigger long after he was dead.

"I didn't stop shooting," I whisper. "Even after he was down, even after he was clearly dead, I kept pulling the trigger. Why would I do that if it was just about protecting myself?"

Leo reaches for my hand, but I pull away. I can't bear to be touched right now, can't stand the way his skin against mine makes me feel powerful instead of horrified.

"Ruby, you were in shock. You were fighting for your life. Adrenaline makes people—"

"Makes people what? Enjoy it?" I stand up and start pacing, unable to sit still with all this energy coursing through my veins. "Because that's what happened, Leo. I enjoyed it. I felt powerful and alive and like I was exactly where I belonged."

"And that scares you."

"It should scare you, too." I spin to face him, and I can see my own reflection in his bureau mirror. I look wild, unhinged, like someone I don't recognize. "What if this is who I really am? What if all those years of being afraid and hiding were just me suppressing my true nature?"

"Your true nature," Leo repeats slowly.

"Maybe I'm not someone who became dangerous. Maybe I'm someone who was always dangerous, and I just needed the right circumstances to bring it out."

"That's not what's going on."

"Isn't it?" I snap, my voice getting higher, more desperate. "Think about it, Leo. You've known dangerous people your entire life. You've seen how they move, how they think. Did you see something in me from the beginning? Is that why you were drawn to me?"

Leo's silence is answer enough.

"Oh God." I sink into the chair by the window, the truth hitting me like a physical blow. "You did see it. You saw something dark in me that I didn't even know was there."

"Ruby, calm down, baby."

"When did you know?" I demand. "When did you realize I had this capacity for violence? Was it when you first kissed me when we were freshmen? Was it when you taught me to shoot? Or did you know even before then?"

"I saw strength," Leo says carefully. "And over these last few weeks, I've seen someone who survived trauma and came out fighting. But Ruby, I've never seen darkness in you. I've seen potential."

"Potential for what? Killing people?"

"Potential for being my equal." Leo's voice is soft, but there's steel underneath. "Potential for standing beside me instead of behind me. Potential for being someone who could handle my world without falling apart."

His words should be comforting, but they're not. Because they confirm my worst fear—that Leo didn't fall in love with me despite my capacity for violence, but because of it.

"So you did shape me into this," I say, and it's not a question. "You saw something you could mold and you turned me into your perfect partner."

"I helped you become who you already were."

"How can you possibly know that when I didn't know myself?" My words are hot. Hard. "Maybe I was supposed to be someone who worked in cosmetics and lived a quiet, safe life. Maybe I was supposed to be someone who didn't enjoy watching people die!"

"People? Do not put Nash in the same box as people. That man was a monster."

"No," I begin, but he steps forward, cutting me off.

"Is that really what you want?" he demands. "To go back to

being afraid? To hide from your own strength just because it scares you?"

The question stops me cold because I don't know the answer. The woman I was three months ago seems like a stranger now—someone completely unprepared for the realities of the world. I can't imagine going back to that person.

But I'm terrified by who I've become instead.

"I don't know what I want," I admit, my voice breaking. "I don't know who I am anymore. Am I Ruby Ryder, marketing executive? Or am I someone who empties clips into people and feels good about it?"

"You're both," Leo says simply. "You're someone who can design marketing campaigns and eliminate threats. Someone who can be soft when it's safe and deadly when it's necessary."

"And you love that about me."

"I love all of you. The gentle parts and the dangerous parts and everything in between."

And that's the problem. Leo loves my darkness. He's attracted to it. Which means our entire relationship might be built on something twisted and wrong.

"What if I can't go back?" I whisper. "What if I've crossed a line I can't uncross?"

"Then you don't go back." Leo stands and moves toward me, his movements careful and non-threatening. "You move forward as someone who knows exactly what they're capable of."

"As a killer."

"As a survivor. As someone strong enough to protect the people they love."

I want to believe him. I want to accept his rational explanations and move on with my life. But every time I close my eyes, I see Nash's face in that final moment. I see the light leaving his eyes because I put it out.

And so help me, part of me is proud of that.

"I need some time," I tell Leo, wrapping my arms around

myself. "I need to think about all of this without you telling me it's okay."

Leo's face closes off, becomes carefully neutral. "What kind of time?"

"I don't know. Maybe I should get a hotel room for a few days. Or go back home. I need to clear my head."

"Ruby—"

"Please," I interrupt, looking up at him, and I can see my desperation reflected in his eyes. "I need to figure out who I am when you're not around to influence the answer."

The words hit him, and I can see him recoil from the implication. That he's been manipulating me, shaping me, turning me into something I was never meant to be.

Maybe he has been. Maybe we've both been too caught up in the intensity of our relationship to see it clearly.

"If that's what you need," he finally says, his voice carefully controlled.

"It is."

He nods, his face like stone. "Then I'll have Davis take you wherever you want to go."

"I can drive myself. I'll have someone bring me one of the office-owned cars."

"Ruby." Leo's voice is sharp now, edged with the kind of authority I've grown used to obeying. "Someone tried to kill you yesterday. You're not driving anywhere alone."

The automatic command makes something cold settle in my stomach. There he is, giving orders. Even after I proved last night that I'm perfectly capable of taking care of myself.

"Fine," I say, because I don't have the energy to fight him on this, too. "But I don't want to see you for a while. I need space to think."

Leo nods once, sharp and controlled. "How long?"

"I don't know."

"Ruby." His voice is soft now, almost vulnerable. "What happened last night doesn't change anything between us. You're still the woman I love. You're still the woman I want to spend my life with."

"But what if it changes everything for me?" I meet his eyes, letting him see the fear and confusion there. "What if I can't love the man who taught me to enjoy killing?"

Leo goes very still, like I've hit him somewhere vital. "Is that what you think I did?"

I look down, then whisper, "I don't know what to think anymore."

The silence stretches between us, heavy with everything we're not saying.

"I'll call Davis," he finally says, his voice carefully empty. "He'll drive you wherever you want to go." As he leaves to make the call, I sink back into the chair and try to process everything that's happened. Twenty-four hours ago, I was a woman in love planning to spend her life with a dangerous man. Now I'm someone who riddled a man with bullets and enjoyed it. Someone who's questioning everything about herself and her relationship.

I close my eyes and see Nash's face again. Feel the weight of the gun in my hands. Taste the satisfaction of watching him die.

And I still don't know if that makes me a monster or just someone strong enough to survive in Leo's world.

Maybe there's no difference between the two.

Maybe that's what terrifies me most of all.

TWENTY-NINE
SAFE HOUSES

My cottage looks exactly the same as when I left it, but sitting in the familiar living room with its soft throw pillows and carefully arranged books, I feel like I'm visiting someone else's life. The woman who chose this furniture, who arranged these photographs, who thought this safe little world was enough—I don't know her anymore.

My phone buzzes for the fifteenth time in three days. *Leo again.* I don't answer, but I can't help listening to his voicemails afterward, torturing myself with the sound of his voice.

BEEP: *Ruby, it's me. Please call me back. I know you need space, but just let me know you're safe.*

BEEP: *I've been thinking about what you said. About me influencing who you became. Maybe we should talk about it.*

BEEP: *Fuck, Ruby, I'm going crazy not knowing if you're okay. Just…please. One text. Tell me you're alive.*

BEEP: *I'm sorry. For pushing too hard, for making you question yourself. I never meant to make you doubt who you are.*

Each message is a little more desperate, a little more vulnerable. And I know that the Leo Grimm who controls everything is slowly dissolving into a man who's lost the most important thing in his world. But right now, I'm not prepared to make that better for him.

A car door slams in the driveway, and I'm already moving toward the kitchen before I consciously register the sound. My hand reaches automatically for the knife block, and I position myself with a clear view of both exits before I realize what I'm doing.

This is what I've become. Someone who hears an unexpected noise and immediately calculates defensive positions.

Through the window, I see Sasha getting out of her BMW, her face creased with worry. I force my hand away from the knives, my heart still racing from the automatic threat response.

"What the hell is going on?" she says, the moment I open the door.

"Nice to see you too," I mutter, but I let her in and immediately get enveloped in one of her fierce hugs.

"Rover said you left LA suddenly. Something about a family emergency that nobody knew about." Sasha pulls back to study my face. "You look like shit."

"Thanks. Coffee?"

"Coffee and answers. In that order."

I busy myself in the kitchen while Sasha settles at the dining table, clearly ready to tackle whatever problem I'm dealing with, just as we've done so many times over the years.

But I've never had a problem like this before.

"Okay," she says when I set a mug in front of her. "Start talking."

"Leo and I had a fight," I say, choosing my words carefully.

Sasha cocks her head. I'm usually more forthcoming in our Help Me Fix My Life conversations. "About who I am," I add, trying to figure out the right words. "About who I've become since we got back together."

Her brow furrows, and I know she doesn't get it. Mostly because I've been holed up in the cottage. Avoiding her. Even avoiding Granny.

"Relationships change people," she says once she realizes I'm done talking. "That's normal."

"Yeah, well, this isn't a normal relationship change." I wrap my hands around my coffee mug and look at the tabletop. "I killed a man. I emptied an entire clip into him, and I watched him die." When I look up, she's blurry from my tears. "I liked it. I felt powerful. Safe."

She nods. "Liam told me." She lifts a shoulder. "Not how you felt, but about what happened. Ruby, it was self-defense."

"It was. But that doesn't mean I should like it."

"Doesn't it? That man killed your parents. He stalked you. And he would have killed you that night if you hadn't taken him out first."

"So, what? What are you saying? That he deserved it? That I should feel proud?"

She shrugs. "Maybe."

"Well, I don't." I look down into my still-full coffee cup. "I felt powerful. Alive. Like I was exactly where I belonged." I blink, and the tears slide down my cheeks as I meet her eyes. "I liked it."

Sasha is quiet for a long moment. "What did Leo say when you told him all of that?"

"That's the problem. He thought it was incredible. He was turned on by it, Sasha. Like watching me kill someone was the hottest thing he'd ever seen. Hell, he probably thought it was foreplay."

Her brows rise. "And that bothers you."

"I kill someone, and he gets hard? What does that say about our relationship?"

As if mentioning his name has summoned him, my phone buzzes again—Leo's name on the screen. Another call I won't answer.

"How many times has he called?" Sasha asks.

"I don't know. A lot." I silence the phone. "I can't talk to him right now. Every time I hear his voice, I remember the way he looked at me that day. Like I was everything he'd been waiting for."

"Maybe you were."

The simple statement hits me like a slap. "What's that supposed to mean?"

"Ruby, I've known you forever. But I've never seen you as alive as you've been these past few months with Leo."

"Because he taught me to be dangerous."

"Because he helped you find parts of yourself you didn't know existed." Sasha reaches across the table. "Do you remember what you were like after your parents died? How afraid you were of everything?"

I do remember. The constant anxiety, the way I jumped at unexpected sounds, the careful life I built around avoiding risk.

"You were surviving," Sasha continues. "But you weren't living. Not really."

"Maybe I was right to be careful."

"Were you? Because from where I'm sitting, it looks like you're plenty strong enough to handle whatever life throws at you."

"Strong enough to kill people, you mean."

"Strong enough to protect yourself and the people you love." Sasha's voice is fierce. "Ruby, what you did wasn't wrong. It was necessary."

"But I enjoyed it," I whisper it, my darkest confession. "That's what scares me."

"So? You enjoyed eliminating a threat. You enjoyed feeling powerful instead of powerless. Those aren't terrible things."

"Aren't they?"

"Would you feel the same satisfaction if you'd hurt an innocent person?" Sasha asks.

The question stops me cold. "No. Of course not."

"Then you're not a monster. You're someone who can be dangerous when it's justified."

I want to believe her, but there's still the question that's been eating at me. "Sasha, what if Leo saw this potential in me from the beginning? What if our entire relationship is based on me being, well, someone who can take down a bad guy and not burst into tears?"

Sasha rolls her eyes. Literally. "Leo Grimm is rich and sexy and smart. He could have any woman he wants. Rich women, dangerous women, women who secretly work as assassins. Literally anyone. If all he wanted was a lethal partner, he had plenty of options."

"Then why me?"

"Because you're smart, kind, loyal, and brave. Because you can be soft when it's safe and deadly when it's necessary."

"But what if I don't want to be that person?"

"Then don't be." Sasha's voice is matter-of-fact. "Stay at Lydia Cos. Find a nice, safe man. Live the quiet life you had before."

The suggestion should be appealing. Instead, it sounds like prison.

"I can't," I admit. "I tried to imagine going back to that life, and it feels like putting on clothes that don't fit anymore."

Her brows rise. "Are you tendering your resignation?"

"I guess I am."

"Good. That means I don't have to fire you. Because you're not a marketing exec anymore, and we both know it."

"But is that growth, or did Leo change me into someone else?"

"Does it matter?" Sasha asks. "People change. Relationships change us. The question isn't whether Leo influenced who you became—of course, he did. The question is whether you like who you are now."

I sit back. I honestly hadn't thought about it like that.

My phone buzzes again. This time it's a text: *I love you. All of you. When you're ready to talk, I'll be here.*

Simple. Direct. No demands, no manipulation. Just a promise.

"He's giving me space," I say, showing Sasha the message.

"Smart man. So what are you going to do with it?"

I stare at the text, then at the cottage around me. This place that used to feel like home now feels like visiting a museum.

"I thought coming back here would help me remember who I used to be. But I can't seem to connect with that person anymore."

"Maybe that's not a bad thing." She sets down her coffee and looks at me seriously. "What do you want to do with your life? Not what you think you should do—what do you actually want?"

I blink, my mouth hanging open as I realize I don't have an answer. For so long, my wants have been shaped by fear—safety, security, a life where nothing bad could touch me. But now that I've tasted something different, I don't know what I want anymore.

"I have no idea," I whisper.

"Then maybe that's where you need to start. Not with who you are, but with what you want."

After Sasha leaves, I sit in my cottage surrounded by the remnants of my former life and try to imagine my future. But every path I consider feels wrong—too small, too safe, too much like running away from whoever I'm becoming.

I pick up my phone to call Leo back, then set it down again. I'm not ready. Not yet.

But I'm starting to realize I might never be ready if I keep hiding in this safe house, waiting for clarity that might never come.

Maybe I need to stop trying to figure out who I am and start trying to figure out what I want to do with whoever I'm becoming.

THIRTY

GET BACK

I'm still at the dining table when Granny comes in with her canvas bag filled with goodies from the farmers market.

"Liebling," she says, pulling me into one of her fierce hugs as I take her bag. "You look troubled."

"I am," I admit, unpacking the bag as she starts making tea. "Granny, do you think people can change so fundamentally that they become someone completely different?"

"Is this about Leo?"

"Tangentially," I say with a grimace. "It's about me. About who I've become since…" I trail off, not sure how to explain without revealing too much. "Since Leo came back into my life."

Granny sets the kettle on the stove and turns to study my face with those sharp eyes that miss nothing. "You seem stronger. More certain of yourself."

"I am," I admit. "But what if that strength came at the cost of who I used to be? What if I've lost something essential about myself?"

"Such as?"

I shrug. "Leo lives in a dangerous world. What if being in his world makes me hard? Gives me sharp edges? What if I stop thinking that the world is basically safe?"

I fold up the bag, then sink into one of the chairs.

She takes the seat opposite me. "You've already thought that, Liebling. You stopped believing the world was safe the same day I did. And yet you have no sharp edges, no hardness."

"What if I did?"

She shrugs. "You would still be you. And," she adds with a smile, "maybe I would worry about you a little bit less. It's good for a woman to be able to take care of herself, no?"

She's not wrong.

"I'm at loose ends," I admit. Then I draw a breath. "I quit Lydia Cosmetics today. Well, technically Sasha fired me."

"And why did you do this?"

I tap my fingers on the table. "I just—after LA, I can't go back to Lydia Cosmetics. I loved it, I really did. Loved helping Sasha build the company, loved the challenge of understanding what makes people want things."

"And now?"

"Now it feels trivial," I admit, hating that I'm talking smack about Sasha's work. Hell, her legacy. "It feels like I'm wasting my time on things that don't actually matter, at least not to me."

Granny pours hot water over tea bags and sets a mug in front of me. "Sasha understands. Part of her love for that company is the connection to her mother. And living her life in a way that her father never allowed. You are as close as sisters, but you do not have the same dreams. Nor should you."

"I know."

"And so we reach the big question," Granny says. "What does matter?"

The question stops me cold because I don't have a ready answer. What does matter to me now? What feels important enough to dedicate my life to?

"I don't know," I admit. "That's what scares me. I used to have clear goals, clear priorities. Now I feel like I'm floating, untethered from everything that used to anchor me."

"Perhaps those anchors were not as strong as you thought."

"What do you mean?"

Granny sits across from me, her expression thoughtful. "Ruby, you have spent most of your adult life trying to build a safe world around yourself. A job that would never put you in danger, friends who would never hurt you, a life that was predictable and controlled."

She's right, but hearing it said aloud makes something defensive rise in my chest. "Is that so wrong?"

"Not wrong, no. But perhaps not entirely honest either."

"Honest about what?"

"About who you really are underneath all that careful safety."

I think about the woman who emptied a clip into Nash's body, who felt satisfaction instead of horror, who craved the power that came with being dangerous. Is that who I really am? Or is that who Leo turned me into?

"I killed someone, Granny," I say quietly, the words spilling out before I can stop them. "The man who killed my parents. And I didn't feel guilty about it. I felt…powerful."

Granny doesn't even blink. "Good."

"Good?"

"That man destroyed our family and tried to destroy you. Feeling powerful about stopping him seems like the perfect response."

"But I enjoyed it. I liked the way it felt knowing I did that. That I *could* do that."

"And this frightens you."

"Shouldn't it? What kind of person enjoys violence?"

Granny is quiet for a moment, sipping her tea while she considers her words. "My parents told me stories from the war. What they learned. And what they impressed most upon me was that there are times when violence is not only necessary but righteous. The world is not always a safe place, Liebling. Sometimes good people must do difficult things to protect what they love."

"But what if I like doing difficult things too much? What if I've become someone who seeks out danger instead of avoiding it?"

"Then perhaps you have become someone who is strong enough to face the world as it really is, rather than as you wish it were."

Her words hit me hard because they echo everything Leo has said. That I'm stronger than I thought. That I'm capable of more than I imagined. That the woman I've become is someone to be proud of, not ashamed of.

But if that's true, then what do I do with this strength? How do I build a life around being someone who can be dangerous when necessary?

"I don't know how to live in the world I used to inhabit," I tell Granny. "But I don't know how to live in Leo's world either."

"Why must it be one or the other?"

"What do you mean?"

"Why must you choose between your old life and Leo's life? Why can you not build something new that belongs to both of you?"

The question hangs in the air between us, and I realize I've been thinking about this all wrong. I've been trying to figure out whether to go back to who I was or embrace who Leo helped me become. But maybe the real question is what I want to do with whoever I am now.

"I don't know what that would look like," I admit.

"Then perhaps it is time to find out."

That night, lying awake in bed, I finally listen to Leo's most recent voicemails.

BEEP: *Ruby, I know you need space, but I miss you. I miss your voice, your laugh, the way you challenge me to be better.*

BEEP: *I've been thinking about what you said about me influencing who you became. Maybe you're right. Maybe I did see something in you and help bring it out. But Ruby, what I saw wasn't darkness—I saw strength that you weren't using.*

BEEP: *Elliott asked me today if I regret teaching you to be danger- ous. And the answer is no. Not because I wanted a dangerous partner,* but because I wanted you to be safe. I wanted you to be able to protect yourself so I wouldn't have to worry about losing you.

BEEP: I love you. The woman you used to be, the woman I helped you become. And the woman you are right now. When you're ready to figure out what comes next, I want to figure it out with you.

By the time I finish listening to all his messages, I'm crying. Not from sadness, but from the overwhelming realization that I've been so focused on questioning our relationship that I've forgotten why I fell in love with Leo in the first place.

Not because he made me feel safe, but because he made me feel alive.

The question now is whether I'm brave enough to build a life around feeling alive, even if it means embracing parts of myself that scare me.

Even if it means accepting that the woman I've become might be exactly who I was always meant to be.

THIRTY-ONE
NINETEEN DAYS

L eo stood at the floor-to-ceiling windows of his Manhattan office, watching the city spread out below him like a chessboard he'd forgotten how to play. Nineteen days. Nineteen fucking days since Ruby had walked out of his life, and he felt like he was slowly losing his mind.

His phone sat on his desk, taunting him with its silence. No calls, no texts, no sign that the woman he loved was even alive except for Elliott's reports that she'd returned to Connecticut and quit her job. Dismantling her life piece by piece, as if the last few months had never happened.

As if he had never happened.

"You look like hell," Alexander observed from the doorway, studying Leo with the kind of clinical assessment that meant he was cataloging weaknesses. "When was the last time you slept?"

"I'm fine."

"No, you're not. You've left a slurry of voicemails for a woman who clearly doesn't want to talk to you, you haven't eaten a full meal in nearly three weeks, and yesterday you nearly put a bullet in Thompson because he suggested we increase security around Ruby without her knowledge."

Leo turned from the window, his hands clenched into fists. "She doesn't want our protection."

"She doesn't want your control," Alexander corrected. "There's a difference."

Alexander was right. Ruby hadn't left because she didn't love him—she'd left because she was questioning everything about their relationship, including whether he'd manipulated her into becoming someone she was never meant to be.

And fuck, maybe he had.

"I can't just do nothing," Leo said, sinking into his desk chair. "She's out there questioning everything about herself, thinking she's some kind of monster because she was strong enough to eliminate Nash."

"So fix it."

"How? She won't take my calls. She won't see me. She made it clear she needs space to figure out who she is without my influence."

"Then give her that space while making sure she knows you'll be here when she's ready."

"I've been giving her space. I've been leaving messages telling her I love her and want to work things out. What more can I do?"

Alexander moved to pour himself a drink from the bar cart, his movements deliberate and controlled. "You could stop trying to manage the situation."

"I'm not trying to manage—"

"Leo." Alexander's voice cut through his protest like a blade. "You've left twelve voicemails in nineteen days. You've had Elliott report on her activities. You've been strategizing ways to prove you're not controlling while actively trying to control the outcome. Do you see the problem?"

Leo stared at his brother, feeling something cold settle in his stomach. "She needs to know I'm not giving up on us."

"Or she needs to know you respect her enough to let her make her own choices without pressure."

"I do respect her choices."

"Do you? Because from where I'm sitting, it looks like you're doing exactly what she accused you of—trying to influence her decision by overwhelming her with your need for resolution."

The observation hit him like a sucker punch because it was true. Every voicemail, every message, every sleepless night spent planning what he'd say if she called—all of it was his attempt to manage a situation that couldn't be managed.

Ruby had asked for space to figure out who she was without his influence, and he'd responded by trying to influence her from a distance.

"Fuck," Leo breathed, dropping his head into his hands.

"Now you're getting it."

"So what do I do? Just...wait? Hope she decides to come back?"

"You do something you've never been good at," Alexander said, settling into the chair across from Leo's desk. "You let go and trust that if Ruby loves you—really loves you—she'll find her way back."

"And if she doesn't?"

"Then you'll know you gave her the freedom to choose, and her choice wasn't you."

The possibility that Ruby might choose a life without him made Leo's chest tight with panic. But worse than that was the growing realization that he might have already lost her by trying so hard to keep her.

"I saw strength in her that she didn't see in herself, and I helped her find it. But what if she's right? What if I influenced who she became because I needed a partner who could handle my world?"

"Did you?"

"Hell if I know." Had he been drawn to Ruby because he sensed she could become that woman? Or had he fallen in love with her gentleness and intelligence and fierce loyalty, and only later realized she had the potential for something more?

"I loved her before I knew what she was capable of. But maybe I stayed because I saw what she could become."

"Or maybe you stayed because you recognized someone strong enough to be your equal, not your responsibility."

"She doesn't feel like my equal. She feels like someone I corrupted."

Alexander was quiet for a moment, swirling the whiskey in his glass. "Leo, the woman who faced down Nash wasn't some puppet you created. She was someone who made a choice to fight instead of hide. You didn't corrupt her—you helped her discover she was capable of more than she knew."

"But she doesn't see it that way. She thinks I manipulated her into becoming someone she was never meant to be."

"Then show her you didn't."

"How?"

"Stop trying to convince her with words and start proving it with actions. Stop calling, stop messaging, stop trying to manage her choices from a distance. Let her figure out who she is without any input from you."

The suggestion made every protective instinct Leo possessed scream in protest. Ruby was out there questioning everything about herself, possibly blaming herself for being strong enough to survive. He wanted to fix it, to explain, to make her understand that she wasn't a monster.

Hell, he needed to fix it.

But maybe that was exactly the problem. Maybe his need to fix everything was part of what made Ruby question whether her choices were really her own.

"What if she decides she's better off without me?"

"Then she makes that choice freely, and you respect it."

"I can't lose her, Alexander."

"Then trust her to find her way back to you if that's what she wants."

Leo scowled. "You realize you haven't dated seriously in ages, and you blew up two potential weddings before they happened."

Alexander spread his hands. "And yet here you are, about to take my advice."

Leo scowled. His brother wasn't wrong.

With a sigh, he stared out the window again, watching the city move and flow around the tower that had been his kingdom for so long. Everything in his world was designed to be controlled, managed, influenced. But Ruby wasn't part of his world—she was her own person, with her own strength and her own choices to make.

And if he really loved her, he had to let her make them.

"No more voicemails," Leo said finally. "No more having Elliott check on her. No more surveillance."

He sighed. "No more trying to manage the situation."

"No more management," Alexander agreed. "Just trust."

Leo's phone buzzed with a text, and for a wild moment his heart leaped, thinking it might be Ruby. But it was just Elliott with another update about Ruby.

He looked at the phone for a long moment, then deleted Elliott's text without reading it and powered the device down completely.

"What are you doing?" Alexander asked.

"Learning to let go," Leo said, sliding the phone into his desk drawer. "If Ruby wants to reach me, she knows where to find me."

It was the hardest thing he'd ever done. But for the first time since Ruby had walked away, Leo felt like he was doing the right thing.

Not the tactical thing, not the strategic thing, but the thing that respected the woman he loved enough to let her choose her own path.

Even if that path didn't lead back to him.

Three days later, Leo was reviewing security contracts when Davis knocked on his office door.

"Sir? There's someone here to see you."

"I'm not taking meetings today."

"It's not a meeting, sir. It's…" Davis paused, something like relief crossing his face. "It's Miss Ryder."

Leo's heart stopped, then started beating so hard he could hear it in his ears. Ruby was here. After twenty-six days of silence, she was here.

"Send her in," he managed.

Leo stood up from his desk, his hands shaking slightly as he straightened his tie. He had no idea what Ruby was going to say, whether she was here to try again or to end things permanently. But for the first time in forever, he felt like he could breathe.

The door opened, and Ruby stepped into his office. She looked different—not physically, but something in her posture, her expression, spoke to a decision made.

"Hey," she said, closing the door behind her.

"Ruby." Her name came out rough, strained. "How are you?"

"I'm…figuring it out." She moved further into the room but didn't sit down. "I listened to your voicemails. All of them."

"I'm sorry about that. I know I said I'd give you space, but—"

"But you love me and you were scared," she finished. "I understand that. But Leo, these last few days when you stopped calling? That meant more to me than all the messages combined." She took a step closer. "Thank you."

"Hardest thing I've ever done."

She grinned. "I believe that." She slid her hands into the pockets of her jeans. "I quit my job at Lydia Cosmetics."

"I heard. How do you feel about that?"

"Relieved. I realized I was playing dress-up in someone else's life." Ruby's smile was wry, self-aware. "Turns out you can't unknow things about yourself. You can't go back to being someone you've outgrown."

"And have you? Outgrown who you used to be?"

"I think so. The question is whether I can live with who I've become."

Leo forced himself to stay still. To just let her talk.

"I've spent the last three weeks questioning everything about myself," Ruby continued. "Wondering if the woman who killed Nash was really me or just someone you created. Wondering if our relationship was built on manipulation or genuine connection."

His mouth had gone dry. He took a sip of the coffee on his desk, then asked, "What did you decide?"

"That I've been asking the wrong questions."

"What are the right questions?"

"Oh, the usual— Whether I like who I've become. If I'm comfortable with my capacity for violence. If the ways in which I've changed feel right."

"And?"

A smile tugged at her lips. "And I like who I am now. I like feeling strong instead of afraid. And I like being someone who can stand beside you as an equal instead of hiding behind you for safety."

The relief that flooded through him was so intense it left him dizzy. "So where does that leave us?"

"I think we need to figure out how to build a life that fits who we both are."

A dam inside him broke, sending relief flooding through him.

"I'm in love with you, Ruby," he said, his voice raw. "All of you. The gentle parts and the dangerous parts and everything in between."

Ruby smiled, the first real smile Leo had seen from her since the night she killed Nash. "So we build something new," she said.

"What will that look like?"

"I don't know yet. But I'm ready to find out with you, if you want."

He was at her side in a heartbeat, pulling her into his arms with desperate relief. She felt warm and solid and exactly right against his chest, and when she looked up at him, he could see the woman she'd become—strong, dangerous, unafraid.

His equal in every way that mattered.

"I want," he said simply, then kissed her like she was everything he'd been waiting for his entire life.

Because she was.

EPILOGUE
SIX MONTHS LATER

"Remember, the goal isn't to win the fight," I tell the group of women gathered in the training facility Leo and I built in Lower Manhattan. "The goal is to survive it. To get away, get help, and live to tell the story."

Eight faces look back at me with varying degrees of determination and fear. Some are here because of stalkers, others because of abusive ex-partners, a few because they're tired of feeling helpless in a world that can be dangerous for women. All of them remind me of myself six months ago—intelligent, capable women who've never learned that they can be dangerous, too.

"What if he's stronger than me?" asks Rosie, a marketing executive whose ex-husband has been escalating his harassment since their divorce. "What if I can't fight him off?"

"Then you don't fight him off," I tell her, moving to the center of the mat. "You disable him. You create an opportunity to escape. You use his strength against him."

I demonstrate the move Leo taught me months ago—how to use an attacker's momentum to throw them off balance, how to target vulnerable spots, how to create the split second you need to get away.

"The most important thing to remember is that you're not trying to be a warrior," I continue as the women practice the technique. "You're trying to be a survivor. And survivors do whatever it takes."

After the class ends, the women file out, chattering with the kind of energy that comes from feeling powerful instead of powerless. A few moments later, Leo appears in the doorway of the training room.

"How'd it go?" he asks, moving to help me put away the equipment.

"Good. Rosie's finally starting to believe she can defend herself, and Maria landed that throat strike perfectly." I stretch my shoulders, working out the kinks from two hours of demonstration. "How was your meeting with the FBI?"

"Productive. They want us to consult on three more cases—women whose stalkers have crossed state lines. Apparently, our success rate is getting attention."

Our success rate. The words make me smile. Six months ago, I would never have imagined I'd have a success rate in helping people eliminate threats. Now it's become the most satisfying work I've ever done.

"What kind of cases?"

"Two are being stalked by ex-partners who've made credible death threats. One is a federal prosecutor who's been receiving increasingly violent messages."

I nod, already mentally shifting into planning mode. These cases require more than just self-defense training—they need comprehensive security assessments, threat evaluation, and sometimes the kind of permanent solutions that most people can't or won't provide.

But Leo and I can. And will.

"When do we start?"

"Next week. But Ruby..." Leo moves closer, his expression serious. "The prosecutor's case is going to be dangerous. Her stalkers aren't just angry ex-boyfriends—they're organized crime with resources and training."

"Are you asking me to sit this one out?"

"I'm asking if you're ready for that level of threat."

Six months ago, the question would have sent me into a panic spiral. Now I feel the familiar surge of anticipation that means I'm ready for whatever comes next.

"I'm ready," I tell him honestly. "Are you ready to let me be?"

Leo's smile is warm and proud and completely without reservation. "Baby, I've been ready since the day I met you."

I laugh as he pulls me into a quick kiss that turns into a very, very long one. The kind I break from regretfully. Especially since the task I'm breaking for is to clean the training room.

He pulls me back, tugging me into his arms, then kissing me deeply. "Speaking of ready," he says, pulling a box from a pocket and dropping to one knee. "I know we're not the most traditional of couples. But I want to do this the old-fashioned way."

He draws a breath as my belly turns to water and my pulse spikes. Old-fashioned sounds just fine to me, and it's all I can do not to scream out my answer.

He clears his throat and looks sheepishly up at me. "I had a speech," his says, "and it's flown right out of my head."

I grin. "Do you remember the basics?"

"I do," he says, and we both laugh.

"I think that's my line," I whisper.

"Eventually," he says, his eyes dancing. "Right now…" He draws a breath. "I love you, Ruby Ryder. I know I should say all sorts of romantic things. But I really just want to cut to the chase."

"Yes, please."

We share a grin.

"Damn but I love you, Red," he says. "Will you marry me?"

"Yes, oh, yes." My voice is a squeal, and I leap on him, knocking him back on the mats, where I join him for some very delicious engagement kisses that I hope will lead to very intense engagement sex. I'm pulling him in for yet another one, when his phone chimes in a pattern I've never heard before.

His eyes go wide, and he pushes back, his body tense as he struggles to get his phone out of his pocket.

"What?" I say, alarmed by the look on his face. "Who texted?"

He takes my hand, his expression entirely unreadable. "Gabriel," he says, his voice sounding numb. "He's alive."

SOME RAVE REVIEWS FOR J. KENNER'S SIZZLING ROMANCES...

I just get sucked into these books and can not get enough of this series. They are so well written and as satisfying as each book is they leave you greedy for more. — Goodreads reviewer on *Wicked Torture*

A sizzling, intoxicating, sexy read!!!! J. Kenner had me devouring Wicked Dirty, the second installment of *Stark World Series* in one sitting. I loved everything about this book from the opening pages to the raw and vulnerable characters. With her sophisticated prose, Kenner created a love story that had the perfect blend of lust, passion, sexual tension, raw emotions and love. — Michelle, Four Chicks Flipping Pages

Wicked Dirty CLAIMED and CONSUMED every ounce of me from the very first page. Mind racing. Pulse pounding. Breaths bated. Feels flowing. Eyes wide in anticipation. Heart beating out of my chest. I felt the current of *Wicked Dirty* flow through me. I was DRUNK on this book that was my fine whiskey, so smooth and spectacular, and could not get enough of this *Wicked Dirty* drink. — Karen Bookalicious Babes Blog

"Sinfully sexy and full of heart. Kenner shines in this second chance, slow burn of a romance. Wicked Grind is the perfect book to kick off your summer." — *K. Bromberg, New York Times best-selling author (on Wicked Grind)*

"J. Kenner never disappoints~her books just get better and better." — *Mom's Guilty Pleasure (on Wicked Grind)*

"I don't think J. Kenner could write a bad story if she tried. ... Wicked Grind is a great beginning to what I'm positive will be a very successful series. ... The line forms here." — *iScream Books (On Wicked Grind)*

"Scorching, sweet, and soul-searing, *Anchor Me* is the ultimate love story that stands the test of time and tribulation. THE TRUEST LOVE!" *Bookalicious Babes Blog (on Anchor Me)*

"J. Kenner has brought this couple to life and the character connection that I have to these two holds no bounds and that is testament to J. Kenner's writing ability." *The Romance Cover (on Anchor Me)*

"J. Kenner writes an emotional and personal story line. ... The premise will captivate your imagination; the characters will break your heart; the romance continues to push the envelope." — *The Reading Café (on Anchor Me)*

"Kenner may very well have cornered the market on sinfully attractive, dominant antiheroes and the women who swoon for them ..." — *Romantic Times*

"*Wanted* is another J. Kenner masterpiece ... This was an intriguing look at self-discovery and forbidden love all wrapped into a neat little action-suspense package. There was plenty of sexual tension and eventually action. Evan was hot, hot, hot! Together, they were combustible. But can we expect anything less from J. Kenner?" — *Reading Haven*

"*Wanted* by J. Kenner is the whole package! A toe-curling smokin' hot read, full of incredible characters and a brilliant storyline that you won't be able to get enough of. I can't wait for the next book in this series ... I'm hooked!" — *Flirty & Dirty Book Blog*

"J. Kenner's evocative writing thrillingly captures the power of physical attraction, the pull of longing, the universe-altering effect one person can have on another … *Claim Me* has the emotional depth to back up the sex … Every scene is infused with both erotic tension, and the tension of wondering what lies beneath Damien's veneer – and how and when it will be revealed." — *Heroes and Heartbreakers*

"*Claim Me* by J. Kenner is an erotic, sexy and exciting ride. The story between Damien and Nikki is amazing and written beautifully. The intimate and detailed sex scenes will leave you fanning yourself to cool down. With the writing style of Ms. Kenner you almost feel like you are there in the story riding along the emotional rollercoaster with Damien and Nikki." — *Fresh Fiction*

"PERFECT for fans of *Fifty Shades of Grey* and *Bared to You. Release Me* is a powerful and erotic romance novel that is sure to make adult romance readers sweat, sigh and swoon." — *Reading, Eating & Dreaming Blog*

"I will admit, I am in the 'I loved *Fifty Shades*' camp, but after reading *Release Me*, Mr. Grey only scratches the surface compared to Damien Stark." — *Cocktails and Books Blog*

"It is not often when a book is so amazingly well-written that I find it hard to even begin to accurately describe it … I recommend this book to everyone who is interested in a passionate love story." — *Romancebookworm's Reviews*

"The story is one that will rank up with the *Fifty Shades* and Cross Fire trilogies." — *Incubus Publishing Blog*

"The plot is complex, the characters engaging, and J. Kenner's passionate writing brings it all perfectly together." —*Harlequin Junkie*

ALSO BY J. KENNER

For all of JK's Stark World and other titles,

please visit www.jkenner.com

Billionaire Brothers Grimm

The Tower

The Wolf

The Beast

The Stark Saga

He'd pay any price to have her…

release me

claim me

complete me

take me (novella)

have me (novella)

play my game (novella)

seduce me (novella)

unwrap me (novella)

deepest kiss (novella)

entice me (novella)

anchor me

hold me (novella)

please me (novella)

lost with me

damien

indulge me (novella)

delight me (novella & bonus content)

cherish me (novella)

embrace me (novella)

enchant me

interview with the billionaire

The Fallen Saint Series

His touch is her sin. Her love is his salvation

My Fallen Saint

My Beautiful Sin

My Cruel Salvation

Sinner's Game

Charismatic. Dangerous. Sexy as hell.

Meet the elite team of Stark Security.

Shattered With You

Shadows Of You

(free prequel to Broken With You)

Broken With You

Ruined With You

Wrecked With You

Destroyed With You

Memories of You

Ravaged With You

Hidden With You

Charmed By You

Tangled With You

Entwined With You

Craved By You

The Steele Books/Stark International:

He was the only man who made her feel alive.

Say My Name

On My Knees

Under My Skin

Take My Dare (includes short story Steal My Heart)

Stark International Novellas:

Meet Jamie & Ryan-so hot it sizzles.

Tame Me

Tempt Me

Tease Me

Touch Me

S.I.N. Trilogy:

It was wrong for them to be together…

…but harder to stay apart.

Dirtiest Secret

Hottest Mess

Sweetest Taboo

Most Wanted:

Three powerful, dangerous men.

Three sensual, seductive women.

Wanted

Heated

Ignited

Man of the Month

Who's your man of the month…?

Down On Me

Hold On Tight

Need You Now

Start Me Up

Get It On

In Your Eyes

Turn Me On

Shake It Up

All Night Long

In Too Deep

Light My Fire

Walk The Line

Royal Cocktail (bonus book)

**Bar Bites: A Man of the Month Cookbook(by J. Kenner & Suzanne M. Johnson)*

Blackwell-Lyon:

Heat, humor & a hint of danger

Lovely Little Liar

Pretty Little Player

Sexy Little Sinner

Tempting Little Tease

Rising Storm:

Writing as Julie Kenner

Small town drama

Rising Storm: Tempest Rising

Rising Storm: Quiet Storm

PARANORMAL

Demon Hunting Soccer Mom

Like Buffy… grown up!

Paranormal women's fiction

ABOUT THE AUTHOR

J. Kenner (aka Julie Kenner) is the *New York Times*, *USA Today*, *Publishers Weekly*, *Wall Street Journal* and #1 International best-selling author of over one hundred novels, novellas and short stories in a variety of genres.

JK has been praised by *Publishers Weekly* as an author with a "flair for dialogue and eccentric characterizations" and by *RT Bookclub* for having "cornered the market on sinfully attractive, dominant antiheroes and the women who swoon for them." A five-time finalist for Romance Writers of America's prestigious RITA award, JK took home the first RITA trophy awarded in the category of erotic romance in 2014 for her novel, *Claim Me* (book 2 of her Stark Trilogy) and the RITA trophy for *Wicked Dirty* in the same category in 2017.

In her previous career as an attorney, JK worked as a lawyer in Southern California and Texas. She currently lives in Central Texas, with her husband, two daughters, and two rather spastic cats.

Stay in touch! Text JKenner to 21000 to subscribe to JK's text alerts.

www.jkenner.com